Here Come the
Pennsylvania Dutch

To Doug and Ollie

Tom Speck

1/25/17

Here Come the Pennsylvania Dutch

"A FAMILY SAGA OF EMIGRATION FROM GERMANY AND EARLY AMERICAN HISTORY"

St. Andrew Galley - 1737

Written by Thomas B. Speaker

PREVIOUS NOVELS BY AUTHOR - SEE AMAZON.COM
THE BATTLE OF WAIKIKI
THE COACH
BORN TO SING

PREVIOUS DOCUMENTARIES BY AUTHOR
THE UNDEFEATED
"The story of the West Lafayette, Indiana, State Champions of 2009"

THE LAST COUNTY CHAMPIONSHIP
"The story of Linden H.S. winning the last Montgomery County Championship"

ISBN: 1505862876
ISBN 13: 9781505862874
Library of Congress Control Number: 2014922952
CreateSpace Independent Publishing Platform
North Charleston, SC

Table of Contents

Johannes Peter Spyker (Senior) 1662-1740

Johannes Peter Spyker (Jonny) 1685 - 1762

Johannes Peter Spyker (Peter) 1711 - 1789

Johannes Peter Spyker

1662-1740

———∽∞∽———

Johannes and Conrad

1675

———— ✦ ————

"Where's America?"

"Conrad," said the stately teacher, Wilhelm Leininger, "you must raise your hand before you ask a question. Now, depart from the others and stand in the corner. Johannes, I see your hand; that's nice. Conrad, do you see the proper way your best friend asks a question to your teacher? Why can't you be polite like your friend Johannes? Now then Johannes, I hope your question is more studious than Conrad's 'Where is America?'"

"Where's America?" asked Johannes even more boldly than Conrad. "Conrad and I are going there. We're tired of constant wars. Thirty years ago we had thirty years of war and the peace at Wesphalia is a joke. We've had thirty more years of war. We have no say in even the smallest decisions involving our lives. We're tired of armies marching through Wurttemberg and taking our crops, livestock, and food. We're tired of the Palatine electors telling us how we should praise our Lord. They say we're not to be Lutherans, but must be Catholic. We're Weisers and Spykers and citizens of Wurttemberg and proud of it."

Although Herr Wilhelm was impressed with young Johannes's knowledge of history and sympathized and agreed with his frustration, he could not allow it in school. "That's quite enough,

Johannes, you are just as outspoken as Conrad. We are never to criticize the counts. They are our rulers. If what you said would get out to one in authority, they would lop off your head. You and Conrad are to stay after school. We cannot have impertinence in my classroom. Johannes, for now you take the other corner. See students, this is how you will be disciplined if you insult our beloved leaders. Whichever Palatinate elector is in charge, we must respect and obey him. Heavens! After all, the Holy Roman Emperor has appointed the counts and they of course cannot be wrong. Life on this earth is not supposed to be fair. Keep in mind, when you die and go to heaven, you will have joy. It makes no difference if it is Lutheran joy, Catholic joy or even Calvinist joy."

Herr Leininger could tell by looking in the eyes of the students that they were as confused as he was. " Now, we must toe the line and be happy with our circumstances."

Conrad and Johannes eyed each other from opposing corners and with grim lips just nodded to each other as if to say, *"We'll show you, we'll show the Count, the count for nothing. We don't care about the Holy Roman Empire or the Empire of France. All they do is trample on us. We feel a responsibility to only our homes and our families. We are from the province of Wurttemberg. We are from the village of Aspach; this is our Empire."*

They didn't dislike Herr Leininger. Many times he was very kind and interested in each student. Their teacher was about fifty years old and as thin as his precisely structured, pencil-thin mustache. He looked tall, because he liked to preen on his toes as he addressed the students. He was however, several inches short of six feet.

It seemed like he became unlikeable only when he discussed or a student discussed the Palatine system or the threat of the French in this area of Germany. The borders were not distinct and Johannes and Conrad considered the village of Aspach and the surrounding province of Wurttemberg to be their homeland.

The one room school had survived through donations from the surrounding villages and farms. It was a log construction with a slate that covered the entire front of the room. In front of the slate was the teacher's "pulpit." In front of the pulpit were several rows of crudely built benches. The students sat there with the youngest in front and the oldest, like Johannes and Conrad, in the rear. In the center of the room was a pot-bellied stove that the older students fueled by bringing wood from their homes.

The students ranged from ages nine to fifteen, but few students were allowed to continue past their thirteenth birthday. Most were boys, but there were a few girls who got to attend for a year or two.

As Wilhelm sat with his two fiercely independent students, Johannes Spyker and John Conrad Weiser (who went by the name of Conrad) many thoughts went through his mind. As he looked at these two thirteen-year old boys he thought, *"I do not want to kill their dreams, but how could they ever go to America. This year of 1675 will be their last opportunity to go to school. Soon they will need to work every day. This is the end of their formal education. They will stay on the family farms, get married, have many children, most who will not survive their first several years, and barely struggle to keep enough food on the table. The various armies during the Thirty Years War and even today will not let them be free to realize their dreams. Every time they get ahead, the armies will pillage and plunder them back into poverty."*

"What a quandary," he thought, *"but still, I must let them dream. I must answer their questions, and tell them about America. Johannes although fragile looking and small will constantly ask more questions, and while he looks fragile, he will never break. Conrad is rugged and strong, but he will let Johannes be the more dominant. Conrad is usually quiet, but he has the strength both on the outside and the inside to accomplish many things."*

As Wilhelm continued to muse he couldn't help dreaming himself. *"These are two strong personalities maybe they will be the ones to lead the Palatines to this New World."*

———— ⊶⊷ ————

"Boys," said Wilhelm Leininger as he lifted his chin and looked each one of them squarely in the eyes, "Where is America? Where is this New World? First I want to tell you how much I would like to see you go to the New World and be free. You need to understand why I avoid this topic during the class discussions. We have students from many families in the province, which is a Holy Roman Palatinate. Most are like you, unhappy with a singular count being our ruler; a ruler who makes decisions based upon the will of the Holy Roman Empire and not about our needs. However, if the Palatinate officials from our area have even a notion that I'm not preaching 'Holy Roman Doctrine,' which is that the Emperor and his chosen elector are always right and we are beneath them, they would close down this school immediately. Even now, just talking to you two, I am taking a chance. If they were little mice hiding under your benches, listening to this conversation, I would be going to prison. I've kept you after school only to talk with you and to answer your questions."

Johannes and Conrad nodded and looked with gratitude at their teacher. Johannes said, "Herr Leininger, you need not worry about us. We will never tell a soul or even a mouse about this conversation." Conrad nodded his head in agreement.

"Let the geography lesson begin! Where is America? This is a recently discovered continent practically on the other side of our world. Let me draw on the slate board Germany, the Netherlands, England, the huge Atlantic Ocean, and America. Let us travel in our minds from our little village of Aspach to the new world. You would boat down the Rhine to Rotterdam. Here is the Rhine River, which is practically in

our back yard." Wilhelm continued to draw and talk at the same time. We float down the Rhine to this city, Rotterdam, which is across from England. One journey I've read about is that of the ship Mayflower, which happened many years ago. The Mayflower left from Plymouth, which is here down at the bottom of England. The ship with over one hundred people on board sailed for two months and arrived here, on the East coast of what is now called America. Presently it is just the English and the Irish, who sail to the New World, but some day ... " The boys could see the dream in Herr Wilhelm's eyes.

The boys were entranced and didn't ask any questions as their teacher continued to explain about the size of the new continent, a strange people, the Indians and other historical facts.

Herr William could have continued for hours. "Johannes, Conrad, you best leave for home. It is getting dark and your parents will be worried. If you like, I can stay after school with you for several class days and tell you everything I know about this America. I would also like to tell you about a man from England, a Quaker named William Penn. Although the Quaker faith is somewhat unique, they pride themselves on understanding that everyone has a right to his or her own belief. William Penn is encouraging people like you and me who want freedom to go to America. Be careful, however, just mentioning the name of William Penn will have you brought before a judge for questioning. That's all I'm going to say about America and William Penn until the next time we stay after school."

The two thirteen-year-old boys got up to leave with eyes full of anticipation. "We'll stay every day possible, but you need to discipline us and make us stay after school, so the others don't know what we're up to," said Johannes.

"I'll pull Margaret's pig tails and you can send me to the corner," said Conrad with a sly smile.

Johannes was quick to come up with his strategy. "I'm going to say 'damn', just like father says, when I answer a question in class. That should get me a nice after-school session." They all laughed as they plotted their American history and geography lessons.

As they separated to go to their homes, Johannes knew he had some answering to do to his parents. "Why are you so late, Johannes" said his mother, who was standing in the doorway and staring at her oldest son, who strolled down the lane, trying to act nonchalant. "We've been worried about you. I thought maybe one of those Romans got you and sent you to Rome."

Johannes, not wanting to disclose his teacher's lesson on America said, "Sorry, Mother, I had to stay after school for talking too much."

"You always talk too much. You watch out or you are going to be a preacher."

"Mom," Johannes said with some hesitancy, "I'm going to have to stay a little later for the next few class days. This is my last year and our teacher wants to give Conrad and me as much learning as he can in this last month of school."

"Education is a good thing. I wish you could go to school many more years, but with your father becoming old and often sick, you will need to take many of his responsibilities. You are the oldest boy and someday this farm will be yours. Get as much learning as you can in these last days of school."

— ഐൟ —

The Palatinate, the area where the Spykers lived, was the land of the Count Palatine, a title held by a leading secular prince of the Holy Roman Empire. These boundaries, which included their Wurttemberg area and their village of Aspach varied according to who was named by the Holy Roman Empire as the Count Palatine.

The land was fertile and supported families for thousands of years. However, the events of the 30 years war and the constant battles between the French and the Holy Roman Empire made their homeland a "living hell." The Spykers could not understand why the outside world could not just leave them alone to farm, worship, and grow their families.

The Palatinate was bordered by the Moselle River in the North, Luxembourg and Belgium in the west, and what today is Koblenz in the East. The Southern border would be today's Alsace, which is now part of France, but throughout history the Palatines considered themselves German and German was their Mother language.

During the Thirty Years War, the Palatine country, including Wurttemberg suffered from fire, war, and the after-effects of pillage by the French armies. This war was based upon both politics and religion. The Roman Catholic armies sought to crush their religious freedom, and the French sought to expand their influence.

Many armies and bands of mercenaries, both friend and foe, made themselves welcome to the food, crops, and livestock of the Weisers and the Spykers and all the farms in the Wurttemberg Province.

———— ✺ ————

"Conrad and Johannes, I see you are in front of me again, even after all the other students have gone home. Can't you behave?" said Wilhelm, with a twinkle in his eye. "Poor Margaret, she screeched to high heavens. I thought she had been scalped by one of those Indians we talked about yesterday. And Johannes, such language in front of some of our nine year olds. This behavior is so bad it makes me want to talk about a New World and William Penn."

The boys were all ears as their teacher talked. "William Penn is a free-thinking man. He is from England and a very wealthy family. Everyone in England, according to the dictates of the King, must worship according to the preaching of the Anglican Church. However, Mr. Penn, who is not afraid to state his own feeling, criticized the Anglican Church, or rather I should say criticized the King and England for demanding that all worship according to the dictates of the Anglican Church. For his beliefs and his desire to have the freedom to think and worship as his conscience guided him, he was imprisoned in the Tower of London.

"Mr. Penn is now talking about a 'Holy Experiment,' a colony in America where there is freedom of mind and soul. He pictures developing a colony in America where there is freedom of religion and the right of self-government. Just think of it boys, you can worship as you wish and you would have a say-so in the laws that will affect your everyday life." Again the teacher paused and the boys waited, hungry for more.

"I have read his book, 'No Cross, No Crown,' and I am convinced he will be successful in developing this colony in America. I hear the colony will be called Pennsylvania. I don't know when this colony will be founded, but when it is, wouldn't be wonderful if you could go and live there, raise your family, and even die in peace."

Over the few remaining days of Johannes's and Conrad's formal education, Herr Wilhelm continued to teach them about America and the "Holy Experiment." As they walked away from the Aspach school on the last day they vowed to keep following this dream of going to America.

Johannes, Conrad,
and William Penn
1677

William Penn

IT WAS THE SUMMER OF 1677 and Johannes and Conrad had been out of school for two years and each was greatly involved in his family businesses. Johannes was doing most of the farming on the Spyker farm as Johannes Sr. was very ill and could only give his son directions on what he should do to keep the farm running smoothly. His advice was golden and Johannes listened to him intently.

His father also worked with him on the other enterprise of the farm, the wine-making business.

"Son," said Johannes the elder, "the farm will keep us in food, but the vineyard and winery will provide us with additional income so we can save money for the difficult times and also buy some extra things that help make life enjoyable. Also it is the wine money that helps keep both our school and church able to provide us with the education you and your sisters have received and the spiritual guidance that is essential to life. You're doing a wonderful job, but I must tell you, I will not be on this earth much longer. You will be the one mainly responsible to provide for the Spykers." Johannes continued to cough each time he gave his son instructions.

"Father, I think you will live many more years, but it makes me feel proud to be able to have the responsibility you are giving me. I do, however, have something that is gnawing inside me. We've talked a little about it, but I need to know more. Someday I wish to go to America. No, not soon, but when I can take the whole family. I keep hearing about America. The story of William Penn is often talked about in the shops in Aspach. Is there any way I can learn more about America and Mr. Penn?"

"You would have my blessing to go to America. I would have felt the same way in my youth. It is a little dangerous to talk too much about America and particularly about Mr. Penn. You see, Johannes, the Count Palatine does not want anyone to leave his Palatinate, particularly successful farmers like the Spykers or Weisers. I will talk with Tom Christ, the owner of the mercantile, and see if he can help you. He seems to have a relationship with William Penn, but he is very cautious about talking with anyone about him.

"I do hear Mr. Penn is traveling around in Germany and Holland talking about his Quaker beliefs, which include freedom of religion and self government."

As often as possible Johannes and Conrad still got together. Conrad was doing an apprenticeship in Aspach learning the bakery trade. Whenever they could, they would go fishing or hunting together.

On a fall day in October, Johannes's mother called him in from his harvesting of corn. "Johannes, your father is very weak and is resigned that he will not survive but a day or two. He wishes to talk with you. You need to see him as soon as you can. I fear the worst."

As Johannes approached his father's bedside, he saw just a shadow of the strong, vibrant man. He grabbed his father's hand. It felt weak and cold. "Father, please try to get better. I'm not ready to have you leave me. Everything you've taught me has helped me continue to make the farm prosper just as you have always done, but I need to know more. I love you so much. I hope I can be half the man you have been; the father you have been to me and my sisters. Mother needs you as well."

In a weak and trembling voice with frequent coughs, Johannes Sr. addressed his son for the last time. It was, however, with a brave and smiling face. Johannes could still see the famous humor that showed in his eyes. "Ah, Johnny my boy. You are twice the farmer I was at your age. I am so proud of you that I can rest easy in the Lord. There is nothing more I can teach you. All Aspach knows you are the one in charge. I pray to God that you someday get to go to America. The farm and our home here have been wonderful, but we can no longer survive happily in this political climate. It will never change. You need to be free, like I once was before the French and the Holy Roman Empire decided we were just their serfs. I've talked to Tom Christ and he knows you will be asking him questions about William Penn. Now, go sneak into the cupboard and get me that hundred proof cough medicine that your mother is always hiding from me. My Gott, Johannes, your mother treats me like a child, and I love her for it. She's babied me for forty years. If you ever get married make sure she looks, talks, and acts like your mother. Now go get my medicine before I cough myself to death and not a word to your mother about me liking her just the way she is."

That same evening, Johannes, Sr. died peacefully in his cough-medicine sleep. In Aspach, families got together in large numbers for every holiday and events of importance like weddings and funerals. The funeral of Johannes Peter Spyker was no exception, particularly since he was so popular and loved by neighbors and family. His humor had helped them all survive the difficult times.

At the funeral, Tom Christ motioned for Johannes to come outside the Spyker home. "Johannes, your father was one my best friends. As I talked with him several days before his death he asked me a favor. He wanted me to let you know when and where a gentleman named William Penn would be coming to our area to talk about his 'Holy Experiment.' Your father mentioned to me that you and Conrad had an interest in the beliefs of William Penn and wanted some day to go to America.

"You must swear to me that you will not mention that I have talked about this with you. Already the authorities in this area are suspicious of me. You see, they forbid anyone to discuss leaving the Palatinate. Also, you should know I am a Quaker, a follower of William Penn, and other people who believe that all men are created equal. Well, I'll not get into too much philosophy as I'm going to direct you to William Penn who will better explain the Quaker faith." He lowered his voice and looked over both his shoulders to make sure no one else could hear.

"Exactly one week from now there is a secret meeting of those who are of the Quaker faith and those like you and Conrad who want to learn about this faith and his philosophy. The meeting will be in the Lutheran church in Speyer. Speyer is on the Rhine River just forty kilometers from here. You will have no problem finding this village. You just follow the Zucker creek the best you can as it winds its way northwest and eventually empties into the Rhine.

Speyer is just north of the creek-river junction and the church is the only building with a spire that towers over the village. The meeting will start at 7:00 P.M. German time, which means exactly on schedule. Share this information with Conrad, but with no one else, not even family members. I've talked to your mother and she gives her blessing and permission for you to go. She wants desperately for you to have a life like she and Johannes shared when they were first married, before Aspach became a battlefield."

Tom continued, "Johannes, when you get to the church and meet Pastor Schuler, please say it was I who sent you. Also say, 'we want to be among Friends'. He will understand."

On that same day, Johannes shared the information with Conrad, who was equally excited. "We will take my two favorite horses and go on an overnight hunting trip." Conrad plotted on going without his family knowing the true plan.

The two fifteen-year-old boys left early the morning a week after the funeral. They were dressed for hunting and prepared to bring home some pheasants and deer. They each had flintlock rifles. Conrad was known in the Aspach area as an excellent shot and hunter. Johannes was not that skillful. Conrad often said to his friend, "Johannes you couldn't hit a bull in the ass with a bass fiddle." This always caused great laughter for both of them as Johannes readily agreed. "You know Conrad, I'm a lover not a warrior." They enjoyed so much being together and looked forward to the adventure ahead. The leaves in Wurttemberg had turned to many shades of orange and yellow and despite the occasional rainfall, frequent in the German fall, the landscape and the occasional views of the Zucker were beautiful.

After several hours of traveling they came upon a strange sight. Two men, both middle age, were struggling with their wagon that was mired in the mud of the Zucker creek. One of the gentlemen had short blond hair and the other long dark hair. Johannes hailed out, "Hello gents. Looks like you're in a mess. Can we help?"

Their help was readily accepted. The two men, despite being somewhat inept in helping Conrad and Johannes free the wagon, kept both teenage boys in stitches. The short haired fellow who introduced himself as George, constantly slipped and fell into the mud as he pushed and slapped the two mules on the butt. "Gott damn, gott damn, gott damn," George swore as he wiped the mud from eyes. The other gentlemen with the long dark locks, who introduced himself simply as William, just laughed and said, "George, friend, with your new make-up, I can't tell you from the donkeys. But I think the Lord likes the language of the donkeys better than yours."

They all continued to laugh and struggle with the mules and the wagons until finally they were ready to be on their way. After a quick dip in the Zucker to clean themselves, they slapped each other on the back and hugged as if they had been friends for years. William explained they were on their way to meet some friends. Then with a twinkle in his eye, he said a strange thing: "Someday we'll meet you in paradise". Then they were off destined to never see each other again.

———— ❧ ————

The Speyer Lutheran church was close to full. Conrad and Johannes took their usual seats in the back of the church, but were all ears and eyes as they waited breathlessly to meet the famous William Penn. The preacher, Reverend Schuler, immediately started the program after the heavy oak doors of the Lutheran church were shut and locked. It was 7:05. "Dear friends, dear Lutherans, dear freedom lovers, I am Reverend Schuler, the Lutheran minister of this church. Why would a Lutheran preacher host a meeting and introduce his guests to a man of another denomination? Because this Quaker wants Lutherans to worship freely. He wants Catholics to worship freely. He wants Reformed to worship freely. In short, he believes all men and women should have the right to listen to the Lord in their own way."

The pastor continued the long introduction, "William Penn, comes from England. His father is the famous admiral, also named William Penn. His father, whom he loves dearly, is a man of war; our William is a man of peace. They often disagree, but our William is not afraid of confrontation. He confronted the English establishment and the Royalty in 1661 by opposing the Clarendon Acts, which required that Englishmen worship only the Anglican Church. He disagreed and encouraged others to disobey this law and was imprisoned. He was imprisoned again in the Tower of London for a pamphlet he released challenging the demands of the Royalty to follow only the Anglican faith. While in prison he wrote *No Cross, No Crown*. In this famous book he argued for an end to pomp and showiness and a return to genuine conviction and virtuous simplicity. The following biblical quotes are used by Mr. Penn to summarize his religious simplicity. 'And Jesus said unto his Disciples; if any man will come after me, let him deny himself, and take up his daily cross, and follow me', Luke 19.23. Further he quotes 2 Timothy 4: 'I have fought a good fight, I have finished my course, I have kept the faith: Henceforth there is laid up for me a crown of righteousness, which the Lord the righteous judge shall give me at that day, and not me only, but all that are longing for his appearance.'"

Again he paused, looking down at them apologetically. "Friends, I am going on in such a lengthy discourse, not to just introduce a man, but to challenge you to be like this man. We also in the Palatines have a cross. We are facing a foe that denies us freedom of religion and freedom to live our lives in a manner that is pleasing to us and to our Lord. Perhaps, this man, William Penn, will give you hope to follow a course that may not be kindly thought of by our count or our Holy Roman emperor, but will allow us to have honor and a crown of glory. Let us give our friend and honored guest, William Penn, and his friend in travel, George Fox, a warm German welcome."

William Penn appeared arm in arm with his compatriot, George Fox. Conrad and Johannes were stunned. They had already made friends with Mr. Penn and Mr. Fox. There was a huge smile on William Penn's face as he recognized them in the back and he said, "Let me introduce the reason we were able to be here on German time. You two young lads, Conrad and Johannes, I believe, come up here in the front row where I can talk to you." Conrad and Johannes, sheepishly, with hesitant steps, made their way to the front where there were still many empty seats as the Lutherans still practiced the art of sitting in the back pews. William Penn gave a warm description of their help as he described them like the 'Good Samaritan' of the Bible who showed kindness to a wounded traveler. The audience also gave them a warm welcome, clapping and patting them on the backs as they made their way to the front.

For one solid hour Mr. Penn held Conrad and Johannes as well as the rest of the crowd spellbound. He told of his struggles to have a free conscience, to accept the philosophy of turning the other cheek, and of loving his neighbor as himself. He then espoused his hopes for his own Quaker colony in the New World which would equally accept all religions and form a representative government of the people.

The Family Farm in Aspach
1685

"JOHANNES YOU HAVE A FINE boy. You finally have a boy to go along with your two girls," said Clara the mid-wife, who traveled throughout the area delivering the children of Aspach. "Someday he will take over the farm and let you rest the same way you did for your father."

"My son," said Johannes, "may farm here for awhile, but some day he will farm in the continent across the Atlantic. This New World has miles and miles of farm land. We don't even know how large it is, but it must be bigger than our continent. And more importantly, they get to keep what they grow, rather than give their crops and food to whatever army happens to be roving in the area. When this baby son of mine gets to America he will be with me, his father Johannes Spyker. We are going to America. I will never give up this dream."

It was ten years since Johannes had finished his education with Herr Wilhelm Leininger and eight years since the adventurous meeting with William Penn. Every day of those years he thought of the opportunity to be free, to not have the ambitious French or the Holy Roman Empire or any other conquering army, dictate his course in life. It seemed like every time Johannes got ahead, a bad year would come and there was no longer the finances to complete the "American Dream."

Johannes looked at his baby boy, all snuggled in the arms of Margaret Spyker. Margaret, who once had to endure the teasing of Conrad and Johannes, was now the wife of Johannes. They were married six years and already had three children; one, a boy, had died several months after birth. The two girls of three and five looked adoringly at their new brother while in the back of Margaret's mind was the thought, *"Please God let him survive and become strong and healthy. I don't care what he does in life, I just want him to be happy."*

"Johannes, what shall we name him. I ask this question knowing the name has been chosen many decades ago." It was a common practice in Germany during the 17th century to name each first born male exactly after his father. This is the way they established the lineage of each family.

"Yes, my sweet, dear young bride. He will be Johannes Peter Spyker the 5th or the 6th or the 7th and his first born will be Johannes Peter Spyker the 6th or the 7th or the 8th. Now, Margaret, Mother Spyker is anxious to see the baby; she has been waiting beside father's grave all during your labor."

Just a few years after Johannes had finished school his father had died and Johannes had become the head of the family. He barely had time to reminisce about the dreams given to him by Herr Wilhelm and his adventurous meeting with William Penn. The farm of thirty acres had to raise enough corn to feed the swine and the dairy cows.

The farm also had to raise enough wheat for all to have bread, but they didn't have to make their own bread. They just gave it to Conrad "The Baker" in exchange for some vegetables, milk, cheese or fruit. Conrad was and always would be Johannes's best friend. Conrad would stop by on his way home from his bakery in Aspach and present them with wonderful bread as well as delicious pies, tarts and various pastry items.

Besides the basic crops, Johannes's mother Anna, his wife Margaret, and his younger sisters Amelia and Lydia were responsible for the large garden of cabbage, carrots, beets, tomatoes, potatoes, beans, pumpkins, Brussel sprouts, and other vegetables.

Johannes, like Conrad, also had an area of expertise that gave the family some extra income. The Spyker farm had devoted five of their precious acres to vineyards. Johannes, with the detailed instructions and training from his father, had become the most well-known wine maker in the Wurttemberg area. He had mastered the art of producing the finest wines and his farm was well suited for wine production with caves by the creek. The Spyker wine was carried in Conrad's bakery store and people from all the surrounding areas came there, not only to buy Conrad's pastry products, but the wine as well.

For all the crops, fruit, and vegetables, each year was a gamble. The weather could smile upon them with rain and sunshine. The armies would stay away to fight in some other God-forsaken area. The next year there would be little rain or there would be another war and the crops would barely sustain the growing family. Now in 1685 the farm had another mouth to feed with the arrival of the howling, screaming, healthy, Johannes Peter the next Roman Numeral.

"Rebecca," ordered Johannes to his oldest daughter, all of five years of age, "go get your grandmother. She will be with grandfather in the cemetery. Tell her that her prayers have been answered; another Johannes is with us."

"Daddy," said Rebecca as she put her hands on her hips, "I don't know how I'm going to do everything. First I had to take care of Catherine, now I have to take care of Johannes, and now you want me to leave my job and go find Grandmother. Fiddlesticks." But away she went with a marked air of superiority.

"I'm going across the field to see Conrad. He and Anna Magdalena are as excited about this coming child as they are their own. I'm only one child behind Conrad. It seems he has a new child every year."

"Yes, hurry and get Conrad and Anna Magdalena." It seemed like they could not just say Anna, but always Anna Magdalena. Margaret and Anna Magdalena spend every moment they could together. The distances between farms made it difficult to have many friends, but Margaret and Anna were as inseparable as Conrad and J ohannes. The ladies were so much alike that Conrad had started calling them "Ding" and "Dong," which was the sound of the Weiser's dinner bell, much to the hilarity of Johannes and the good natured thumb-nosing of the two almost sisters.

"Tell Conrad he can't bring his smelly pipe in to see the baby. Maybe you two should sit outside, while Anna Magdalena and I adore the new born child. You two can introduce yourselves to Johannes and then toast each other's manhood with that apple cider that is no longer apple cider."

Life was difficult for both families. But life, when no roving armies preyed upon them, was good and it was a blessing to have each other's family as best friends. They shared each other's happiness and shared each other's grief. They played together and prayed together. God was a member of their families.

It was June in the Wurttemberg province. Wurttemberg was part of the Holy Roman Empire, but the territorial rights were constantly threatened by France and Louie the fourteenth. It really made no difference which army came through the area, all were vultures. Johannes and Conrad considered themselves just citizens of Aspach and the Wurttemberg area. They could care less if they were part of the Holy Roman Empire or were part of France with an idiot king who called himself "The Sun King."

Johannes's heart sang as he trotted toward the Weiser farm to get Conrad and Anna Magdalena. Conrad, since his uncles ran the Weiser farm, was not as involved in farming as was Johannes. He had chosen and enjoyed the occupation of baker. Every morning he made bread in the stone ovens of the Weiser farm and then carted the bread and other bakery items to Aspach. In Aspach he was known as Conrad "The Baker".

Their farms were several miles apart and Johannes traveled cross country to the Weiser farm. He had at his heels his faithful Wolfhound, "Lucky". He had initially named him Lucky Louie, but decided to keep the last name secret. Lucky was nine years old, old for a dog, but he was still swift and the protector of the Spyker farm. Lucky now had the added responsibility of protecting the newest Johannes Peter Spyker.

Johannes smiled to himself and then started laughing out loud when he remembered Lucky coming in to see the new child. Lucky had cautiously stepped to the bedside, enjoyed the loving pat from Martha and then tilted his head quizzically as he viewed his new charge. He then had turned to look at Matilda and everyone in the room as if to say, "no one, had better mess with this child, or you will have to deal with me".

"God is sure good to the Spykers," thought Johannes as he came to the deep but narrow creek named the Zucker, which eventually flowed into the Rhine River. As he approached the Zucker creek, he saw the dark shadows of good size bass and channel catfish. *"Tomorrow, we will have fried catfish for dinner."*

He took hold of a knotted rope, which was stuck in the fork of a tree, and swung across the creek to land in the Weiser farm area. He parked the rope in another tree fork. Sure enough, Lucky was waiting for him, just shaking a few drops from his large ears.

"Conrad, he's here. The newest American farmer," shouted Johannes for the whole family to hear.

"Anna, get your bonnet; we're going to see the new King of Wurttemberg."

They nearly flew across fields and forests and the Zucker creek to see the new man of the Spyker house. Conrad carried a cloth bag with one of his famous pumpkin pies and some freshly baked sourdough bread. They were still a quarter mile away, when Lucky, happily announced their arrival.

The two friends sat on the back porch on the swing and chairs crafted by Johannes. "Why can't the Sun King just leave us alone? We could have a happy life with only the weather to worry us. Now, Johannes," said Conrad, "Louis the Fourteenth wants more and more land. Every day someone from another village comes into my bakery house and tells me of the 'mad man's' newest ambitions. The War of the Reunions is over, the King has got more land, but he still wants to gobble up someone else's homeland. The Spanish and the Holy Roman Empire have said, 'no more, Louis'. Soon our area in Wurttemberg will become the stepping stone across the Rhine to Philippsburg. The Spanish and Holy Roman Empire have vowed not to let this happen. Then here we go again, another senseless war." Conrad ended, just shaking his head.

"There's only one solution for us. America. I'm not afraid to fight to defend my home and family, but this constant battle for some unknown objective or to satisfy someone's ego makes no sense. I fear things will never change in the Palatinates or for that matter in all of Europe."

Conrad leaned over and quietly shared with Johannes, "Don't mention this to Margaret, for she will surely tell Anna Magdalena; the Palatine authorities in Affstatt have notified me that I may have to join the military outfit to protect the Palatinate from the greedy French and Louie XIV. I'm not the head of the farm, so I am subject to being impressed into the service They not only want me, but our beautiful stable of horses. Johannes you are lucky as they will not impress you into service because you will help them feed the Hapsburg Armies. I only hope you don't have to feed the French aggressors as well."

As they frequently passed around the jug of potent apple juice, they discussed their immediate future. All they saw was war and tribulations, with an occasional glimpse of the land of the free.

Christmas Eve at the Spykers
1687

———— ∽∾∾ ————

THE SPYKER HOUSE WAS ALIT with candles and a beautifully decorated Christmas tree on this Christmas Eve of 1687. The house was filled with friends and relatives from all over the Aspach area.

"Let us drink to the new year," said Conrad as he raised his glass of the Spyker's Riesling wine. All the adults joined in while the many children played in the cellar of the Spyker's fine big house. They tried to be jovial, but knew that another war was imminent and it was coming soon to Wurttemburg. The European world was a mess. The "Sun King," Louie the XIV was not content with his successes after the War of the Reunions and the resulting Truce of Ratisbon, which extended French borders. Now he had his eyes on the Rhineland.

"Let's drink to the 'Sun King', damn his greedy soul," continued Conrad. Conrad tried to be brave, but then he had to wish them farewell. "My friends, my dearest neighbors, tomorrow my family, all six of us will leave Aspach. I have been ordered to Affstatt to join his Holy Roman Empire force, the Blue Dragoons. My family will join me and travel with me to the ends of the continent. We are to train to help protect the Holy Roman Empire from the French. Eventually we will form in a unit and go east to Turkey, Hungary and Serbia to extend the Empire. I wish I could stay and help defend our homes from the vultures from France and the grasp of the Holy Roman Empire."

Anna Magdalena tried to hush Conrad, "Shh, the walls have ears."

But there was no hushing Conrad, who was angry and sad. "I pray that someday soon this madness will stop. Every king, every count, every baron wants more land and they have no idea that God gave us this land. We have tilled it, planted it and treasured it. It has given our families food for centuries. And now each king wants to say, 'Aha! I have more land than you, ha, ha, ha.'"

Johannes quickly jumped in and with tears in his eyes, raised one of his glasses of wine, which he had produced with tender love and expert care and the best Riesling grapes in the world, "To Conrad, to Anna Magdalena, to their four lovely daughters. Go with God's protection and come back to us in Aspach. We will defend your farm and your family with every ounce of strength we have. Conrad and Anna Magdalena, if we don't see you in Aspach, we will see you in America."

The atmosphere was too bleak for Anna Magdalena and Margaret, but they had a diversion planned. Just before the children's bedtime, and all the children would be sleeping in the Spyker loft that night, Anna Magdalena stepped in front of her too serious husband, "Before we all jump into the Rhine river we'd like to bring you the future of Wurttemberg. Let me present, Rebecca Spyker and the Asbach Singers."

Out popped Rebecca, with her frilly red and white Christmas dress and with her blond curls abounding, "Let me introduce the Weiser, Spyker, Christ, and Kaderman children. I of course am the choir master. We are little Christmas trees growing in Wurttemberg and some day we will be very tall and strong Christmas trees. We may be growing in Wurttemberg or we might well be growing someday in America."

Out came, in perfect marching order, all the children from five to nine. Rebecca curtsied to the parents and then spun around to face her choir. With a serious look on her face and then a posed smile, she brought both her hands in a downbeat: *"O Tannenbaum, O Tannenaum, Christmas Tree, O Christmas Tree, Your branches green delight us! They are green when summer days are bright, They are green when winter snow is white. O Christmas Tree, O Christmas Tree, Your branches green delight us! ... ."*

The parents clapped, smiled, and laughed with joy. All thoughts of war and leaving departed into the Christmas Eve night.

The Nine Years War

1688

"LUCKY'S BARKING AND BARKING AND here comes a man riding a horse," said Catherine, the youngest Spyker daughter, who would soon turn six. She was very excited and ran around and around to every member of the family including Johannes Peter Spyker, "the younger", who was now a toddling two year old. Very few people visited the farm, particularly on a fast riding stallion.

Although the rider was still a mile away, Johannes said, "It looks like Conrad, he rides like Conrad, by golly it is Conrad." He was excited and happy, it had been almost ten months since he had said goodbye to his best friend.

"Let me hug all the Spykers and pull Margaret's pigtails and then I wish to talk with you and Margaret in private." Everyone was overjoyed to see Conrad, even young Johannes, or Jonny as they had nicknamed him. Jonny came fearlessly wobbling to his "uncle" Conrad.

It was October and the farm was in harvest season. The corn was almost head high and the ears were heavy and already turning brown, ready for harvest for the pigs and the cows. The wheat was golden and swaying in the breeze, the vegetables were being stored for the winter, and the grape vines were drooping with hanging ripe, purple and green fruit. The wine-making was in full swing and all the children were enjoying trampling on the grapes to make them into a sodden mass. The juice was being collected to start the process of fermentation into the popular Spyker Riesling wine. It was a glorious day and there was no more beautiful farm than the Spyker's. Their large house was built solidly of field stones. It was a fortress that would not collapse in wind or war.

After all the greetings, Johannes opened a bottle of his Riesling wine and Margaret brought them cheese, bread, and crisp apples to enjoy with the wine. "Margaret, you need to stay and hear what I'm going to tell Johannes. It is not very good news. We have been in a constant war with the French armies that are coming into the Rhineland. The battles have not been fierce. It seems that they are but testing the Palatinate forces to see how strong our resistance will be. Our forces have been supplied by people like you, the farms that are in the area of the fighting. Now the French armies are adopting a new strategy, which is to begin at the end of this year of 1688. Our commanders who have spies in France have told us that Marshal Duras Vauban, the head of the Army for Louie XIV, has instructed advancing troops to burn and destroy the farms in Wurttemberg to keep them from supplying food for the armies of the Palatinate. This means by the end of the year and by the beginning of 1689, French troops will be coming to Aspach to destroy our farms."

Johannes looked at Conrad and then with a look of resolution looked skyward, as if seeking divine intervention. Margaret, hugged Johannes's arm and buried her face in his shoulder. Finally after a long quiet period, Johannes grasped Conrad's hand, "Thank you my friend. We will prepare for the worst. We will not leave our farm, but we will immediately start planning for the worst possible situation. No matter what, after the armies have left, the fields will still be here and the house will still be standing. We will prepare to protect ourselves and prepare to once again start over. Our fathers, Conrad, have had to start over many times. We will do the same.

We will not run. We cannot fight, but we will still be here when Louie's mongrels have gone on to ravage other farms."

"I must go to other Aspach farms," said Conrad, "and then get back to my force and my war, my lovely war. Our commander gave me just one day to spread this disastrous news. Most of our Aspach farmers are preparing to leave, but some like you are staying and preparing. Our Weiser farm is going to close and all the Weisers are going to relatives in Switzerland."

Margaret could not stand the thought of losing their farm and she quickly switched the subject. "How is your family, how is my Anna Magdalena?"

"We are managing. Life is not good around an Army camp. We had another son and buried another son. Conrad, Jr. was born in June and seemed healthy until he contracted the measles. In army camps, diseases spread quickly and the young and innocent do not have the strength to survive. Anna Magdalena is a strong women and never complains, but you can see the sadness in her eyes. She needs you, Margaret. When will this war be over? I think, never," said Conrad rhetorically.

Margaret just held Conrad and they wept together. "Someday you will have your Conrad, Jr. and he will be strong and good just like his father."

The Spykers started preparing immediately. "The forests are thick close to the creek where there are limestone caves. Martha, we will explore these caves and find several where we can store our belongings and store ourselves."

Although the situation was dire, it was almost like a grand adventure to ready the family for the oncoming vultures of "The Sun King." In the caves they wrapped and hid caches of every seed and seedling that represented their farm. Their heirlooms passed down from decades they stored as well, but they would leave most of the furniture and would rebuild their future after the French had left.

"Remember, the story in our Bible about Noah and the ark?" related Margaret to the family.

"We must take a mother and a father of our pigs, cows, horses, and chickens; and even now keep them by the caves. When the French come the animals will go in the back of the cave out of sight and sound."

"Why are we taking a mother and father?" asked six-year-old Catherine.

Rebecca gave Catherine a knowing smile and answered, "I will explain everything to you after your next birthday."

With everything prepared the family started having drills. They could vacate their home with all the essentials and be in their cave-home in less than an hour.

Nothing happened and life went on as normal. Fall turned to winter, which was a mild one. Spring approached. Maybe their Aspach area would be spared. Then came the news, on March 2, 1689, the city of Heidelberg and the surrounding farms were sacked. All the farms and households were destroyed. The French were headed to Aspach.

"Dad," shouted Rebecca, "look at the smoke coming from the Weiser farm."

"Family, this is it. The time we have been preparing for has arrived. Everyone grab the items you have been assigned, and go to our cave-home. Hurry. Leash and muzzle Lucky."

In less than an hour the Spyker home looked desolate, like no one had been there for months. They did not move out of the cave for two days. The forest was filled with smoke, and they heard shouting and laughing and gun fire. The night sky was filled with orange flames and they heard the bleating sounds of pigs and cows and the neighing of horses. All of a sudden it was quiet. Deathly quiet.

"We will wait one more night and then I will climb the tall oak on the edge of this forest and see if the soldiers have gone."

When the Spyker family returned to their farm, they held hands as if to say, we are all in this together. There was smoke and ashes where their out buildings had once stood. The animals were gone or lay still in the fields. The log fences were gone. The house was a shell of field stones with no roof. The loft was gone. The furniture was charred pieces of sticks. They had done a thorough job of destroying a homestead.

"Someday we will rebuild. But now if we rebuild and plant our crops and raise our animals, they will return and destroy us again. The forest, the creek and the caves will be our home until the war is over in this area," stated a stoic Johannes. He had one goal, to keep his family safe.

Little did he realize the war would continue for over seven more years. The end of the war would be in 1697 with the Treaty of Ryswick in a small town outside The Hague in the Netherlands.

A Hope for Normalcy
1697

———— ✎ ————

THE WAR WAS OVER. No one won. No one in Alspach cared who won. It was a time to rebuild, to get back to the normal life that they remembered from Christmas Eve, 1688, at the Spyker's home.

It was a weary looking Conrad and family that appeared on the Spyker farm in August of 1697. Although the Treaty of Ryswick was not yet signed by all belligerents, the war was over and Conrad's army of the Blue Dragoons was dismissed.

Johannes had already rebuilt the rooms and the loft. He had restored the storage buildings and had log fences containing the few pigs, cows, horses, and chickens. It was a long way to normalcy, but it was a start.

"Conrad, you and your family will stay with us until we can get your farm rebuilt," stated Johannes with firmness. "We want to hear all about your adventures since we last saw you that October day. The day we knew life was going to drastically change."

The two families spent a lot of time together that day talking about the last eight years. "Let me introduce the three newest members of our family. Strange things happen when you're stuck at campsites waiting for the next battle, not knowing if your husband is going to return the next night. This is Margareta, where did I get that name?" joked Anna. "She is almost six years old. This little girl of four is Maria Sabina and finally here is our son ready to take over the bakery business. He is already two and walks like his father. Conrad, Jr. can you say hello to your new friends?"

It was a wonderful visit. Both families had high hope for the future. Conrad, Sr. would reopen his bakery business in Alspach. His brothers would be back soon from Switzerland to take over the farming. All would be well until the next war and the next war, and the next war.

"Tomorrow," continued Margaret, "we will show you our cozy home of the last eight years. The pre-historic cavemen had nothing on us. We raised our animals down by the creek side. We planted our cabbages on the banks of the Zucker which also provided our fish. We enjoyed the rabbits, and pheasants that God always provided, with the best hunting dog ever, Lucky Louie, who is a lot smarter and braver than his namesake."

Indeed it was a beautiful day in late summer as the two families walked to the banks of the Zucker creek. The parents were all in their mid-thirties. The Spyker's girls were now teenagers and their son Jonny was now twelve years old. The Weiser family was girls galore. They ranged from four to sixteen and finally a boy, Conrad,. Jr. had survived.

They carried their picnic baskets filled with the best sausages, Weiser breads and pastries, fruits, and a couple bottles of Spyker's Reisling wine. Jonny carried Conrad on his back and told him about fishing in the Zucker creek. "We will catch some fine fish and cook them on a huge bonfire." Little Conrad had never seen a fish and had no idea of the adventures ahead.

They explored the caves and realized the good life they had, even in the most primitive conditions. They had survived and survived well. As they explored the caves and showed them to the Weiser family, Rebecca, Jonny, and Catherine realized they missed their home of the past eight years.

"Dad, come quick," shouted Jonny.

Johannes and the other parents feared some major disaster as they raced to the Zucker creek bank. There was Jonny with his makeshift fishing pole of a slender green limb, almost bent in half by the heft of the small mouth bass that was diving and then exploding above the water. Little Conrad was clapping and shrieking; the most excited Anna had ever seen him.

"My God, it's Louie Fifteen. The fish we've never been able to land. He's the king of the Zucker creek. Hold on, keep your line tight. Don't horse him in. Let him tire himself out," instructed Johannes.

Johannes senior was just as excited as Jonny and little Conrad. They had seen this fish and occasionally hooked him over the last three years, but the five pound bass had only teased them and eventually spit out the hook and laughed in their faces as he disappeared into the ten foot depths of his favorite hole.

A full half-hour later, Jonny finally dragged the then worn out king, to the bank. Little Conrad went to touch the fish but as it flopped a couple feet into the air, he cried out, "Mommy, help." All laughed and it was an often repeated story to young Conrad's dismay.

Jonny, hoisted the still lively and large bass, looked at Johannes who only nodded, and gently put Louis back into his home. At the end of this wonderful day, Conrad said, "Johannes, we would get in the way in your house that you are resurrecting. Could we stay in your war home?"

The Weiser family enjoyed the next two months before winter in the cave. Finally their farm was rebuilt. Conrad's brothers and family had returned. Conrad's stone ovens were again perking and life seemed to be back to normal.

The War of Spanish Succession
1701

—◦◦◦—

AFTER ONLY TWO YEARS OF freedom from war, King Louis the XIV was back at it again. The Spanish empire was huge, with territories all over Europe and in North America, however, the leadership was in disarray. Consequently they were militarily weak and financially unsound. Louis the XIV saw the opportunity to install his choice for King of Spain and increase his empire. Once again the Grand Alliance of the Holy Roman Empire along with Great Britain, the Dutch, and others knew they could not tolerate this new expansion of France. In 1701 the War of the Spanish Succession began. Once again there were war and armies in Bavaria and Wurttemberg. Once again the families of Wurttemberg, including the Spykers and Weisers, suffered the ravages of war. Although there was no immediate threat to their farms being decimated, the roving armies took liberties with their food supply and their peace of mind.

The war raged on. Would it ever end, would there ever be in the lifetime of Johannes and Conrad a lengthy period of peace? Both returned their thoughts back to Herr Leininger's America. Now they knew that the famous Mr. Penn, their friend, had founded his Pennsylvania colony. Pamphlets, secretly appeared, encouraging the Palatines to go to Pennsylvania. William Penn wanted the industrious German to come to his colony. He knew with their work ethics and desire for justice that they would make his colony strong and a successful "Holy Experiment."

Early in the winter of 1706, the war was not the most important concern of the Weisers and the Spykers. The village of Aspach and surrounding areas suffered an epidemic of smallpox. Smallpox was caused by a virus and not understood by anyone. There were, however, similarities between smallpox and cowpox. Cowpox was a lesser disease than smallpox and did not cause death or massive disfiguration of the human skin. Another phenomenon that was discovered, but not understood, was that those who worked with dairy cows got the cowpox disease but did not contract smallpox.

The epidemic viciously attacked the village of Aspach and surrounding villages. Conrad, who was showing his leadership abilities, mobilized the farm families to assist in helping the many that suffered the scourge of smallpox. All members of the Weiser and Spyker families came to Aspach to tend their neighbors. "Someday, someone a lot smarter than I will find a preventative for smallpox. It will have something to do with the lesser cowpox illness," opined Conrad. "Until then God has given us the miracle of being able to help those with this disease without getting the sickness ourselves. I also know we need to keep those who have the pox away from those who are still healthy."

The Spykers, Weisers, and other farm families who had dairy cows and had milked them for their families from the time they were barely able to reach the teats from their stools, tended and cared for the suffering.

Johannes had a disconcerting thought, "Margaret, you are not to help with the ill. You have never milked the cows. This was the one task you avoided from childhood and when we were married you asked not to have this task. I'm not sure why, because you have done more farm work than any women I know. You are not afraid of work, but this one task ..." Johannes was so concerned he could not finish his thoughts.

"To quote our Rebecca, 'fiddlesticks'. I don't know anything about this myth you and Conrad have cooked up, but I need to help others as they would help me." Margaret as well as all the family did not let fatigue or concern for their own health stop them from trying to help their neighbors survive or to comfort the sick and dying.

After a week of the smallpox rampage, Catherine came to her father, "Dad, we must do something about mother. She's looking ill and she can hardly stay awake." Johannes realized his greatest fear had come true. Margaret was ill with the smallpox. They put her to bed and tended to her every need. Margaret became sicker and sicker. Each one took turns trying to keep her fever down with cool cloths. They made chicken broth and forced her to drink, despite her lack of appetite and her terribly sore throat.

"Dad," said Johnny, "do you think Mother will die?" Johnny, who was already married and had his own stone house on the Spyker farm, could not conceive of life without his beautiful mother.

"Everything is in God's hands," said Johannes, who knew in his heart that his wife of twenty-five years, would not survive the night.

"Johannes," whispered Margaret in the strongest voice she had left, "bring the children into me. I want to say goodbye."

Events Leading to Emigration
1708/1709

―⟁―

"WE DESERVE BUT GRIEF AND shame, Yet his words, rich grace revealing, pardon, peace, and life proclaim. Here our ills have perfect healing; We with humble hearts believe Jesus sinners will receive.

When their sheep have lost their way, Faithful shepherds go to seek them; Jesus watches all who stray, Faithfully to find and take them. In his arms that they may live Jesus sinners will receive. . ."

The roof just about came off the little Lutheran church in Aspach as the fifty some families belted out their favorite song, "Jesus Sinners Will Receive." The Reverend Schmidt came to the pulpit. Everyone in the church wondered who the good Reverend would damn to hell today. He had already sent Louis XIV, Marshall Villars and many other French and Holy Roman Empire leaders to the netherworld.

"Good morning, congregation" boomed the Reverend Schmidt.

Jonny whispered to his dad, "Did he say good morning sinners?"

Johannes, Sr. tried not to laugh, but his son, with his great sense of humor always got him to laugh. At first, laughing did not come easy for Johannes after his wife Margaret had died, but Jonny kept at it, knowing that laughter would be the only cure for his father, who had lost the joy of his life.

"Ah," said the Reverend with a smile on his face. He was in a great mood this Sunday morning. "I see the Weiser family is here. I can tell because the first four rows are filled to the brim. Ah, Mr. Spyker, you are finally smiling after your loss. You must be anticipating a wonderful sermon today.

"Today, I am not going to give my usual fire and brimstone message to get you sinners back on track. I have received a letter from my friend William Penn. Although he is a Quaker rather than a Lutheran, he loves our church and religion as he does all religions. He only wants all souls to have the right to choose and worship as their conscience tells them.

It is with great pleasure that I now read his letter."

Dear Reverend Schmidt, my old friend and compatriot,

Are you still sending the French to hell and the Palatines to heaven? Until your congregation receives their heavenly goals, send them to America. Send them to Pennsylvania.

Pennsylvania has grown rapidly and we now have nearly 18,000 inhabitants and Philadelphia over 3,000. It is beautiful here and my tree plantings are providing the green urban spaces we have envisioned. Shops are full of imported merchandise, satisfying the wealthier citizens and proving America to be a viable market for English goods. Most importantly, religious diversity has succeeded. You can worship as Lutherans and all other denominations and religions are respected.

Despite the protests of some, I have insisted that our grammar schools be open to all citizens. This is producing a relatively educated work force. High literacy and open intellectual discourse has led to Philadelphia becoming a leader in science and medicine.

There is land for all who wish to farm. There are jobs for those who wish to pursue a craft, such as black smithy, milling, carpentry, shoe repair, weaving, and every craft needed in our community. We have need of food merchants such as bakers and shop owners that sell meat, fish, produce, and everything for the kitchen table.

You will not have armies camp on your farms and take your crops. You will not have fear for your life from roaming nomads. We live at peace and will not make war on anyone. ... . Reverend Schmidt continued to read and although it was as long as his fire and brimstone sermons, all remained attentive and excited as they dreamed of distant shores where they could finally live in peace.

After the church service the Weisers and the Spykers joined together on the Spyker farm for a meal. It was however a sparse meal as both families had been ravaged by the roving armies of the War of Spanish Succession. As they shared fellowship they kept an eye on the horizon for the next army to send them scurrying for the Zucker creek caves. There had been no peace. During the War of Spanish Succession, the French commander, Marshall Villars, had invaded their homeland. Once again they were ruined and once again started to rebuild.

Besides the armies and the never ending war, nature also dealt them a crippling blow. The winter of 1708/1709 was the coldest in five hundred years. The Rhine froze. Animals perished. No one was ever warm. Even the firewood would not ignite because of the cold. Life was miserable.

A number of their children and grandchildren perished. Maybe it was a blessing for them as they did not know a warm meal or a warm bed. It was hardly a week without a burial. All the vineyards were ruined and Johannes would have to start again on his wine producing. There would be many years without any profits from the vineyards.

The bakery of Conrad survived. Conrad only traded his bread for things his family needed. He often gave the bread away to needy families. They were beat. Where was God? It was time to leave, to give up. Not to give up and quit, but to give up and find a new life.

The letter from William Penn once again stirred in each family a new hope. Why not go to America? Even if you died on the journey, you were better off than dealing with the attrition and slow death that God had wreaked in Wurttemberg and the whole of the Rhine Palatine area.

Spring came mercifully to Wurttemberg, but it was still uncomfortably cold on that April afternoon of 1709. "Johannes, we have decided to leave Aspach." Conrad announced, "Queen Ann of England has been rumored to give us free land in America. All the Weisers, except my daughter, will travel down the Rhine to Rotterdam and then on to England and God willing, America. We will sell our farm to my daughter and her husband, who wish to still try to survive this God-forsaken area. Will you and the Spykers come with us? We are leaving in May and maybe in 1710 we will be in America. We don't know how we will do all this, but there is no reason to stay."

After a week of discussion among the Spyker family, Johannes went to visit his friend. "Conrad, someday, but not now. Both Rebecca and Catherine have small children and I am delighted to announce that Jonny will give me a grandchild in several months. The time is not right. The kids wanted me to go without them, but I can't leave them, particularly Jonny at this time. We will wait until the rabble has gone back to France and once again rebuild. "I'll help you get prepared, Conrad, and I insist on giving you some of my wine money."

The Weiser family prepared continuously for their June departure to the Netherlands, England and the New World. All the Spykers joined in with as much help as they could. *What a momentous task,* thought Jonny as he looked at Conrad and Magdalena and the eight surviving Weisers. They were all going. Only leaving in their burial homes the seven Weiser children who had not survived birth and the early years of vulnerability. Jonny particularly looked at Anna Magdalena who looked ill and frail and thought, *"She will not survive the journey."*

On May 1st, 1709, Anna Magdalena died after many painful months of having gout.

"Lord, bless this women and see her immediately in heaven," ordered Reverend Schmidt as he conducted the funeral of Anna Magdalena. The Aspach Lutheran church was filled. "She followed the two greatest commandments, Love thy God with all thy heart and all thy mind and all thy soul, and love your neighbor as thyself," continued the Reverend.

She was buried on the Weiser farm beside her seven children who had preceded her in death. Conrad, Jr quietly came up to Johannes Spyker after the funeral and the burial, "Mr. Spyker, I don't think Father is physically and emotionally strong enough to help our family make this trip to the New World. I'll be able to help him as much as possible with all the children, but I don't think he and I can manage alone. Maybe we should cancel the trip. Is there any way you can reconsider and come with us and be part of our family?"

Again Johannes discussed this possibility with Jonny. Jonny knew that his father would not survive many more years with all the continuous struggles with the armies and the difficulties of nature in the Wurttemberg area. Only the thought of emigrating to America gave Johannes the hope to keep on going. "You must go, Father. I can take care of the farm and continue our efforts with wine-making. It is important for you to go now, while you are still strong. Someday we will come, but you must go and prepare a place for us and all your grandchildren."

After much prayer and talks with Rebecca and Catherine, who like Jonny encouraged him to go and fulfill his dream, a dream he had since the early days in Herr Leininger's school. Johannes made the decision to go. His idea to go was enhanced by his thought that once he got established in the New World, he would have his children and grandchildren join him.

—— ∝∝∝ ——

On June 24th, 1709, at the break of dawn, all the community of the Aspach Lutheran church gathered at the Spyker farm. Reverend Schmidt gave them the blessing, "Lutheran children, go with your Lord Jesus and bring Lutheranism to the New World. Greet my friend William Penn with a kiss and a hug. Go with hope in your heart and know that our community in Aspach is with you in spirit."

There were many tears and goodbyes as Johannes, Conrad, and eight of the Weiser children hopped aboard the large wagon driven by Jonny and the beautiful horses from the Weiser stable. Naturally the good pastor, Reverend Schmidt, could not miss an opportunity to travel, preach, and damn the heathens who wouldn't listen. He traveled with Jonny in the shotgun seat.

Johannes, Conrad, and Conrad, Jr. had built two large scows for their journey down the Rhine. These they also loaded onto the wagon. A scow is a flat bottom boat with a blunt bow. It is similar to a raft but has sides to help contain all the supplies.

Conrad and Johannes both had left their worldly possessions with their families. They had only the necessities of life, which they hoped would last until they finally were able to establish a home in America. Both men were fairly wealthy as far as citizens of the Palatinate, because of their crafts of baking and wine making. They took this money with them in their money belts, which were heavy with currency, gold and silver. Surely this money would last until they had settled on farms and established baking and wine making careers. They had no idea of the expenses involved and the many months their journey would take.

They left Jonny at a landing just north of Strasbourg. The scows held and floated beautifully. They were works of good craftsmanship. Conrad, Conrad, Jr. and three young children in one scow and Johannes, George Weiser, and three other children rode in the second scow. There they began their journey to the New World.

Good Bye Father
1709

———— ∞ ————

"REVEREND SCHMIDT, DID I DO the right thing encouraging my father to travel in harm's way?" Jonny asked to the preacher, who was riding back with him from Strasbourg. It was late afternoon on June 24, 1709 and Jonny and the Reverend were returning from taking his father and the Weiser family to the banks of the Rhine. His father and the Weisers were beginning an adventure that included many challenges to its success. They were starting a trek to the New World that would take most of a year. From Strasbourg they would embark on scows carrying only the necessities of life and their faith. They would first go to Rotterdam with hopes of soon going to London and then to America, which was described in pamphlets as a "land of milk and honey."

"My son," boomed the Reverend who always spoke as if he was giving a sermon, "God will travel with them and they will bring the word of God to the heathens they call the Indians. You did the right thing and whatever happens is God's will. We will pray for them every day and God's will be done. You also did the right thing by not going. Your sweet wife Elizabeth is heavy with a child and now is the time for you to raise a family and rebuild the Spyker farm."

Jonny left Reverend Schmidt off at the Lutheran church, waited until the Reverend entered his house, then dismounted, took off his hat and went into the church. Tears flowed copiously down his cheeks as he prayed and reflected to the Lord. *"Dear Heavenly Father take care of my beloved father who is my best friend. Carry him and our great friends, the Weiser family, safely to a new land and a new life. If it be thy will, help me and Elizabeth, our new child and other children we will have, join him someday in a world that is free of constant war."*

As Jonny knelt on the hard wood floor of the church he thought of his father. He thought of the training sessions to get the family to the caves when roving armies threatened their very existence. He remembered the snug feeling of being in the cave in his mother's arms with his father telling him and his sisters that all was well. He remembered the look of anger but determination on his father's face when they returned to their burned out home. How he enjoyed working with his dad rebuilding their homestead. His father could do anything. This thought made Jonny smile as he knew that he would be like his father and never give up.

"Soon," he thought, *"I will be harvesting the vineyards as father travels to America. The wine will be so fine that everyone will think Father is still here. The corn will have heavy ears almost bringing the stalks to their knees. The wheat fields will be a swaying panorama of gold. How I love to see my sweet, beautiful, wonderful Elizabeth in her bonnet as she carefully picks the green beans from the garden."* Again Jonny smiled as he remembered Elizabeth looking up at him from her green bean picking and patting her round four month belly.

This caused Jonny to again talk to himself and the Lord, *"Life can still be good and dad will be with me every step of the way. I will make him proud, but oh how I will miss him. I soon will be a father and what a great teacher I had."* Jonny rose, bowed to the crucified Christ and left for home.

The Journey to London

1709

———— ✦ ————

"W<small>HOA THERE MY GOOD FELLOW</small>," challenged a huge man with his whole face covered with hair. Only his eyes and his mouth showed through the black forest of his beard. "You cannot pass this point without paying the toll required by our majesty, King Louie." The French now controlled the Rhine and intended to make the most of it. They didn't care that the Palatines were leaving, however, the Palatinate electors did care. It was the usual conflict of interest for these Palatines, the French wanted them to leave, the Count and his army tried to prevent them from leaving.

This event occurred many times during their float down the Rhine to Rotterdam. It must have been a whole family of river men that all looked alike. All were menacing and Conrad and Johannes dutifully reached in their purses for a silver piece. It took them a full month to get to Rotterdam and their money belts were getting lighter each day. Only Conrad, Jr. who was only thirteen challenged the toll collectors. "Yes and what happens if we don't pay the toll? This river belongs to all people. We should not have to pay to float down the great river that the Lord has given to us."

Conrad tried to quiet his son, who was headstrong, but brave and would indeed fight the river man if he had his way. The river man laughed so hard his huge belly shook. "Oh my fine rosy-cheeked young lad. You don't have to pay the toll, we will just roast you for dinner tonight."

The Weisers and Johannes continued to travel down the Rhine and continued to pay the tolls. Conrad, Jr. fumed inside and vowed to do all he could to make life fair for everyone.

In early August they completed the first leg of their journey. They joined thousands of other Palatines who had the same dream. Conditions in Rotterdam were not good, but the Weiser family and Johannes Spyker made the most of it and remained in good spirits. It was just a couple of weeks before they found that they would be going to England. Queen Ann, who needed inexpensive labor in the American Colony had them sent by boat over the short distance to England with the goal of sending them to America. Also she thought that bringing Protestants to England would help fuel the anti-Roman Catholic sentiments. It was also her thought that sending many Protestants to Ireland would help quell the Irish Catholic rebellion.

The Weisers and Johannes were sent to the tent city of Blackheath, which was just outside of London. Here they were to wait until ships were made available to take them to the Ireland or the New World.

"Mr. Spyker," said Conrad, Jr., who was taught to address elders in a respectable manner despite the familiarity, "what is all this religious concern, Catholic and Protestant? I don't see the difference, but it seems the religious matters are more important than how good or how bad is each person. To me God is God and Jesus is Jesus."

"You ask a good question, Conrad. Yes God is God and Jesus is Jesus. If we ever get to Pennsylvania, where William Penn has established his colony of religious freedom, it will make no difference. Some of the reasons for the French and the Palatinate electors fighting in our homeland of Wurttemberg are related to religion. I do think, however, the main reason was the greed and ego of King Louis XIV. He wants more land and more power and we are caught in the middle."

Johannes continued his explanation, "We are Lutherans simply because Martin Luther rebelled against the Catholic church and when the Catholic church expelled him, the church split into those who protested the ways of the church and those who remained faithful to the Catholic church. Today there are few differences between the Lutheran church and the Catholic church. England became Protestant initially because of foolishness. Henry VIII wanted to get rid of a wife, and since the Catholic church would not annul his marriage, he had England switch to Anglican. Conrad, you are so right. This business of wars over religions is not right. Your father and I, even before we were your age, wanted to go someplace where God is God, and Jesus is Jesus, and even if a person didn't believe, he or she had that right. We would have the freedom to live without religious consequences. We know Pennsylvania is that place, we think all of America is that place."

Conrad seemed pleased with such a complete and thoughtful answer.

⸎

Each day the tent city was uncomfortable, but the dream of going to America kept Conrad and Johannes from losing hope. Finally 3,000 Palatines were rounded up for transport. No, not to America, but to Ireland. They were sent there in hopes of causing the Catholic faith to be less dominate in Ireland.

"I'm glad we're not going to Ireland," said George Weiser, the twelve-year-old son of Conrad, Sr. . "But I don't understand why we were not chosen since we were some of the first Palatines in London."

"Son," said Conrad, Sr., "we were not chosen because we are Lutherans and our faith is very similar to the Catholic church. Now the Calvinists really dislike the Catholics, so these are the ones Queen Anne hopes will divide the Irish from their faith as it is vital to their system of government. We are lucky. We want only to go to America. I do fear, however, we will not be sent to Pennsylvania. It has been rumored that the English, who own the American colonies need us in New York. We'll just have to wait and see. Our Lord has a plan for us, but some day in one way or another, I am taking you and my family to Pennsylvania."

Johannes and Conrad and other Palatines were getting anxious to depart for America . Finally in December, they were assigned to one of the ten ships that were to take the Palatines to the colony of New York.

Conrad, Sr., who was becoming one of the Palatine leaders in London, was called to a meeting with the Duke of Marlborough and other Palatine leaders from different areas. "Gentlemen, by orders of Queen Anne," toned the Duke, "you will depart England before the first of the year. We have provided ten ships for you and they will take you to New York. The newly appointed governor of New York has made arrangements for you to reside in the New York colony. Here you will help supply England with badly needed naval stores. We will give you forty acres that you need work just three years to provide naval stores and then the land you use will be yours for whatever purpose you wish."

Conrad excitedly came back to his family, Johannes and the other Palatines, whom he represented, and told them the good news. Everyone had many questions of which only a few Conrad could answer. "When do we leave?" "How long will it take?" Where will we reside on the ship?" "What will we eat?"

What Conrad didn't know was that each ship captain would be paid ten pounds per head for each of thirty-three hundred Palatines. The more the captain could squeeze on the ship the more he made. The less the captain had to pay for food, the more money he made. The Palatines had no idea how difficult and dangerous this Atlantic crossing might be. Yet they looked forward to it eagerly.

By the first of December, Conrad was able to tell the people for whom he was the leader, "Fellow Palatines, we will sail on the Lyon and our captain will be Captain Alexander Stevenson. We will depart on December the 29th. If the weather holds and the winds are favorable we should be in New York by early March."

The Lyon of Keith
1710

—∞∞∞—

They departed from London on December 29th, 1709 and sailed from London down the Thames for America. However, after just a day of sailing, "Dad," said Conrad's sixteen-year-old daughter Anna Margarete, "why are we going the wrong way? I've saw these same shores about two hours ago." Anna was right. The ships, all ten of them, had turned around and were heading back to London. Conrad immediately made an appointment to see the Duke of Marlborough.

"Several of the captains were not happy with the agreement and decided to return until more favorable means were decided. The main problem, however, was with the gentleman on your ship, the newly appointed Governor of New York, John Hunter. He was not happy with the amount of provisions you Palatines would be given. It was in your best interest. It will be worked out and it will be just a matter of weeks until all problems are resolved." Truth be known, Governor Hunter could have cared less about the Palatines. He just wanted to establish how long he could keep them indentured and how much he would thrive from their work in providing naval stores, such as turpentine, tar, pitch, and ship spars.

Weeks of debating turned into months and it was not until April 10th, 1710, that the ships departed again from England. All were in high spirits as they left England fading on the horizon. The Lyon had on board about three hundred souls. Forty-eight of them, many of them children under ten years old, did not see the shores of New York.

The people were crammed into the ship to make as much money for the captain and his bosses as possible. Johannes gave up his bed to let the Weiser daughters have more room. He slept in hallways and on deck and everyplace possible. Although it was uncomfortable not to have a bed to sleep in, Johannes was able to breathe fresh air, as he often slept on the open decks of the Lyon.

"Ah, isn't this pork wonderful," said Conrad Sr. with a factious smile on his face. And how 'bout these beans, aren't they simply delicious?"

"Yes, Dad, this is the most wonderful meal we've had since yesterday, and the day before yesterday, and the day before yesterday."

"I get the idea my beloved Anna Barbara, but we must keep eating to survive. You are too skinny."

The Weiser family along with Johannes were able to keep from getting too depressed because of the constant humor and bantering between Conrad and Johannes.

"Kids," said Johannes, "did you know your father thought his desk was in the corner in Herr Leininger's school? He spent most of every school day there."

"You were so small you couldn't see above your inkwell. I thought the quill was your nose," countered Conrad.

"Your father was the reason my Margaret had such long hair. He pulled her pigtails every time our teacher turned to the slate board."

"Johannes, I still remember the first time you sat on one of our horses. How did it feel to be facing the tail?"

"Yeah, and I remember when you were told to join the Dragoons. You asked if fire would come out of their mouths."

"Kids, did you know that whenever Johannes had difficulty sleeping, he couldn't wait to get to one of Reverend Schmidt's sermons? I can still remember the good reverend looking out the window to see if a storm was coming. He never could understand why there was thunder, but no clouds."

"Conrad, Jr., you know why I have false teeth? I've had to eat your father's cement bread too many meals."

"Yes, Johannes, and congratulations on your new product last year, frozen wine. What will you think of next?"

"Ah, Conrad, my always best friend. I still remember your famous answer, which will go down in the history of education. During our days in school, Herr Leininger asked your father 'what is the name of the present pope?' and he also asked jokingly, 'what religion is he?' How well I remember your father proudly standing with a puffed-out chest and saying, 'Sir, the pope is Martin Luther and I think he is a Lutheran.'"

These conversations kept the younger Weisers and all around them entertained. But solemn days would be coming. The adults mostly fared well, but the children had not developed immunities, and those like Anna Barbara, who were young and small, began to get ill and lose their appetite.

About a month out to sea in May, "Ship Fever" started to break out. The sick were mainly children. Anna Barbara, age nine, was ill with the fever for over a week. Red spots started appearing all over her body. She suffered greatly no matter the attention that her father and everyone gave her. "Barbara, you must eat, you must drink the water."

Johannes refused his portion of water for almost a week and kept giving it to Conrad for Barbara. No matter, she kept getting thinner and thinner. Despite the prayers and the efforts, Anna Barbara died at sea.

Conrad, who had seen his wife die as well as many of their children, had great difficulty getting over this death. He could not smile and kept constantly checking his other children to make sure they were not ill. Conrad could not accept the death of Anna Barbara and could not even force himself to cry or to complete his grief. He refused to eat and divided his food amongst his seven remaining children. No matter how hard Johannes tried to console him, Conrad refused to regain his optimism. It was if he wanted to die also.

Finally after a couple of weeks, his son Conrad, Jr., now fourteen years of age took matters into his own hands. "Dad, you have told me many times, never to give up. I've listened to you and admired your spirit and desire for freedom. Otherwise, we would not be on our way to a better life. We cannot make it without you. Maybe we should not have left Wurttemberg, maybe we should just have stayed in Germany and suffered from the hands of the French and the Holy Roman Empire."

Conrad, Sr. kept looking at Conrad, Jr. for a long time and in his mind he thought, *"Here is a boy, no a man, who is stronger than I. He must survive and become the face of our ancestors in the New World."* Finally he broke down and sobbed and held on to his courageous son.

This is America
the Land of the Free?
1710

"Mr. Spyker, aren't those geese?" asked Conrad, Jr. "Why would we be seeing geese so far out in the ocean? Look, there's a tree limb."

"Land ahoy!" boomed one of the seaman.

It was June 13, 1710 when the Lyon limped into the New York harbor at the mouth of the Hudson River. Many on board were ill and the ship's captain and a Lutheran minister, Reverend Schuler, former pastor at the Speyer Lutheran church, had buried forty eight souls at sea.

The ship's captain and the newly appointed Governor of New York, Robert Hunter, who had sailed with them, but in far superior quarters, boarded a small dingy and went to get clearance for the ship to dock on the Hudson bank. After several days the captain returned and asked for an immediate meeting with the various Palatine leaders. He addressed them, "Gentlemen, we cannot land in the mainland at this time. The health authorities are afraid the illnesses on board will cause an epidemic with the present population. We will go to the island that you see off the coast, Nutten

Island. The health officials will visit us weekly and determine when the quarantine can be lifted."

"Where will we stay?" asked Conrad.

"You can stay on the ship, or make your own shelter on the Island. Your Governor has arranged for fresh water and food to be brought periodically. This will help you get well and ready to survive in a new world. Right now Governor Hunter is surveying the lands to find tracts that will be well suited for the production of naval stores. The banks of this river, the Hudson, are covered with pine trees, which are necessary for tar and turpentine."

The Palatine leaders were resigned and went back to their communities and related that it would be several weeks before they would be settling in the mainland.

Conrad and Johannes discussed the situation. They had experienced the "several weeks" when departing London, which turned into "several months."

"We will not stay on the ship but we will build shelters and make our situation as livable as possible. We doubt if we will be going to the mainland of New York for a long time." said Conrad to his children.

They took their belongings from the ship, and with crude tools and lots of hand power built lean-to sheds sizeable enough to comfortably house all of them. Their living quarters were the envy of many others on the ship. Soon others were coming to Johannes and Conrad for their help in constructing their own living quarters.

As Conrad predicted, weeks turned into months. While the quarantine was continuing, Governor Hunter was negotiating for land for the Palatines to farm for the required naval stores. Finally he negotiated with Robert Livingston for land on the East side of the Hudson River. Little did Governor Hunter know that the trees were not suitable for producing naval stores.

Finally, in October, the quarantine was lifted and Governor Hunter brought the Palatine families to the east side of the Hudson to their dwelling place for three years, the Livingston Manor. It was not the dream Johannes and Conrad had envisioned. They still were not free. For all practical purposes they were indentured servants, supplying naval stores for England. Each family was given ten acres of land instead of the forty they had been promised. Both Conrad and Johannes were approaching fifty years of age, and despite all the disappointments, both were unwilling to give up their dreams of freedom. The freedom to decide their own destinies.

Schoharie, New York

1713

———— ⊷⊶ ————

DURING THE DAYS AT THE Livingston Manor, Conrad, Jr., could not stay cooped up on a small farm. He worked hard, but then would disappear for days at a time. Conrad had a knack for languages and became friends and was able to converse with many of the younger Mohawk, who lived in the area.

The Mohawk were part of the Iroquois Nation. Although they did not seek war, they were feared by other Indian tribes. They were friendly to the White man who came in peace to the Mohawk Valley. They described to Conrad the lands that lay north of Livingston Manor in the Catskill Mountains. It was called the Schoharie Valley, which means "floating driftwood." It was a seven day journey to get to this land, which they described as fertile and able to grow bountiful crops.

Conrad made friends with a young Indian boy about his age, Orenda. Orenda helped Conrad learn his language and also told him about the Schoharie Valley. No one knew how young Conrad could easily learn the Indian languages, but it was a gift that was valuable to the Palatines. Besides learning the language of the Mohawks and other Indian nations, Conrad was able to adapt to their way of life.

One day Orenda asked Conrad, "Would you like to see this valley where you can grow pumpkins bigger than a house? I will take you there. We will travel for seven sunsets."

Conrad went to his father and asked his permission. "Son, you go with my blessing. Maybe this will be a place someday where we can move our family and farm and create the life we wanted in America."

Orenda helped Conrad pack the way of the Mohawk, carrying everything he needed to sustain himself for a week. Early in the morning a couple of days later, they set out and traveled almost due north from their farm in the Livingston Manor. Conrad made a map of everything during his journey. He saw where they could travel by boat on large streams and lakes, and charted the easier paths that Orenda traveled. They came to the Catskill Mountains, found a deer path that made climbing less treacherous. It was a path that few would see, but the Mohawks knew it was the best route. It became known as the Catskill Pass.

After they descended from the mountains, Conrad saw the green valley of Schoharie. To the north of the valley was a large river, called the Mohawk. To Conrad's eyes it truly was a place where you could grow pumpkins as big as a house.

Conrad excitedly told his father and Johannes about the valley. "Johannes," said Conrad, Sr., "I'm going to explore the area and see if we can buy this land for our Palatine families. When our indentured services or 'freedom' according to our English friends is complete, maybe this is where we will settle and finally find the life we are seeking. I do not wish to settle here along the Hudson."

It was difficult for Conrad, Sr. to get away because of his responsibilities, not only for his own farm but for the other Palatine farms for whom he was made captain. His every move was watched by Governor Hunter and the authorities under the governor.

"Johannes, let's be honest. We are no better off now than we were in Wurttemberg. The name of our 'thorn' has just changed from the French to the English. I'm being watched, maybe you could go with my son and explore this area. If you find it a place for our future, you would negotiate with the Mohawk to buy and deed the land."

Despite all the expenses of the journey to America, both Johannes and Conrad, as well as many of their Palatine neighbors, still had enough finances to buy land. This was their goal. Ownership of land was their idea of belonging, of creating a new life for themselves and their families. Johannes, particularly, wanted this ownership so he could send for his family.

———⌾———

Johannes, with the help of Conrad, Jr., now sixteen years old, and a respected friend of the Mohawk in the Schoharie Valley, traveled many times to the valley. Orenda introduced him to his uncle, Atsila who was the chief of the Mohawk in the valley.

"You cannot purchase land. No one can purchase land. It is not our land. The land belongs to the Spirit or the one you call God. You can settle here and we will keep peace with you. We will respect your homes and farms and you are to respect our lands," said Atsila. Neither Johannes, nor Conrad realized that although this land was the home of the Mohawk, it was also land claimed by both the Dutch and the English as if the Mohawk had no rights.

———⌾———

The scheme of using the Palatines as quasi-indentured servants did not work. After almost three years of back-breaking work on the Livingston Manor, it became obvious that these trees could not produce the naval stores required for success of the project. The governor, who had put so much trust in Robert Livingston, who was also commissioner of Indian Affairs, had not yet gained the riches he envisioned. The only person who "won" in the project was Robert Livingston. Most realized after the three years that he was a "scoundrel." Finally the English gave up and the Palatines could have the land without commitment.

"Conrad and Johannes, you cannot leave your farms along the Hudson. I forbid it and all England forbids it." lectured Governor Hunter when he learned that Johannes and Conrad were going to lead Palatine families away from the civilized banks of the Hudson. "After, all you have beautiful farms that we have given you. Stay, colonize New York for your good and for the good of your Motherland, England."

Johannes was never afraid to speak out and never afraid of a fight after all the hell the French, English, and the Holy Roman Empire had put him through over the years. "My dear Governor, you brought us to America in the most impossible conditions with greedy captains who were not concerned about our welfare. We lost many of our children. Even now you have made apprentices of some of our children without our consent. You have taken them from their families. You promised to give us forty acres, we have less than ten acres. We've tried to harvest naval stores out of inappropriate forests. You have given up this impossible venture of naval stores for land. England is not our Motherland, we are Germans. You have failed and now we wish to venture on our own."

In the Spring of 1713, despite the efforts of the small armies the Governor had watching the Palatines, Johannes. and Conrad, Jr., who now despite his youth was a respected leader of the Palatines, silently and stealthily left the banks of the Hudson for the land of the huge pumpkins.

It took them almost two weeks of winding their way through the forests, over streams, rivers, and mountains to reach the Schoharie Valley. On the journey they encountered many wild animals, deer, moose, wolves, and bear. They were ably led by young Conrad's friend Orenda. The Indians they met were friendly and helped them with food and water. It was a happy journey. They all, old and young, made the journey successfully.

On the day they reached the peak of the Catskills they saw down below them plush green grass land, small ponds and streams, and dense forests. "This is our home. This is where I will bring Jonny and the rest of my family," said Johannes. He was overwhelmed with gratitude, thinking his journey finally ended.

Johannes staked out forty acres, as did each family. The first year was just one of raising the bare amount of beans, maize, and potatoes. The winter was very difficult as they were able to store only enough food to survive until spring. It was this winter when Johannes Spyker realized he was too lonely to be happy.

Conrad, Sr. was involved in politics with the Governor of New York, and subsequently returned to England to represent the Palatines claim in the New World. Conrad, Jr. decided with his father's blessing to spend a year with one of the Mohawk tribes. It was both the Conrads' idea that he learn, not only to speak the Mohawk language fluently, but also able to understand the Mohawk ways. Conrad, Jr. became successful in both goals and was able to negotiate and retain good relationships with the Indians.

Lomasi
1714

"This is how I wish the readers to picture Lomasi"
- AUTHOR

ONE COLD SNOWY DAY IN January, 1714, Johannes went to visit the camp of the Mohawks and Atsila, Chief of the Maqua Tribe. "You should stay with us this winter," said Atsila, "and learn how to survive our winters. Winter should be a happy and a joyous time of making friends. You should be warm, well fed and learn to dance and sing. You should learn the ways of the Mohawk. You are still a young man, Johannes, but you are acting like an old man.

"Next spring you will also learn how to better supply yourself with food; how to grow the same crops that we grow, and how to hunt and fish in our bountiful land. Man cannot live on corn and beans alone. "

Johannes decided to stay with the Mohawk and live in the same longhouse as Atsila and his family. The longhouses were not tents, but large wooden frame buildings where many families stayed together in communal living. They were covered with the bark of elm trees.

Johannes struggled with the language, but slowly learned how to communicate successfully with his "roommates." He was never to become as fluent as Conrad, Jr., who had the gift of youth in learning languages, but he learned enough to be accepted by his new family, albeit with much laughing at his difficulties in speech and his strange German ways. Johannes did not abandon his flock of fifty Palatine families, but visited them frequently and often brought them meats, berries, and herbs to supplant their meager first year's crops. He did, however, learn to appreciate his family in the longhouse.

One day as Johannes was enjoying ice fishing by himself, but with no luck, he saw a lonely man, dressed in bulky fur and a large beautiful hat of many rabbit furs, fishing a short distance away. Gaining confidence in his speaking and wanting to make new friends who also enjoyed his favorite sport of fishing, he said, "You're doing well. Look at all the long fish laying on the ice. How are you doing so well and I can't even catch a cold?"

The fisherman laughed at his struggles with the Mohawk language, and then turned and smiled. She was not a fisherman, but a fisherwoman. Johannes could not tell if she was shapely as the furs made her look bulky. She had golden skin that looked like it had been kissed by the sun. Her hair was the black typical of the Mohawk, but also shiny and healthy. Johannes in his mind guessed her to be in her mid-twenties, but later he was to find that she was thirty-two.

"Let me show you. You must reach the bottom of the lake with your line," she said. The lake was about the size of Johannes's now ruined vineyard. "You must use these flint weights to get to the bottom. In the winter, fish are lazy and only lay close to the bottom and hope some food slides by their long-pointed noses. I will help you. My name is Lomasi and I am from the village of Tehandaloga. I know you are from the village of Ganegahaga, which is the village of our chief."

Johannes met Lomasi several more times during the next few weeks and they became friends. He learned that her mate, Kessegowaase, named such because he was the swiftest of all the Mohawk in Schoharie, had died in warfare against the Cherokee.

Johannes was as perplexed as he was lonely and thought: "*How could I have deep feelings for another women after Margaret? What does she look like other than her beautiful face? Surely she is not bulky outside the bearskin. She has a slender face with eyes like a young doe.*" Her eyes held Johannes in a mesmerized state. She was tall as was typical of the Mohawk Tribe and moved gracefully. It was a confusing but an energizing experience for Johannes, who was now fifty-two years old. Johannes had no idea how to make their relationship other than friends.

Their relationship continued through February and three results came about: Lomasi was finally able to laugh and enjoy life after the death of her brave husband, Johannes was no longer lonely, and Johannes caught a lot more fish.

One March day, Johannes returned to his village of Ganegahaga in high spirits. He had a wonderful morning and afternoon with his beautiful mystery. "You seem in high spirits my friend. I see you caught many fish. They will be wonderful this evening at our dinner. Is catching fish that exciting for you, or is there something else that has put a smile on your face and a bounce in your step?" chided Chief Atsila. "Maybe tonight will be wonderful at dinner and after dinner, who knows?" continued the chief with a some-what secret smile.

Johannes dreamed deeply in his sleep that night, covered warmly with fur skin and sleeping on a huge and plush bear skin "mattress." During his sleep, he started picturing Lomasi walking toward him in a doeskin dress with long black braided hair. The face of an angel, yes, an Indian angel, she smiled and continued to walk toward him. Johannes was becoming more warm and comfortable and gently woke to the feeling of a warm body next to him. He turned and drank in the dark doe-like eyes and smiling face of his lovely Lomasi. As he gathered her into his arms he realized she was not bulky at all.

The next day was a wedding. A marriage, blessed by the God of Johannes and the Spiritual God of the Mohawk.

Soon it was time for Johannes to plant his crops and rejoin his community of Palatines. Lomasi made her home with Johannes among the Germans. She helped teach both men and women how to farm successfully in this new country. Although Johannes and Lomasi never conceived, they can be called the "founding father and mother" of the first German-Schoharie settlement.

Schoharie to Tulpehocken
1723

THE GERMAN PALATINES STAKED OUT their land in the valley. They cleared the fields and planted their crops. Over a short period they brought in livestock and horses and had what they thought was an ideal life. After all, the Mohawk had acknowledged that this was their land. They had tried to purchase the land but were told, "You settled it. You farmed it. It is yours."

Peace once again escaped Johannes Spyker and the other Palatines. The land had been claimed by England. Governor Robert Hunter, once again, made life miserable for these original settlers, who by the sweat of their brow and back-straining work had settled and civilized the valley of Schoharie. He had become bankrupted in his futile effort to provide naval stores for England. Soon he would be replaced by a more benevolent governor, but to recoup his losses, he sold a patent to the Vrooman family in Albany, who in return sold the land to five partners also from Albany, New York. This patent included ownership of the majority of the Schoharie valley, which included the land of Johannes Spyker and the fifty families he had led to this fertile valley.

"Johannes, you can stay and continue to farm this valley, but you must now purchase the land from the Vroomans and the other partners who own the patent to this land," said the governor. "If you object, we will send our sheriff to have you arrested as we already have arrested your friend John Conrad Weiser."

The argument would continue over several years. Conrad, Sr. would go back to England to plead the case of the Palatines to Queen Anne. His efforts, were to no avail, and Conrad returned to Schoharie a broken and disheartened man. It was as if this was the final blow for Johannes's best friend. Later his son Conrad would take up the fight and become, along with Johannes Spyker, the leader of the German Palatines in the Schoharie Valley.

Governor Hunter was recalled to England and replaced by Governor Henry Burnett, but not until Hunter had successfully refuted the ownership of the Palatines, and made for himself a small fortune. Finally after the years of struggle with varying parties claiming ownership of the land of the German Palatines in Schoharie, Governor Burnett formed the Council of 1722. Besides Governor Burnett, major leaders of the Palatines, including Johannes and Conrad, Jr., the governor of Pennsylvania, Governor William Keith, and Indian leaders were members of this council. Governor Keith had been appointed governor of Pennsylvania upon the death of William Penn. He was appointed by William Penn's wife and was a disciple of William Penn. He believed in the philosophy that all people could worship and live in peace.

The purpose of the council was to decide the ownership of the valley. Two alternatives were made clear to Johannes and Conrad. If they wanted to stay in the valley, they must lease or purchase the land that they thought was theirs. The cost was prohibitive. Secondly, they found a friend in Governor Keith from Pennsylvania. "Gentlemen," said Governor Keith to Johannes and Conrad, "I agree with you that this is an unfair and complicated decision of land ownership. You will never own your farms and homes, which you thought were yours. Even if you purchase, someday in the near future new claims will again arise and you will be faced with tangling ownership issues. You have developed farms, your crops are becoming bountiful, you have brought in livestock and skillfully increased your herds. Others may not see your value to America, but the colony of William Penn does. We want you to come to Pennsylvania. We will give you land, more than you have in Schoharie. You will get the legal papers for ownership of these lands. They will never be refuted. You are the people that will make Pennsylvania the best of the colonies. Come to Pennsylvania, come to the Tulpenhocken area, the Western Frontier of Pennsylvania."

Although not an easy decision to again relocate and rebuild, the Schoharie Palatines thought what Governor William Keith had said was appealing. "Finally, someone wants us. Someone sees how hard working, honest, and skillful we are. Conrad," said Johannes, "I think we should go to the colony that your father and I heard about, the 'Holy Experiment' of William Penn. I do not want confrontation. I want to live in peace. I want to bring my children to America. I will talk with Lomasi. She is wise and if she agrees we will go and go soon."

"Johannes," said Conrad, Jr., "if we decide to go, you will be the leader of the first group. I must stay and interpret between my Palatine friends and my Indian friends. I do not think it should be a large group. But if you go and find it as Governor Keith says, we will follow."

It was decided, Johannes and Lomasi would lead a party of fifteen families to Tulpehocken. "We should go, Johannes," said Lomasi. "Chief Atsila also thinks we should go. He is sad that the land he gave you has been taken away by White men not honest like you. You are my family. I know the forests and the streams to the "land where the turtle sang and wooed," to Tulpehocken. I will help you understand the Indians in this area. They will know that

79

we come in peace and will not stay in their area, but continue to the colony that you call Pennsylvania."

It would not be an easy journey. It would be four hundred miles as the crow flies. They would be going through dense forests and fording large creeks and rivers. It would be a slow journey that would take over a month. They would be bringing with them their cattle, over two hundred heads of the strongest bulls and cows and a fine stable of horses.

Johannes, along with the help of Lomasi and several other of the families that would be going, worked the rest of the year preparing for the journey. They would depart after the winter, when the birds began to sing and the water fowl returned to the lakes and rivers of the Mohawk Valley, in the spring of 1723.

In early May the journey began with fifteen families, the cattle, and the horses. The majority would ride where possible and several herdsmen would drive the cattle on land close to the waterways. When they arrived at the shores of the Susquehanna, they camped for several days, while they built canoes and large rafts. The canoes would carry the majority of the people and the rafts would carry the supplies and utensils needed to start a new life in a new and remote area of the Pennsylvania colony.

The canoes and the rafts would always keep the cattle and horses in sight, thus it was a slow journey. They passed the village of Harrisburg, which one day would become the capital of Pennsylvania. The Indians they met along the way were peaceful and Lomasi was able to help them communicate.

Shortly after Harrisburg, they came to the Swatara Creek and continued down that smaller water path. Eventually they reached the Tulpehocken creek and shortly thereafter they came to the foothills of the Blue Mountains. They were home.

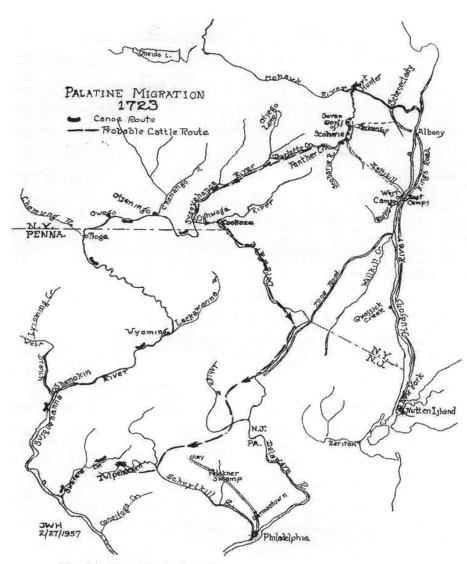

Map of the Palatine Migration from Schoharie, New York, to Tulpehocken, Pennsylvania, showing the water route taken by the canoes via the Susquehanna River, Swatara Creek and the Tulpehocken Creek, and also the "overland" route taken by the cattle-drivers. The broad band of the Appalachian Mountains extends across the western (left) side of this map. To avoid the dangerous trails in these mountains, the cattle-drivers turned east at Oghwaga to Cookoze (located above center of map), then turned southeast, following the broader and safer valley of the Delaware River to Tulpehocken.

(The map and the information below is provided by the Historical Society of Burks County. It is part of an article written by John W. and Martha B. Harper,

"The Palatine Migration – 1723"
"From Schoharie to Tulpehocken"

Map of the Palatine migration from Schoharie, New York to Tulpehocken, Pennsylvania, showing the water routes taken by the canoes, via the Susquehanna River, Swarta Creek and Tulpehocken Creek and also the "overland" routes taken by the cattle-drivers. The broad band of the Appalachian Mountains extends across the western (left) side of this map. To avoid the dangerous trails in these mountains, the cattle-drivers turned east at Oghwaga to Cookoze (located above center of map), then turned southeast, following the broader and safer valley of the Delaware River to Tulpehocken.)

"We are The Pennsylvania Dutch"
1724

———— ∞∞∞ ————

JOHANNES AND LOMASI STAKED SIXTY acres when they arrived. Later they staked another one hundred acres that remained as forests. This land would someday be for Johannes's sons. They cleared the land, kept five acres of grazing land for their ten cows and bulls, five acres for Johannes's new vineyard, one acre for a vegetable garden, one acre for a homestead, and planted the rest in corn and wheat. By the summer of 1724 they were seeing that the land was rich and productive for all their products, corn, wheat, vegetables, grape vines, and excellent grass lands for dairy and beef cattle.

Johannes knew exactly how to build a house. It would not be anything like the dwellings he had lived in since arriving in New York. He carted back from the Blue Mountains, boulders about two feet in diameter and lovingly mortared them in his new home. He crafted a loft and dug a basement. It was similar to his home in Aspach.

The community of fifteen families was soon joined by other friends from Schoharie. Soon they together built a Lutheran Church and installed their friend from the Lyon Ship, Reverend Schuler, as the pastor.

One day a year after their arrival in Tulpehocken, "Johannes, a letter from Aspach," cried the courier from Philadelphia. Mail arrived only once a week and seldom did the German pioneers receive any mail. This was a major event in the community. Johannes held his breath, praying the letter would be from his son Johannes Peter Spyker, or Jonny as he had always lovingly called his son. Thank God, it was. He read the letter to Lomasi:

Dear Father,

It has been almost fifteen years since you left with the Weisers to America. I've longed to hear from you so I could respond back. Finally, in June, I received one of your letters. I see by your frustration that you have written frequently, but this is the only letter I have received. Your struggles have made our family weep, but we celebrated the letter knowing that you are alive.

We are happy you met Lomasi. Mother would be happy also. Someday, with God's grace we will see you and Lomasi. However, it still is not time for us to leave even though the situation is not much better than when you left.

Dear father, this will be a long letter to bring you up to date on my family and your grandchildren. When you left Wurttemberg in 1710 . . .

Johannes Peter
Spyker (Jonny)
1685 - 1762

Jonny and Elizabeth
1700

———◦∞◦———

Jonny and Elizabeth sat and listened intently to the teacher in the one room Aspach school. Actually Elizabeth listened intently, Jonny looked intently at Elizabeth and thought

"She's the prettiest girl in the school, probably the prettiest girl in the world."

Elizabeth was one of five girls in a school of twenty students. This was the same school her father, Basil Nead, had attended. The teacher was a stern man who tried not to show his deep love for his students. He thought, like his father, Wilhelm Leininger, Sr. that discipline was a necessity in a world of uncertainty. *"The uncertainty,"* he thought *"of who will overrun our farms and take our crops today? Will it be the French, the Holy Roman Empire, the Spanish, Austrians or Prussians? What difference does it make?"* The Leiningers had been the teachers of the Aspach youth for forty years.

Wilhelm, Jr. continued to muse *"Why do they call the war that started in 1618 the 'Thirty Year War?' Why don't they call it the 'Fifty Year War' or the 'Never Ending War?' No leader cares about our people, only about who has control of our Germany. Who has the bragging right? Dear Lord, I'm thirty-five years old and have never tasted the concept of William Penn's freedom. Someday I will pack up my family and go to America."*

Wilhelm's reverie was interrupted by a shriek from Elizabeth, "Herr Wilhelm, Jonny has put a frog down my back. I hate him and wish he would go to Reverend Schmidt's hell." Tears flowed down her rosy cheeks as she shook her glorious golden locks with anger.

"Jonny, go to your corner. The corner we now call 'Jonny's corner.' It is reserved for you. You spend more time there than in your 'pew.' After school we will administer three strokes of Jonny's paddle. My Gott, my young heir to the Spyker throne, you are the smartest student in our school. Hopefully someday you will have a son that will torment you as much as you torment our darling Elizabeth."

"*I can't help myself,*" Jonny thought. "*I like her attention even if it's because she yells at me and says she hates me. I wonder how she will like the garden snake that is in her lunch pail?*" Jonny looked more like his mother than his father. He was strongly built and masculine for his fifteen years of age. He kept his dark hair at shoulder's length and had deep dark eyes that seemed to have a look of mischief.

Elizabeth had long blond hair and blue eyes. Her eyes were not the eyes of mischief, but the eyes of an angel. "*I really don't hate Jonny,*" she thought. "*He's so fun when he's not mean to me. Mother says boys only tease the one's they love. He must love me a lot.*"

All of a sudden Elizabeth was seventeen. It was Christmas Eve at the annual Spyker's party. The house was filled with friends and relatives of Johannes and Margaret. Despite the ever present danger of roving armies, there was much joy and laughter in the house. It was to be the last Christmas Eve party for Johannes and Margaret. The Christ and Kaderman families were already there with their extended family, which included grandchildren from cradle rockers to the "why" five-year-olds.

Rebecca and Catherine, daughters of Johannes, Sr. and Margaret, were there with their husbands and a roving band of children, many crawling faster than the Weiser horses. The house was jumping and the noise was loud enough to wake up Pope Clement at the Vatican.

"Margaret, I'm so happy you invited my good friend Basil Nead," said Johannes. Soon they heard the small bell on the front porch as Basil was ringing out "Oh Tannebaum."

"Jonny, would you answer the front door. It is our friends the Neads. The name didn't register with Jonny as he answered the door and bowed and said a greeting to Basil and Sophia. Jonny was always the effervescent one when meeting anyone. All of a sudden – "silence"– as following her parents was a golden angel with a knowing smile on her pretty face. He hadn't seen Elizabeth since the last day of Herr Wilhelm's school as she had gone to Switzerland to live with her Aunt and Uncle and to continue her education. "Well hello Jonny," said an angelic voice. "Where should I put the garden snake I brought you for Christmas?" They both laughed and Jonny regained his effervescence.

"Dearly beloved, we are gathered together on this 23rd of September, 1709, here in the sight of God, and in the face of this congregation, to join together this man and this woman in Holy Matrimony," Reverend Schmidt proclaimed so the whole world could hear. These were his two favorite young people in his congregation and he wanted the good Lord to pay special attention. It was as if he said, "Do you hear me Lord?"

"Johannes Peter Spyker, do you take Elizabeth Margaret Nead to be your wedded wife to live together in marriage? Do you promise to love, comfort, honor and keep her for better or worse, for richer or poorer, in sickness and in health, and forsaking all others, be faithful only to her so long as you both shall live?"

"I do." said Jonny, with tears in his eyes as he looked at the empty space in the pew next to his father.

Another Johannes Peter Spyker
1711

"OH MY DEAR HUSBAND," SAID Elizabeth with tears in her blue eyes, "we have lost our child. We have lost the most important person in your life." Jonny gathered Elizabeth in his arms and wept with her, but said sternly, "No, you are the most important person in my life. We will have other children, but we will never have another Elizabeth."

Elizabeth had miscarried a couple of months after Johannes, Sr. had left. They were not to hear from him for fifteen years. Although Jonny never lost hope, it was a void in his life. It was not too long until Johannes Peter Spyker the 16th or whatever was again on his way.

October 27th, 1711: "He's here. He's handsome. He's healthy and so is his beautiful mother, my Elizabeth." The whole town of Aspach and the neighboring farms saw a young man riding "hell bent for high water" telling the joyous news. Jonny was at the side of Elizabeth during the entire period of birth. Elizabeth came through everything just fine, but Jonny suffered. It was amusing to see a strong man, crying, fainting, reviving, crying, and fainting again, while Elizabeth just smiled through her pain and tried to comfort her husband. Finally after his "labor" was complete, Jonny got on his knees, "Thank you dear Lord, thank you dear Jesus. If it be your will, let Johannes Peter Spyker with his brothers and sisters someday greet the eastern sun in America."

Elizabeth was beaming with joy, and although she understood the necessity of calling the first born Johannes Peter, she wanted him to be unique. "Jonny, this child will always be Johannes Peter Spyker, but what would you think if we called him Peter?"

"Peter it is and what a proud name for this leader to be. The name will always remind me of the first disciple of Jesus, Peter the fisherman."

Peter was never the typical kid in the community of Aspach. He resembled his grandfather in stature and in appearance, however, some strange combination of genes had gained him bright red hair and freckles. He was a charming and charismatic child even as a five-year-old. He particularly enjoyed engaging adults in conversation and wanted to learn everything.

After Sunday service when Reverend Schmidt greeted the congregations at the exit of the church, and no one dare pass him by, Peter would question the reverend about his sermon. "Reverend Schmidt, you said we were all sinners. How did you know that I steal cookies from the cookie jar? Am I bent for hell? I'll bet Jesus took cookies from Mary's cookie jar."

The Reverend Schmidt would tousle his red hair and admit, "Peter, I also took cookies from my mother's jar, but Jesus forgives us. All we need to do is ask for forgiveness."

Peter, with his amazing blue eyes, looked directly at the rotund preacher, "So Reverend Schmidt, if I steal cookies tomorrow, and then ask for forgiveness, then I'm not bent for hell?"

Reverend Schmidt laughed so hard that his whole body shook like a bowl of jello and he had trouble gaining his breath. "Peter, are you sure you are not a Catholic?"

Elizabeth, who was well educated, even gaining a college degree while she was in Switzerland during the wars between the Holy Roman Empire and the French Empire of the Sun King. She read every night to Peter and soon found him at five years old able to read even the readings meant for adults. Peter's favorite book was *The Fables* by La Fontaine. Elizabeth started reading *The Fables* to Peter and after several weeks found him reading the book by himself. "Peter, are you really reading the Aesop fables or just looking at the words?" Peter then proceeded to read out loud, although hesitantly, several pages to his mother.

Peter was seven-years old and Elizabeth and Jonny both wanted to give him the opportunity to go to school. Elizabeth took Peter and went to see the teacher of the Aspach school, with the familiar name, Wilhelm Leininger. "I'm sorry Mrs. Spyker, but we do not allow students to be in our Aspach school until they are eight. You must understand, even eight-year olds are not ready to read, spell, understand, or cipher. We will be delighted to have him as we have the other Spykers as soon as he turns eight. It would be so difficult for Peter and would not be fair to me and the older students to struggle with a seven-year-old as we try to move forward to get the younger students to read words and the older students to read stories. If he is like his dad, he would be a lot of fun, but learning would be secondary. Regardless, Jonny was one of my favorites; I still enjoy thinking about his seeking your attention by devious means."

Peter sat quietly through the conversation. When the conversation seemed to come to a halt and the decision of "no" seemed to be made, Peter chimed in, "Herr Leininger, I really want to start school this year and my father has made me promise not to cause a disturbance that would make me sit in the 'Jonny Spyker' chair, which must be that one facing the corner. Herr Leininger, I see you have a Holy Bible on your desk. Can I read something from it?" The teacher was amused about his promise and skeptically gave him the black Lutheran Bible. "Herr Leininger," continued Peter, "do you have a favorite passage?"

Wilhelm, curiously said, "I do, I do indeed. I've always loved the 'Sermon on the Mount'. It is in Matthew, Chapter 5, particularly verses 3 through 8. It always gives me comfort during difficult times."

Peter quickly thumbed through the Bible to the Gospel of Matthew and began reading, "Blessed are the poor in spirit, for theirs is the kingdom of heaven. Blessed are those who mourn for they shall be comforted. Blessed are the meek, for they shall inherit the earth. Blessed are those who hunger and thirst for righteousness, for they shall be filled. Blessed are the merciful, for they shall obtain mercy. Blessed are the pure in heart, for they shall see God." Peter finished and all were silent, particularly Wilhelm, who was in a state of shock. He had never had a student that read so fluently without hesitation.

After the period of silence, which seemed forever, Wilhelm said simply, "Peter, we will see you the first day of school."

Johannes Benjamin Spyker (Ben)

1723

———— ❧ ————

"HERR WILHELM, I FINALLY HAVE a brother," said Peter. "I can't wait to teach him all the things that boys do, like swinging over the creek, playing ball, playing tag, hunting, and fishing. I'll be the best big brother in the world."

"That's wonderful; I of course am delighted and pray that he stays healthy. I also hope he torments your father the same way he tormented your mother when she was just twelve," laughed Wilhelm. "That's how I knew it was true love."

It was 1723. John Benjamin Spyker was born on September 30. Life had been a turmoil for Jonny and Elizabeth and their children. They had great joy and they had great sadness. They would build, plant, harvest, celebrate with their friends of Aspach and in a blink of an eye the roving armies of the French or those representing the Holy Roman Empire would come steal their crops, vegetables, and livestock, and burn their farm.

They made the Zucker creek caves their home three different times, when the armies came to plunder their farm. They remained strong and even stronger each time they left the caves and rebuilt their lives; this was their make-up. They had faith in God and they had the German and Spyker persistence and ability to get things done.

Elizabeth was very weak after John Benjamin was born. Jonny always had difficulty at each birth, while Elizabeth remained strong. But not so this time. They had a son born just two years before who they had named John Benjamin. That poor baby boy was never well and despite all the love and caring by the family, survived only a year and was laid to rest beside Jonny's mother Margaret in the family cemetery that overlooked the Zucker creek.

After the death of their first John Benjamin, the village doctor, Hans Lentz, said to Jonny, "Jonny, listen to what I say. Elizabeth can never again go through another child birth. She may be able to live a fairly long life, but not if she goes through another difficult birth. She has had two miscarriages, bore Peter, gave you three sweet girls, Margaret, Rebecca, and Catherine, but the birth of John Benjamin and now his death has weakened her physically and spiritually for bearing another child." Jonny agreed completely with the doctor. He saw his Elizabeth of previous vitality, despite the always a good face she put on, now becoming somewhat frail and often tired.

"Fiddlesticks," a popular Spyker expression, exclaimed Elizabeth. Jonny had related the doctor's insistence that Elizabeth would endanger her health if she again gave birth. "There is nothing wrong with me and I can have ten more children and the only one who will suffer will be my dear husband Jonny. Besides I love you and I want to give you another son, another Benjamin."

Elizabeth conceived and gave birth to a very healthy "Benjamin," but as the doctor predicted, Elizabeth was getting weaker every day.

God's Will Be Done

1726

———— ⚬∞⚬ ————

ELIZABETH SURVIVED THE PNEUMONIA AFTER the birth of Benjamin, although still a young women of thirty-two, she lacked the health to live many more years. It was the spring of 1726 when fifteen-year old Peter ran to the Spyker vineyard and called, "Dad, come quick, mother has fallen and she is too weak to get up. The girls are with her and trying to make her comfortable."

———— ⚬∞⚬ ————

Old Reverend Schmidt had difficulty with God. *"Dear Lord,"* he thought to himself as he prepared to comfort the Spyker family on the death of Elizabeth. *"Elizabeth would have been thirty-eight years old this summer. She had a beautiful family and she loved life and her husband. Oh God, why didn't you take this grumpy old man? I don't know how many times I've told you to take the old first. Why Lord don't you follow the seniority system? Sometimes Lord Jesus, you just don't listen to me."*

With a heavy heart, Reverend Schmidt looked out on the filled church and prepared to help ease the sorrow of all those present, particularly of those in the first two rows which were filled with Spykers and nee Spykers. His eyes blurred as he looked at little

Catherine, now seven- years old, at Rebecca nine, Margaret just a teenager, who was holding a confused three-year-old, Benjamin, and also at a strong young man of fifteen, Peter. *Thank God for Peter and Margaret,"* he thought, *"they will help Jonny with the farm and the family."* Before his funeral sermon that would exalt the life of one of his favorite persons, he read from the scriptures, John 5:24 - 29: *"I tell you the truth, whoever hears my word and believes him who sent me has eternal life and will not be condemned; he has crossed over from death to life. I tell you the truth, a time is coming and has now come when the dead will hear the voice of the Son of God and those who hear will live. For as the Father has life in himself, so he has granted the Son to have life in himself. And he has given him authority to judge because he is the Son of Man. Do not be amazed at this, for a time is coming when all who are in their graves will hear his voice and come out—those who have done good will rise to live, and those who have done evil will rise to be condemned. By myself I can do nothing; I judge only as I hear, and my judgment is just, for I seek not to please myself but him who sent me."*

After the church funeral, they placed the solid oak casket carrying Elizabeth Nead Spyker into Jonny's wagon. Jonny and his children led a procession of other wagons to the Spyker cemetery overlooking the Zucker creek. As they laid Elizabeth to rest beside her son, mother-in-law, and all the other Spykers and nee Spykers, Reverend Schmidt, intoned one more simple scripture verse:

"Peace I leave with you; my peace I give you. I do not give to you as the world gives. Do not let your hearts be troubled and do not be afraid."

It was over. It was just beginning. "Children," said Jonny with a loving but determined look, "what would your mother, my Elizabeth, expect from you?"

Peter said, "Father, she would want me to help you with the farm and also take care of my younger brother and sisters. I will never forget her. She was the best mother a person could have. She made me laugh, she consoled my sad days and she set an example that I will follow, 'with God nothing is impossible', and I mean nothing. Someday I will fulfill her dream of our family being with my grandfather in America. You and I, Dad, and all of us will go to America. Mother will be with us."

"Dear father, I feel so sad for you," said thirteen-year-old Margaret, who already was becoming a beautiful women. I know how much you loved mother. I've learned from mother, and I will help you and Peter raise our family. I will take care of Benjamin as if he were my son. I know my sisters will help me. Also I can cook, I can garden, I can milk, I can do everything even as well as Peter. Mother always said I was a strong young girl and would become a strong woman. Today I am a woman."

The two younger girls, could only sob and hang on to Margaret. Benjamin, was in his father's arms and asked, "Will mother come back soon?"

———— ⚭ ————

The years after the death of Elizabeth, although difficult, soon led to an adjusted structured life, so typical in every Spyker family. The family seemed a military hierarchy with father Jonny being the captain, and Peter his son and Margaret being the lieutenants. Peter took it upon himself to mentor Benjamin, and Margaret became the mentor for Rebecca and Catherine. Frequently Rebecca, a "tomboy," rebelled and insisted she wanted to be more with Peter and do "boys" play and work. "Fiddlesticks," said Rebecca, "I'm tired of sewing. I want to work with the cows and horses. I want to plow fields and build fences." By her tenacity, Rebecca always got her way. She sewed and cooked when needed, but quickly was out pitching hay to the cows and fishing with the boys.

Benjamin copied everything Peter did, and by the time he was five, became the "king of questions," and patient Peter became "the answer man".

"Why don't the cows eat the big ham I just put in their food bin?"

"Why do the clouds take away the sun?"

"Why is it cold some times and hot some times?"

"Why are there stones in the field?"

"Why don't the vines have ears of corn?"

"Why does Margaret have blonde hair?"

Finally the patient Peter, got a question he longed for. "When can I go to school like Rebecca and Catherine?"

"By Gott, you can go to school tomorrow. Herr Wilhelm has always expected another Spyker to come to school and drive him nuts." Instead of school the next day, Peter said, "Benjamin, let's go fishing. We've worked hard all week and now it's time to see if we can catch 'King Louie.'"

"Who's King Louie?"

"Where did you get those fishing pole?"

"How come fish swim underwater?"

"Why don't fish drown?"

They grabbed their fishing poles, which they bought from Aspach's merchant store, a long one for Peter and a short one for Benjamin. As they were strolling across the field toward the Zucker creek with their fishing poles and a can of worms each, they saw behind them a cloud of dust. It looked like small tornado, but was a small, red-faced, smiling, Rebecca with her pole and worms. "I bet I catch the most and biggest fish."

Christmas Eve

1736

THE SPYKER'S CHRISTMAS EVE PARTY was legendary. It was Christmas Eve, December 24th, 1736. Although the year had been difficult with foreign army raids, religious pressure from both the Calvinists and the Catholics, and a dry, hot summer that severely stunted the vineyards and the crops, it was still time to celebrate the birth of Christ. Jonny was now fifty years old. He had not remarried despite pressure from his peers and his daughters. The opportunities were plentiful, but "I have found no one like my Elizabeth."

Peter was still single even though he was twenty-six and there was an equal amount of pressure, particularly from his sisters. The opportunities were plentiful, but "I have met no one like my mother Elizabeth."

Margaret, who was twenty-three was married to Georg Kolb. It seemed half the town of Aspach were Kolbs. They already had two sons. Rebecca was married to Daniel Liebengut and had a child on the way. Catherine, although not married was promised to Jacob Frize, and they had planned a spring wedding.

The house was filled with Libenguts, Frizes, Stohrs, Kolbs, and half the farmers close to Aspach. Even the new preacher, Filib Schmidt was there. He had followed in his father's footsteps. His famous dad had demanded God to obey the seniority rule, to die before another younger member of his congregation. Finally the Lord had answered him and he was buried beside the Aspach Lutheran church. Although many had witnessed his closed casket funeral, there were some who insisted they saw a "chariot come to carry him home."

At the Spyker Christmas Eve party, it was the time to toast the yearly successes, promises, dreams, and the future. Etched even then in the memories of many of the guests was the toast offered by Johann Conrad Weiser at the beginning of the War of the Grand Alliance, when he said goodbye to Aspach to join the Holy Roman Empire's Blue Dragoons. The memory of many of these toasts was preserved as part of the history of the Spyker family.

"Friends, Peter, Benjamin, my lovely daughters, grandchildren, dear friends it is time for me to go to America. My father is seventy-four and longs to see his family. The soil on my farm is tired and the vineyards are dying. There is no reason to stay, except my daughters, and I know they will follow me in a few years. Peter and Benjamin have said they will go with me. Who else?" asked Jonny as he held up one of the last glasses of his famed Riesling wine.

It was amazing; half the room stood up and cheered as they also hoisted the Spyker wine. "We will go to America." was the shout from every corner of the room.

"Is it too early to call you father?" said Jacob Frieze. "I hope not, as your daughter will become my bride this spring and if you wait for us we will also go."

Planning the Next Spyker Emigration

1736

———— ✦ ————

IT WAS SETTLED, A NUMBER of the farmers of the Aspach area were going to America. They looked to Jonny and Peter to lead them. Although Jonny was the father, Peter had gained a reputation as a natural leader. Also Peter was studying law from every book he could get his hands on. When he was twenty-two, he traveled each winter to Heidelberg to study law for a month. Jonny took great pride in his oldest son's natural leadership ability. Jonny remembered well the healthy pink baby that was born after his namesake brother had died only a couple of years before. Peter was almost six feet tall with bright red hair and deep blue eyes. He was muscular in build and although he usually had a somber look on his face, when he smiled everyone could not help smiling with him. *"He will become a respected leader not only here in Aspach, but in America as well."*

They had made the decision. They would emigrate to America. All together there were ten adult men, besides Jonny and Peter, between thirty and fifty years of age that made the decision to emigrate. Some were widowers, some had spouses who would go, and four also had young children who would go. Thankfully none of the children was less than ten. They knew from the letters Jonny had received from his father that it was unlikely that children under nine would be able to survive. They knew that diseases at sea claimed almost all younger children. All together there would be thirty-five people leaving the Aspach Lutheran Church and going to the Colony of William Penn, the colony of Pennsylvania. These ten men were named by Jonny the "Lutheran Ten."

However, the Elector of Wurttemberg had made it clear, no one was to leave his electorate. They were to remain and supply the Holy Roman Empire with all the necessities to sustain the economy of the province and to help defend it against the ambitions of the French.

They had to have clandestine meetings. If any surprise visitors were to intrude on the meetings, they would quickly open their note pads and discuss the finances of the church. At the first meeting an important decision was made. The "Lutheran Ten" unanimously asked Jonny to be the leader. They wanted him to chair the meetings and guide them in the successful path to the Colony of Pennsylvania.

Jonny stood up and addressed the group, "My fellow Lutherans. I respect and appreciate your confidence in me. However, there is someone in our group with a legal background, which we will desperately need in Rotterdam, Philadelphia, and Tulpehocken. This person has shown he commands respect with each of you and he has the youth and vitality to lead us on this difficult journey. As you know, I am talking about my son Peter Spyker. Peter should be our leader."

Jonny sat down to silence, but after a brief period of thought, Jacob Lentz, Peter's best friend and a respected doctor, stood up and said, "Thank you Jonny, you are right, I agree Peter should be the leader." Jacob, who always liked to add a little humor to each situation, continued, "now that I've taught him everything he knows, he should do a good job."

The other men expressed their support for Peter. Peter nodded his acceptance, and in his usual quiet, but confident demeanor, stood up, hugged his father and walked to the church pulpit. "Let's get started, we have a long journey, and it starts now."

Johannes Peter
Spyker (Peter)

1711 - 1789

The Lutheran Ten

1737

—∞∞∞—

THAT NIGHT AFTER THE FIRST meeting, Peter reflected on the task ahead and wondered if he was prepared for the responsibility of leading his family and friends to a new life. He started to smile as his reflections took him back to his youth. He knew that even in his youth he was preparing himself for this responsibility.

His best friend was Jacob Lentz, who was the son of the village doctor, Hans Lentz. Even in their first years of school they started talking about going to America and how they would follow Conrad Weiser, Sr. and Peter's grandfather in bringing the people from Aspach and the Wurttemberg Province to Pennsylvania.

Jacob, like his father, was a doctor. "Peter," lectured Jacob, "are you aware of how many people on each ship to America don't make it? They die of diseases right on the ship. It's not just the hard times or the weather, but it's that most diseases are contagious. That means that once someone is sick they pass the disease on to another person who passes it to another person, and so on." Peter was always amazed how analytically his friend thought. "There's got to be a way we can discover a medicine that will kill the miasmas that travel from one person to another."

"Okay, Jacob, you stumped me. What in the world is a miasma?"

"I'm not sure but I've read it's something in the air that is invisible and is passed from one person to another. That's my explanation of diseases being contagious. Someday, I'm going to create a medicine to kill these miasmas."

Peter was always impressed with his friend's scientific knowledge. Peter also loved knowledge. He, however, was more interested in the understanding of communication than in scientific knowledge. Peter loved words and tried to understand everything he read, and he read every chance he got. He had read every pamphlet that William Penn had written. He had read all the writings of Voltaire, Rousseau, and Samuel Johnson. He also enjoyed novels about adventure like "Robinson Crusoe" and Jonathan Swift's "Gulliver's Travels."

He started thinking back to his days of school with Herr Wilhelm Leininger, Jr. Wilhelm had always challenged him and seemed to be much stricter on him and Jacob Lentz. He recalled his last day of school. "Jacob, Peter, you probably wonder why I've always pushed you two the hardest. It's time for me to tell you why" said school master Wilhelm. "You two are the best students I have ever had. You are interested in so many things. Everything came easy for you two, so I had to push you and challenge you. Today, I am proud of you. You, gentlemen, are no longer kids. You will be the leaders who take our families out of this subservient way of life and take us to the freedom of a new world."

"Yes, I am ready. Yes I will take my family and this community to America." said Peter to himself as he felt confidence overflowing within him.

At one of the meetings Filip Schmidt, after the invocation, made a surprising announcement. "I am going to step down as the preacher for the Aspach Lutheran Church. The young man I have been grooming, William Kurtz, will take over. I've decided there is no way this group of rugged pioneers, godly men, but apt to stray when hoisting a few beers or glasses of wine, can survive without my spiritual guidance. I am going to America and will open an Aspach Lutheran church in the midst of you sinners in the colony of Pennsylvania." All the "pioneers" clapped, whistled and shouted, and several came out with typical witty remarks.

"Reverend Schmidt, you can't build a church large enough for all us sinners."

"Can we have beer along with wine for communion? Should we bring our own?"

"Please don't let Jonny in the choir. Already, I'm losing my hearing."

"Just build pews in the back. You won't need any in front."

"Will we have Bingo, or will I have to go to the Catholic church?"

"Reverend Schmidt, we must have a separate room for Johann Kolb, his snoring keeps me awake."

"George, be quiet now already. When I wake up, only you are left in church."

Despite the good humor or in some cases coarse humor, many thought, "With the good Lord for us, who can be against us?"

———— ∞ ————

At one of the meetings after Jonny had received a letter from his father, he shared joyous news with his fellow sojourners. After the prayer by Filip, Peter gave the floor to Jonny to relate information from his father, Johannes. "As you know, my father is in Tulpehocken, Pennsylvania and is praying for not only his family, but for many from his home village and farms, to come and make his home even a better place. Johannes insists that we travel on the St. Andrew ship because the ship's captain is John Stedman.

My father relates that Mr. Stedman, unlike many of the captains, is an honest man and truly cares about his passengers. My father writes that Captain Stedman does not overload the ship for maximum profit as so many others do, and that the Captain provides as clean and comfortable quarters as possible, and provides substantial meals and healthy water.

"Here is some great news, Father and many of his neighbors, want so badly for us to come that they have made down payments to Captain Stedman to hold up to forty berths. The ship will leave in early June. Peter will make the journey to Rotterdam and finalize everything with Captain Stedman in April and then return to lead us to Rotterdam and the St. Andrew ship." The plans were set. All were committed to the journey.

Aspach to Rotterdam

1737

—— ∞∞∞ ——

THE JOURNEY TO AMERICA STARTED at the Aspach Lutheran Church. The date, May 25, 1737. "Brothers and Sisters, my dear friends, we gather here together with the captain of our ship, the Lord Jesus Christ," started Reverend Filip Schmidt. "He will lead us on a journey to freedom of religion and freedom to lead our lives in the manner with which we wish." Young Schmidt like his father loved to preach and preach and preach, however, he was not so demanding of the Lord as his father. Filip continued to pray out loud until the dark skies threatened to show signs of an early sunrise.

They had to leave early. They had to leave in the dark of night to avoid any chance of representatives of the elector, Duke Maximilian I of Bavaria, trying to stop them. Anyone caught or suspected of emigrating to America would be imprisoned. Fortunately, Peter, on his journey to Rotterdam and return, had discovered and become acquainted with many houses of Quakers along the emigration route. These would be safe houses to hide them from the armies of the elector. Once they got past Koblenz they were safe from the elector, but then faced the many perils of a three month or more sea voyage.

All the sojourners were there with great anticipation and greater anxiety. They knew the travels to the New World would be difficult. They knew that a number of them would never make it. They had received warnings from ancestors of the difficulties of a three month sea voyage. Jonny had received a final letter from his father in Tulpehocken, Pennsylvania, with many words of caution and advice on how to survive at sea. As Jonny looked at his sons, Peter and Benjamin, he prayed silently that his family would survive. Jonny sensed the strength in Peter and the courage in young Benjamin. He knew also that he was up to the task. *"Although I am over fifty years of age, I have the lithe, strong, and healthy body of a young man and the inherited determination of my father. Yes, God, we will make it. Nothing can stop us,"* were his thoughts on this farewell date.

His daughters and grandchildren waved goodbye and assured Jonny, Peter, and Benjamin that they would soon join them in William Penn's Colony of Pennsylvania. His sons-in-law loaded them in their farm wagons and drove them to the Rhine River, where they were to follow in the footsteps of Johannes Peter Spyker, Sr. Like the senior, they would float down the Rhine in boats to Rotterdam. They would pay the same tolls to the river men of the French empire. Then they would board the St. Andrew ship captained by John Stedman.

The five scows of Aspach Lutherans departed on a clearing above Strasbourg in the early morning of May 26th. The band of Lutherans were in high spirits as they sailed down the calm and peaceful Rhine. There were tolls to be paid as they traveled from Strasbourg down the Rhine, but these were expected. After four days they neared Karlsruhe and were awed at the beautiful Karlsruhe Palace, the new home of Charles III, who was the military commander for the Holy Roman Empire in Baden-Durlach.

They knew to drift by the palace at night and to be very quiet so as not to alarm the military guards. Soon they passed Karlsruhe and everything was going smooth and peaceful. The Lutheran escapees from the Holy Roman Empire could taste freedom. Every mile brought them closer to Koblenz, which ended the Palatine and Holy Roman Empire control.

When they were miles past Karlsruhe the relief caused them to rejoice. Reverend Schmidt led them in a rousing version of 'Washed in the Blood of the Lamb.' Everyone was singing for joy; all five boats of Lutherans were near to each other. With now reckless abandon they practically shouted the final verse: *"Have you laid down your burdens? Have you found peace and rest? Are you washed in the blood of the lamb? I've laid down all my troubles. I've found peace and rest. I'm all washed in the blood of the lamb."*

Yes "peace and rest." Suddenly Peter dropped his river pole and stood up and pointed, "Look, here comes a horseman right toward our boats. He can't be more than a mile away. We need to pole to the other side and seek shelter. He may have others with him."

They all moved as quickly as the clumsy scows would allow to overhanging trees on the west bank. Those who had guns loaded the powder and tamped down the bullets. No sooner were they ready for action, "Put down your guns, I know who it is," said Peter. "Why is Jacob Frieze risking his life riding like a damn fool? We best prepare ourselves. It must be bad news for Jacob to endanger himself and his favorite black stallion."

With caution they rowed and poled themselves back to the east bank. Jacob stopped at the bank and waited for all to gather round. "This morning at Sunday service ten renegades, hirelings of Duke Maximilian, pushed open the doors of church during the homily, pushed Reverend Kurtz aside and demanded from the pulpit, 'Where is Peter Spyker? We have a warrant for his arrest. The duke has been informed he is planning to lead a group of you

Lutherans,' he stated and then spit as if in disgust, 'to the promise land, to the joke they call America. No one and I mean no one can leave this Electorate without direct permission from the governing body of Duke Maximilian the First.' Jacob was out of breath as he related the story.

"Jonny, despite threatening us, even the women and children, they received no information, just blank stares. The Lutherans of Aspach are a brave bunch. However, it will not be long until this gang decides to ride down the river and block and capture you before you reach the territorial limits of the Palatinate in Koblenz. You can't go on."

Peter quickly took control of the dire situation. "We must go to the west bank, unload our boats, and drag then inland to help build shelters. We can no longer travel on these boats. On my travel to Rotterdam, I learned of safe houses to protect emigrants from just these types of circumstances. These are houses of people of Quaker faith that believe in religious and individual freedoms. They long for the privilege of helping people to emigrate to America, and to join their leader, William Penn, in the colony of Pennsylvania. Father, take everyone inland as far from the river as possible in the hours of daylight that are left."

Jonny, was impressed, but not surprised, at the "take charge ability" of Peter. Jonny did, however, worry about many things, such as survival in the forests, concealment from the renegades, and further transportation to Rotterdam, but he had confidence in his oldest son.

"Dad, I'm going to take Jacob's horse and ride to Speyer which has several 'safe houses.' If all goes well I'll be back by daybreak. This is just a momentary delay. No one can stop us from our destiny." With that Peter saddled up the black stallion and rode at an easy pace, until the fine horse was rested and watered and ready to gallop to Speyer.

The resilient Lutherans traveled inland about ten miles, built shelters from the wood of the scows, covered them with leaves and prepared for a quiet night. No fires were permitted, but there was sufficient food from their packs for a cold dinner.

It was just forty kilometers to Speyer and Peter made the distance in just three hours. He knocked on the door of James Mather, the man Peter knew to be the leader of the Quaker group in Speyer. "Peter, how nice to see you again. Won't thee come into my home. You appear tired and worried. Rest, have something to eat. My Hilda will be glad to see you and will prepare for you even better than she prepares for me."

Peter quickly related the foreseen dangers of his tribe of Lutherans. "Can you house and hide thirty-five people?"

"We can hide one hundred people if we need be. It is our task in life; our joy to help thee get to America. I'll quickly seek out my brothers and sisters and will be back before you can finish Hilda's rhubarb pie and churned ice cream."

True to his word Peter watched five horse-drawn wagons arrive at Herr Mather's home. "Peter," related James, "we will drive our wagons and ford the river just one mile below my farm. With you leading the way we will gather our Lutheran friends and bring them to five safe houses in our Speyer village. You can stay safely with us until danger has past and then we will take you past Koblenz out of the reach of the electors. We will bring you to a place where you can again build your boats and continue your journey to Rotterdam. Peter, this is the most excitement and fun we have had in months. Thank you for bringing us this challenge."

Jonny had set out scouts in all directions to look for their would-be capturers or the "good Lord willing" his son with a plan to bring them to safety. Scout, Jacob Lentz, was watching the first light of morning, when he heard a slight creaking. He quickly scaled a tall maple tree, hooded his eyes from the light of dawn and joyously saw Peter on the black stallion. Even more joyously he saw five wagons cautiously approaching the encamped families of Aspach. Jacob quickly climbed from his nest and leaped to the ground. Soon he was able to hail Peter. He jumped on the back of the stallion with Peter and led him and his entourage to the families who were just starting to rouse from a cold and wet night's rest. Soon they all were on the road to the safe houses of the Quakers.

———∞———

On June 16, 1737 the trip of Aspach Lutherans came to the confluence of the Rhine, Waal, and Lek rivers. They had reached their first destination. The next day they all viewed the ship, the St. Andrew. They knew that this would be their home for at least three months and they knew for some the sea might be their final resting place.

"Ah Peter, we have been waiting for you," said Captain John Stedman. "I was worried you would not make it. Your grandfather has become a great friend of mine and I long to take you and your fellow kinsman to the delights of his eyes. We plan to depart Rotterdam just two weeks from now on June 30th." The reunion was grand as the captain hugged young Spyker.

"Thank you, Captain, it is a great joy to see you again. With your permission I would like to bring the ten leaders to meet with you tomorrow. I should warn you ahead of time, although good and godly men, they all are as stubborn as a German mule."

The meeting was set and early the next morning Peter made the introductions to Captain Stedman: "Captain, this is my father Johannes Peter Spyker, also my name, but he is called Jonny; with my father is his youngest son and my brother Benjamin. Now then let me introduce, Johannes Stohr, Jacob Lentz, Heinrich Hartman, Jonathan Hager, Johann Kolb, Philip Liebengut, Daniel Reiss,

George Conrad, Johann Gist, Andreas Heit, and last, the soul of our group, Filip Schmidt, our pastor." As Peter introduced each, he individually stepped forward, doffed his hats and bowed.

"A fine group of able looking men," stated the captain as he also doffed his hat and bowed to the group. "With such a group we will have a successful sail. I look forward to working with all of you. And Reverend Schmidt, I look forward to hearing your fine sermons each Sunday morning. Peter has told me that if I don't run the ship with God as my co-pilot, you will bring fire and brimstone upon my shiny bald head. I should also tell you what a fine lawyer and negotiator is young Mr. Spyker. Your deposit of fifty pounds for family has been made by your friends in Tulpehocken. I expected another one hundred and fifty pounds. Mr. Spyker said fifty. I said one hundred. Mr. Spyker said fifty. I said seventy five. Mr. Spyker said fifty. I said seventy five. Mr. Spkyer said, if you insist, seventy five. By the way Mr. Spyker has my shirt."

You could see the men relax and smile as they immediately felt comfortable with Captain John. Despite the fact that these were brave and often stern men, they still enjoyed moments of humor. "Captain," said the reverend, "yes, I want God as our co-pilot, but if there is a storm, I'd just as soon have you at the helm."

The attempt at humor quickly brought out the group jester, George Conrad, with his seemingly naive questions. "My good captain, thank you for putting us at ease. I do have just a few questions. First of all, what time is dinner served each night and should we dress for dinner? My wife, Judith has brought just three formal gowns, so hopefully not too many dinners will be formal." George quickly continued on with a straight face and a look of concern. "Will we be having music with our dinners? Also, I should inform you, we prefer white wine with our Halibut and red wine with our prime roast beef." Before Captain Stedman could react, he continued with, "Captain, when you have time we would like to invite you to participate in our bridge games."

At first, the captain thought he might be serious, but when he saw the smile on everyone's face he knew this was going to be a fun group. "Captain," Philip Liebengul said interrupting the litany of requests by George, "do you have an anchor? We'd like to tie it to George's leg and see how long he can stay under water."

They all had a good laugh. It was like the quiet before the storm as they realized the peril of the upcoming months. "Steward," requested Captain Stedman, "bring me thirteen tankards of our best rum. No, better make that twelve, I don't think Jonny would like to see son Benjamin wobbling down the gang-plank. Maybe make it eleven, as likely the rum might tarnish the halo above the Reverend Filip's head."

Quickly, Reverend Schmidt retorted, "Captain, go ahead and make it thirteen, I'll have two."

It was a joyous beginning, but before the end of the visit, Captain Stedman became serious as he informed the group of all the do's and do not's for a safe voyage. Among the rules and regulations, the captain stressed several. "You are the ones who will determine the success of our voyage. You are the ones who must be responsible for your family. At times you must be a dictator. You will get each day portions of fruit, salt meat, hard biscuits, and sufficient good water. No matter how sick people may be, they must eat their portion and they must drink their portion of water. No exceptions. In some cases you may have to literally stuff food and water down loved one's throats. To be liked and not demanding in these issues will kill them. Fruit will help them avoid scurvy and the salt meat gives them strength for survival. The water is clean and they must drink their entire portion each day.

There will be a tendency to not keep one's self clean, or more commonly to be lax in keeping one's quarters and clothing clean. If you and your family don't follow my rules of cleanliness you will suffer typhoid and will not complete the journey. You must get your family into fresh air and hopefully some sun each day, no matter how hot or cold the temperature on deck. When you are on deck, exercise is a must." Other rules and regulations were stressed and then the captain finished with, "We are indeed fortunate to have you strong, determined, Lutheran men on board. I can be responsible only for my crew. You must be responsible for your families. Also you may have to be responsible for others that do not understand the necessities of diet, cleanliness, and exercise. Others may see you as a cruel dictator, but you will be saving the lives of your family and your neighbors."

As the men went back to their families, they were stern in the face and strong in the heart. Each thinking his family will survive, will arrive safely in America, will be free. They knew it would not be easy. Each man's strong will and faith in the Creator would be the measure of success.

St. Andrew

1737

The Saint Andrew

The SAINT ANDREW galley was a three-masted ship with square sails and a square-sterned galley- type hull design of about

150 tons. Built 1733 in Philadelphia. Fitted with accommodation for passengers including compartments. 8 or 9 pairs of oars, if fitted. 8 deck-mounted guns, later increased to 20. Around 15 crew. Transported emigrants mostly from Rotterdam to Philadelphia from 1734 to 1752. Masters: John Stedman, Robert Robinson, James Proud, Charles Stedman, John Evans, Robert Brown, James Abercrombie, John Brown, Andrew Breading. Owned by 3 London merchants, managed by Charles & Alexander Stedman, Second Street, Philadelphia.

"The Ship St. Andrew, Galley, A Hypothesis" by Alfred T. Meschter. Schwenkfelder Library & Heritage Center www.schwenkfelder.com

---

0700, Monday, June 16, 1737: heavy seas, cloudy and rainy weather: the anchors were weighed and the bowlines were lifted from the dock posts. The St. Andrew, Captain John Stedman and about three hundred lives, including thirty-five Lutherans from Aspach, set sail for America. The ship, though full, was not packed as many of the other ships. Most carried at least four hundred men, women and children.

The ship would take just a short day trip to Cowes, England on the Isle of Wight. Here the official papers would be submitted and both papers and passengers would be scrutinized by the English government before the long journey ahead. Although it was a short trip, the huge swells, buckets of rain, lightning and wind, made it a terrifying start for the first-time sea-goers. Many got terribly sick that first day and it was with great relief when the ship docked on the Isle of Wight. It was a blessing to stay four days in Cowes. This well-timed stay gave the passengers a chance to recover from their first bout of sea sickness.

The St. Andrew and all the passengers cleared the rigid inspection. Many ships were delayed before permitted to sail and there were often passengers who were not permitted to re-board. They would be sent back to their homeland. However, the reputation of Captain Stedman and the legal knowledge of Peter Spyker helped them easily clear the final customs. On July 4, 1737 the ship sailed west. There would be no land on the horizon for over three months.

———— ∞ ————

The quarters, although more spacious than most ships, were cramped, causing families to have little privacy, which often led to conflicts. The ship was out a couple of weeks when the first severe bickering started. The berths and living quarters were on the second and third level of the ship. These levels had few open windows, which once were oar locks for rowing. The St. Andrew was a galley, but one that no longer used rowing as a means of moving the large ship through the water. It had three strategically placed sails that helped move the ship swiftly through the great sea, if the wind was present and in the favorable direction.

Each area of the ship had several oar holes in which the fresh sea air could filter into the living quarters. The temperature in July was very hot as the sun blazed down on the ship in the cloudless skies. The Lutheran group had its own section. The group, although good neighbors, became very irritable with each other. The four Lutheran families with children began to quarrel. The squabbles were mainly about who could have the living and sleeping quarters by the small windows. After several days of bickering, the men of each of the four families almost came to blows and the spouses threatened to tear each other's hair out. Peter knew something had to be done. Some of the Lutherans, not affected, as they did not have children, began to take sides. It was a powder keg situation that was ready to explode. Finally Peter, called a meeting of the "Lutheran Ten."

"Gentlemen," started Peter, "we will not be able to survive this journey as long as we keep trying to kill each other. We loved each other when we met in the Aspach church to start this adventure. Now, if tempers continue to escalate, I fear we will not be able to live together in peace and certainly we will have a difficult time surviving the journey. We need to support each other, to lift each other up. But all we are doing now is tearing each other down."

The discussion started. Peter was not a dictator and he was a good listener. All the men gave their opinions and suggested solutions. The debate continued for over an hour. During one of the recesses, Peter shared with his father the frustration of the argument. "Peter." said Jonny, "They all keep saying the same thing, 'we must compromise.'"

Later after there seemed to be no end to the argument Peter heard himself saying, "I keep hearing all of you saying there should be some kind of compromise. My father, my brother and I, do not need any kind of special location in our quarters, as we do not have others to worry about, and can go up on the main deck at our leisure. We do have to be aware of the sailors who are doing their duty in guiding the ship, but as long as we stay out of their way, can enjoy the deck just one level below the sky. We can have all the air, sun, and breezes we want. We can even sleep on the main deck. I think this should also be true of you other men who have no children. Your wives can also be free to come and go to the upper deck. The only problem is the four families who have children. I understand well the need to protect your children and to give them opportunities to breathe fresh air. Our quarters have two windows and there are four families with children. Can we schedule a rotation, where each family has one week with one window and one week without?"

Everyone looked at each other and wondered, *"Why didn't we think of that? It seems so obvious."* This procedure was followed and once again there was peace in the galley. This was just one of the common sense solutions Peter exercised during the journey.

———⚬∞⚬———

One dark, warm, August night, Peter was on the main deck. It was very peaceful. Although warm, there was a gentle breeze and the stars were out in all their glory. Peter was musing about the trials ahead once they arrived in Philadelphia. He had just rounded one of the small jetties, that served as a life boat; he was looking at the stars when "whoops" he ran into another individual who was also looking at the stars. Peter steadied the other person, who was quite small in comparison, "Geez, I'm so sorry, I wasn't paying any attention to where I was going. Are you okay?" A cloud passed the moon and there in the moonlight was the most beautiful woman he ever seen. He was spellbound as he looked into her dark eyes. She was young with long blonde hair, slender with a beautiful figure that only God could have sculpted. She lifted her chin and looked into the eyes of Peter, who seemed to tower above her five and a half foot frame.

"Yes I'm fine," she said as she struggled to regain her composure. Seeing the handsome and strong man in front of her, she all of a sudden broke into a delightful smile. "Thanks for bumping into me. I mean thanks for not letting me fall when I bumped into you. Gosh this was the most fun I've had today. I mean it was fun that I didn't fall. I really don't know what I mean."

This caused Peter to break into one of his few full smiles, but his smile seemed to light up the sky, much more than the moon and the stars. "If I didn't hurt you, this is the best thing that has happened to me all day, maybe all week, actually since this journey has begun." They both laughed together and Peter realized he was still holding on to her shoulders. He did not want to let her go, ever.

"You are Peter Spyker. Everyone talks about you. I've seen you talking to the captain and also heard how smart you are and how much others respect you. I've always thought you were stern and somber, but now that I see you up close, so close you almost knocked me off the ship, you seem warm and gentle. Wow, I've said too much. My father would ground me to my quarters and put a guard around me twenty four hours a day if he heard me talking like this, especially talking like this to a stranger. Please forgive my impertinence. My mother always says I talk too much without thinking. Goodbye. Still it was nice to bump into you."

Peter didn't want her to leave. She was the most attractive woman, no young lady, he had ever set his blue eyes on. "Wait, you can't leave until you tell me your name and promise that we can meet again."

"My name is Susan Wagner and this has been the best night of all. Goodbye Peter, if you promise not to knock me off the ship, I'd love to see you again."

For the next month Peter and Susan happened to bump into each other during the night. They continued to play the same game each night. "Whoops, sorry," Peter would say. " I didn't see anyone coming. It sure is nice to bump into you."

"Gosh, isn't this a coincidence," said Susan. This is the 13th straight night you've run into me. Oh how I love it."

Their relationship had matured to the point that they were even holding hands as they walked around the ship. "Peter, are you ever going to kiss me? Maybe you haven't even kissed a girl before."

"Ha, I've kissed many a girl. At least one hundred, maybe even one thousand, but I'm afraid to kiss someone that I like so much. Maybe you wouldn't want me to kiss you and I would feel so sad. I guess I'm afraid, because you mean so much to me."

"Try me."

Peter leaned over to give her a chaste peck on the lips, but Susan would have none of it. She gently put her hand behind Peter's neck and pulled him toward her. He felt like a fine leather glove that fit snugly to her shapely body. Peter saw shooting stars as her lips massaged his. The kiss would have lasted until day break, but Susan's curfew was at the ship's bells of midnight.

"Peter," said Jacob, "I've called your name three times and you seem not to hear me. Lately you've acted like you were in a daze. My wife heard rumors that you meet a young lady every night and if someone asks you about it, you just blush and say, 'A beautiful young lady.' Let me take your temperature." Jacob put his hand on Peter's forehead and diagnosed, "Yes Peter, I fear you have a bad case of love-sickness. Let's visit the good captain and ask for his sure-fire cure, several tankards of rum."

"Oh, Jacob, it's never been like this. You know well how I act to the ladies whom I've visited in the past and the ladies who try to set a marriage trap for me. This is so different. How do I tell this Susan that I love her?"

"Oh, God, quick, let's get to the captain's quarters before it's too late."

Throughout August, the romance continued. They were in love and planning the next fifty years of their life together. "Peter, what will you do when you arrive in Philadelphia?"

"Do you mean after I marry you? Actually I want to take you first to Tulpehocken and we will be the first marriage by Filip Schmidt in the Aspach Lutheran church. Then I will build a solid fieldstone house with enough rooms for six children. Soon after our first child is on the way, I will join the law firm of Marshall Nead. He is a good friend of my grandfather and wants me to join his firm. Susan, I want to help all of the citizens of Tulpehocken and maybe even the entire colony of Pennsylvania attain the freedoms they want.

— ❧ —

The seemingly endless journey continued into September. Though disease had taken a few lives, as expected, there was no major outbreak of illness that threatened most voyages. It was the first week of September, and several of the younger members of the Lutheran families started getting sick with high fevers. There were two levels of living quarters and each had its own doctor. Jacob Lenz was the doctor on the second level. Jacob tended them and advised Captain Stedman that they had influenza. "Captain," said Jacob, "we must quarantine these patients as influenza is contagious and can spread rapidly." The quarantine seemed to work and there were just a handful of cases. Dr. Lentz didn't have any sure remedy for the flu, but just hoped each person's immune system and tender care would help him or her survive. His main remedy was for the patients to drink lots of water. Of the twelve cases diagnosed, only one died, Heinrich Hartman, and his was an unusual case.

Heinrich, a man about fifty who was a friend of Jonny's, had been ill even before he boarded the St. Andrew. His family traveling with him was his wife Regina, his son Henry, and Henry's wife Magdelena. Because of his illness, Jacob had discouraged him from going. "Heinrich," said Jacob, "the voyage will be too difficult for you. Even the slightest disease on ship will affect you more than others."

Besides Dr. Lentz, his family and particularly his wife Regina, who was ten years younger than Heinrich, tried to keep him from traveling. "Heinrich, we can stay here in Rotterdam and sail on another ship when you are well. America will still be there."

Despite all the pressure put on Heinrich to postpone the travel, he would not give in. "Dear Regina, I fear if we wait we will never go. As much as I want to go to America, I want more for you, Henry and Magdelena to have the freedom we have always dreamed of. The Hartmans did sail with the other "Lutheran Ten," but Heinrich was too weak to fight the flu that he contracted. He died and was buried at sea. Although he never reached the New World shore, his family not only reached America, but along with the Spykers, were some of the early settlers in Tulpehocken.

Unfortunately the other level of living quarters continued to have people suffer from influenza. Finally, Captain Stedman asked Jacob to talk to their doctor about quarantine. "Dr. Heitz," said Jacob when he sought out the doctor for those quartering on the third level, "You must quarantine them as this is contagious and others will get the illness."

"Ah, Doctor Lentz, you are just a young puppy. When you get the experience that I have for over twenty years you will realize that purging the bad blood is the answer to healing." Jacob argued strenuously with Dr. Heitz, until it became a shouting match and all Jacob could do was retreat and pray that those patients and others living on the third level would somehow survive.

Peter finished his day of visiting with the men and families of the Aspach Lutherans. He helped Jacob tend the several who were ill. Fortunately all seemed on the road to recovery. Peter also conversed with the "Lutheran Ten" and listened to their plans and advised them of legal technicalities they would have to address when they arrived in Philadelphia. He was aware that all would need to swear an oath of allegiance to England. He had eaten his meal of salt beef and hard biscuits and even had a few carrots that were supplied by ship's mess. He anxiously waited for his appointed time to "bump" into Susan.

Finally he climbed to the main deck, greeted some of the sailors with whom he had become friends and eagerly walked to his favorite jetty. He rounded the small boat, but no Susan. He continued his walk, again greeted some of the other sailors, and anxiously rounded the jetty again. It was a very dark night. This time as he bumped into "Susan," he realized "Susan" was much smaller than usual. "Hello Mr. Spyker, I'm Emily, Susan's younger sister. Susan wanted me to meet up with you as she won't be here tonight. She's not feeling well and doesn't want you to catch the 'bug' she has. She's sure she will be better tomorrow."

The next night, September the 2nd, 1737, he rounded the jetty again. He had worried all day about Susan and prayed she would be well. Again, it was Emily, "Mr. Spyker, Susan, won't be here again. She's feeling even worse and the doctor is afraid she has the flu. She says to tell you, 'not to worry,' she'll be fine in a couple of days. She says she's drinking her water, just like you told her to do and also letting the doctor purge her. She's sure this will help her get better soon."

It was then that Peter realized that Susan and her family had their quarters on the third level. Peter quickly sought out Jacob, "Jacob, my Susan is sick and I'm afraid she has the influenza. You shared with me your worries about how the doctor on the third level tries to cure his patients. Jacob, Susan is on the third level."

They rushed to the third level and finally found Susan and her family. "Oh, Peter, I wanted so much to see you these last two nights, but I feel so weak. Our doctor is very good and has worked hard to cure me. He's purged me twice each day, but I just seem to be getting weaker."

Peter knelt down and took Susan's hand while Jacob rushed to find Dr. Heitz. "Doctor, please, I beg you," Jacob pleaded in the most diplomatic manner possible, "let me take Susan and her family to our level so we can keep an eye on her every second. I know you care for her and want her to be healed, but she is getting weaker. When I visited with her I found her pulse very weak. I think good food and water, along with fresh air, will help her survive."

Doctor Heitz became very angry, "How dare you interfere with my medical practice? You are to stay out of this third level. I am the best doctor in Bavaria; all my patients will tell you that. I have a reputation that you will never gain because you experiment with faulty practices and ignore the scientific methods we have worked so hard to establish. Your lack of accepted practice could kill many on this ship. I will go to the captain and ask him to reprimand you and even put you in quarters if you keep interfering." The doctor then shoved Jacob away.

When he shoved Jacob, Peter could no longer contain himself. He grabbed Doctor Heitz and hurled him into the ship's wall. Quickly, several men close to the situation got between Peter and the doctor. They held him until members of the ship's crew came and bound Peter and took him to the captain's room. Jacob followed and they soon found themselves in front of Captain Stedman.

"Release him at once and unbind him," shouted Captain Stedman to the members of his crew. He closed the door and once he had dismissed the crew members, he listened and discussed the situation with Peter and Jacob at length. "While I agree with you and see the different results in both levels in the treatment of disease, I must be careful not to cause a revolt. Let me talk to Doctor Heitz and then I will summon you both. Now you must return to your quarters."

After several hours, while Peter suffered his greatest anxiety ever, he and Jacob were summoned back to the captain's quarters. "Gentlemen, you are not going to like my decision. I could possibly save Susan, but I would lose the whole third level and we would be in a state of revolt. If I interfere with their long practiced methods, we all will have hell to pay. All we can do is pray that the Almighty Lord looks down on your Susan and somehow cures her of this disease. Although I respect, like, and appreciate you two gentleman above all on this ship, I cannot allow you to interfere again. To do so, I regret to say, would cause me to imprison you both and subject you to arrest for mutiny upon arrival in Philadelphia. God, how I hate myself for making this decision."

Peter could not eat or sleep and avoided everyone. He stayed on the main deck and avoided all contact with everyone, even his best friend and his father. Although he prayed constantly, in his heart he expected the worst.

Each night he took the same path that enabled him to always meet Susanne. He hoped, if not Susan, at least Emily and some good news. There was no Susan and there was no Emily.

One week from the last time he had seen Susan, the ship's bell rang out, the signal that a burial at sea was to take place. There was no prior word announcing the name of the deceased. Peter went to the deck where there were many people. He could hardly walk, but Jacob helped him to the side of the crowd of witnesses. *"Surely it is not my Susan,"* he continued to say to himself. Then following the covered corpse he saw Emily, who was sobbing. He knew as the deceased sank into the sea, he would never see Susan again.

<hr />

Despair, depression, rejection from God, were some of the many anguishing emotions Peter felt. He could not share how he felt with anyone. Not his father, not Jacob, only with his mother could he share. *"Dear mother, I need you so much. No one knows the pain I am feeling. Will I ever recover? Losing you took part of my soul and now losing Susan has taken another part of my soul. Tell me what to do. Tell me how to recover from this loss. How do I regain my strength and my confidence? Soon we will be in America, I am no longer looking forward to this adventure. I am lost.*"

"Peter," consoled his father, Jonny, "I wish I could help you. You do not eat. You no longer encourage our flock. You have lost the glint in your eye and our people have lost the one who kept them looking forward to each day. You kept them straining to see America and to hope and pray for a life where they could know what it meant to be free."

Peter nodded to his father and then put his head down and walked away.

"I cannot bring Susan back, Peter," said Jacob, "but I can promise you I will work every day to erase the invisible creatures that have killed Susan and so many of our other loved ones. So help me God, I will stop the quackery of purging, the blood-letting that weakens and causes death."

Peter hugged his friend, but could not bring himself to feel any glimpse of new hope. He walked away.

One evening as he followed his once joyful trail, he reminisced about bumping into Susan. He started sobbing, and no matter how hard he tried to be the masculine image he perceived himself to be, he kept sobbing. *"Good Lord, help me, I want to dive into the ocean and join the only love of my life.*" As he neared the ship's rail, a little, but strong hand grabbed his coattail. "Peter," said Emily, "My mother wants to talk with you. She found Susan's diary and she smiled for the first time since Susan became ill. She wants desperately to talk with you. You must come, Mother has not stopped grieving, but with the smile and the request she made, our family thinks there is hope for her."

"Peter," said Marie Wagner, "I have to confess, we didn't want Susan to fall in love with you. We will be settling in the colony of South Carolina and feared you would take Susan away from us to Pennsylvania. Oh how wrong I was to interfere." Peter had followed Emily to the quarters of the Wagner's where he met a little older version of Susan. She spontaneously hugged him as though he was her son.

"I knew Susan was keeping a diary, but until just yesterday knew I couldn't read it without breaking down again with grief. When I read about her "bumping in" love life, I realized how wrong I was not to share with her the happiest days of her short life."

Peter held Marie in his arms and consoled and comforted her. This was his nature.

Peter went to see Marie often in the remaining month at sea. Somehow, Peter's efforts to console Marie and her family helped him heal and soon he was again looking forward to America.

Philadelphia
1737

———— ∞∞∞ ————

THE SPYKERS WERE STANDING BY the ship rail one early morning in September, 1737. Jonny was now fifty-two years old, Peter was twenty-six and Benjamin fourteen. Jonny and Peter were deep in thought, while young Benjamin constantly scanned the horizon.

Jonny was trying to imagine what his father would look like now that he was seventy-five years of age. *"Father said he would be there in Philadelphia when he knew the ship was coming into the harbor. Will I recognize him? I pray his health is good. Although father described Lomasi, his wife, I don't know how to picture her. I know she's an Indian. Dad says the Indians are not from India and have been in America forever, and that it is more correct to call them Native Americans. Father says she is beautiful. She's so much younger than dad. I'm sure we will become good friends."*

Peter had his own thoughts, *"God how I wish I was standing here with not only my dad and my brother, but Susan as well. Although I no longer feel the gut-wrenching pain I felt before getting to know her mother, I still would love to feel her pressing against my side.*

I look forward so much to meeting my grandfather. He must be a lot like my father, strong, resolute, but tender and caring. I can't wait to take my place in our new home. I want to help all of us have the opportunities that William Penn has promised. Through my law practice, I will do everything I can to make sure all of us share in the true meaning of freedom."

While Jonny and Peter were deep in thought as they often were on the many days of watching the horizon for something other than endless seas, Benjamin was eagerly looking for the promise land. Benjamin looked a lot like his father when he was fourteen. He was small in stature and somewhat frail as compared to his older brother Peter. Most thought he was just ten or eleven years old. He was just barely five feet in height. Despite his physical appearance he was aggressive and never afraid to stand-up to someone much larger than he. He had dark, dark, hair and eyes that were just as dark. He was not the student Peter was, in fact, he still did not know how to read or write with great efficiency. He had started school at a younger age than most students, but his days in school were frequently interrupted by fishing and hunting trips that were not known by his father. Even while sitting in the classroom, he fantasized on catching the largest bass in Zucker creek and shooting down a colorful pheasant. Despite his lack of "school-learning," he was quick to interpret events in his environment. His judgment and his decisions, based upon the events and sights of the moment, often exceeded those expected of a teenage boy. It was Benjamin who was the first on the St. Andrew to discover America.

"Dad," said Benjamin, "Do you remember when you read me the story of Noah in the Bible? That bird, just overhead, is carrying a green branch. This reminds me of when Noah knew that the water was going down and soon they could get off their boat. Don't you think that's a sign that we will soon get off this ship?"

Peter and Jonny simultaneously looked above and saw the first signs of land. "Ben," exclaimed Peter, "you've given us the message we've been looking for. We've been at sea over three months and now we are soon to be in America."

The Noah message from Benjamin quickly spread throughout the ship. Soon the ship was lilting to the west as most joined the

Spykers at the rail. It was about an hour later when one of the seaman, high in the mast, yelled, "Land Ahoy." The journey was over, but the landing in America was just beginning.

Peter could not believe his eyes as the St. Andrew sailed into Philadelphia harbor. He expected it to look a lot like the Rotterdam harbor from which they had left; a few boats loading and unloading their goods. Peter did not realize that Philadelphia was the second largest harbor, next to London, in the Colonial Empire. Ships with three and four masts were tethered throughout the great inlet. Boats loaded with wheat were departing for London and the Caribbean. Everyone seemed busy and there was a constant bustle of humanity as everyone was saying hello or goodbye. *"I expected America to be small and quiet, with just a few houses, and the Philadelphia harbor to be a lot like Rotterdam,"* thought Peter. *"It seems confusing. How can we possibly fit into this overwhelming scene that is so different from our little farming community of Aspach?"*

Soon after the ship had lowered and secured the anchor and just inside the harbor, a small boat with important looking dignitaries came from the wharf and tied alongside the ship. They boarded the ship and with Captain Stedman went behind the closed doors of his cabin. Soon the dignitaries left and Captain Stedman asked for all the group leaders to gather around him on the main deck.

"Gentlemen, as you look upon the distant shore you think it is America; you think it is the colony of Pennsylvania. Yes it is, but it is also England. America is just one colony in the English Empire. Most of you are from Germany and Switzerland, but now before you can step forward on this new land, you must renounce your allegiance to your Mother land and swear your allegiance to the colony of Pennsylvania, King George II and England.

"You may not agree with everything you hear in the oath administered by James Logan, who presently represents England as well as the royal colony of Pennsylvania, but it is a small price to pay to say 'aye.'"

Then to add a little humor in this tense climate, Captain Stedman added, "You know I am a citizen of the Netherlands, a country that often does not always agree with the policies of England. However, I needed to reside in this royal colony so when I took the oath I simply said 'I swear by my 'Dutch Uncle.' As they did not understand 'Dutch Uncle' they blessed me in 1712 as being loyal to the Queen of England. Now gentlemen, put on your most loyal faces as we go ashore and march up the hill to Second and High Street and the Pennsylvania courthouse."

Both Jonny and Peter knew they could swallow any pride necessary to reside in Pennsylvania. They could easily agree to the Oath of Allegiance, at least outwardly, but had learned the Palatine habit of crossing their fingers behind their backs to negate their verbal responses. The Palatines had to do that often when confronted by both French and the Holy Roman Empire soldiers. Their concern was with Benjamin. They knew Benjamin to be outspoken, blunt and overly honest when confronted with any questions. After all, the whole community of Aspach had enjoyed Benjamin's famous answer to Herr Leininger's question: "Ben, why have you missed so many days of school this month?"

Ben's response still brought chuckles to the community: "Dear teacher, I have been fishing for that answer all month."

As all the males from the ship alit from their small boats on the boardwalk, they found that walking on land other than aboard the ship was a wobbly experience. Benjamin, who seemed to be at home on land and sea, laughed to himself and thought, "We look like drunken sailors." The large group longing to be a part of America, marched up the hill and entered the courthouse of Philadelphia.

"Ladies and gentlemen," intoned James Logan, "you come from distant lands; lands that are not part of the greatest empire the world has ever known. You do not come from England. We want you here only if you can change your allegiance and be totally loyal to England and King George II. Thus it is my duty and privilege to administer to each of you in this group an oath of allegiance. After you have sworn your fealty to England we will ask you to sign two documents. The first will be the document for loyalty to England and the second for the document to enter the colony of Pennsylvania."

After the interpreters had helped each male understand, James Logan continued with the help of interpreters, "Raise your right hand and repeat after me in a loud and distinct voice: "I, say your full name, do solemnly swear I will conduct myself as a good and faithful subject to England and King George II. I will not revolt against his Majesty nor will I settle on lands that are not my own. I also swear that I will abjure allegiance to the pope. I swear this so help me God."

After the interpreters had completed the translation, Mr. Logan asked, "Are there any questions or do any of you disagree with any part of this oath?" Both Jonny and Peter cringed when they saw Ben's hand rise in his typical aggressive manner. Despite the efforts by Peter to get Ben's hand down, he was recognized by Representative Logan. "Yes young man."

"I am happy to swear allegiance to England and Pennsylvania, but I do not understand why you would ask us to be against another religion. I'm not Catholic, I'm Lutheran, but William Penn has taught us to respect all religions, so why should anyone who is Catholic be asked to no longer follow their religion?"

Jonny expected the worst and Peter thought this might be his first legal challenge in the new colony. They were amazed at Logan's reply. "My bright young man. I admire your courage. You've said something that is on many of the minds in your group.

I'm required to administer an oath with which I do not totally agree and you will be required to sign something with which you don't totally agree. This is called politics. This is the reason I am more a representative of William Penn than I am of the British Empire. I don't think I will ever be made governor."

The interpreter quickly repeated the comment to everyone in German, but then hastened to add, "Quickly, please sign the two documents and get back to your ship for the debarkation."

Jonny and Peter signed the two documents of allegiance in their strong handwriting and then witnessed Benjamin, who despite deficiencies in writing had beautiful handwriting, just checked the box indicating agreement, but did not sign his name.

Tulpehocken
1737

———⚬∞⚬———

THE THREE SPYKERS STOOD BY the rail as the St. Andrew was moored to the wharf. As they looked out, each wondered if Johannes would be there to meet them. Jonny thought: *"It's been twenty-eight years since I last saw father. Will I recognize him? Will he recognize me?"* Jonny scanned the crowd on the wharf. Many were merchants, men that would work with the immigrants, some in a wholesome manner and some in a greedy manner.

"There," shouted Jonny to Peter and Benjamin, "I think that's father. He has a lady with him. See her dark hair and how tall she is. She's just as tall as father. That's got to be Lomasi. That other person might be Conrad Weiser, Jr., as he looks just like his dad. I was kind of a mentor to Conrad. I'll never forget the first time I took him fishing." Jonny was beside himself with excitement.

Jonny waved and waved and all of a sudden the man who looked like his father broke into a giant smile and waved even harder than Jonny. As they ran down the gangplank twenty- eight years passed into nothing. They were a family again.

Johannes introduced Lomasi and she shook hands with Jonny and Peter and then hugged Benjamin as if he were the son she had always wanted. In a limited German language she expressed, "Welcome to America. Your father has talked so much about you

Jonny that I think I know you already. You're a little too old for me to call you son," laughed Lomasi, who was just a little older than Jonny. "So I'll call you Jonny and we will be great American friends." Jonny couldn't get over how young Lomasi looked. She looked no older than Peter.

Johannes could not control himself and neither could Jonny as they hugged and sobbed. "Okay dad," said Ben, "That's enough. Everyone is looking at us and everyone is also starting to cry. If you keep this up, I might even cry. Besides you told me Lomasi would teach me to fish and hunt in this new country. Let's go fishing."

"Ben," said the older Johannes, "Lomasi indeed could teach you to fish, just like she did me a few hundred years ago, but this man next to me is the true outdoorsman. Jonny, do you remember Conrad, who was the son of my best friend Conrad, Sr."

Conrad jumped in before Jonny could answer, "Speaking of fishing, my father loved to tell the story of my first encounter with a fish. Jonny, I can't tell you how many times Dad told everyone that his brave son wasn't so brave after all; 'heck, he was even afraid of a fish.'" Johannes, Jonny, and Conrad all laughed as they remembered how scared Conrad was of the flopping Louis.

Johannes eagerly related many of the tales of Conrad, Jr.. Peter and Benny were all ears as they looked at Conrad in admiration as their grandfather told of the heroics of one of America's most renown pioneers.

"Conrad's father," continued Johannes, "my great friend is still alive, but the years have been tough on him. He lives in New York colony close to Schoharie, which is where I ended up after leaving the Livingston Manor and before I came to Tulpehocken. I haven't seen him since he went back to England on a fruitless effort to get King George I to cede land in Schoharie to us Palatines. He literally gave his life for us and received no reward for it but poverty and heartbreak. I pray that I may someday see him again and renew our friendship. Conrad, Jr. stayed in Schoharie in the

New York Colony when I went with Lomasi and other families to Tulpehocken. He learned the language and the lifestyle of the Indians and is now the person who negotiates between the settlers and the Indians. Conrad is probably the most loved and respected White man to the Indian Nations. He maintains peace in not just Pennsylvania but in Virginia, New York and all over the American colonies."

Johannes finished his discourse on Conrad, "I know Conrad is one hundred percent American, but I think his soul is half White and half Indian. That's why he is trusted by both the immigrants like us and the Indians, who he calls Native Americans."

Conrad did not go back to Tulpehocken with the Spykers at that time. He remained in Philadelphia to meet with James Logan concerning some boundary disputes in Western Pennsylvania.

The Spykers put all their belongings, meager as they were, into the large wagon that Johannes had brought. They were ready for the journey to Tulpehocken and a new life. The long trip from Philadelphia to Tulpehocken allowed them to renew their relationship and share many stories.

Although Johannes spoke to his son and grandsons in German, he would speak to Lomasi in both English and the language of the Iroquois. Peter, who was well educated and had taken some English while at Heidelberg, was curious as to why his grandfather preferred to speak English rather than German to Lomasi.

For a period during the ride, Jonny fell silent and went deep into his thoughts. He replayed the journey in his mind which seemed both like a million years ago and just yesterday. *"Mein Gott in himmel, how did we survive the journey? Oh how I wish I had Margaret with me, but yes, she is with me. I can feel her presence. My father looks wonderful, but he is so old. I pray he can stay with us for a long time. I thank God for Lomasi, I can see she makes him happy. Dear Gott in himmel, we are here, thank you!"*

Benjamin was still the question man that Jonny and Peter remembered from the time shortly after their mother's death. Peter laughed as he saw Ben talking to Lomasi and thought, *"Now she's the answer lady."*

Lomasi, who had been somewhat quiet as the Spykers talked among themselves, smiled at Ben, and thus the questions began. After several, Ben asked, "Lomasi, Tulpehocken is sure a funny name. What does it mean?"

You could tell Lomasi was delighted with the question. "Benny, I love young people who have your curiosity. Tulpehocken means 'The Land of the Turtle,' which sounds simple, but has a much greater meaning than that. My people use many symbols to replace words. We do not use as many words as you do. The turtle is a very important symbol. It represents Mother Earth. The meaning of the turtle symbol signifies good health and long life. The turtle has great longevity, living up to one hundred and fifty years. Also the turtle is important in our explanation of the creation of our world. Here's the story. The turtle in the beginning was called an Earth Diver. This Earth Diver swam to the bottom of the water that stretched across the world. He then surfaced with the mud that the creator used to make the earth. Another important symbol of the turtle is his hard shell. This represents perseverance and protection."

Lomasi continued to explain the way of life for her people, "You see Benny, our nation did not have the advantage of knowing your God and the knowledge in the Bible. I think, however, there are many stories in your Bible and in our lore that might be similar. We often believe in the same things, but just use different terms. I'll tell you more stories of my people in our times together. I'm so happy you are here and are going to be living with us. Wait until you see the beautiful home Johannes has built with the help of his friends and a little help from me as well."

With this explanation by Lomasi, Ben felt satisfied and sleepy from the events of the day and the continuous sojourn to a new life. He closed his eyes and slightly leaned against Lomasi. Lomasi put her arm around Ben and snuggled him close. It was a tender sight to see these new friends so content with each other.

———— ✺ ————

The horse and wagon came across a small bridge over the Tulpehocken creek. "Son, we are home." They were met by a young man of about thirty who took the reins and led the horses and wagon to the front door of the Spyker home. As they climbed down from the wagon, Johannes introduced Thomas Jones in both English and German. "Thomas and his wife Mary are staying with us until they get their home by the creek built. Thomas is a miller and is building a mill along with his house at the rapids of the Tulpehocken about ten kilometers from here. He's been with us close to a year."

Peter explained further that the Joneses were Quakers from Portsmouth, England where Thomas had been a miller. They had not felt welcome in England, in fact were threatened because of their faith. When they came to Philadelphia, they found it was too large for them and that not all the people, including the proprietors, were tolerant of their Quaker faith. Thus they migrated further west to establish the mill.

"He and Mary just showed up at our door one day about a year ago. Now they are part of the family. We have a mutual agreement. They stay with us until their homestead is ready and they are teaching Lomasi and me the English language. Jonny, it is important for all of us to learn English as soon as possible because we are an English colony and this is the language we will need to succeed in America."

Peter eagerly replied to his grandfather, "Now I know why you and Lomasi spoke English on our trip from Philadelphia. I am so thankful. I want to speak English and I know this will be the language of my law practice. But Lomasi, I also want to learn your language."

Johannes had a twinkle in his eye, "Now for your first lesson and then a good meal and a good rest.

"Ich liebe dich," said Johannes. "Konoronhkwe," said Lomasi. "I love you," said Thomas.

"Now," concluded Johannes. "You have had your first lesson and it's time for a wonderful meal prepared by Mary and then time for rest. You are home. Tomorrow is another day and Ich liebe dich."

Christmas Eve in Tulpehocken
1737

———— ⊗⊗⊗ ————

IT WAS DECEMBER 24TH, 1737, the first Christmas Eve in the New World for Jonny, Peter, and Benjamin. Johannes and Lomasi had prepared their home just as Peter remembered it in Aspach. The home was filled with friends that had come with Johannes from Schoharie. Also there were many who had come with Peter and his father on the St. Andrew, like the Stohrs and the Hartmans. Regina Hartman was there with her son and his wife. Regina had grieved for her husband buried at sea, but was a strong woman and she helped her son and his pregnant wife make it all the way to Tulpehocken, which was her husband Heinrich's desire.

Dr. Jacob Lentz and his wife were there with their young children, as well as the ever exuberant Pastor Filip Schmidt. Filip was an assistant pastor at the Reed Reform church with Pastor Reith, who had come with Johannes from Schoharie. Filip, was still insistent that they build their own Lutheran church, the Aspach Lutheran church. He had prayed incessantly for the proper land to come to him. He wanted a church that everyone could view from kilometers away. A church on a pinnacle.

It was a wonderful gathering of Palatines of Germany, who no longer had to fear the roving armies of the French and the Holy Roman Empire. With neighbors far apart, it was only at these types of gatherings that they got to visit and share their lives with each other.

Also there were a few Native Americans from the Iroquois Nation at the party. They were friends of Johannes and Lomasi. The Iroquois Nation's habitat was many miles north of Tulpehocken, but a few had become spouses of the Palatines, as did Lomasi. The most numerous tribes of Native Americans in the Tulpehocken area were the Delaware, who were wary of the immigrants and not too pleased that they were encroaching upon their hunting grounds. Conrad had many negotiations between the Delaware and the immigrants and the Delaware and the Iroquois. The Iroquois and Delaware were frequently at war with each other. Conrad was amazingly able to keep the peace until 1754, when the Delaware made war on the settlers.

In different nooks and corners you could hear important conversations going on. Among the guests were some of the best known families in the Tulpehocken area. Both Womelsdorfs, Daniel and his son John, were there. Daniel was one of the earliest settlers who had come to Tulpehocken before Johannes and his followers had come from Schoharie. As they had the largest land tract in the area and others were purchasing land from them, the settlers started calling the settlement Womelsdorf.

Daniel was in his fifties and his son John was the same age as Peter, just a little less than thirty. They were talking with Conrad Weiser and at his side was young Benjamin. Ben always wanted to be by his hero; the best hunter, the best fisherman in Pennsylvania.

"Conrad," said John Womelsdorf, "should we be afraid of the Indians who hunt in the forests beside our farms and the land that we have deeded? It seems more every day are coming to our creek to water their horses."

"John," answered Conrad with a little smile on his face so not to be confrontational, "this is their creek and their forests, although deeded to you by the chief in your area, they will never recognize it other than their own land; the land that the Great Spirit gave them centuries ago. You can go a long way in keeping the peace and your family safe by sharing with them in every way. Let them hunt the forests, fish the stream and roam freely. If you can accept this, I will talk to the great Chief Cannassatego, and he will make sure you remain safe. A couple of weeks ago, I would have told you to be afraid of Chief Cannassatego, as he was losing control of his tribe to some of the young war-like Delaware. The Chief was sick and planning to depart with plans to go to his 'Happy Hunting' ground. He was sick and ready to die. However, our doctor, Jacob Lentz, went with me to see the Chief. Lo and behold, young Lentz mixed together some herbs and administered them to the Chief over several days and now he is well again and in control of the tribe."

John, the son of Daniel Womelsdorf, quickly supported Conrad, "Thanks be to Doctor Lentz. My wife Anna and I have become friends with several of the Indians who come to the Tulpehocken creek beside our farm. They bring us game and fish and we supply them with salt, milk, and vegetables from our garden. I'm not close to being fluent in their language, but Anna is almost as fluent as you, Conrad. They really appreciate Anna speaking their language and oh how they laugh at my attempts. The other day I was trying to be a preacher and convert them to our religion. I was trying to explain heaven and God to them. I threw in all my Indian words and my inept sign language and they just kept looking bewildered at each other. I even had Anna confused. Then she understood what I was trying to teach them and helped explain my efforts.

"Conrad, you should have seen them laugh. They almost went rolling down our yard into the creek. Then they comforted me. Two of them even put their arms around me, knowing I was confused and frustrated. Anna said, they were simply trying to correct my ignorance and helping me understand the Great Spirit and the Happy Hunting ground and that I shouldn't be embarrassed by not understanding these ideas."

Benjamin listened intently. Finally he could restrain himself no more and jumped in, beseeching Conrad, "Let me live with the Native Americans, like you did; maybe for a year or least for several months. I know I can learn their language and help you keep the peace. I'll hunt and fish with them and live just like they do. If I learn their ways I can help all of us Palatines know best how to live together with the Native Americans. After all, this was their land long before we arrived, and we can't just expect them to move. In some ways we are acting just like the French who came into Wurttemberg and expected us to supply them with food and get out of their way when they had to make war.

"Conrad," continued Ben in a pleading voice, "I already have a friend that is a Delaware." Ben proceeded to tell his story. "I was trapping rabbits just a few kilometers from grandfather's house. As I was releasing a rabbit from one of my traps, a large rabbit leaped nearby. I tried to kill it with my sling-shot, but it escaped and all of a sudden –"*zip*," Ben made the noise of an arrow passing close to him, "an arrow pierced the rabbit right through the neck. I was scared and wanted to run swiftly to the house. Just then I heard a roar of laughter and out from a stand of trees appeared an Indian – I mean an Native American, about my age. I think he laughed because of my lack of success in hitting the rabbit. We communicated the best we could with sign language and his few English words and my few Native American words. He said, 'wie gehts' and I said 'konoronhkwa.' Neither one of us knew what the other was saying, but we both just laughed. We became friends and I have met him often. We have hunted and fished together all through the fall. His name is Kitchi. The neatest thing, Conrad, is that he has helped me learn a few Delaware words and he is teaching me how to use a bow and arrow."

Conrad and the Womelsdorfs were impressed with Benjamin's sincere request and his experiences with his friend. "Ben, for fifteen-years old you already understand the importance of keeping peace with the ones who have been here long before us. I cringe when we call them Indians. They are not from India, but from America, long before we came to America.

I will call them Native Americans. I was fourteen years old when my father had me live with the Iroquois. Even before then, I like you, had a friend, like Kitchi. His name was Orenda and he was a Native American from the Iroquois Nation. He's the one that first showed me Schoharie and the beautiful Mohawk valley. I lived with Orenda and the Mohawk of the Iroquois nation for several years. Because of this I can speak and understand their language. I also know their ways; their nature, their pride. They are a great civilization and we must learn to live with them or maybe better said, we want them to be able to live with us. We can learn so much from them. Ben, I wouldn't hesitate to suggest this to your father if the Native Americans in this area were Iroquois, but they are not, they are Delaware.

Conrad explained his concern, "The Delaware are not as welcoming as the Iroquois; they are very skeptical of everything we settlers do and for good reason. Later I will tell you the story of the 'walking purchase' where the government in Pennsylvania cheated the Delaware out of many acres. Regardless, it would be a good thing for you to live with the Delaware. I am only one person and today we need more Conrads to work with the Native Americans. Ben, let me talk first to your father and then to Chief Cannassatego." Benjamin was grateful and satisfied with Conrad's understanding of how he felt. Both Womelsdorfs just nodded their heads and realized how vital Conrad was to their very existence in Tulpehocken.

—&—

While this conversation was going on, Jacob Seltzer was sharing his culinary notes with Johannes and Lomasi. Jacob had opened a restaurant some thirty kilometers east of the residence of Johannes and Lomasi. It was in the settlement that many were calling Womelsdorf. The restaurant was already becoming popular and a wonderful gathering space for civic meetings that the settlers needed to have. Anytime Conrad, Daniel Womelsdorf, Marshall Nead or other community leaders wanted to get the settlers together for an important issue, they simply said, "Meet you at Seltzer's."

The guests had just enjoyed a fine dinner of venison from Seltzer's restaurant, as well as the many meats and fowl provided by guests from all over Tulpehocken. Besides the meats the neighbors brought many other dishes to complement the meal. However, special treats were the vegetables and fruit from the Spyker garden and vineyard. Lomasi was the gardener and a gifted chef to Johannes. For this dinner she had also prepared biscuits with corn meal that seemed to melt in one's mouth. During the meal, all the adults enjoyed the Spyker wine and the beer from Conrad's brewery he had established in the cellar of his house.

Although Lomasi was the gardener, Johannes was in charge of the orchard of apples, peaches, pears, and plums. The Spykers and their neighbors were never without fresh fruit in season or preserved fruit when you could not just go and pick a fruit off one of the trees. Johannes loved his orchard, but treasured above all his vineyard. In Aspach he and his father before him, and his father before him, always had a fine vineyard and the knowledge for making fine wine. Johannes had found, when he was in Schoharie, wild grapes that were similar to the Riesling grapes in Aspach. The grapes were as white and aromatic as those from his vineyard at home in Aspach. When he emigrated from Schoharie he brought a number of vine sprigs in the hope that they would take hold in the Tulpehocken area of Pennsylvania.

It took him several years of providing these sprigs with tender love and care, but now his vineyard was a sight of beauty and his wines were sought after throughout the Tulpehocken and other areas of the Pennsylvania colony.

All during the meal the Spyker wine and the Conrad Weiser beer flowed continually. The meal had been topped off by the pies prepared by Jacob's restaurant. The favorite was the shoofly pie. "Heavens," exclaimed Johannes as he patted his full belly and belched with satisfaction, "how do you make your venison as tender as if God himself had prepared it for his angels? And Jacob, the shoofly pie is fabulous. I think I have already gained twenty pounds."

"Johannes, you have to be patient with deer meat. It is more flavorful than beef, but it takes a long time or it will be as tough as the soles of those boots you are wearing. First, trim as much fat from the venison as possible. I prepare the venison myself and not a speck of fat remains on a Seltzer-prepared cut of venison. Johannes, you leave that fat on that deer and you will have plenty left over because no one will eat it.

"Now you want to soak the meat in a mixture of water, vinegar, and salt. Soak it for about an hour. Next, after the first soaking, you are going to dry rub into the venison a mixture of these herbs: marjoram, thyme, parsley, garlic, and mint. Lots of mint. Rub it in hard. Then, Johannes, you must prepare a marinade of vinegar and your wine. You may not realize it but many of my recipes at Seltzer's contain the Spyker wine. Soak the meat for three hours and you are almost ready to roast it in a fine clay oven. But before you do, brush your venison with a light coating of olive oil over the entire surface of the meat in a thin layer to increase the moisture in the meat and preserve juiciness while cooking. Then 'wunderschoen!' you have a meal just like you would have at Seltzer's restaurant."

After the venison recipe, Jacob went into great detail about making shoofly pie. However, the mixture of molasses, soda, flour, butter, ginger, cinnamon, nutmeg, and cloves became too mind-boggling for Johannes, particularly the "throw in a little of this and a little of that." Johannes simply said, "Jacob, I'm too old to remember this recipe. I'll just get all my shoofly pies from the Seltzer restaurant."

"Johannes, you are always welcome to a piece of the Seltzer shoofly, but more than one piece and you will lose the fingers that reach out so eagerly for my pie," laughed Jacob.

"Now, Lomasi and Johannes, it's my turn," said Jacob. Our restaurant makes biscuits just like everyone else. People say they are okay, but we never receive compliments about them. They always say nice things about the meals and the desserts, but no, not a word about my biscuits. This evening I tasted the best biscuits I've ever had. I want them to be a special item on my menu, the Spyker Biscuits. Please, I beg of you, teach me, Johannes, how you make these delicious biscuits."

Johannes smiled put his arm around Lomasi and said, "Jacob, you must call them 'Lomasi Biscuits.' The Iroquois have been making these biscuits for hundreds of years, but no one, and I mean no one, can make them as deliciously as my lovely Lomasi."

Lomasi, leaned into Johannes and smiled bashfully. "Jacob, I will teach you how these are made, but you must not share this secret with anyone else or off goes your head." Once again they all laughed together, particularly as jokes were not the nature of Lomasi.

"The secret is honey, Spyker corn meal, and Weiser beer", said Lomasi and then she outlined the typical ingredients and then re-emphasized the addition of honey from the bees of Tulpehocken, and a slight amount of Weiser beer with the buttermilk. "Please, do not over stir the mixture, leave butter lumps in it. Jacob, make sure your oven fire is as hot as possible, dab out your biscuits on a cooking sheet, and put into the oven no more than ten minutes. Also Jacob, in the spring and the early summer, put blueberries in some of your biscuits for a special treat." After their discussion, they all joined arms and went into the Spyker kitchen for another round of shoofly pie and Lomasi biscuits.

One of the most interesting conversations and one that would be significant for years to come was in the parlor. Dr. Jacob Lentz and Peter and the others were smoking cigars and sipping fine port; port that was from Spain and had been imported via Philadelphia by Jacob Seltzer. They talked about their progress and their future. "Peter," said Jacob, "I love doctoring with the settlers in this area and often with the help of Conrad I am even able to minister to the Delaware.

"Just last week I treated an important Delaware chief named Cannassatgo. He had severe gout and no longer could function as the tribe's chief. His disposition was so bad that he wanted to go to war with everyone. Conrad took me to the chief and I recognized the symptoms of gout, which coincidently was the malady that caused Conrad's mother to die. I've had good success with herbs of tansy root and germander in this treatment and it was immediately effective on Chief Cannassatgo. He was so thankful that he thought I must be some sort of god. He now wants me to come to their village each week and take care of the sick. In return he will award me with a hundred acres of land just north of Tulpehocken creek.

"That's wonderful, Jacob. You are so valuable to all of us. I'm clearing the land that father has bought for me and hopefully even this spring can start to plant corn and wheat. Also I want desperately to have a home and farm that is as beautiful and sturdy as our home in Aspach.

Besides farming I am working with Marshall Nead. To be honest, I'm learning more from Marshall than I am contributing. He is, however, pleased with me and will petition Thomas Penn, son of William, for me to become a Justice of the Peace in Tulpehocken."

"Peter, what will you do with a grand house? You would get lost in it and we would not be able to find you. You need to find a wife and fill the house with little Spykers. I've got just the right lady for you. She's a great cook, a wonderful housekeeper, and she has a terrific personality." They both started to laugh as this proposal had been repeated many times from all who felt obliged to get Peter married off.

After their moment of hilarity, Jacob continued, "I have a lawyer job for you. As I mentioned, Chief Cannassatgo wants to award me acreage, acreage by the way that is not in a great place for hunting, hence the Chief is happy for me to own it for my continued services. Peter, I know it is important to do this legally, to have a solid deed. I honestly do not want as many acres as the Chief has suggested, since I am not and never will be a farmer, but just want to keep enough acres for our house, a garden, and land to pasture a few head of cattle and horses that I will use for my travel to my patients. I would like to have you deed me just ten acres and then have you take the rest for your farming. The acreage I think will abut on the present area that you farm."

"Jacob, thank you, I will work on this deed as soon as Christmas is over. You are overwhelming me with your generosity. I will accept only if I pay you through the years with the produce from my farm and the wine from my vineyard. I've got an additional thought. What would you think of some of the land being deeded in common to build the Aspach Lutheran church?"

"That's a wonderful idea." As if on cue, Jacob looked out the massive window to the west. "Peter, look out the window, look in the distance, about five kilometers to the west. Look at that ridge that is much higher than the rest of the land. This is part of the parcel of land that will be part of the deed. Would it not look great to have our church at the highest point in Tulpehocken? Throughout Tulpehocken we could see the church and the spire and the cross as if it were sitting on top of our world."

They were so excited about their plans that they sought out the good Reverend Filip, who was trying to Christianize Lomasi. They saw Filip frustrated, as Lomasi was explaining in her simple language that both nations, White and Iroquois, had a great spirit and a heavenly hunting ground. Lomasi was, however, interested in learning the story of Jesus.

"Filip," said Peter putting his arm around Filip's shoulder. "You can build your church." Peter and Jacob shared the outcome of their conversation, and Filip was more excited than he was the day when he declared he was going to America.

"My good Christian friend," Lomasi said to Filip, "I will come to your church and learn about Jesus."

━━━ ◦◦◦ ━━━

Peter and Benjamin, although having their own enjoyable conversations, wondered where was their father? The Christmas Eve meal started in the mid-afternoon and lasted for hours. The Spyker house, although large, was busting at the seams as over fifty people, men, women and children, devoured huge helpings of venison and turkey along with all the trimmings. During this long afternoon meal, Jonny was sitting across from Regina Hartman, the widow of Heinrich.

Regina and her family had traveled with other Palatine Lutherans to the Tulpehocken area and deeded a farm twenty some kilometers northwest of Johannes and Lomasi. Her son Henry was a farmer and also a blacksmith. His wife Magdelena was pregnant while on board the St. Andrew. Now they had a child, a strong healthy daughter, the first child from the St. Andrew born in

America. Henry and Magdelena, along with Regina, were also at the feast and Magdelena was again pregnant.

Henrich and Regina Hartman had always been friends of Johnny and Elizabeth at their get-togethers, the Christmas Eves, and the occasions of funerals and marriages. Jonny had comforted Regina as best he could after her husband had died. He had also made arrangements for Regina and her family to have transportation from Philadelphia to Tulpehocken. Then he had lost track of her. Jonny did not know how Regina had come to be invited to the Spyker's Christmas Eve, but he was delighted.

As Jonny looked across the massive table at Regina, he was struck, as he always had been by her appearance. She was beautiful in Jonny's eyes. Regina, surprisingly could have been taken for a lady of the Iroquois nation. She was tall, with long, dark, shiny hair, and a sun-kissed complexion. Her eyes were also dark, almost appearing black, and she had perfect white teeth when she smiled, which was seldom. Regina was a little younger than Jonny, perhaps, forty-five years of age.

During the meal, Regina and Jonny had acknowledged each other. "Jonny, it is so wonderful to see you and to come to your father's house. We were blessed when Lomasi visited us and insisted that we join them. I told her, 'Jonny has always been a blessing to me, both in Aspach, and particularly in my grief on the St. Andrew.'"

It was difficult to carry on a conversation across the table with all the buzzing going on amongst good friends. After they had completed the dinner, Regina came over to Jonny and they hugged as good friends. "Regina, I'm so full that I need a good walk. Would you join me in a walk along the Tulpehocken creek?" It was not cold, less than zero centigrade, and the snow was only a foot deep. It was beautiful outside in the vast unpopulated countryside. "Oh, Jonny, I would love to take a walk with you. I've never seen anything as appealing as your father's farm with all the snow and the water trickling through the ice on the creek."

They enjoyed each other's company as they strolled for over an hour until the sun started to disappear in the cold Pennsylvania sky. When they walked back to the house, they were arm in arm. "Regina, could I visit you at your farm. I'd like to see you again. I think we can become good friends."

"Jonny, we are good friends," said Regina as she kissed Jonny on the cheek just before they came back into the house.

———

As Conrad was talking with the Womelsdorfs, Conrad's wife was busy with her own project. Conrad's wife was a lively little lady whom he loved dearly called Anna Eve. They had brought with them their seven children ranging from fifteen to two. As in the early Christmases in Aspach, the children had a great time playing together and then performing Christmas carols. Anna Eve was the organizer of this traditional program and her daughter Anna Madlina was the conductor.

It was getting late in the night and time for the younger children to climb the ladders to the large loft and wait for the sandman. The loft was entirely covered with the soft downy quilts made by the Palatine ladies. It was like sleeping on a cloud. But before bedtime, Anna interrupted all the conversations. "My dear neighbors, my best friends, Palatines, Germans, and those who have been here for hundreds of years, our friends from the Iroquois Nation; our children have prepared a program for you. This is similar to the program that Johannes and Peter described. Jonny tells me that he remembers like it was yesterday the Christmas Eve of 1705 when he re-met his Elizabeth, the mother of Peter and Benjamin. The children will sing one song from Germany long ago and one song from America our new home and our new hope. Here's my Anna Madlina and the Tulpehocken children."

As in days of yore, out marched the children ranging from five to twelve, with Anna Madlina Weiser, twelve-years-old, as their leader and conductor.

Anna introduced the first song. "Look outside in the countryside and look in every home in Tulpehocken and you will see Christmas trees. These are signs that Saint Nicholas will come to our house tonight and that Jesus is always with us. We have decorated our trees as a present to the new born baby Jesus." Anna, with great poise, turned to the choir, silenced them with her two index fingers at her lips, and then with great emphasis opened her hands to start the carol. *"O Tannenbaum, O Tannenbaum... (They sang the song in German.)*

O Christmas Tree, O Christmas Tree, Your branches green delight us! They are green when summer days are bright, They are green when winter snow is white. O Christmas Tree, O Christmas Tree, Your branches green delight us! ... ."

All the adults were delighted and applauded and applauded until the conductor held up her hands to them as if to say, "Thank you, but that is enough."

Anna, after her polite silencing of the audience, "We dedicate this song to Mr. Johannes Spyker, the elder, and Lomasi in thanks for this wonderful Christmas Eve in their home. May we have many more. It is a song we have learned in America, written years ago by Isaac Watts, an Englishman. We are going to sing it in English, which we are studying every day in our homes. Children," with that Madlina gave a strong down beat and the children with sweet but strong voices began: *"Joy to the World, the Lord is come! Let earth receive her King; Let every heart prepare Him room, And Heaven and nature sing, And Heaven and nature sing, And Heaven, and Heaven, and nature sing.... .*

And wonders of His love

And wonders of His love
And wonders, wonders, of his love... ."

The children left and climbed to the loft, waited for sleep to come, and anxiously waited for the next morning.

For Johannes Spyker, Sr. this was his twenty-seventh Christmas in the New World. It had been twenty-seven years since he had seen his son. He had never seen his grandchildren until this September, 1737. Now with the coming of Jonny, Peter, and Benjamin he could truly have "Joy to the World," Johannes felt very tired that late night and early morning of Christmas 1737. He was getting old and each day he felt like resting in the Lord. *"Dear Lord, yes I'm tired and worn out,"* he prayed, *"but let me stay until I see that my son and my grandchildren are successful in this New World."*

Benjamin (Ben) and Kitchi

1738

<hr>

AFTER THE CHRISTMAS EVE CONVERSATION where Benjamin had asked Conrad if he could live a year with the Delaware, Conrad had talked with both Jonny and Chief Cannassatego about this venture. Jonny was very reluctant, "Conrad, Ben is still very impressionable. He will not be sixteen until this summer. Elizabeth would expect me to keep him under fatherly reins until he was older."

"I understand how you feel," replied Conrad, "but I've been impressed with Benjamin's maturity, particularly as it is related to the outdoors. As you know, Ben and I have hunted and fished together frequently. Many times we stayed several nights in the forests and beside streams; he is very capable of living the Native American life." Conrad, would not use the word Indians and always referred to them as Native Americans or their tribe names, such as Iroquois or Delaware. Conrad's preference had rubbed off on Jonny and his family and they also used the term Native Americans.

"Jonny, let me tell you about an experience Ben and I had recently as we were hunting deer. I've not shared this as it might have alarmed you, Johannes and Lomasi. This happened in November before Ben's request to live with the Delaware, and is the reason I took his request seriously. We planned to be out for just one overnight and wanted to bring back two deer for our holiday parties. I knew deer would be coming to the juncture of the Maiden creek into the Tulpehocken for their morning drink from the crystal clear creek. We went to overnight on the banks of the Maiden so we could rise early, kill our deer, and get back to Johannes's house before dark. As we were setting up our campsite, out of the woods came a huge black bear. I foolishly did not have my flintlock loaded. To protect Ben, I led the bear on a merry race along the banks of the Maiden creek and finally had no choice but to cross the creek with hopes the bear would not follow. I was cold and wet and miserable, and all of a sudden as it looked like the bear was going to continue after me. Ben appeared with his flintlock and fired into the bear, killing him."

Conrad continued to tell the story, "We were safe, I should say, I was safe, because Ben had the situation well in hand. He built a blazing fire, had me strip and warm by the fireside as he hung my clothes close to the fire to dry. He skillfully skinned the bear. Later after I was reasonably warm he nursed me to a normal temperature with a little rum in a cup of water that he had heated over the fire. We were fine through the night with the still warm fire and now dry clothes. The next morning we killed our two stag deer, packed the meat and the bearskin, and traveled back to civilization. Now you know why I have confidence in Benjamin to do well with the Delaware tribe and also why Lomasi has a fine black bear rug in front of the fireplace."

Jonny was impressed, but not surprised, as Benjamin was always a capable outdoorsman and an independent young man. "Conrad, let me think about this and I'll give you my answer in a day or two. I must ask Elizabeth in my prayers."

It was just two days later when Jonny consented to have his youngest son live with the Delaware.

Now, with Jonny's approval, Conrad approached Chief Cannassatego. He presented his case and his reasoning. Chief

Cannassatego then related a story. "Conrad, if you were to ask for one of our young men to come and live with the Americans, I would have said no. Let me tell you a story told me by a chief close to Boston. The Bostonians thought it a good idea to foster good relations by having three young Delaware men attend your Harvard University. They would learn the way of the White man and gain knowledge that they could bring to our nation.

After three years at Harvard, the educated Delaware youth returned to their tribe. Conrad, they were good for nothing. They could not kill a deer, catch a bear, or surprise an enemy. The chief told the Massachusetts commissioners, 'Have your White children come live with us. They will learn the ways of the Delaware and we will make men out of them.'"

Conrad, nodded his head in agreement. The chief then made a request of his nearby wife and shortly appeared a young Delaware lad of about fifteen-years-old. "Conrad, this is my grandson Kitchi; someday he might be chief over all the Delaware in the Tulpehocken lands. He wants to speak to you in English, a language he is learning from his best friend."

Kitchi addressed Conrad in a mixture of German, English, and Delaware. Although he did it with great difficulty, he made his grandfather proud of his efforts. "Mr. Weiser, I have a friend who is teaching me to speak your language and teaching me how to use a sling-shot. I am teaching him how to speak the language of my people and how to hunt with a bow and arrow. I would be honored if he could be my brother and live with me and our tribe. His name is Benjamin Spyker."

───── ⌾ ─────

Peter was impressed with the story from his father, and understood the reasoning for Benjamin to live with Kitchi and the Delaware. After hearing the story he traveled with Jonny and Conrad to thank

Chief Cannassatego for this great gift of educating Benjamin in the ways of the Delaware.

"Chief Cannassatego," said Peter, "in two years I will have a fine house on the land that you have sold to Doctor Lentz and to me. It would be an honor if you would at that time have Kitchi come to live with Benjamin and me for a year. He would learn our ways and also learn that we are not as greedy and insensitive as the proprietors in Philadelphia. I know my brother will return to us a better man and I want to assure you that if Kitchi later comes to live with us, he too will be a better man, a man who will help all of us live peacefully in this beautiful Tulpehocken valley."

Chief Cannassatego knew that Peter had in mind "the walking purchase", when he mentioned the greed and insensitivity of the proprietors.

Peter Spyker in Philadelphia
1738

———— ∞∞∞ ————

MARSHALL NEAD WANTED PETER TO continue his law education to help make him a Justice of the Peace who would know as many nuances of the law as possible, particularly of those related to the frontier. During one of their meetings after the first of the year 1738, Marshall said, "Peter, you are not presently married, but I expect some day you will be married with a family. Now is the time, while still without family responsibilities to expand your legal education. You have come to us with a good foundation in law with your studies at Heidelberg and your vast readings. Now you need to expand your knowledge with American ideas. I have a good friend in Philadelphia who is one of the top lawyers in Pennsylvania. His name is Thomas Hopkinson. I would like you to work with him for a couple of months."

Marshall continued to explain his expectations, which excited Peter. "Not much happens in Tulpehocken in January and February. I have talked to Thomas and he is open to having you work with him. Thomas is married with a young son, Francis, but his home is large enough for boarders. Actually you two remind me of each other, about the same age and both deeply concerned about our new country and our new citizens. Thomas is from England. He came to Philadelphia just a few years ago in 1731, but he is already a successful lawyer. He is the judge of the Vice-Admiralty and on the Governor's Council. Besides a lawyer, he is a merchant and imports needed products into the colonies, such as gunpowder. Peter, you can learn a lot from Thomas."

Peter readily agreed and in the middle of January he saddled up a horse from his father's stable and left for the long ride to Philadelphia. He was warmly welcomed into the Hopkinson's household and started his "apprenticeship" with Thomas almost immediately. Both Thomas and his wife were wonderful hosts and spent the first day helping Peter get settled for life in Philadelphia. However, when it came to work, Thomas was a no-nonsense person.

Thomas had Peter join him in his office early the morning after Peter's arrival. "Peter, let me give you an outline of what you will be doing." He proceeded to explain that he would be an aide to him in his work by taking notes and by doing research from the law books when necessary. "However, you won't have to make the tea," he joked. "I think you have the opportunity to learn a lot in this position. You will be doing many things to help me both in my law practice and as Justice of the Vice-Admiralty."

Thomas explained that the justice position was assigned by the proprietors of Pennsylvania. It mainly involved making decisions about maritime activities, such as disputes regarding importing and exporting. Often the cases involved smuggling, and in those cases a conviction allowed him to keep five percent of the smuggled goods as payment. There was no jury. He was just given the responsibility of listening to both sides and making a decision. At this time in the English colonies, the importing and exporting of goods was essential to the colonists' livelihood and comfort; consequently it was an important duty.

"Today, I will have in front of me, a merchant, Mr. Alan Baldwin who sells spirits. He is very successful and very wealthy. Bringing him to my court is one Conrad Weiser. Mr. Weiser represents

Teeyeegarow, an important Iroquois chief, who wants me to take away Mr. Baldwin's license to import rum from Barbados. Supposedly merchant Baldwin is selling rum to some Iroquois chieftains and then once the chieftain is intoxicated he supposedly bribes him with more rum allowing him to buy land from the chieftain's tribes at a very minimal price. It is a very difficult decision, particularly as Mr. Baldwin is a relative of Thomas Penn, the proprietor of Pennsylvania."

"This is really interesting to me," spoke Peter quickly. "Mr. Hopkinson, Conrad Weiser is a great friend to our Spyker family."

Thomas Hopkinson, quickly interjected, "Please call me Thomas".

Peter preceded to tell all the life experiences regarding the Weiser family and the Spyker family.

"Peter, as a judge, I must hear both sides. I presently feel very much as Conrad Weiser does, but I'll need to weigh the monetary damages to Mr. Baldwin's very large importing business against the humane dealings with the Indians. Another factor that weighs heavily on me is the large amount of taxes that Mr. Baldwin pays to the proprietary government. I'll ask you to be a good listener and prepare me a pro and con document for me to review after the hearing. I'll need as much empirical evidence as possible to make this decision. Let's go to court."

What a day it was for Peter! Conrad was happy to see him and made him aware that they would remain friends regardless of his mentor's decision. He was, however, furious with Alan Baldwin. "Peter, people like him make it difficult for me to keep the peace."

When Teeyeegarow walked into the court everyone stood up, not just in respect, but in awe. He was the most stately person Peter had ever seen. He was at least six-foot-five with a powerfully built body. Yet, by the lines in his face, one knew he was an old man; an old and respected man. Throughout the long day Peter, kept copious notes. In his mind he thought, *"There is no doubt Alan Baldwin is an unscrupulous man. Why do we treat the Indians, no I mean Native Americans, the way we do? Surely, Justice Hopkinson will rule in favor of the chief."*

Several witnesses from both sides gave their testimonies. All were given an opportunity to state their cases and Justice Hopkinson questioned them very thoroughly. Finally at the close of the hearing, Judge Hopkinson said, "Gentleman, thank you for being here. I will consider both sides, both arguments. My new assistant, Peter Spyker has been taking notes and he and I will discuss this case and I will render a decision one week from today. Conrad, please explain all of this to Chief Teeyeegarow. Also, please convey my respect for him and the Iroquois. We hope we can be as helpful to them as they have been to us."

Hearing this compliment to the Iroquois chief, Mr. Baldwin stood up with his lawyer, "They're just savage animals and I'm sick of hearing you take their sides. Mr. Penn will hear about this. You better make the right decision or you'll be out of this lucrative job."

"Mr. Baldwin," said Thomas, "you are out of order and I will fine you immediately and hold you in prison until my verdict if you do not apologize to Chief Teeyeegarow."

Meekly, with disgust in his eyes, he said quietly, "I'm sorry."

On the way home from court, Thomas said to Peter, "It is easy to let our emotions make our decisions, but Peter, to be an effective judge, and one reason Mr. Nead sent you to me is to help with research. Peter, my office contains an effective library. Many of the books come from a Junto to which I belong. In case you're not familiar with a Junto, it's a group of people with similar interests who work together to help each other. The next couple of days I would like, when we do not have court business, for you to do research to see if there are similar cases. It's easy to say now, yes, Mr. Baldwin should be outlawed from purchasing rum, but is this taking away rights that are due an Englishman?"

"Tomorrow, you will get a chance to see another side of Thomas Hopkinson, the lawyer side. I'm representing a women, whom the government wants to fine for infidelity. She's had a child out of wedlock."

"Hear ye, hear ye, the court will come to order," said the black-robed judge as he banged his gavel into his desk. Peter was awed and excited about being in a formal English court. Lawyer Hopkinson had explained to Peter, because of the nature of the Puritan majority in Philadelphia at that time, fines were freely handed out for immoral conduct. The young lady could not afford a lawyer and was at the mercy of the court. The lady, Sadie Steele, was only twenty and looked even younger. She was very comely and had a sweet smile.

These cases were usually automatic and she would be fined for birthing a child out of wedlock, but Thomas, when he learned of the case, wanted to make a statement regarding the Philadelphia attitude of chauvinism.

The government perfunctorily made its case. "She's not married and has sinned greatly by having a child out of wedlock, thus she owes the proprietorship three pounds. Our case rests and I see not why the defendant needs a lawyer, unless he's the father and wishes to pay." This caused a number in the gallery to laugh.

Lawyer Hopkinson stood up and said, "I resent this seemingly harmless joke, but this is the essence of why I am here defending this young lady. Sadie, will you take the stand." As was customary the judge had her put her hand on the Bible and swear to tell the truth.

"Sadie, please sit down and tell us about yourself." Sadie explained her circumstances in life. She was an orphan who had lost her mom and dad in a fire when she was just five-years-old.

She had a little education as she had started school to become a secretary. "I now can read and write very well. I love to read and I love taking care of my child. My child is in the second row with my girl friend." All eyes turned to see the baby boy in the arms of a young lady about Sadie's age. After her brief but sad story of her young life, Thomas started asking her questions.

His first question was somewhat delicate, "Why did you not get married when you found yourself with child?"

Sadie answered the question with more detail than expected. "I had met a man that I liked. We courted for several months and he said he wanted to get close to me." She hesitated and said a little sheepishly, "You know what I mean." Then she continued, "I told him not until we are married. He said since we will be married soon, we are the same as married. We did get close and soon I was pregnant. I told him we were having a child, and he told me that, unfortunately, he had decided to marry someone else because his mother insisted he marry a girl who had lineage."

"Sadie, as your child had no father, and you have little money, why did you not give him to the orphanage?"

Sadie was well-spoken. She quietly smiled at the judge and others in the court. "I love my child. He is mine. He will not want for anything. He will get an education and someday be a fine citizen of this colony."

"If you are fined, how will you pay?"

Sadie answered, "I have saved up enough money for my next term in secretary school. I will not go to school this term, but use the money for the fine."

"I don't see the father." Thomas looked around acting a little bewildered. "Surely he is here. After all it is his child."

"No, his mother has forbidden him to see me again."

Thomas paused for several seconds for effect and then said, "So he was not fined for having a child out of wedlock, but you are to be fined. I'm sure he paid half the fine or one and a half pounds, right?"

Sadie, shook her head. "No he didn't."

"Your honor, I do not see the man who had this baby out of wedlock. How can we fine him for sinning or for breaking the Pennsylvania law?"

The judge and the government lawyer met and talked quietly for a lengthy period of time.

"Miss Steele, Lawyer Hopkinson, as judge I cannot overturn the law. My brain says the fine must stand but my heart says no. She will be fined, but the fine has been paid. I paid one and a half pounds and Lawyer Smith paid one-and-half pound."

While there was a pause, Mr. Smith stood and said, "I apologize to you Mr. Hopkinson and Miss Steele for my crude remark at the beginning of our trial." Thomas nodded his acceptance.

"Speaking off the record," said the judge, I am going to address both the assembly and the proprietary council and see if this law can be changed. Thomas, can you be our spokesperson in this endeavor?"

After the court decision, Thomas addressed Sadie. "I am impressed with your deep concern for your son. We need mothers like you who will raise sons who will be a credit to our colony. I will pay your tuition to school until you have received your secretary degree."

When they were finished in the court for the day, Peter looked at Thomas with admiration. "You must go to church a lot. Our church is always preaching about loving your neighbor. It seems like in every sermon I hear this message."

Thomas looked at Peter and simply said, "To quote a good friend of mine, 'A good example is the best sermon.'"

Peter was learning a lot being in court with Thomas and doing research in his considerable library. In his research regarding the Vice-Admiralty case, he did not come across a precedent that favored the Native Americans. One recent case really concerned Peter. It was grossly unfair to the Delaware, the Native Americans in his back yard. The case was called "The Walking Purchase."

The proprietors of Pennsylvania negotiated a treaty with the chief of the Delaware nation, Chief Lappawinsoe. The Delaware agreed to sell land west of the junction of the Delaware and Lehigh River. The Native Americans used a walk as a distance as they did not know kilometers or acres. The typical day walk was about fifty kilometers. The agreement was made for the proprietors of Pennsylvania to buy land equal to a "day and a half walk", which would be approximately seventy-five kilometers. The proprietors hired three extremely fast men and had them sprint in a relay for a day and a half. They covered one hundred thirteen kilometers in a day and a half and staked out the purchase. When the Delaware attempted to use the Pennsylvania courts to appeal this unfair situation, the courts ruled in favor of the proprietors. Now Peter realized why the Delaware in Tulpehocken were not friendly with the settlers, why they were wary of them. Now he realized why Conrad had such difficulty keeping peace with the Delaware.

Peter came to Thomas with the results of his research, "Thomas I don't think we will be able to rule in favor of Chief Teeyeegarow. I can find no cases where the courts have upheld an appeal from Native Americans when they were in conflict with citizens of Pennsylvania. Based on my studies, if you rule against Mr. Baldwin, he will appeal to the proprietorship judge and the case will be reversed. I personally feel Mr. Baldwin should lose his rum license, but I can understand why you would hesitate to rule in his favor."

Thomas, who had a dry sense of humor and was extremely intelligent, answered Peter in a curious way. "Peter, to again quote my good friend, who is the master of quips, 'there is more than one way to skin a cat.'" Peter couldn't wait to hear how Thomas planned to 'skin the cat.'

The court day came and Judge Hopkinson said, "Chief Teeyeegarow and your interpreter and council, Conrad Weiser, please stand. Mr. Baldwin, please stand. I have made a decision on this case. As you know, for better or for worse, I alone as judge of the Vice-Admiralty will make the decision."

The judge continued, "I have decided not to take away Mr. Alan Baldwin's rum license. He can continue to import rum from Barbados and sell this product to anyone who wishes to purchase."

Conrad's face fell and he explained the verdict to the chief, who remained stoic. Mr. Baldwin smiled and started to express his thanks.

"Please let me finish," interrupted Judge Hopkinson, "I do have a couple of stipulations. Mr. Baldwin you can sell your rum to the Iroquois nation, but only via Chief Teeyeegarow. I'm sure he will be happy to purchase it and distribute it to his people. Also, you may purchase land from the Iroquois but you must go through Conrad Weiser to make this purchase as he will be able to interpret the details to the chief and other chiefs of the Iroquois. I'm sure you would not want one of the Iroquois chiefs to misunderstand you and sell more land than they wish or at a lesser price than its value."

What was once a smile now became a frown. What was once a frown now became a smile. Peter now knew there was more than one way "to skin a cat."

Benjamin Franklin
1738

Benjamin Franklin

"Peter, you've worked hard and helped me prepare well for our court cases and your detailed work has helped lessen my stress. Now it's time to enjoy a little of Philadelphia life. We're going to have a welcoming party. You've been here two weeks and we have caused you to be a hermit. We've invited several of our friends this Saturday to enjoy a meal with us and some relaxing and entertaining conversation. You will know what I mean by 'entertaining' when you meet my friend of many quips, Ben Franklin. He and his wife, Debbie, will be here along with the Reverend Jedediah Andrews and his wife, Annabelle. Reverend Andrews is the Presbyterian minister at the church where Benjamin belongs. The good reverend is on a quest for Benjamin's soul," he said with a smile. "You'll enjoy the bantering between the good reverend and 'Poor Richard,' an alias of Mr. Franklin. Also our good friend, Gabriel Seidel will be here with his wife Appolina, whom we call Polly, for obvious reasons, and their young daughter Maria. Maria, although young, brightens our surroundings with her beauty. She's amazingly charming for just sixteen-years-old. Gabriel is one of the leading architects in Philadelphia and he is making plans at the present for a building that will someday house 'Thomas Hopkinson, Attorney at Law.'"

It was a party Peter would never forget. Peter did not know what to expect from Mr. Franklin. He had heard a few things about him and knew him to be a printer. Precisely at 7:00 came a rap on the door and in entered a man with long dark hair to his shoulders. He was wearing round spectacles with thin wire rims. Although not needing a cane for walking, he carried one with a highly polished gold handle. It was with the cane that he had rapped on the door. One could feel his presence as he walked into the room and stoutly shook Peter's hand. Mr. Franklin was at least six feet tall with a barrel chest and a barrel waist. "Ah, Mr. Spyker, I have heard many nice things about you. Thomas must be buttering you up for the kill." His laugh was contagious and he immediately put his arm around Peter. "Peter, I need to get you aside before my favorite preacher comes and puts you to sleep with his sermonizing. Contrary to what you will hear from my friend and soul advisor, 'God helps those', he paused for several seconds, 'that help themselves.'"

Several steps behind Benjamin as he entered the house was his wife, Debbie. She was a nice looking lady, but seemed a little flustered by the commotion caused by her husband. When introduced to Peter, and after hearing Ben's advice about helping yourself, she said, "Mr. Spyker, I hope you have brought some salt tonight, because you must take everything my humorous husband says with 'a grain of salt.'"

Soon Reverend Andrews and his wife arrived and were introduced to Peter. "My young man, tomorrow is Sunday and I will have a wonderful sermon on virtue. I would hope you and the Hopkinsons will be there sitting next to my friend Ben, keeping him awake. Virtue is a foreign word to Mr. Franklin, but hopefully after my exciting and enlightening sermon, he will become my disciple. I'm having Ben read my sermons before I deliver them. He is a talented writer, but it disturbs me when he crosses out the Presbyterian doctrines that I succinctly place in my sermon."

Then the reverend turned to Ben and stated for all to hear, "I'm not sure I understand, the statement you have added to my sermon for tomorrow, 'look at others for their virtues and thy self for thy vices.' " With that Reverend Jedediah and Ben separated from the others to discuss tomorrow's sermon. Peter almost laughed out loud when he heard Mr. Franklin say to the reverend as they were walking away, "My dear reverend, I read your sermon and it is a dandy. You should have them nodding shortly into your second doctrine."

"Peter," asked Mary, "could you answer the door? Thomas is off refereeing the Jedediah and Benjamin debate. That must be the Seidels."

"You must be Peter," said Polly Seidel. "We've heard so much about you. Thomas says you will be an outstanding lawyer. This is my husband Gabriel, and this is my daughter Maria Margaretha." Peter shook hands with Gabriel and right behind him was Maria. Peter almost said to Maria, "It's nice to bump into you," as he recalled meeting Susan on the St. Andrew.

She was fairly tall for a girl, about five foot six; she had dark, long, shiny hair that fell past her shoulders and blue eyes, and although slim, she had an exquisite figure. Peter quickly thought in his mind, *"Hold on there, boy, she's too young for you."* Maria smiled up at Peter and offered her hand. He felt like kissing her hand, but just grasped her hand and bowed slightly, "Thanks for coming along, it's nice of you and your parents to welcome me to Philadelphia."

"Nice to meet you also, Peter," said young Maria. "I wasn't planning on coming until Mary told my mother how handsome you were. She was right." Peter kept thinking, *"God how she reminds me of Susan, particularly with her openness."* Regardless Peter couldn't help blushing and avoided her mischievous eyes.

"Okay everyone," broadcast Mary, "time for dinner. Matilda has everything ready and I've put names by your places. I don't want all the men sitting together, and since I get to sit by Thomas each night, I'm sitting by Ben. You'll notice I've put Ben and Jedidiah at opposite ends to keep them from fighting." Everyone laughed and made their way to the dining room and the well set table with ornate crystal goblets and brilliantly shining silverware. In the middle of the table was a crystal vase with a dozen yellow roses. As they made their way to their assigned seats, Thomas patted Matilda, their housekeeper, on the shoulder and said, "Matilda, thank you. Everything looks great and I know your dinner will be as scrumptious as usual."

They all sat down and Reverend Andrews said the prayer. After about five minutes of beseeching the Lord, there was a pause, which was probably for Jedidiah to catch his breath. Benjamin quickly said, acting like the prayer was finished, "Let me add, bless the cook, amen." Maria, could not help chuckling until her mother gently kicked her under the table. The meal was "scrumptious," but the conversation was even better.

During the dinner, Maria, who was sitting next to Peter was very talkative which contrasted with Peter, who though quiet, was a good listener. Peter found her charming and much more intelligent than one would expect of a sixteen-year-old girl. "Are you familiar with the school that Mr. Franklin and the others from his Junto have established?" This was an educational program, which someday would become the Academy, and eventually the University of Pennsylvania Law School. Maria explained further the educational program and added, "I am the only woman in the program, but Mr. Hopkinson encouraged my father to let me enter. He thinks I might become the first women lawyer in America. My father, who is a sweetheart, said 'okay and I'll probably be the first person she prosecutes.'" This caused Peter to laugh, which entertained Maria greatly and encouraged her to get a little more personal.

"Peter," said Maria, "Why do you have to live so far away? Why don't you move to Philadelphia and help me with my studies?" As Peter smiled, Polly, Maria's mother interrupted. "Maria, I'm sure Peter doesn't appreciate such a forward young lady. Now eat your dinner and let Peter enjoy his meal as well."

Peter thought, *"I don't mind at all. This is the most I've enjoyed talking to a young lady since Susan."* He didn't want to disagree and just smiled at both of them and then, did for him, a strange gesture. He put his hand gently on her arm, and said quietly, "I think you would be the one to help me with my studies."

"Ben," said Thomas, "I read in your Pennsylvania Gazette, that you felt the proprietors should be taxed twice as much as 'Poor Richard' since they lived in houses and 'Richard' lives in a hut. Will you not be criticized by the proprietors for saying that? Of course, if you didn't ask for the proprietor to be taxed, then the assembly would criticize you."

"Thomas, Mary, Peter and the fine people at the table, will you indulge me a short story to answer Thomas's question?" Naturally Mr. Franklin did not wait for an answer. "A father and son were going to market. The father rode their horse and the son followed. The people seeing them criticized the father. Thus the son rode the horse and the father followed. The people seeing this criticized the father. So neither rode the horse. The people seeing this criticized the father. So they both rode the horse. The people seeing this criticized the father. So then they threw the horse into the river." Benjamin concluded his story and went back to his plate.

The others at the table looked at each other quizzically. Then they all laughed heartily except Jedidiah. Benjamin looked up and said, "I'll explain this to you later, Jedidiah."

After dinner, the gentlemen went into the library for cigars and port while the ladies went into the parlor for some nice gossip. Maria jokingly asked her father, "Dad may I join you? I'd sure like a cigar." Although Polly laughed with the others, she shook her head and pulled her daughter into the parlor.

Some of the discussion after several sips of port involved Thomas Penn. This led Peter to share with the others, "My grandfather, Johannes and the elder Conrad Weiser, had a great experience with William Penn." Peter related the story of his grandfather and Conrad going to Speyer to hear Mr. Penn talk about emigration to America. At the conclusion of the story Peter said, "It would be an honor for me to meet William Penn's son. I'm sure he would enjoy hearing this story and how much my grandfather admired his father. To this day grandfather speaks of Mr. Penn in revered terms. Do you think there would be a way I could meet Mr. Penn, while I'm in Philadelphia?"

All of a sudden, silence. Then Benjamin Franklin cleared his throat and said, "I'm sure I can arrange for you to see his secretary to convey this message and maybe there's an outside chance the Honorable Mr. Penn would meet with you." Then Ben Franklin made a strange statement, that confused Peter. "'Kings and bears often worry their keepers,' however, I will arrange this and let you know a date and time. Also, Peter, I wonder if you could come with

Thomas to our Junto meeting which is on Thursday, next?" Peter was happy to agree and thanked Mr. Franklin.

The conversation continued, and Peter enjoyed particularly, as did the others, the wit of Mr. Franklin. He couldn't wait to share some of these clever remarks with his father and grandfather. Several of them seemed to flow as a result of comments made by the reverend, a devout teetotaler. He seemed much concerned about Gabriel and Thomas having a third glass of port. "Gentlemen, I know you enjoy your port; however, my doctor says it can be bad for your health."

Benjamin nodded vigorously at Jedediah's remark as if in agreement, "Reverend that is great advice, but are you aware there are more old drunks than old doctors?" Even Jedidiah laughed at this, "Ben you are a joy. Perhaps you can help me add some humor to my sermons."

During the course of the evening, Peter decided to mention his building project to Mr. Seidel, the architect. "Mr. Seidel, I was interested to know that you are an architect. I'm getting ready to start building a house in Tulpehocken. I'm trying to make it look somewhat like our house in Aspach, but want it to be more of a modern design. Our house in Aspach, which had been home to the Spykers for several generations, was solidly built but not very classical."

Gabriel became interested immediately. "Peter, what will you be using for the main structure of the house?"

"Our house in Aspach was built with field stones and was a couple of stories with both a loft and a basement. I want this same permanent type of structure and also want to have a loft and basement. I want it to be like our home, but different. Does this make sense?"

"It does and you are wise to build a house with a strong stone foundation and structure. I would imagine there is ready timber in your area. Have you thought of incorporating wood into the outside appearance of the house? This would give you a very classical look, but still maintain the solidness you want. Also, you may want to think of using bricks for your chimney. This looks nice and more importantly it is the safest material to use. There are many fires caused by poorly built chimneys. Peter, if you would be interested I could take you to see some of the houses in Philadelphia that I have built." Peter was excited to have such a knowledgeable person take an interest in his building project. They made arrangements for Peter to come to Gabriel's home the last Saturday Peter would be in Philadelphia.

The evening ended and all departed in a congenial mood. As the Seidel family left, Polly and Gabriel shook hands with Peter, but not Maria; she gave him a huge hug and left with another remark not appreciated by her mother. "Please don't let those bears eat you. I want to see you again." A pleasant glow enveloped Peter as he watched her depart.

The Philadelphia Junto
1738

⸺ ❧ ⸺

"MEMBERS OF JUNTO," SAID THOMAS as he addressed the members of the organization, "it is my pleasure to introduce Peter Spyker. Peter is with me through February as an intern to my law practice. He is recently from Germany having arrived in Philadelphia in late September. Immediately upon arrival he traveled to the frontier of Pennsylvania to Tulpehocken, which is at the foot of the Blue Mountains in between the Swatara Creek and the Schuylkill River. Mr. Spyker joined his father Johannes who has been in Tulpehocken since 1723. Peter is a lawyer in training with the well-known Marshall Nead. Let the questions begin."

Thomas had described the Junto club to Peter. It was a club of working men founded by Benjamin Franklin in 1727 for the purpose of bringing tradesmen and artisans together. Thomas had explained to Peter about the division in classes in Pennsylvania, or for that matter throughout the British colonies. Without lineage and wealth you were not of the elite class of society. Thus the Junto club was formed to help the young energetic workman succeed in a society that was heavily tilted toward the elite, those who had wealth and position and did not care to work with their hands.

Thomas further explained that the club allowed the "middle" class to discuss important issues, also to devise ways to improve themselves as a group, and to work with one another to help each person in his career. "The members wish to glean as much information from each other and from guests to help them further their careers. So Peter, they may well grill you particularly when they find you are from a frontier area, an area that is foreign to them."

"Mr. Spyker, my name is Robert Grace; why did you become a lawyer? What would be the needs of a lawyer in the wild West?"

"Mr. Spyker, William Coleman here. I'm a merchant. What are needs in Tulpehocken and other frontier areas that our Junto might provide?"

"Peter, Gabriel Seidel here. I've had the pleasure of meeting with young Spyker at the Hopkinson home. A number of us are concerned about the Indians on the frontier. Are they friendly toward you? Do you see them threatening our movement to the West? I see in the near future that more and more settlers are going to move west from the coast and also immigrants like yourself who want their own land are going to look west. Do you think we can co-exist with the Indians? It seems we want to settle and they want to have much land to roam."

Peter answered all these questions in detail and the group seemed satisfied. Now stood Benjamin Franklin and Peter didn't know whether to get ready to laugh at his wit or to be asked questions from the most intelligent person he had ever met.

Mr. Franklin said, "I also had the pleasure of making the acquaintance of Mr. Spyker as did Gabriel. It was delightful to meet you on Saturday. You can be of real service to our club and I think we can be of service to you and the citizens in Tulpehocken. I think it is essential for our Junto to have a direct contact with the Western Frontier. As Mr. Coleman mentioned we need to know not only the products but also the services that are needed in Tulpehocken. I think there would be a good purpose to have you communicate with our club. We have several off-shoots of this

Junto Club, and how advantageous it would be if you could start a Tulpehocken Junto."

All the members sat up with interest and Peter, quickly expressed, "I agree, Mr. Franklin, however our members would come from as far as forty kilometers away. But I think we could meet once a month. We have a good central location at the Jacob Seltzer pub in the Womelsdorf area." Peter's head was spinning as he thought it a great idea.

"Peter, I would be excited to visit you each month at least at the beginning to help you get started." Thus the idea of the Tulpehocken Junto was formed. As much as this was exciting, just having Benjamin Franklin visit this frontier area would be a benefit to all the settlers in Tulpehocken.

The questions continued for several minutes and finally the chairman, Joseph Breintnall, brought this part of the program to a close. "Thank you, Mr. Spyker, or Peter if we can be informal. We are delighted to have you here and the information you have given us is enlightening. I would not be surprised if soon you have the first William Coleman Mercantile store in Tulpehocken."

The chairman continued, "Besides Mr. Spyker, we have another guest. He wishes to become a member of our Junto. His name is George Taylor and as you can see he's a very young man. Mr. Taylor will tell you a little about himself, and then we will go through our routine of 'grilling' George. Although this can be entertaining, it helps us know if Mr. Taylor would be a good fit for our club and as a second benefit today, it will give Mr. Spyker a better understanding of our Junto. "

George Taylor proceeded to tell the members that he was just twenty-two years old and recently emigrated from Northern Ireland. He was an iron master for Warwick Furnace company and had recently been promoted as the companies head bookkeeper.

After the self-introduction, Mr. Breintnall addressed George Taylor. "George put your hand on your breast and answer these questions for our members." The chairman asked four questions, and each was addressed by Mr. Taylor.

"Do you have any disrespect for any current members? Do you love mankind in general regardless of religion and profession? Do you feel people should ever be punished because of their opinions or mode of worship? Do you love and pursue truth for its own sake?"

As Mr. Taylor was answering each question appropriately, Peter also agreed in his heart with the premise of each question and the value of a Junto in Tulpehocken.

After the meeting Mr. Franklin discussed more details with Peter on the forming of a club and then advised him that he had made arrangements for him to meet with Mr. Thomas Penn, or at least his secretary.

Thomas Penn

1738

———— ⊗⊗⊗ ————

PETER ARRIVED AT THE PENN building on Walnut Street. It was an ornate building of Tudor architecture with a steep pitched roof, tall narrow windows and doorways, and a large chimney that seemed to be the centerpiece of the structure. As Peter made his way through the large building, he was awed by the obvious wealth and prestige of the Penn family. This seemed in contrast to his grandfather's story of William Penn, who despite his fame was very commonplace.

"Yes can I be of service," said the prim gentleman sitting at the desk guarding the inner sanctuary of Thomas Penn, who served as the proprietor of the colony of Pennsylvania.

Peter introduce himself, "I have an appointment with Mr. Penn. I believe it was arranged by Benjamin Franklin."

"Oh, do you come to assassinate Mr. Penn?" joked the secretary. "The last time Benjamin was here sparks were flying everyplace. I thought the building was going to catch on fire. Well, never mind, just a little humor. I see you have an appointment. Please be seated and I will make Mr. Penn aware of such an honored guest."

Peter could not help disliking the prissy secretary and thought about throwing him out of one of the narrow windows, however, he maintained his composure and had a seat in the straight-back wooden chair. The clock ticked away the lengthy wait and then, another obvious secretary, this time a prim and proper lady, came from behind the tall heavy door. "My Spyker, I presume, would you follow me, his honor will see you?" Peter thought for sure she was going to say 'his Royal Majesty.'

The secretary advised him to have a seat in front of the large mahogany desk, where sat a gentleman with a white powdered wig, who maintained his concentration on a document in front of him. "Ah, Mr. Spyker, thank you for the visit. My friend Mr. Franklin said you wanted to share a whimsical story about my father. I hope it's brief as I have mountains of documents to peruse. You should know, I did not know my father that well. He was always gone and at best we had a tacit relationship."

"Thank you Mr. Penn, it is an honor for me to meet you." Peter then told the humorous and heart-warming story about Conrad and his grandfather meeting with William Penn. "Mr. Penn, if it weren't for your father, we probably would not have come to Pennsylvania or even America. He's the person who created for us a dream of freedom and thank God we had the perseverance to realize this dream."

Thomas Penn responded to Peter, "Thank you. I know many people feel this way. Yes he created a colony, but he also created a mountain of debt for me and my family. It has taken most of my life to get the Penns out of debt. Also, I am so thankful that my brothers and I have been able to choose another religion than my father's. The Quaker religion is a religion of mild, meek, do-nothings. Still I appreciate your visit and your kind thoughts about our family. One last thing and then you are dismissed. Please tell Mr. Franklin, if he doesn't stop smearing my name in his horrible low-class newspaper and insisting that we, my brothers and I pay taxes commensurate with our holdings, I will have his paper shut down.

We, the Penns have done so much for this colony and for America that to think we should owe money to the government is absurd."

Thus ended a conversation that made Peter understand the silence from Benjamin Franklin and others when he mentioned the name of Penn.

The Seidels

1738

———— ∞ ————

Just a few days after the Junto meeting and the meeting with Thomas Penn, Peter went to see Gabriel Seidel. It was an easy walk from the Hopkinson's home. Peter kept checking the addresses and the name plates. Soon he came to a beautiful house made of stone with wood crisscrossing the structure on all four sides. The windows were narrow but tall with brown shutters on each side. *"Yes this is what I would want,"* he thought as he appraised the house at a distance. As he approached he notice the sign-board hanging from a square wood post that also served as a lantern, which would guide one to the house at night. The sign-post said, "Gabriel Seidel, Architect".

The solid large oak door had a golden-looking brass knocker, which he clapped several times. The door opened to a beautiful sight. "Yes, have you come to take me for a stroll along the Schuylkill?" Maria fluttered her long eyelashes with her hands together as if to pray. Peter couldn't help laughing.

"No," said Polly, "Mr. Spyker is here to see your father and you are off to your piano lessons." As Polly half dragged Maria away, she looked back, raised her arm and waved as if she was on stage and departing behind the curtain. Again Peter laughed and thought, *"Yes, she's still a silly young girl, but someday soon she will be a charming lady."*

Mr. Seidel greeted Peter and was not surprised when Peter said, "I want a house just like this."

Gabriel took Peter through the house discussing every detail that went into building a house of this nature. He talked about materials, tools, and manpower. It took more than an hour and then Gabriel said, "Let's see some other houses of German architecture and then join me to meet Mr. Franklin at our neighborhood pub, 'The Mayflower.' Talk about quaint architecture, you'll love this pub that is a replica of 'The Mayflower' on Rotherhith Street in London. I may be German but I love the English pubs. Ben and I meet here along with several other friends just about every Saturday at the tea hour. Let me assure you, Ben will have some great ideas for this house of yours."

It was another exciting day for Peter and he started wondering if maybe it would be fun to live in Philadelphia. At the close of the visit, Gabriel said goodbye and sent him on his way with an exciting promise. "Peter, I'm going to work up some plans for your house and get them to you before you leave next Saturday. Then if at all possible, if you wish, I'll visit you sometime this summer, hopefully before you are too far along building your house. I would imagine it will take you through the summer just to get your materials gathered and your basement dug."

Peter's two-month stay in Philadelphia came to an end. It was possibly the two most important months he would ever spend in America. He tripled his knowledge of law. He learned of a plan to better life in Tulpehocken. He met the man who would be one of the most important in establishing America's independence. He had the detailed plans for building his home, and he met a young lady who helped him forget Susan.

Building the Spyker Home
1738

———— ∞∞ ————

IT WAS APRIL, 1738, PETER had returned from Philadelphia with a thousand ideas. He had the detailed plans to build the home of his dreams. The weather had cleared and the snow was almost gone as Peter, Jacob, Conrad, and Chief Cannassatego walked the land that the chief was selling to Jacob Lentz in return for his weekly medical care of the Delaware in Tulpehocken. Much of the land was covered with boulders and fieldstones. The land contained very little forest area suitable for hunting. Most of the land was rolling plains speckled with ponds, and with the Tulpehocken creek and several smaller creeks running through it. It would take a great deal of work to make it suitable for farming.

The most level of the acreage would be the ten acres where Jacob would build his homestead and the highest point, the high ridge on the most western edge would be for the Aspach Lutheran Church. As they walked the land, they designated landmarks that would be the boundaries. Conrad, who among his many traits was a surveyor, made notes that would be in the deed prepared by Peter and lawyer Nead.

After two weeks, the deed was prepared and now Peter started visualizing his property. The plans provided by Gabriel Seidel were imbedded in his mind. He was going to carefully follow each detail. As he walked his property he visualized the house he would build.

After much walking over several days, he saw "his house" set on the rolling terrain. The house overlooked a pond and a small creek that fed into the Tulpehocken. He knew it would take over a year, perhaps two, to build, but he was ready to go to work. Peter had talked with both his father and his brother and assured them that this would also be a home for them. "Peter" said Jonny "Thank you. It will be a lovely house as you do everything well. I will work beside you and help you in every way. However, I will stay in my father's house. Your grandfather is old and I must help Lomasi take care of him and take care of the farm. Benjamin might eventually stay with you, but as you know he will live with the Delaware for a full year. It is important for someone from the Western Frontier, besides Conrad to be able to communicate with the Delaware."

Now was the time to build. It was early May and Peter with rolled up sleeves was ready to tackle the boulders and other field-stones on his land. It was a task that could not be done by him alone. He would need physical help and help from craftsmen. The initial physical help came from his dad, but they made little progress wrestling the stones from the ground and cutting timber from some of the small forests on the tract. One day as they were struggling taking stones from the ground and putting them into the horse-drawn wagon, they saw on the horizon two Native Americans coming toward them. There was no alarm because the Delaware and the settlers were at peace.

As they came close, Jonny recognized his son Benjamin. "Hello Dad, Kitchi and I have been having a guilty conscience watching you and Peter slave away. So here we are ready to help. Chief Cannassatego gave us his blessing to help a few hours each day if we didn't pick up the 'White man's' ways."

Benjamin now looked as much a Native American as he did a White man. His hair was long and glistening and tied in a pony tail. He wore a band around his forehead, several strings of shells around his neck, and a loin cloth. Over his shoulder he had strung his quiver of arrows with his bow hanging cross-ways across his trunk.

As he and Kitchi were struggling along with Peter and his father over the field stones, Benjamin shared his new life with them. Although he had been living in the Delaware camp for just a month, he was satisfied with the Delaware life-style. "Dad, I'm learning the Delaware language and now talking to you seems a little foreign. Also everyone is impressed with my progress with bow and arrow and all other phases of the tribal life."

As Benjamin shared his stories with his father and Peter, Kitchi seemed to understand what they were talking about and kept agreeing. He then placed his arm around Benjamin and said, "Nim, brother, Demothi, name Ben." Ben explained that the tribe had given him a Delaware name, Demothi, which means 'he even talks while he walks.' Ben further explained that Kitchi was calling him his brother.

Peter laughed and said, "Ben, Demothi suits you well. You even talk when you sleep."

The Tulpehocken Junto
1738

—⚬⚬⚬—

THE FORMING OF THE JUNTO became a blessing to Peter. As he continued building his house he realized he needed help from some of the craftsmen in the Tulpehocken area. Peter needed someone to saw his timber, including the many cross-woods for his selected German architecture. He found a man who had a lumber mill. He knew he was not capable of the fine craftsmanship for the cabinets and the furniture, so he needed a cabinet maker. He wanted the brick chimney that he had discussed with Gabriel and so he needed a brick mason. While talking with the craftsmen about his needs, Peter discussed the Junto.

The Junto was formed and the first meeting was on July 4, 1738 at the Seltzer restaurant in the Womelsdorf settlement. The original members were from as far as twenty kilometers from the Seltzer restaurant and many of them were recently contracted by Peter to help him build his house. The members, as was the case in the Philadelphia Junto, were craftsmen, artisans, entrepreneurs, and professional men.

The Seltzer Restaurant was built in the 1730's.
It was purchased in 1785 by Conrad Stouch and is now a
historic restaurant in Womenlsdorf, called the Stouch Tavern.

As the group gathered, Peter stood up and greeted them and then explained in some detail the purpose of a Junto and how they could help each other. He explained that the first order of business for each meeting would be for each to give a brief introduction, and then relate any new information or needs regarding his business.

Then, he explained, one member at each meeting would be given about twenty minutes to discuss his occupation and suggest how other members of the Junto could assist him in improving or increasing his business.

Peter continued in his effort to organize this Tulpehocken Junto, "Okay, let's have each of you introduce yourself and tell us your occupation and make other remarks that will help us get to know you. At the end of this meeting today, we need to elect a president." Quickly several suggested out loud that Peter should be the first president.

"Mr. Franklin, the founder of the Philadelphia Junto, strongly advised that the founder not be the initial president, because then it becomes like a proprietorship, where the founder becomes like a king. Gentlemen, we want this to be a democratic organization." All nodded their heads in understanding as they had negative feelings toward the present Pennsylvania Proprietorship.

Then the introductions began. "Jacob Seltzer, restaurateur. As I look around I see that I am already using or need to use the services and skills of many of you. Just last month Dr. Lentz helped my wife deliver our twin girls. When one goes to sleep the other wakes up and screams for her mother. Then when that one goes to sleep the other wakes and screams. Doc, can you put one of them back?" That seemed to set the tone for good fellowship and good humor.

"Jacob Lentz, doctor. Jacob, I did not put them there, however, I'm was delighted to give you two beautiful girls that keep you up all night, and when they turn sixteen they will still be keeping you up all night. I came to Tulpehocken last September on the St. Andrew along with Peter and several others I see here. Gentlemen we made it. Now, let's together, build one fine community. I am at your service at any time day or night. Sickness does not have hours."

"George Weiser, baker. I am the long lost son of Conrad Weiser, Sr. When we arrived in New York in 1710, my father was forced to indenture me to an English merchant. I served my indentured service and came west to be with my brother Conrad, whom all of you know. My father was a baker and now I'm a baker. The shoofly and black raspberry pie that you have had today is my gift to you. I am so pleased that Jacob Seltzer is now having me do his baking.

I am a bachelor, but if you know a good German girl that can bake and brings a huge dowry send her my way."

"Henry Hartman, blacksmith. I also came from Germany to America on the St. Andrew with Peter and Doctor Lentz. I, like many of you here, am also a farmer, but am pleased to bring my blacksmith skill from Germany to Tulpehocken. My father passed away on the St. Andrew, but my mother is with me. And Peter, I've seen a gentleman who looks like you, maybe twenty years older, visiting my black smithy shop recently. He must be a florist. He brings my mother flowers each time he comes."

Peter quickly interjected, "Henry, my father will do anything to get his horses shoed for free. Are you sure those flowers are not for you?"

"Thomas Jones, I am a grain miller. I am grateful to Peter's grandfather for taking my wife and me in while we built our home and mill on the Tulpehocken just a few kilometers from here. We are up and running and ready for your corn, wheat and anything else that needs to be ground into meal. I do have an additional occupation and that is a teacher of English. Although I speak German with ease, I'm from England and able to help you or your children learn English.

However, sometimes I don't think I do such a good job. I worked with George Weiser recently to speak English to an English lady he was courting. He said to her with sincerity 'I love you like a pork liver sausage.'

"That's true," said George. "Before Hilda hit me with a rolling pin, she practiced her German on me. 'George, you are a dummer esel.' Now I'll find a nice German lady."

The next gentleman stood up while all were still laughing. "Well, I'm the elder of the group. My name is Isaiah Katterman and I came from Schoharie ten years ago just after Peter's father, Johannes. I own the Katterman Lumber Mill, which is at the confluence of the Tulpehocken and the Schuylkill. Peter came to me about a month ago with wagons of timber for the lumber on his new house. I love the forests and the trees and want to preserve these same forests for our children and grandchildren, so I have a request. When you cut down a tree, plant a new one. Beside my lumber mill I have a tree nursery. When I do a job for you, I'll give you new seedlings. There is no charge for these unless you do not plant them. Then they cost plenty."

In every group, there is always one loquacious one. "Hello gentleman, I am a brick mason. My name is Byson Smythe. My name is spelled s-m-y-t-h-e, let me explain." After a lengthy genealogy of the Smythe family, he got back on track. "I am not the only brick mason in the area. There is one other, an older fellow, he's also good. He recently completed a chimney for the Reed's church. The beautiful chimney was started shortly after the Mayflower landed in 1620 and just last week he plastered the last brick."

The hearty laughter really got him going. "Let me tell you about bricks. Do you remember the story of Moses and the Egyptians?" After the story which was longer than the Book of Exodus, he continued. "I'm from Switzerland, but my parents are originally from Germany."

After a history of the Thirty Years War, Peter cut him off. "Hey George, good stuff there, but we've got one more introduction, and I've promised that meetings would be no more than an hour and a half."

"Ah, sorry Peter and others. My wife always tells me if words were pounds, I would be richer than that fellow, Midas."

Finally the last charter member got up and introduced himself . "Peter, this group is such a good idea. I'm Joseph Zollberger. I also came over on the St. Andrew in 1737. As far back as we can trace our ancestors there has always been a craftsman of wood in our family. I am, so to speak, 'a chip off the old block.'" This comment was met with derisive laughter and some good natured nodding of heads. "Sorry, for the old joke. But I am a cabinet maker and a furniture maker and really happy to be included."

After the introductions Peter advised that to make this formal, they would need to take the same pledge as the Philadelphia Junto,

"Do you have any disrespect for anyone here?"

"Do you love mankind in general regardless of religion and profession?"

"Do you feel people should ever be punished because of their opinions or their mode of worship?"

"Do you love and pursue truth for its own sake?"

To the four questions all nine of the charter members answered the appropriate 'no' or 'yes' response. Peter explained this would be asked of any new members that were invited.

The meeting concluded, but not before, the new president needed to be selected. "Gentlemen, do we have anyone wishing to run for the office of the president?" said Peter.

Henry Hartman stood, "No I'm not running. I think the president should be at every meeting. Those of us that live ten kilometers or more away, may have problems. However, since the meeting is at the Seltzer Restaurant, Jacob will always be there. I nominate Jacob Seltzer to be the president of the Tulpehocken Junto."

It quickly became a unanimous vote and Jacob took the gavel from Peter. "Thank you Peter, for helping us found this club, that will help each one of us. Next meeting will be the first Thursday of August. Let's see if we can bring some new members. Gentlemen you are dismissed. Please have a stein of beer on me before you leave. Just one stein, however. You know what old Johannes Spyker says, 'you shouldn't drink and ride'." Naturally all laughed.

Before Peter left for the Spyker farm, he wrote a long note to Benjamin Franklin with all the details of the Junto. He gave it to Jacob Seltzer, who would give it to the next courier to Philadelphia.

Franklin and Seidel Come
to Tulpehocken
1738

THE NEXT WEEK AS PETER, Jonny, Demothi, and Kitchi were digging the foundation to Peter's house, they saw a horseman approaching them from the East. "I think it's the mail courier" said Peter. It was the mail from Philadelphia and Peter had two letters.

"My Spyker," said the courier, "I hate to get rid of this one letter. It smells lovely. It even makes my horse smell lovely."

The first letter was from Benjamin Franklin. He would be coming in a week. He wanted to attend the Junto meeting and then stay for several days to visit with the settlers from the Tulpehocken area.

The "lovely lavender smelling letter" was from Maria Margaretha Seidel.

"My dear, Peter," the letter continued for several pages and finished with, *"I'm so tired of Philadelphia. It is so crowded. I think someday I will come west, maybe to Tulpehocken and maybe I'll stay forever. Your devoted servant, ha, Maria."*

Peter just smiled and remembered an enchanting young lady.

The Monday before the August 1st Junto meeting Peter was alone with his thoughts as he viewed the foundation of his home.

He felt he was ready to start the next process, the building of a strong foundation. Although he could visualize the finished house, he was perplexed on how to start from the ground up. As he wiped the sweat off his forehead, he saw a cloud of dust in the horizon. Soon the wagon with two men came close enough for Peter to identify Benjamin Franklin, then he recognized Gabriel Seidel. *"What a blessing,"* he thought, *"Somehow the Lord has provided me just the person to help me start the foundation."* Peter excitedly hailed them and insisted that they stay at his grandfather's house. "Johannes and Lomasi will be thrilled to have you stay and tell them about all the new developments in Philadelphia. We in Tulpehocken seem to be a year behind Philadelphia in learning the news of America and Europe." Before going to the Spyker farm, both Benjamin and Gabriel walked with Peter throughout his acreage and discussed his building project.

Peter shared with them his concern about building the foundation. Then Gabriel brought Peter over to the wagon and showed him bag after bag of lime he had brought from his building sites in Philadelphia. "Peter, here is the solution to your problem. Tomorrow we will begin to create cement."

It was a fruitful week for Peter. Benjamin attended the Junto and got the members even more fired up about their newly formed club. He also visited many of the settlers as far away as one hundred kilometers. His goal was to inform them of the governmental structure of the colony of Pennsylvania. He instilled in them the dream of a representative democracy that would be different than the present proprietary government which they presently had. It was an easy sell as the settlers on the Western Frontier of Pennsylvania were fiercely independent and wanted to control their own destiny. To a man they requested to have someone from their frontier area represent them on the Pennsylvania Assembly.

Before departing back to Philadelphia, Benjamin sat down with Peter. "Peter, as you know I have visited many of your fellow settlers here in Tulpehocken and beyond. They are like you in that they came to America for freedom and also to have a say so in their government. When I return I will talk with the assembly about honoring their request. But first I need to have a person whom I can recommend to them as the first assemblyman from the West. Peter, will you be that man? You will need to come to Philadelphia four times a year."

With the thoughts of his exciting visit to Philadelphia and of a young lady that sent him lavender letters, "Benjamin, I feel it is my duty as a citizen of Pennsylvania to accept this grave responsibility." He said it with a little twinkle in his eyes.

While Benjamin was making his visit to the settlers, Gabriel and Peter spent each day working on building the house. Gabriel showed Peter that when you mix lime, gravel and sand with water in just the right portions, you create cement. "Cement is the building material we will use to create the foundation for your house." Gabriel was ready with many details that gave Peter confidence he would be building the finest house in all Tulpehocken.

During the stay, Jonny and Gabriel became friends. They had much in common and discussed their hardships in Germany and the blessings of coming to America. It however, was not just political talk. They also enjoyed their nightly games of checkers, which often lasted into the wee hours of morning.

"Dag nabbit, Jonny, you beat me again. I'm considered one of the best players in Philadelphia and you beat me two out of every three games. You make sure Peter brings you to Philadelphia with him each time he comes. We've got a checkers club and when you come I'll tell everyone that I'm trying to teach you the game. We've got one gentlemen, maybe I should say rogue, Theodore Schnapps, who wants to bet everyone each time he plays. He's pretty good and does win fairly often. Let's have you play him and play him very badly. He'll want to play you for money after he sees what an easy mark he has."

The First Assembly Meeting
1739

———— ∞∞∞ ————

JONNY, LOVED GABRIEL'S IDEA OF accompanying Peter to Philadelphia. It was also good for Peter as he used his father for a 'sounding board' both before and after the meeting. Jonny amazed Peter with his sage advice.

"Father, our people in the West want the roads from several of our settlements improved so we can more easily get our products to Philadelphia. The assembly doesn't understand the needs of our people, and just keeps putting us off."

They rode quietly for awhile and Peter assumed his father just didn't have an answer. Finally Jonny said, "Everyone always thinks and acts according to what is best for them. They don't see how good roads will help them in Philadelphia. You must show them the advantages to the Philadelphians of these improvements. Here's a thought. The road to Boston, although longer, is getting better, not good, but better. When you discuss this idea, let's make the road to Boston really good and getting better. Tell them how much the frontier people are enjoying going to Boston and are starting to buy most of their products from Boston."

Peter followed his father's advice. In the meeting, Jacob Spitznagle, who previously paid little attention to Peter and the Western concerns, interrupted Peter's compliments to Boston,

"My dear Peter, you are a Pennsylvanian, your people should buy from Philadelphia."

"Yes, you are right, Jacob," answered Peter, "but it's so convenient to get to Boston. Our wagons don't break down from the ruts in the road and it's wide enough for a wagon from the west to meet a wagon from the east without stopping and getting off the road." The discussion ensued and before the end of the meeting, Benjamin Franklin asked for a vote on a motion from Jacob Spitznagle. "Gentlemen, do you vote yea on spending one thousand pounds to improve the roads from Philadelphia to our Western Frontier?" It was an unanimous, yes.

Peter continued to consult with his father on each subsequent trip. It also made him think back to many decisions he had made, particularly on emigration to America. He realized that although he made the decision, his father often planted the seeds for his decisions.

It was a joy for Jonny to spend time with his son on these journeys to Philadelphia. Jonny also enjoyed being with Gabriel Seidel and his wife Polly and their daughter, Maria Margaretha. *"Margaretha reminds me so much of my daughter, Rebecca."* The thought made him smile and he said to himself, *"Fiddlesticks."*

The first meeting for Jonny also gave him the opportunity to make another great friend, although this friendship came about in a most unusual way. "Jonny," said Gabriel as he rubbed his hands together, "it's time for us to go to the checker's club and time for Mr. Scnapps to meet his maker or should I say breaker."

Gabriel introduced Jonny Spyker, "Friends and enemies," they all laughed. "I want you to meet my new friend from the frontier. He wants to come and learn about our game and enjoy your company. If you play him, please don't laugh at his clumsy attempts. I've been to his place in Tulpehocken, which is at the brink of civilization, and I've tried to teach him the game. When I brought my checker game out, he was thrilled. He took two of the checkers and placed them under an uneven table." The group laughed, pretty sure Gabriel was joking, and gave Jonny a nice round of applause.

"Gabriel, you couldn't teach a cow to give milk," said Theodore Scnapps in his usual boisterous voice. "Let me work with him. I'll teach him how to win, although it may cost him a pretty penny or two." Now the group was in it, and roared appreciatively. Gabriel laughed also and thought, *"Now the hook is set."*

The evening was great fun for Jonny as he played with several and lost quite handily. He kept getting better. When it came time to play with Theodore, he really played his 'almost' best and barely lost. "Okay, Mr. Jonny," said Schnapps, "how about a friendly game, say ten pence?"

"Heavens no, I'll let you have a pence, just to be a good sport", said Jonny. They played several games and Jonny saw that Theodore was letting him win a game or two. The hook became more snug. "Okay, Theodore, it's time for me to leave; I can hardly stay awake and poor Gabriel is already nodding. I've got just a pound left and might as well get rid of it. Now Theodore played his best, but surprisingly Jonny "stumbled" into a win.

Jonny gathered his pound and got up to leave. "Better lucky than good, I always say", said a somewhat humbled Theodore. "Hey we have a rule on the last game, if you're behind you can go double or nothing. How 'bout it my lucky friend?"

"Sure and you're right. One more game and home to bed. I came into this world with nothing and I might as well leave this world with nothing." All applauded Jonny's attitude and the final game began. While they were in the early hops, Gabriel, had passed around the true story and all gathered to see the game. Jonny won easily, no contest, everyone roared and laughed. Theodore found he enjoyed the ploy as much as anyone else. He laughed, clapped Jonny on the back and said, "I've been sharked." Surprisingly Jonny and Theodore became great friends and Jonny let him win occasionally.

The Peter Spyker House Warming
1740

This is the Peter Spyker house today. It is a national landmark in Stouchsburg, Pennsylvania. The picture is courtesy of the owner Robert C. Nelson

It took Peter another two years to build his Spyker home, but finally in the late summer of 1740 it was completed. To celebrate the building, Peter threw a party the likes that had never been seen in the Western Frontier. The guest list was large and familiar. All the members of Junto were there, which now included fifteen men and their families. Benjamin Franklin and his wife were there as well as Conrad Weiser and his wife Anna. Also the Seidel's were there, which included a now more mature Maria Margaretha, who was nineteen years old.

Over the last two years every time Peter went to Philadelphia for the assembly meeting he along with his father stayed at the Seidel house. During the free time from the assembly, he spent time with Maria. Once again as on the St. Andrew he was shy about showing any true feelings about Maria. He just enjoyed being with her. He kept saying to himself, *"How I wish she was older or I was younger. She would be the one I'd love to spend my life with. Maybe in a couple of years... ."*

His father was there with Regina Hartman at his side. He had never seen his father happier and Peter thought, *"Will these two get married? They seemed so right for each other. My father needed a companion and his mother would be happy for Jonny."*

It made him feel good to see his grandfather Johannes there, supported by Lomasi. Johannes was getting fragile in his eightieth year, but Lomasi still looked to be just a lady in her forties.

An interesting trio came with Benjamin from the Delaware tribe in Tulpehocken including Chief Cannassatego, Kitchi, and with them an attractive young Native American girl of about sixteen years.

Peter noticed as did Jonny that the Native American girl never left the side of Benjamin. Her name was Lolotea. Lomasi explained to Jonny and Peter that this meant "Blessing from God". Lomasi also mentioned that she had often talked with Benjamin and Lolotea, and they wished to get married in two years, when she was of age to be a bride.

Benjamin had become an ally of Conrad and was even summoned as was Conrad to Philadelphia to meet with the assembly and proprietorship to assist them in the relations with the Native Americans; a relationship that was often strained by poor decisions by the colonists. Often Benjamin sat down with Native American chiefs and their White counterparts to settle differences. Benjamin, although only eighteen, was becoming a respected and mature young man.

During the party, interesting conversations were taking place that would affect the history of the Spyker family. "Maria," said Peter, as he was showing her around the grand house, "this is the master bedroom."

"This is nice. How nice of you to show me 'our' room." said Maria with a coy look on her face. Peter chuckled as he always enjoyed her subtleties. As he laughed, Maria turned to him with uplifted face and closed eyes. She was irresistible and Peter kissed her as passionately as he had learned from a young lass on the St. Andrew. "I do love you, Maria. I want to marry you, but we must wait for a time and have a lengthy engagement."

"Fiddlesticks," said Maria as she continued to embrace the only man she had ever loved.

Once again Peter could not help laughing as he remembered the favorite expression of his sister in Aspach. God, how he loved this adorable Maria Margaretha.

Maria enjoyed Peter the most when he laughed at her personality. "Double Fiddlesticks", she said with her hands on her hips.

"Stay here for a moment, don't move. I have something for you." Peter went to his bureau of sacred items and found his mother's diamond wedding ring that his father had given him. It was one of the few diamond rings in all of Palatine and it had been in the family's possession for several generations. Jonny had told him shortly after Elizabeth's death that this family heirloom would be for Peter's bride.

Returning to the master bedroom, he found Maria standing in the exact pose like a statue with her hands akimbo. "Peter, you told me not to move, but I'm not sure how long I can stand like this."

"Don't ever move," said Peter as he got down on his knees. He opened the palm of his hand and showed Maria the beautiful sparkling diamond once worn by his mother. "Maria Margaretha Seidel, will you become Maria Margaretha Spyker? Will you change your name, but nothing else about you?"

Maria was stunned. For one of the few times in her life she had nothing clever to say. "Oh Peter, I've dreamed about this moment, but thought it would never happen. Yes I will marry you and we will have ten children all named Peter."

They went arm in arm down the stairs. Peter invited everyone into the large living room and after they had assembled, "Mr. and Mrs. Seidel, Gabriel and Polly, may I have your permission to marry your daughter. I loved her as a beautiful girl the first day I saw her come into the Hopkinson home and I now love her as a beautiful woman who has come into our home."

All Gabriel could do was nod his approval, but Polly, like her daughter, always had something memorable to say: "Peter, thank God. Maria has told me one hundred times over these last four years that she is going to marry Peter Spyker. You have our permission to be our son." Everyone in the room applauded.

Soon after the room quieted down another man stepped forward, "This may not be the appropriate moment, but I have an announcement that I've been waiting to make all day," said Henry Hartman, son of Regina Hartman. "Peter, once again you've upstaged me . As I mentioned several times to Peter over the last two years, there's a man who looks a lot like Peter, although several years older, who keeps coming to my house and bringing my mother flowers. Two weeks ago he asked me for my mother's hand. I of course said yes and asked if I could announce it at the Peter Spyker housewarming. Let me announce that next week Johannes Peter Spyker, Jonny, will wed my mother Regina Hartman." Many were surprised, but not Johannes and Peter. They had encouraged Jonny to put his widower status aside and marry someone he had loved from the day of his first Christmas Eve in Tulpehocken.

Tears of Joy, Tears of Sadness
1740

———— ✺ ————

DURING THE SUMMER THE LUTHERAN Church of Aspach had been completed and Filip was looking for just the right moment to have his church-warming. The church stood high and proud over the entire area of Tulpehocken. On the morning of Saturday, September 7, 1740, the church was filled for its first wedding, that of Johannes Peter Spyker, Jonny to all, and Regina Hartman. This was another moment of celebration on the frontier. It seemed like usually it was just weddings and funerals that were occasions when neighbors from a radius or forty kilometers or more would gather together. A time for joy, a time for sadness.

Reverend Filip Schmidt was in all his glory as he stood in front of the altar of "his" church; his dream that he had envisioned from the day he left Aspach, and sailed on the St. Andrew. As he stood like a ramrod, but with a grin that no one could erase, he saw coming down the aisle on the arm of her son, Regina Hartman, soon to be Regina Spyker. Beside him on his left stood the best man, Benjamin, youngest son of Jonny, and next to him a proud, tall, and strongly built, Peter Spyker. On his left he could see Lomasi who was usually stoic, but now shed a small tear. Next to Lomasi was the very pregnant wife of Henry, Magadelena Hartman.

If the child was a girl, she would be called Regina. As Regina reached the altar and joined arms with Jonny, Magadelena stepped forward and sang: *"Allein und doch nicht ganz alleine . . .*

She sang it first in German and then in English: *"Alone, yet alone am I, Though in this solitude so dear; I feel my Savior always nigh, He comes the weary hours to cheer: I am with Him and He with me, Even here alone I cannot be."*

This was the Hartman's favorite song that they sang everyday as a family, and would, as years go by, sing to their sons, George and Christian, and their two daughters, Regina and Barbara. "Regina, my mother, my friend, you now have Jonny as well as your Savior. You will never be alone." After Magadelena had said these poignant words to her mother-in-law, they all turned to the smiling Reverend Schmidt for the ceremonies.

Early in February of 1741 at the monthly Junto meeting Dr. Jacob Seltzer addressed his best friend Peter. "Peter, you know I've been visiting your grandfather frequently. He will not be with us much longer. All I can do is keep him comfortable. He goes into pneumonia frequently and then shakes these bouts, but I fear not much longer. You need to help him get his affairs in order."

Just a week later, Benjamin rode up to Peter's house, "Peter, come quickly, Grandfather will likely not survive the night." Peter rode with Benjamin and gathered with Lomasi, Jonny, Regina, and Dr. Jacob Lentz around the fragile and pale Johannes. "Peter, thank you for coming. I want to spend these last hours with my family. However, I want you all to quit crying and hear my last words. There is no need to be sad. I have lived the most beautiful life ever. My life is like a history book that will keep on telling for centuries. I still can see my days in Aspach school with Herr Wilhelm and Conrad. Poor Wilhelm, we nearly drove him crazy with our pranks." Johannes chuckled along with his son and grandsons. He then coughed and closed his eyes for a spell.

Soon he grasped firmly on Jonny's hand and opened his eyes. "It was first Wilhelm and then our amazing visit with William Penn in Speyer that pointed my way to America and eventually to Pennsylvania. Ah, Jonny, do you remember our Christmas Eve parties, joy in the middle of misery? Those damn French armies, and the Holy Roman Empire armies were no better. They took our crops and our livestock and they burned down our house. They thought we'd give up on life, but we survived in those snug caves on the Zucker."

Again Johannes weakened and closed his eyes. All thought he had breathed his last. But soon he opened his eyes and said with a smile and a faint voice, "Not yet. I haven't finished my reverie. See Peter, I'm no lawyer, but I can still say those fancy words. Where was I? I would never have come to America, but my Margaret left me and Conrad needed me."

All were amazed at his recollection as he continued, "The journey on the Lyon, the awful days in New York where we often thought of going back to the French and the pope. However, we knew if the French and the Empire could not keep us from freedom, neither could Queen Ann and the English. Let me rest." Again he stopped closed his eyes, but soon opened them again surveying his family. "I'm thinking about the first time I saw Benjamin and Peter." He winked at Benjamin and again closed his eyes. Doctor Jacob put his hand on Johannes's chest. "He's still with us. I've never known a man I've respected more."

After several minutes which seem eternal, Johannes again opened his eyes smiled his beautiful smile. "The Lord just told me to hurry and finish my story. His angels are waiting. Thank God for the Weisers. Young Conrad discovered the Garden of Eden, Schoharie and Conrad Sr., my friend said, 'Johannes, go and take others with you.' We loved the Mohawk Valley, but the English were not through giving us grief. I'll never forget the night when the most beautiful angel, Lomasi, snuck into my sleep and kept me warm."

"Now Johannes," said Lomasi with tears in her large dark eyes. "You are not to tell everything. Look at the influence you might have on Benjamin." Johannes laughed and all joined in.

"No one thought we could bring our homestead from Schoharie to Tulpehocken. We brought families and we brought livestock. Without Lomasi, we never would have made it." Again Lomasi interrupted, "No, without Johannes we never would have made it."

Johannes smiled and took Lomasi's hand, "Conrad told me the St. Andrew should be in Philadelphia within a few days. The ship had been sighted by another ship that had arrived just before the St. Andrew. We took our fastest horses and finest wagon to the port of Philadelphia. When the St. Andrew arrived, there was no son, no grandsons. I searched and I searched, but no one looked like my Jonny. Then high on the top deck"– here Johannes raised himself almost a foot in his bed and stretched out his hand in greeting– "I saw a hand waving and waving at me. By his side was a young boy and a handsome young man. My family was with me in America."

Johannes fell back in his bed and closed his eyes. Jacob, felt his chest, and whispered, "He's arrived on another distant shore."

The funeral of Johannes Peter Spyker, the first Spyker pioneer in America, was a grand celebration.

Peter and Maria the Early Years
1742

———— ∞∞∞ ————

Despite the desperate pleading of Maria, the Seidels were able to contain their daughter for another two years after her engagement. On December 2, 1742, they were married in Philadelphia in the Presbyterian church which was in Buttonwood Hall on Market and Bank Streets. The Seidels were Presbyterian and attended the church regularly along with many other Philadelphia notables such as Ben Franklin. Later, Maria was to become Lutheran along with the Spykers and the many other citizens of Tulpehocken.

"Poor Richard" described the wedding in Benjamin Franklin's *Pennsylvania Gazette*.

THE WEDDING OF THE YEAR

On December 2, 1742, Buttonwood Hall was bursting at the seams as all witness the exchanging of vows between Johannes Peter Spyker and Maria Margaretha Seidel. The Reverend Jedediah Andrews officiated. The righteous reverend was in rare form as he called down the wrath of God one hundred times and even mentioned love twice.

The groom, Johannes Peter Spyker is the son of Johannes Peter Spyker and the grandson of Johannes Peter Spyker (deceased). Do you

*wish to know his great-grandfather's name? Peter, as he is called, to dis-
tinguish him from the other Spykers of the same name, is a farmer and
lawyer in Tulpehocken country on the Western Frontier of Pennsylvania.
He is also an assemblyman in our Pennsylvania Assembly.*

*Maria Margaretha Seidel is the daughter of Philadelphia's ren-owned
architect, Gabriel Seidel and wife, Apollo nee Murphy Seidel.*

*Weeping copiously was Philadelphia's number one citizen, Benjamin
Franklin, as the bride and bridegroom exchanged these vows:*

*"As God unites us in the presence of our family and friends, I give you
my firm commitment to be faithful and loyal to you, in sickness and in
health, good times or bad, in sadness and in joy. I do promise to love you
unconditionally, to help you make your dreams come true and to respect
and honor you. I cherish you, my dear (Peter/Maria) for as long as we
both shall live."*

*And if that was not enough, they continued: "I commit to never leave
you, to follow you. For where you go, I shall go, and where you remain, I shall
remain. Your people will be my people, and your God will be my God. Where
you die, I shall die and be buried beside you."*

*Guests at the ceremonies, besides the aforementioned Benjamin
Franklin, who was resplendent in his dinner jacket, which made him look
like a penguin, included some of the following famous men of Philadelphia:
Conrad Weiser who looked uncomfortable without his raccoon hat, John
Kinsey, Speaker of the Assembly, and Isaac Norris, past Speaker, who
were there to witness the wedding and to collect some votes as well. Peter
Spyker is a member of the Pennsylvania Assembly and John and Isaac
had their hands full to keep him from fleeing to the frontier wilderness.*

*The Penn brothers, Thomas and John, good friends of the Seidels, but
not so good friends of Mr. Franklin, were in attendance to make sure Mr.
Franklin would not talk behind their backs. Also making an appearance was
James Logan, past governor and mayor of Pennsylvania.*

*Many other dignitaries were there as well and they will soon be at
the office of "Poor Richard" as to why they were not mentioned as famous
men of Philadelphia.*

The reception after was at the landmark, Seidel house. A house viewed by thousands as the vanguard of architecture in these American colonies. Food and drink flowed in great quantities as the guests toasted the beautiful couple. For a brief period in our Pennsylvania history, Barbados rum was not available to the rum runners for their sale to the Indian nation.

We wish them good fortune and God-speed as they make their way to the Western Frontier and the Spyker house in Tulpehocken.

———⸺———

It was a tired but very happy couple who arrived at the Peter Spyker home in Tulpehocken. Maria couldn't wait to get into her new kitchen. She had planned the first dinner for Peter to be special.

Authors note. This is the actual picture of the kitchen in the Spyker house. The house owned by Robert C. Nelson has retained much of the historical appearance as the original. Thanks to Mr. Nelson for contributing this picture.

This first dinner was a great success and just the beginning of the amazing culinary art of Maria. That night they retired to "our" master suite, as Maria had named it at the housewarming of 1740 and the day of their engagement.

"Peter, I love this house, however, all visitors would exclaim, 'What a nice bachelor house?' May I change the decor, not only in the 'master - mistress' suite, but throughout the house so all will know Maria has slept here? I'll do all the sewing and painting and decorating. I will do so with great joy as this is my home and I'm one hell of home decorator. Now that I've got you, you should know occasionally I use damn and hell."

As usual, Peter could not help laughing. '*God, how he loved this woman.*' "Maria Margaretha, I don't care if you paint the whole house pink both inside and outside."

"Now that we have that settled Mr. Spyker, blow out the candle and let's get started on our first of ten children."

———◦◦◦———

They settled into their house and into a lifestyle suitable for the Western Frontier. The Spyker house was on two hundred and forty acres. About one hundred and fifty were tillable for crops and Peter had planted both corn and wheat each year. Immediately surrounding the house was a pasture for the livestock with a barn and stable for the horses. Close to the house was also the garden, now called "Maria's Garden." As in Aspach, Peter had set several acres aside for his vineyard. The house and the property was the finest in all of Tulpehocken.

Peter had an office inside for his law practice, but his main law office was with Marshall Nead in Finney's Fort a half-hour ride from his house. Finney's Fort was presently being surveyed by the Penn brothers and Conrad Weiser. They wanted to petition the courts in Philadelphia to establish Finney's Fort as a city.

They would name the city Reading, after the Penn's county seat in Berkshire, England.

The law office of Nead and Spyker was in a clapboard building on Centre street. Peter was making a name for himself as a reliable lawyer handling deeds, wills, property disputes, and the usual mundane legal matters requiring a lawyer. There were occasions when he served as a defense lawyer for his constituents. The most famous case to come to the Ft. Finny court was that of "a horse named Sparky."

Michael Lauer, a member of the Junto and the owner of a lumber mill in Tulpehocken was accused of stealing a horse. This was a very serious offense in the frontier as horses were the means of transportation for all frontiersmen. A farmer from Bethel, named Tom Barnes, had his horse stolen. It was a roan-colored horse with a white triangle on its forehead. Several witnesses swore they saw a man who looked like Mr. Lauer lead the horse from the pasture of its owner. When the sheriff investigated the case he came to the Lauers, received permission to search Michael's barn, and there was a roan horse with a white triangle.

"Peter", said Michael, "You know me well. I would never steal a handful of oats much less a horse."

Peter believed Michael, but he himself was confused how the identical looking horse had ended in Michael's barn. The only persons who could attest to Michael's ownership of a horse similar to the roan was his family. After much discussion with Michael, Peter, knew his strategy.

The case lasted just one day in the court. The farmer presented his case against Michael and his witnesses attested to the fact that they saw a person that looked like Michael Lauer lead the horse away from the farmer's pasture. The sheriff was called to testify for the prosecution and had no recourse but to tell the court that the horse found in Lauer's barn was the one described by farmer Jones.

Peter had Michael's family testify that they owned the horse described by the sheriff. Peter could tell by the look on the judges face that the testimony meant nothing to the veracity of the case.

"Judge Johnson", said Peter, "Would it be permissible to ask farmer Barnes the name of his horse?" Before the judge could answer, farmer Barnes volunteered with a laugh and the simple statement, "This horse has no name. He's just a roan-horse with a white triangle on his forehead, the very one found in Mr. Lauer's barn."

Peter then called Michael Lauer to the bench. "Mr. Lauer, you heard farmer Jones relate that his horse has no name. Do you have a name for your horse?"

"I do; his name is Sparky."

"Judge Johnson, the horse that has allegedly been stolen is being held outside the courthouse to be returned to its owner. Can we go outside and make sure farmer Jones can identify his horse?"

The judge agreed and all preceded outside. Farmer Jones, examined the horse and verified, "This is my horse. I'll take him back after your decision." Peter and Michael Lauer stood about twenty-five yards away from farmer Jones as he was nodding his surety that indeed this was his horse.

Michael simply said "Here Sparky." At which time "Sparky" broke away from the handlers and trotted to Michael and nuzzled him with obvious familiarity. The judge simply said "Case dismissed."

While the home life between Peter and Maria was often joyous there was also great sorrow as three of their children died before their seventh birthday. It seemed Doctor Jacob Lentz was visiting the Spyker home every month. Their first child, Philip was born in October of 1743 and survived just four years and nine months. Although this caused great grief, soon Maria was expecting again and gave birth to John Peter. He was never healthy and contracted whooping cough and lived just for a year and a half.

Thankfully, Benjamin, their third child was healthy. Marie and Peter decided to break the trend of naming the first born Johannes Peter Spyker. Benjamin was named after Peter's brother, but was always called Benny. He was born in March of 1747.

Just two years after Benny, a daughter was born, Anna Elizabeth. She also remained healthy. Then a year after Anna Elizabeth came another daughter, Catherine, who was born in December of 1750. Catherine although loved greatly and treasured by both parents and siblings was never healthy. Dr. Jacob had cautioned Peter and Maria shortly after birth that her lungs were not well developed and that she would likely not survive a year. Catherine was always happy but struggled to live and departed from the Spykers after seven years in March of 1758.

Maria Barbel was born just before the new year of 1752. She was the entertaining one in the family and always made everyone laugh. On the eve of the French and Indian War another son was born, John Henry. John Henry was always vital and healthy. The Spykers were no different from most of the families on the Western Frontier in that life was a struggle and the chances of their children surviving into adulthood were just over fifty percent.

Each year, despite the hardships and sorrows, they celebrated the success of their harvest in November, a Thanksgiving celebration with many neighbors and relatives coming to their home. On these occasions they were able to put aside their sorrows and enjoy the fruitful harvest and successes of the year. However, the Thanksgiving of 1753, although still a celebration, was a precursor to war coming into the colonies and new dangers in the frontier.

War Comes to the Frontier
1754

———— ✦ ————

It was the early summer of 1754 and tensions were mounting between the French and the British over the ownership of the Ohio Valley. Benjamin and Peter had been called to Philadelphia to meet with Benjamin Franklin, Robert Morris, who served as deputy governor of Pennsylvania; Lieutenant Governor of Virginia, Robert Dinwiddie; and the military commander from Virginia, a young officer, George Washington.

Peter was called to the meeting because he was the assemblyman from the frontier. Peter had been an ex-officiate member representing the Western Frontier, but with the establishment of Berks county in 1754, Peter became a full voting member of the assembly.

Peter's brother, Benjamin was also requested to be at this meeting because he was one of few Americans, along with Conrad Weiser, who understood the culture of the Native Americans. Benjamin was now starting to take Conrad's place when advice regarding negotiations with the Native Americans was needed. Conrad was often ill, and now more than ever wanted to remain in his frontier home with Anna Eve and their children.

Although Benjamin had no children, he considered Peter's sons and daughters to be like his own children. Particularly his namesake seven-year-old Benny was like a son. He had helped teach him the way of the Delaware, to hunt with a bow and arrow, and to speak in their tongue.

Both the brothers, although fairly content in 1754, had suffered times of sadness. Peter's farm had made him one of the wealthiest persons in Tulpehocken. He was successful in his law practice as well, and this added to his wealth and his prestige. Benjamin had lived off and on with the Delaware for several years. He had married Lolotea when she was eighteen. However, Benjamin and Lolotea were blest with just one year of married love. Lolotea had contracted smallpox and died very quickly. Despite his influence and friendship with Chief Cannassatego and his brother in spirit, Kitchi, the father of Lolotea blamed Benjamin for his daughter's death. "My daughter died of White man's disease. Damn the White man."

Lolotea's father, Mattawa, was the younger brother of Cannassatego. When Chief Cannassatego died, Mattawa became the Chief and no longer welcomed Benjamin to live in their camp.

Later Benjamin had married a widow, Margaretha Yeiser. They had no children and Benjamin was gone much of the time as a trader with the Native Americans and as a saddler. There was no better, maker and repairer of saddles and other leather products for horses and his presence was in demand throughout the Western Frontier. Although his marriage was comfortable, his greatest joy was in the presence of Peter, Maria and their children.

As they rode together, along with their father, to Philadelphia, they discussed the events leading up to this meeting. "Ben, those damn French," said Peter. "We had to leave our home in Aspach because of them and King Louis the Fourteenth. Now the French are building forts in our area and stirring up the Delaware and other nations to want us out of this land."

"Well," said Benjamin, "The British are not much better. All they want is for us to supply England with desired products and to buy their products, even if we don't need them. We once were caught between the French and the Holy Roman Empire, and now it's the French and the British."

Benjamin, who more than anyone else understood the mood of the Native Americans, conveyed his feelings about the war potential in the Tulpehocken area. "The attitude of the Delaware and some of the Iroquois is changing and not for the better. We have not always treated them fair and the French have reminded them of this and have started rumors of other cases of our mistreatment of the Native Americans. I'm not sure we can trust them anymore. I care for them and many of my Delaware friends, but I am a settler in America. I'm caught between, but some day the Delaware may become my enemy."

"I understand your feelings," said Peter. "The new governor-general of New France, Marquis Duquesne, is building military forts right under our noses. These forts are an act of war to all of us in the West. I hope we can make the assembly and the proprietorship aware of our concerns and I hope we can get them to provide us with some soldiers to protect us. If war comes with the French and their bribed allies it will happen on our soil, not in Philadelphia. We cannot fight them with pitchforks. We need arms, ammunition and soldiers. Ben, I will not let anyone, French, Indians or both, drive me and Maria from our home. I will die rather than flee."

Jonny had been listening to the concerns of his sons and now joined in, "Lomasi tells me there will soon be war. She says the Iroquois, her people, are torn between the French and the British, but do not trust either. She says although some of the Iroquois Nation might side with the French, her concern and caution is that the Delaware in our area will not hesitate to burn and kill. Lomasi is one of us, although her heart breaks when she thinks of the possibility of her people fighting against us. Sons, your father has no advice. Try to keep the peace, but be vigilant and ready to fight. I will fight by your side."

They became quiet as they covered the last few miles to Philadelphia.

Prelude to War
1754

———— ❦ ————

THE MEETING WAS HELD IN the Penn building and chaired by Robert Morris, who was deputy governor of Pennsylvania. Mr. Morris was appointed by Thomas Penn and represented the views of the proprietorship. Benjamin Franklin had met Peter and Ben the evening before at the Tun Tavern. Benjamin Franklin had made his feelings known to them and Peter in turn made the feelings of the Western Frontier settlers, whom he represented, known to Mr. Franklin.

"Peter, I understand your feelings," said Mr. Franklin. "We need to protect our frontier and I am also worried about our relationship with the Indians. It seems to be deteriorating fast. I know much of it has to do with the unfair treatment of them. We must protect the frontier, but I cannot convince the assembly to fund this operation without financial help from the proprietors. How can they sit on the prime properties in Pennsylvania, which has been given to them, then ask us to tax all other property owners without themselves paying one penny of tax?

"Tomorrow at the meeting you will hear me express these sentiments. Eventually we will be able to tax the proprietors and then we will be able to supply the frontier with their needs to protect themselves from the French and their allied Indians."

Mr. Franklin continued on as he felt indebted to Peter and the frontier, and wanted him to understand why he would not whole-heartedly support immediate arms and soldiers to the Western part of the Pennsylvania colony. "I have high hopes for a meeting we will have in Albany, colony of New York. All the colonies will be there with a representative and we are going to try to unite as one body in our support of England in the conflict with the French and the Indians. Ben," continued Benjamin Franklin, "Conrad Weiser wants you to come to the meeting. He is feeling poorly and also discouraged about the continual breakdown in relations with the Indians, whom he insists upon calling Native Americans. He relates how your youth, energy, and negotiating skills are needed to help our colonial representatives understand the problems ahead. It is so complex. There are Indians that favor the French and Indians that favor the English. How do we keep more and more Indians from going to the French side and how do we get the French allied Indians to come to our side?" Benjamin Franklin finished, and it was plain to see he was frustrated.

"I will be there," said Benjamin Spyker. "But, Mr. Franklin, I have little hope for our ability to convince the Native Americans who are allies with the French to come to our side. Every day in Tulpehocken I see the hostilities of the Delaware increase. My friend, my brother Kitchi said that we should keep vigilant. Many in his tribe want to kill the settlers they think have taken their land. Land has been sold by the governor of Virginia to settlers without regard for the Delaware. I will do my best with you at the Albany meeting and with my negotiations with Native Americans, but I must keep my attention mainly focused on the possibility of war and the potential of atrocities committed against my people in Tulpehocken." It was a somber mood as Ben and Peter went back to the Seidels for a night's rest before the potentially explosive meeting the next morning.

Next morning, Robert Morris stood and called to order the meeting as he described 'for the survival of the Colony of Pennsylvania.'

"Gentleman before proceeding, would each of you stand and introduce yourself. Some of us are not familiar with some here. Mr. Franklin, would you proceed. I'm sure you will have something clever to say." It was obvious there was no love lost between Benjamin Franklin and Robert Morris.

"My clever statement, Mr. Morris is philosophical. I doubt you will understand it. 'Be civil to all; sociable to many; familiar with few; friend to one; enemy to none'. I am Benjamin Franklin, President of the Pennsylvania Assembly and printer of the *Pennsylvania Gazette*."

With that Benjamin sat down and on his right the next gentleman rose, towering above the seated meeting members.

"I am George Washington. I am a surveyor and also commander of the armies of Virginia and right now I am a humiliated warrior, but I love Virginia and I love America." After this short and somewhat confusing statement, he sat down.

After all the introductions, Governor Dinwiddie said, "Gentlemen, we are at war with the French. It seems like we are always at war with the French. My people from the Virginia colony have settled in the Ohio Valley. They have made their homes there. They want nothing but peace. However, the French feel it is their land and they are building forts to claim the land for France and to protect this land from any invasion by our English soldiers. I've asked Major Washington to be here today as he has firsthand knowledge of the situation in the Ohio Valley and the frontier. He introduced himself as a humiliated warrior. I disagree, but George will you explain the situation on the frontier as you see it?"

George Washington stood up and addressed the committee. He was six foot two inches tall, but seemingly taller as he stood straight with excellent posture. He was twenty-two years old, had dark brown hair, and a long narrow aristocratic nose.

A twenty-two-year old George Washington

He smiled slightly, "Governor, thank you for your confidence in me, but I stand before you as a puppy with his tail between his legs. The French whipped me, but they have not seen the last of me and when they do they will be running away from my troops. On October 31, 1753, Governor Dinwiddie sent me to Fort LeBoeuf to advise the French to leave the land claimed by Britain. They very politely said no and goodbye. Later the governor sent me back with troops. We were successful in this foray as we attacked Fort Duquesne, killed the Commander, Coulon de Jumonville, and a number of the French soldiers. We also took a number of prisoners. Governor Dinwiddie mentioned that we are at war with the French. This was the first battle. I was extremely confident and full of myself. I had won the war. Soon the French returned and drove us from our Fort Necessity, captured our troops and yours truly. They released me on condition that we, the English, would build no more forts in the Ohio Valley. Thus I stand before you, no longer the victor of the world. I ask this committee, Governor

Dinwiddie, King George, and the English Parliament to give me the opportunity to free our land of the French, to push them north of the Great Lakes. Gentlemen, I'm just a young soldier, but my vision is that we should have no western boundary."

George Washington sat down. Peter knew in his heart that this was a young man destined to lead the colonies in their ventures against the French and any other foe that might infringe on the colonies right to be free. The discussion continued. All agreed the French should be driven north of the Great Lakes. This was the agreement, but the means was in disagreement, particularly the raising the funds to support the war efforts.

Robert Morris, who mainly sat quiet and listened, did give the committee members some news that sounded encouraging. "Mr. Penn has asked England and Parliament for help with our war with the French and their Indian allies. General Edward Braddock has been assigned to come to America with two divisions of soldiers. This will be discussed more fully at the Albany Congress in June of this year."

The discussion continued and was often heated. Benjamin Spyker at one point criticized Governor Dinwiddie for selling land in the Ohio Valley without regard to the Native Americans.

The other disagreement without resolution was on taxation. Benjamin Franklin insisted the proprietors pay their fair share of taxes and Governor Robert Morris, who represented the proprietors, explained to him that the proprietors felt they had no debt. "Benjamin, right or wrong, the proprietors feel the colonist are indebted to them. They founded the colony. They owned the colony and to quote Mr. Penn, 'by God, whoever disagrees with our decisions can go elsewhere.'"

After two days of meeting, little was resolved. At the conclusion of the meeting as Benjamin Franklin and Peter were preparing to leave, Robert Morris, asked both, "Would you two gentlemen be kind enough to meet with me at the Tun Tavern? I have something I wish to discuss with both of you. I of course will buy."

The Tun Tavern in 1754.

As Benjamin Franklin and Peter entered the Tun they saw sitting in the very back, trying to be inconspicuous, Robert Morris. "Benjamin, Peter, have a seat. What will it be? I'm sure after our farcical meeting you need something stronger than water." After a pitcher appeared from the blowsy bar maid, Robert said, "Benjamin, I am not your enemy. I must be discreet and ask you both to allow this conversation to go no further. I am appointed by the proprietors to govern the colony in the manner in which they wish it to be governed. I often do not agree with their policies. Yes, I could resign, but then you would get a governor who cared little about the colonists. To be truthful, I am a governor in name only. Mr. Penn is the governor, and he will continue to re-elect himself. Benjamin, I hear you. The proprietors should pay property taxes in the same proportion as our other citizens. Even now I am making some headway."

Morris turned to address Peter, "I hear you. I've almost convinced Thomas Penn that if we want to retain our Western Frontier, we are going to need to invest in arms and men. Here also I'm making headway. I'm using what I think is a Benjamin Franklin strategy. Just last week, I suggested to Mr. Penn, that maybe it would be best if we let the French have the Western Frontier of Pennsylvania. Then, I said, we would not have to spend money to maintain the safety of the settlers. You would have laughed. Mr. Penn almost had apoplexy. His face got red and steam came out of the top of his head." Robert Morris seemed to mimic the mannerisms of Mr. Penn, as he quoted him, "'Damn it Robert. You can spend every dime of my money to keep those bastard French out of my Pennsylvania.'"

Benjamin Franklin almost choked on his ale he laughed so hard. "If you would persuade, you must appeal to interest rather than intellect," quipped Benjamin. "You were wise Robert, because I've attempted to appeal to his intelligence and found it lacking."

———⊗———

Although Benjamin Franklin had high hopes for the Albany Congress, it was a dismal failure. His goal was to get the colonies to unify and defeat the French and the Indian allies. Each representative feared that their colony would be giving up some of their freedoms if they united into one body. Every attempt by Mr. Franklin to get them to come together in some way to defend the colonies met with failure. He at one point presented a sketch to the committee of a snake divided into many segments, representing the colonies if they did not unify.

The committee voted against the plan to unify and thus the plan of unity died. The only positive outcome of the conference was that the representatives did agree to request military help from England. They were delighted when this request was granted by the English Parliament.

The Massacre at
the Monongahela River
1755

*A portrait of General Bradock as he prepared to
"squash" the French and the Indians*

GENERAL BRADDOCK, WHO WAS A much decorated and successful officer serving in Ireland, was assigned by the British Parliament to sail to America, and once and for all put a stop to the French occupation of English land in the Ohio Valley. The Parliament also sent, with the general, two brigades of England's finest warriors.

The colonists, particularly the governors and proprietors, were jubilant as they saw this as the answer to rid the French from the Ohio Valley and to subdue the Indian threats. The celebration in Virginia and the colonies in general was short lived. General Braddock, although a highly decorated and successful soldier was also a pompous ass.

Immediately upon arrival in Virginia, he agreed to accept the armies from the colonies to join his British brigades, but then he quickly relieved colonial officers of their responsibility and rank. This included George Washington, Commander of the Virginia army. The officers could join the forces, but would have no leadership responsibility. Over each colonial army he placed one of his officers from England.

General Braddock would permit George Washington to go as his aide, ostensibly so he could teach him how to wage war. Washington requested Ben Spyker to be with the troops as a scout, and once again Ben left his home and went to Alexandria, Virginia.

At a meeting several days after the training had been completed, General Braddock addressed George Washington. He was befuddled with the lack of success by the colonists. "Mr. Washington, noticeably not calling him colonel, I do not understand why you colonists are having so many problems ridding our colony of the French and their Indians allies. We will march right down their throats and show them how a war is fought. When we are finished, the remnants of the French will stay put north of the lakes and the Indians will find different hunting grounds."

George Washington, being just twenty-three, was intimidated by General Braddock, but tried to get him to understand that this would be different than fighting on the continent. "General, in due respect, I don't think it's wise to march directly to the fort; the Indians don't fight fair. With me is Benjamin Spyker, who has lived with the Indians and understands them well. Ben, maybe you better than I can explain the type of battle we will be facing."

Ben, who was never afraid to speak his mind as he had done the first day in America, addressed the General. "General Braddock, sir, if you march those redcoats directly at the fort, you will get your asses shot off. Behind every tree will be an Indian. They may not shoot their rifles as effectively as our soldiers, but they can knock the feather off each British hat with their arrows. I think we should ..."

General Braddock interrupted with his face as red as his beautifully manicured coat. "My dear Mr. Washington and my dear Mr. Spyker, I have conducted battles with the Imperial British Army for forty-five years. I know war. I know battle and I know how to win. I've invited both of you along to learn, because after this campaign, my soldiers and I will go back to England and count on you to wage war to keep the French out of our land. Mr. Washington, you may come as my aide, but Mr. Spyker, we cannot have anyone dressed like you, dressed like an Indian, accompany us. You will not be permitted to go with us." That was the end of the conversation. George Washington stayed, but Benjamin, who refused to dress in a red coat, decided to go back to Tulpehocken. His enmity toward the English increased even more.

After the meeting, when Ben was preparing to leave, a soldier from the Virginia contingent came to Ben's quarters. "Sir, Colonel Washington would like to meet with you in his quarters."

"Ben, said Colonel Washington, "I understand how you feel and I am also disturbed at the attitude of General Braddock. However, I am more concerned about our colonies and my soldiers. Would you consider getting involved in this battle without the knowledge of General Braddock? Would you consider scouting ahead of our brigades and letting me know when we are approaching a dangerous situation? I'm not sure even with your knowledge I will be able to convince the general to proceed any differently, but I must give it a try."

Ben, who continued to pack his belongings into the saddlebag, looked up at George Washington with a look of acceptance.

"Colonel, for the sake of our colonies and you, I will try to keep you informed. I hope to God we can sway the General, otherwise I fear we will lose a lot of men, and jeopardize our chances of chasing the French from our land." Ben immediately set out in the direction of Fort Duquesne and the Monongahela River. He saw the dangers. The places where the French and Indians would most likely lay in ambush.

The journey of Braddock's army of fourteen hundred men proceeded slowly, almost leisurely. They marched in perfect formation with beautiful red coats as if to say, "Here we come," and as Ben had said, "shoot our asses off." As they approached the Monongahela, Ben got word to George Washington that the French and their allies were waiting for them at the river. "George, you've got to convince General Braddock of the danger. They must spread out and even encircle the area and come from all sides. And for God's sake George, they must approach with caution and ready to seek immediate cover."

Washington, who was severely ill with a high fever, had stayed back from the main contingent. After getting the communication from Ben, he saddled his horse and joined General Braddock and tried to convince him of Ben's strategy.

"Be damned, George, you must have courage," said the general. "When we initially receive fire, we will have the first rank kneel down, fire at will, and then the second rank will also fire at will over the top of our kneeling soldiers."

"I hope when they kneel, they say lots of prayers," thought Colonel Washington. The British and colonial troops marched confidently forward as they had for one hundred years on the flat war fields of Europe. As soon as they crossed the Monongahela River, the woods exploded with musket fire and whooping Indians who hailed arrows from every angle. The Indians and the French had the audacity to let loose their musket fire and arrows and then protect themselves from the fire of the redcoats by hiding behind

trees. General Braddock was seething with fury. How could an enemy be so devious? Shortly, he fell with a gunshot wound and was no longer able to lead his troops. The troops were in disarray and Colonel Washington took command. No amount of courage from Washington or his men could avoid the inevitable. It was a disaster. The battle lasted but three hours. The British suffered nine hundred casualties. General Braddock saw his last battle as he did not survive his wounds and was buried on American soil.

The British soldiers retreated hastily, however, the soldiers from Virginia stood their ground and started to fight, "Indian style," shoot and hide, shoot and hide. Leading them besides George Washington was an unknown soldier, not dressed in red but as a frontiersman. After the battle, there were numerous accounts about George Washington and this unknown frontiersman.

One of the Virginia militiamen, soldier Paulding, gave this account of Colonel Washington: "George Washington is more than a soldier. He must be a spirit from God. He was shot three times through his uniform and came away unscathed. He had three horses shot out from under him and then he settled to fight on the ground. I saw him take hold of a brass field-piece as if it had been a stick. He looked like a fury; he tore the sheet-lead from the touch-hole; he placed one hand on the muzzle, the other on the breach; he pulled with this, and he pushed with that, and wheeled it around as if it had been nothing."

One of Colonel Washington's original company leaders who survived asked the Colonel, "Who was that fierce frontiersman? I thought he may have been an Indian, until he killed three Frenchies and a handful of Indians who were after your hide, Colonel. He shot one with his flintlock then flung it at another. Then out of nowhere appeared his bow. He shot arrows so fast you would have thought one was going to pass another. Just when he ran out of arrows I thought an Indian was going to hatchet him, but he swung onto a tree limb and landed on the back of a

Frenchie's horse and took out half a dozen more Indians. Who was that amazing warrior?"

Two outcomes came from the Battle of the Monongahela. George Washington was established as the leader of all the colonial forces and the Indians now had no fear to terrorize and try to drive out the settlers in the Western Frontier.

Tragedy Comes to Tulpehocken
1755

PETER, MARIA, AND THE CHILDREN were enjoying a party with all the Spykers. It was Sunday, October 16, 1755. Jonny and his wife Regina, Benjamin and his wife Margaretha, and the matriarch, Lomasi, were at the table giving thanks to the Lord for the bounty. Before them was spread two huge golden-baked turkeys shot by Benjamin, who had hunted the previous morning with Benny, who was eight-years-old at his side. "Maria, that son of yours shot the beady eyes out of 'ole Tom turkey' there; that's why it looks like 'Tom' is winking at you."

"Thanks Ben, now I'm not sure I can eat turkey today. He looks good sitting on the platter, but you've made me see him proudly walking through our field. Poor Tom. Besides my Benny's going to be a teacher."

All laughed and Peter said, "Let's say a repose over the soul of 'poor Tom' and then let's eat. I'm starved." In front of them, besides the turkeys, were yams, mountains of green beans, yellow squash, Lomasi's corn meal biscuits, stewed cinnamon apples, pumpkin pies, shoofly pies, and of course several bottles of Spyker's fine cooled Riesling wine.

They had just finished their dinner and were getting ready for their coffee when in the distance they saw a rider streaking for their house. Benjamin, ever cautious after his experiences with the French and Indians at the Monongahela, grabbed his flintlock. As the rider drew closer, Regina gasped, "It's my daughter-in-law Magdelena and my baby grandson Christian. I think something must have happened at their home."

Magdelena handed baby Christian to Jonny and fell off the horse, sobbing with grief. Regina gathered her into her arms and waited for what she knew would be tragic news. "Mother, you have lost your son and your grandson. My daughters, Regina and Barbara have been kidnapped. Thieving, murderous Delaware came to our home when I was away visiting Mary Lauer, who has been ill for over a week. When I returned, I saw our home and our barns smoking and almost burned to the ground. Outside our house was our dog, Wasser, completely hacked to death. He must have tried to warn my husband and son. When I went in what remained of our home, there were the charred bodies of Henry and George."

Regina upon hearing the news fainted and fell to the ground. Peter quickly took hold of Magdelena, while Johannes knelt down with Regina. "Your daughters," said Peter, "you said they were kidnapped?"

"They were gone. Nowhere in sight. They must have been taken. Please get them back."

This was the most personal experience for the Spykers, but this scene was happening in other homes in the Western Frontier. The Indians had become convinced by the French that the settlers would rob them of all their land. Rum had been used to bribe the Delaware to drive the settlers from the west and help the French attain control of the Western Frontier of America. The Indians had no tolerance for alcohol, and this with the continuing lies fed to them about the English, made them uncontrollable.

The Spykers quickly formulated plans to defend Tulpehocken. Benjamin Spyker, who previously had loved and respected the

Delaware, became the most active Indian fighter on the frontier. He was determined to get revenge and find the daughters of Magdelena. "Peter," said Ben, "I must go see Conrad Weiser. He and his sons will help us protect our people."

"Ben, give me a brief moment, so I can write a letter to give to Conrad. Please tell him to forward it to the assembly and the governor." Peter, as the assemblyman from the area, knew his letter would be a call to action.

Before Benjamin left for Womelsdorf and the Weiser's homestead, Lomasi made a request. "I know my people will help us. Please let me go to Schoharie and talk with them."

Although some of the Iroquois nation aligned with the French, the Mohawk, Lomasi's people, remained loyal to the British colonies. "My people will be able to find Regina and Barbara and will take up arms against the Delaware." Jonny looked at Benjamin and Peter, who gave their silent nod in agreement.

"Lomasi," answered Benjamin, "you cannot go alone. Peter and Jonny must stay here to protect our families. Give me some time and I know Conrad will send one of his sons with you."

Benjamin saddled up and rode to the Womelsdorf settlement to talk with Conrad Weiser. After the conversation, Conrad gathered his saddlebag and gun and said to Benjamin, "It's time for me to get off my butt. I wanted to be a homebody and watch my children grow, but I knew this was coming. I will no longer negotiate or try to appease the Delaware in our area. Ever since Chief Cannassatego passed, they have turned into renegades. They no longer want to live in peace. I will hunt them down, particularly those who killed my friend Henry Hartman and I will kill them. I know their ways and I know they are afraid of me, and I will find them and they will pay for their sins."

Benjamin had never seen Conrad this way. He was quietly furious and had tears in his eyes; he was ready to take charge. "Benjamin, you travel to all our neighbor homes east of Tulpehocken Creek and I will travel west. Let's all get together at your homestead by Wednesday afternoon prepared and armed for war. Hopefully we can soon get help from Philadelphia.

"Ben," continued Conrad, "there have been other Indian massacres in our area, The Paxton family by Hunter's Mill were all killed and scalped. I have previously sent a letter to the governor in Philadelphia asking for immediate help. Now with this new barbaric act, I will forward the letter from Peter to the governor as well."

Conrad briefly read out-loud the letter from Peter.

... . We are, at present, in imminent danger to lose our lives and estates; pray therefore for help, or else whole Tulpehoken will be laid waste by the Indians in a very short time. ... . We hope members of the Assembly will get their eyes opened, and manifest tender hearts towards us; and the Governor the same. They are, it is hoped, true subjects to our King George II of Great Britain, or are they willing to deliver us into the hands of these cruel and merciless creatures?'

I am your friend,
Peter Spyker

*Letter, reprinted in part from "A History of the Speicher, Spicher, Spyker Family... ." compiled by Paul I. Speicher.

"My son Samuel will courier this letter to the Governor. He will have it in his hands by tomorrow morning."

Benjamin had also told Conrad about Lomasi's request. "Ben, I agree with Lomasi the Mohawk are honorable Native Americans. They will wage war on the Delaware and help us find the Hartman girls. My older son Peter will join her and keep her safe along the way."

Lomasi was grief stricken. She and Peter Weiser rode rapidly but with great caution to Schoharie. She could not understand the culture of the Delaware. When they arrived at the home of Mohawk tribe, she was received with honor and assured they would help. The Mohawk did wage war against the Delaware and all Indians allied with the French. They did not find the Hartman girls, but learned Regina had been kidnapped along with another girl in the Tulpehocken. Unfortunately they also found that Barbara had been killed in an attempt to escape. When this information was given to Magdelena a week later she went into a period of grief that her mother-in-law Regina, felt she would never recover. *Perhaps if they could find her daughter Regina ... .*

On Wednesday, October 19, over two hundred frontiersman from Tulpehocken and the surrounding area gathered at the Benjamin Spyker home. They were mostly well armed, though about twenty had nothing but axes and pitch-forks. They were ready to defend their homes and ready to take the war to the Delaware.

Conrad addressed the anxious crowd, "Gentlemen, God-fearing men, friends, I am not surprised to see you here. No one has declined Benjamin or me in this call to arms. We will divide into seven groups." Conrad proceeded to outline the strategy that he and Benjamin had planned. "Before we depart I have asked Reverend Schmidt to say a prayer."

Reverend Schmidt started his prayer with the 23rd Psalm and asked all to join in. *"The Lord is my Shepherd, I shall not want .... ."* When they had finished, he asked all to go to their knees, *"Dear Lord, You brought us to Tulpehocken and to other communities on this frontier. You brought us here to raise our families in the belief of your son, Jesus Christ, who died for our sins. You brought us here to spread your Gospel to all corners of America. We need you now by our sides. We need you to help us defend ourselves from the enemy and to relieve our homes and our families of constant danger. We cannot do it without you. Lord protect each of us as we go into battle and give us all courage. If we must die, let us die bravely and in the sure knowledge that we will inherit the Kingdom of God. Amen."*

With that, Reverend Schmidt rose from his knees, grabbed his flintlock rife, and said to all, "I am going with you."

The frontiersmen fought bravely. Conrad and Benjamin showed them amazing courage, which created in each the same courage. They quelled the Indian savagery and brought a tentative peace to Tulpehocken and the nearby communities. The war, however, continued throughout colonized America and the Ohio Valley.

William Pitt "The Elder"
1756

William Pitt

ALTHOUGH THE PENNSYLVANIA FRONTIER REMAINED at a tentative peace, the French and Indian War raged in the Ohio Valley and Canada. The Pennsylvania Dutch *(Dutch is a misnomer as they were Germans)* needed someone to come forward and reverse the distinct possibility of Pennsylvania becoming a French colony. That notable historical figure, that "savior" was William Pitt.

"You're fired." This was a phrase heard often by William Pitt as he was always critical of the British government and the king. However in 1756, after the British war efforts were dismal and General Braddock had been so soundly defeated at the

Monongahela, King George II reluctantly named him Secretary of State.

William Pitt was not a person who lacked confidence. In fact his self-confidence almost became overwhelming to King George when he stated, "I know that I can save this country, and that no one else can." Despite King George's distaste for William Pitt, the populace had forced his hand and he had put "The Great Commoner" in total charge of the war effort.

As Peter Spyker traveled to Philadelphia for a special meeting of the assembly in 1758, he was not sure the English would retain the American colonies. The war effort in many areas was still favoring the French. Peter, however, was proud that their make-shift army, ably led by Conrad Weiser and his brother Benjamin, had kept the Indians from forcing the Pennsylvania Dutch from Tulpehocken and other areas of the Pennsylvania frontier.

No longer were there tragedies like the one where the Delaware had burned the Hartman farm, killing Henry and his son. The Delaware in Tulpehocken feared Conrad Weiser. The frontier army had not just defended Tulpehocken, but they had taken the war right into the settlements of the Delaware and drove them farther west.

"Dad," said Peter as they rode calmly on the Philadelphia trail, "What will our life be like if the French drive the English from America?"

Jonny, who read every news article from Philadelphia and from England that he could get his hands on was very knowledgeable on world affairs. "The French do not want to settle. They do not want to farm the land, they just want to trade with the Native Americans. They want to trap the fur bearing animals and increase the coffers of Louis XV. They do profess the noble idea of Christianizing the Indians and some of the priests who have come to the wilderness have done a remarkable job. The Catholic fathers are sincere in their efforts, but I do not feel Louis and his government care about the souls of man. If the French win, our farms will be overrun and the Native Americans will again bring nomad living to Tulpehocken. Peter, as I look into the future and see America become more and more populated, I know that settling the land by farming is the only way America will become a strong nation. We cannot be a nation of nomads. England must win this war."

Jonny continued his insight and Peter knew he was listening to a man of great wisdom. His father would have been a great leader of America, but he chose to instill this wisdom into his sons. "Peter, it will never seem fair that we are driving the Native Americans from their lands. Years from now, centuries from now, we will be criticized for this, but it is the only way. The Native Americans can change, settle the land, and claim their individual homestead. Then we can live together in peace. If they cannot do this then they will be forced to make way for civilization.

"I also have a personal reason for defeating the French and their allies. Every day, Regina's daughter-in-law, Magdelena grieves for her family who were tortured and died horrible deaths. The only thread to her sanity is her son Christian and the hope that her daughter, Regina, is still alive. Peter, every night before she goes to bed we hear her singing the family song, *'Alleia und doch night ganz alleine, ... Alone, yet not alone am I, Though in the solitude so dear; I feel my Savior always nigh, He comes the weary hours to cheer; I am with Him and He with me. Even here alone I cannot be.'"*

"Regina says that her daughter-in-law feels the song will bring back her daughter.

With the defeat of the French and their allies perhaps she will be returned to Magdelena."

Peter nodded his agreement with his father. "Father, I know this war is not just about America, but about global concerns. Perhaps England is more concerned about the continent and India and will eventually disappear from America."

"No Peter," said Jonny. "America is the most important piece in the giant chess game that is being played between France and England. Without us, neither country will be able to dominate the world. Don't forget about Spain. They own the land south and west of our Georgia colony. They are involved in this global war. It would be best if America was only colonized by one country. Actually Peter, I think even now as you continue your political career and continue to represent the Western Frontier of Pennsylvania, you are finding that England only cares about England and how America can maintain the great Royal empire. Maybe someday America will be an independent country."

0900, Tuesday, January 15, 1758.

"Gentlemen, will you come to order," called Assembly Speaker, Isaac Norris. "This is a called meeting of the Pennsylvania Assembly. Certain events call for quick action. You will soon understand why I have called this meeting." Isaac Norris served as the speaker for the assembly. Isaac Norris was a Quaker who had misgivings about his philosophy of war since the French and Indian allies were threatening to displace the English in America. With mixed feelings, Isaac introduced Nathaniel Grubb to introduce a splendid looking gentleman at his side.

"My fellow Englishman, until recently I have feared greatly that we will soon be French colonies. These last two years have been depressing. As you are aware, I once held Quaker belief that there should be no war for any reason. The actions of the French and their Indian allies and the murdering of many of our frontier families have caused me to change my philosophy. Recently I traveled back to England and met a man who has the courage to stand up to Parliament and to King George and assert that we must save America. He was designated reluctantly by King George as the Secretary of the State. As a result of the lack of success in driving the French from the Ohio Valley and Canada, they have now given him the sole responsibility for guiding the war effort. Gentlemen, he didn't choose to spend his energies in India, Prussia, Austria, or Africa, but he is with us here today as a sign that America is the most important possession in the conflict." Nathaniel realized his compatriots were waiting anxiously to hear from their guest rather than him. So he turned to Mr. Pitt and simply said, "William Pitt."

Peter and the assemblymen waited eagerly, hopefully, finally, for some good news. They all greeted the secretary with some quiet applause. William Pitt stood up and looked at each assemblyman as if he was talking to him personally. Peter thought, *"He's been called the 'Great Commoner' in England, but he sure looks aristocratic to me."* William Pitt had a beautiful coiffure wig of powdered white. His silver and black baroque coat gleamed with the finest silk from India. His cotton shirt had lace ruffles at the neck line and at each cuff. His trousers were form fitted and his black boots were leather with a shine that would reflect like a mirror. He was in Peter's mind, *"A dandy."*

"My dear Englishmen, England will take care of its countrymen; England will take care of its most prize possession, America. Here is my strategy for conducting the war efforts."

Pitt held his hand in front of the assemblymen and finger by finger enumerated his thoughts:

"Number one, North America, not Europe, is the most important possession in the creation of a great empire. We must liberally subsidize the Prussians to handle the bulk of the conflict on the continent while concentrating on America.

"Number two, France is our number one enemy. We must concentrate on defeating them. We cannot spread ourselves too thin. Defeat France and the other enemies will not have the resources to challenge the greatest empire in the world."

As William Pitt enumerated his philosophy and his strategy for conducting the war, Peter saw Mr. Pitt as a vision of his father, who had just voiced the same ideas.

"Number three, The present officers in charge of armies in North America are like General Braddock, God rest his soul, inept. I am firing everyone of them and replacing them with men that will listen to George Washington, Conrad Weiser, and Benjamin Spyker.

"And finally, we can provide men and arms from England, but you Americans are the most knowledgeable about fighting this war, which is different from the wars we have fought for centuries on the continent. We will supply you with the monies necessary to provide the colonial governments with soldiers and supplies, and your officers like George Washington will retain their rank and leadership responsibilities."

As if shot from a cannon, all thirty-six assemblymen stood up and gave thunderous applause. "Here, here," resounded from the chamber and would not have stopped until Speaker Norris pounded the gavel.

After the chamber had quieted, William Pitt continued, "My fellow Englishmen, thank you for your support. I have a request. When our officers come to Philadelphia, don't stone them. Recently, Colonel Bouquet came to your fair city. As he was riding through the city, a group of your Quakers lashed him with whips. This is the third time this has happened to one of our officers. I know they detest war, but to quote your favorite citizen, Benjamin Franklin, 'They who can give up essential liberty to obtain a little temporary safety deserve neither liberty nor safety.' I do find it a little incongruous to abhor violence and then whip a defenseless man.

Now that I've got that off my mind, let me make you aware of the logistics of our struggle." With that, William Pitt, pulled out a huge map of North America, which was tacked to an easel.

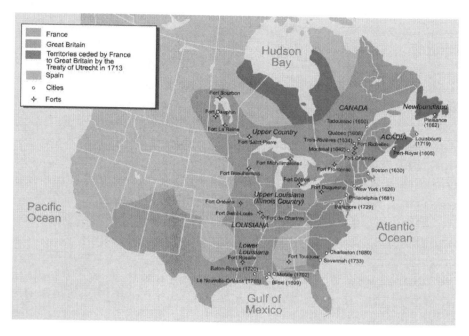

"To control the Ohio Valley it is essential that we take Fort Duquesne. To control Canada we must take the city at the mouth of the St. Lawrence, Louisburg." As he talked he used a long wooden pointer to point to Fort Duquesne and to Louisburg and then to other important locations in conducting the war.

As William Pitt continued, the assembly for the first time understood the magnitude of the war effort. They also understood the brilliance of William Pitt. After almost an hour of geographical and historical education, Mr. Pitt concluded with, "Someday my fellow Englishmen, this map will have only one color. It will be colored England."

Again the assembly stood and applauded until all were tired. At the end of the session, Nathaniel Grubb came to Peter Spyker before he could leave. "Peter, Mr. Pitt would like to meet with you. Could we meet at the Tun Tavern at noon for a lunch?" Peter was quick to reply yes, and wondered why this renowned person wanted to see him.

Peter arrived to find Assemblyman Nathanial Grubb and Secretary Pitt already seated at the best table in the house and surrounded by waiters and bar maids. "Peter, have a seat," said Nathaniel, "we have taken the liberty of ordering the lunch. It will just be a light repast," continued Nathaniel with a twinkle in his eye as he patted his extremely rotund belly. Soon in front of the trio, was a 'light repast' of roast beef with Yorkshire pudding and roast lamb with green beans and mint sauce.

The bar maid, a full-bosomed lady in her early twenties, addressed Mr. Pitt since he was the one ordering the lunch, "Can I bring you, fine sirs, a wine recently imported from France?"

"No, my dear," said Mr. Pitt as he winked at the maid, "I don't care for a French wine, but could you bring us the head of a Frenchman on a platter? Do you have a Louis XV?"

The bar maid was confused, and Mr. Pitt quickly said, "Just bring us a flagon of your best British ale."

All laughed at Secretary Pitt's wit. Peter relaxed enjoying the dinner, and the heady ale, while he waited for the occasion of his summon.

"Mr. Spyker, can I call you Peter?" started Mr. Pitt when they were through the early stages of the dinner. "The only frontier that presently has relative peace and is not under constant Indian attacks seems to be the Tulpehocken area. Why is that? I questioned Benjamin Franklin, George Washington, and others extensively about this phenomenon. They all have given me three answers: Peter Spyker, Benjamin Spyker and Conrad Weiser. Peter, help me understand this?"

Peter went into great detail about the situation after the murder of the Hartmans and the Paxtons and then described the call to arms. He described the leadership of his brother and of his friend Conrad.

William Pitt listened intently, nodding frequently, and finally replied, "Colonel Bouquet along with John Forbes will be conducting the warfare in your frontier. I would like you, Benjamin Spyker, and Conrad Weiser to meet with Colonel Bouquet, advise him the details you have outlined today, and then join him as officers under his command. We will have complete peace in North America by 1760."

Before departing from the Tun Tavern, William Pitt arranged a meeting with Peter, Benjamin, Conrad, and Colonel Bouquet at the Seltzer Restaurant in Womelsdorf. "We wish to come to the frontier, not only to meet with you three, but to view your frontier army and talk with many of them as well. I don't believe in conducting war from a desk." The meeting and subsequent visit was arranged for the first Monday in February, 1758.

Colonel Henry Bouquet
1759

Colonel Bouquet

WILLIAM PITT WASTED NO TIME in organizing the armies to wage war on the French and the Indians. To restructure the army, he used the phrase directed at him by King George and the Parliament. "Lord Loudan, you're fired!" Lord Loudan was the officer appointment by Parliament to replace the deceased General Edward Braddock. He was obviously a political appointment by the parliament before William Pitt was put in charge of the war. Lord Loudan had no genius for either civil or military affairs. His goal was to use his command to fill his pocket. His battle tactics were to state not to act. Referring to Loudon's tardiness, Benjamin Franklin said: "He is like Saint George on a sign-post; always on horseback, but never goes forward."

On Monday, February 3, Peter gathered with his brother and Conrad Weiser at Seltzer's Restaurant and Tavern. Jacob, who had been informed of this sensitive meeting and the two men who were coming from Philadelphia, had placed them in a private room in front of a warm and blazing fireplace.

"Peter," said Jacob as he opened the door and peered in, "I'm quite sure your guests have arrived. One looks like a peacock and the other like a little furry bear in winter. Both are wearing red jackets with beautiful gleaming sabers."

"You have described William Pitt brilliantly. I do not know the other. Send them in and bring us all some hot rum toddies. I'm sure they are near frozen from their ride from Philadelphia."

All stood as William Pitt and Colonel Henry Bouquet stepped in. Both were shivering and after short introductions, stood with their backs to the fireplace and rubbed their hands together. The February of 1759 was almost as cold as the February in 1710 that Jonny had often talked about.

As they sat down to a hot, steaming rum toddy, and after a quick but long swig, Secretary Pitt thanked Jacob, who was leaving the room. "Thank you Mr. Seltzer, you have just saved my life. Please give me the recipe. I'm taking it back to the White Hall in London and will sell it for a thousand pounds."

Conrad had sized up the short, rotund Colonel Bouquet, who had a face as round as a Tulpehocken pumpkin and thought, *"He sure doesn't look like a warrior."* Colonel Bouquet had gained the reputation of a fierce and astute warrior. He had entered the Swiss military at seventeen-years old and had been a professional soldier ever since. It didn't take long for all to realize that although the Colonel did not have the bearing of a soldier, he was indeed prepared for the task ahead.

After William Pitt's introduction and assurance that Colonel Bouquet would have the responsibility for waging war against the French and Indian allies in Pennsylvania, the colonel addressed the group. "Although I have only recently heard of the reputation of the Spykers, all England has heard of the Weisers. They tell me that Conrad was the best Indian negotiator and now is the most feared Indian fighter in America. I've heard the story how you and Benjamin Spyker have caused the Delaware to turn tail and head for the West. I have thoughts about the overall conduct of the war, but I bow to you gentlemen on the specifics of fighting on the frontier."

The ideas went back and forth among the five principals. Peter expected the two Englishmen to be giving instructions and was surprised to find both of them were excellent listeners. Colonel Bouquet listened and asked piercing questions. Finally after almost an hour of give and take, the Colonel said to all, "We are planning an attack again on Fort Duquesne. The attack will be soon and it cannot fail. If it does, we are in danger of losing America to the French. This might be the most important battle for England in all of history. Benjamin, I've heard from George Washington that you gave him excellent advice and information during the failed battle of Fort Duquesne by General Braddock, God rest his soul. I know the advice was not heeded. Give me that advice now. I will listen."

Benjamin, who had been awed in the presence of these two prestigious individuals had been fairly quiet. Now he was glad to be heard. "Colonel, I have just four pieces of advice, which I feel are crucial. They will be the difference between defeat and victory." Peter listened and was extremely proud of his brother, who now stood to emphasize these thoughts.

"Colonel, we can hardly call it the battle of Fort Duquesne, because our soldiers did not get within twenty kilometers of the fort. We were soundly defeated upon arrival at the Monongahela River. Once the battle was waged, the right flank had no idea what the left flank was doing. The soldiers in reserve had no idea to come forward and assist. It was bedlam. There was no communication between the commanders. So, first, Colonel and Secretary Pitt, we must devise a clear means of communication."

All could see Colonel Bouquet and William Pitt nodding their heads at each other in complete agreement.

"Colonel Washington requested that I scout ahead of our soldiers to help us avoid ambushes. I believe I was effective, but my advice was not heeded. I witnessed a needless defeat and many deaths of our soldiers. It could have been avoided. Colonel, fighting in the frontier is different than waging war on the continent. The most effective fighters in the battle were not the English or the French it was the Indians. Their clothing blended into the surroundings. They knew where to take cover and they knew how to be silent warriors. We should not wear red and we must not march in perfect files staying close together.

Although my scouting could have helped, we need more than a singular scout; we need many, because the route to Fort Duquesne is a big, well camouflaged area, with numerous areas for ambush. This brings me to my final thought. As I mentioned, there are always areas that are sites for ambushes. Why don't we occupy those sites in advance of the main troops?"

This thought received the, "Why didn't I think of that?" look from all the men present at the table. "Mr. Spyker," addressed William Pitt to Benjamin, "your ideas are sound and will be implemented. Although Colonel Bouquet will be the officer in charge, General John Forbes is in charge of the planning. I will instruct him of your advice and he will implement these ideas.

"I'm afraid," continued Secretary Pitt, "we have disgruntled your George Washington. General Forbes has decided and Colonel Banquet and I have agreed that we should use a different path to attack the fort. Previously we had used Fort Cumberland as a starting point, marched to Fort Necessity and then gone north across the Monongahela River toward Fort Duquesne. We are now going directly from Raystown, which is west of Philadelphia, straight west to Fort Duquesne. This is a more direct route. I also think General Forbes is a little superstitious and feels this will reverse our luck. Regardless, this is the route. Colonel Washington, although disagreeing, has assured us he will fully cooperate with General Forbes and his 'black cat' ideas."

The meeting concluded. Peter then took William Pitt and the Colonel to the Spyker home to meet his family and to spend the night before a full day of going to the homestead of some of the frontier soldiers. On the ride from the restaurant to his home, Peter had talked about his family. "We are really happy to have you gentlemen at our house tonight. My son, Benjamin, or Benny as we call him has been excited for days. He's heard so much about the 'Great Commoner,' as you, Mr. Pitt, are referred to in Benny's school. His teacher, Wilhelm Leininger is a stickler for details and has taught his students the history of the Pitt family. Benny can't wait to ask you about the diamond in your family and also to learn about your father. My wife Maria is also excited. You might have met her father, Gabriel Seidel, the well known architect in Philadelphia. She is used to political talk and will grill you on the plans for the war. I think she should have been a lawyer."

As they neared the house, Mr. Pitt was amazed, "Peter, what a beautiful house. I've not seen a house more beautiful in Philadelphia." Soon, out to meet them, was Benny. He hailed them and grabbed the reins of their horses. "Dad, I'll take the horses, sponge them down, and take them in the barn." Peter introduced Benny, "Mr. Pitt, Colonel Bouquet, this is my twelve- year-old son Benjamin, named after his uncle who was with us today. He's like him in many ways. Benny, like his uncle, is a good hunter and marksman. He can out-shoot me with gun or bow. When Benjamin was his age he held the record for the number of questions in an hour. Benny now has broken his record."

"Ah Dad, that's not true. How was the ride from the Seltzer? What did you have to eat at the Seltzer? Did Jacob ask about me? What's the name of Mr. Pitt's and Colonel Bouquet's horses? How's Old Conrad? Is he feeling any better? Was the creek in Womelsdorf frozen? Did you see any deer on the way? Did you see any turkeys? Did you see any pheasants?" Here Benny switched gears, "Dad, I shot two 'Tom' pheasants this morning. I used bow and arrow, so they don't have any shot in them. We're having them for dinner tonight."

"Son, put the horses away before they die of old age."

After a quick wash and stowing of their gear, Colonel Bouquet came down to the dining room. Not so Secretary Pitt. As usual he primped and dressed to the hilt. When he came down the stairs he was resplendent in his dress with powdered wig, laced shirt, and fine silk jacket. They all joined in the large dining room around a beautiful oak table, large enough for ten people. Maria had met each and given them her hand, which was elegantly kissed. They, as most men, were immediately attracted to Maria. William Pitt or Colonel Bouquet didn't need to say a word, but one could tell by the appreciative look in their eyes they thought she was stunning.

Previous to the arrival of her husband and his famous guests, Maria had instructed the children in proper behavior. "Benny, you can ask the questions you want, but not at the supper table. Son, I don't want to keep you from learning. I think some day you will be a teacher."

Maria knew she had no need to be concerned about her daughter Anna Elizabeth as she was becoming a charming young lady. Then Maria's thoughts turned to her seven-year-old Maria. "What do you do about a girl named Maria," kept running through her mind. She carefully instructed seven-year old Maria and six-year old Henry, how to address the gentlemen. "We say Mr. Pitt." She emphasized the t's as Maria had trouble with the t sound. "Now, the other guest is a famous soldier and we don't say Mister, but Colonel – like a kernel of corn. Then we say Boo – kay. Together let's say kernel boo–kay." They did well. Maria also strongly suggested that they only talk when being talked to. She had her doubts that this would work with little Maria as she was as outgoing as she herself had been at seven, and then forever.

Also at the table was George, who was two years old. He was in a tall chair, but as usual just wiggled and wiggled, and although he didn't talk, he leaned forward and looked constantly at the two guests. Little Maria did her best to keep George in line. She was the boss of George and Henry and frequently looked at each with stern looks. All looked eagerly at the fare in front of them, pheasant with wild rice. "Let's join hands and Peter would you say the prayer," said Maria who was obviously in charge within the household.

Peter gave the usual short family prayer, "Come Lord Jesus, be our guests, and let these gifts to us be blessed."

Before they started eating, William Pitt addressed Maria and the family. "Maria, you have a beautiful family. Thank you for letting us come to your house and your table. This is the reason we will defend these colonies. With families like this and men as resolute as your husband we cannot fail."

It wasn't long into the meal when little Maria could contain herself no longer, "Mr. Pith" she said with her seven year old lisp, "You are the most beautiful man I have ever seen. I wish I had a coat like that for my doll."

Mr. Pitt laughed and the others joined in. It was a wonderful occasion.

———— ✦ ————

The next morning at sunrise, Benny brought the horses around to the front for the men to start their reconnoitering journey among the frontier families. "Benny, saddle a horse for yourself. Mr. Pitt has insisted that you ride with us. He wants you to ride with him and ask him as many questions as you wish." Benny was thrilled, was gone in a flash, and then came out with a smaller roan horse ready to travel.

Benny enjoyed his question and answer ride. He learned about the famous Pitt diamond, which his father Thomas Pitt had purchased in India. It was four-hundred -ten carets and eighty-two grams in weight, the largest diamond ever discovered. His father had purchased it for twenty-thousand-four-hundred pounds and later sold it for one-hundred-thirty-five thousand pounds, making him one of the richest men in England. Because of this, he was always referred to as "Diamond" Pitt.

The visits throughout Tulpehocken and surrounding area went well. Colonel Bouquet understood the caliber of these frontiersmen and asked each to join his army in repelling the French from the Ohio Valley.

Their final visit was the most significant. "Gentlemen before we return to my house for dinner and a refreshing night's rest, I would like you to visit my father's household. My father brought us to America. Although he is not involved in politics, he is the most knowledgeable person I know regarding world politics. The house was built by my grandfather." Peter then identified the other members of the household told them about the tragedy that had resulted in their living together.

"My Grandfather Johannes is my namesake. Although we use different first names my grandfather, my father, and I are all Johannes Peter Spyker. Johannes, who passed away about twenty years ago, was one of the earliest Palatine settlers in Tulpehocken. He and our friend Conrad, who was with us yesterday led a settlement of Palatines from the Mohawk Valley to Tulpehocken in 1723."

It was a meeting that moved Colonel Bouquet to a final determination to drive the French and their allied Indians from the frontier of North America. The story of the Hartman family remained with Colonel Bouquet until the final surrender of the French in North America.

Peace in North America
1760

———

In 1760 the war for all practical purposes was over in North America. Fort Duquesne had been burned and vacated by the French in early 1758, Louisburg was captured in 1758 by General Amherst, and in 1759, Quebec fell to General Wolfe.

The army of the frontier, although never an official British army, continued to be called "The Frontier Army". Although it was not an official army, Colonel Bouquet and William Pitt considered the army as vital to the war effort. Conrad and Benjamin remained as the officers in charge.

Early in 1759, Conrad became ill and Benjamin became the colonel in charge of the army. When Colonel Bouquet felt confident that the Western Pennsylvania frontier was secure he asked Colonel Benjamin to march his Frontier Army to join the forces of Brigadier General Prideaux to march up the Mohawk River and attack Fort Niagara. Benjamin and his soldiers joined General Prideaux along with over one thousand Iroquois, who had remained loyal to the British. On July 25th, the French surrendered Fort Niagara. After the Fort Niagara battle, Colonel Benjamin and the Frontier Army continued north to Quebec. Quebec fell late in 1759, but Ben and his army could not depart for home until the April thaw. Finally in April, Benjamin returned to

Tulpehocken and his home thinking that he would never again face war.

When Benjamin returned he found his mentor, Conrad, very ill. On July 13, 1760 Conrad died. The funeral in Womelsdorf was the largest ever in frontier Pennsylvania and attracted dignitaries from all over. Conrad's wife Anna Eva had asked Benjamin to give the eulogy.

Benjamin looked over a sea of mourners on the Weiser farm in Womelsdorf. He could see George Washington, William Pitt, Colonel Bouquet, James Hamilton, Governor of Pennsylvania; Isaac Norris, still Speaker of the Pennsylvania Assembly, and many members of the assembly. Also off to the side was a contingent of Iroquois. He recognized the young Mohawk leader, Tagawininto, who was the son of Theyanoquin. Benjamin had met Theyanoquin when he had attended the Albany Convention in 1754. Theyanoquin had died at the hands of the French at the Battle of Lake George. The Iroquois loved Conrad Weiser as much as the Delaware hated him.

"Dear friends and family of Conrad Weiser. We are here to mourn a man of two great nations, America and Iroquois. There would be no Tulpehocken community without Conrad and my grandfather, Johannes. They settled the land and with Lomasi were able to live at peace with our Native Americans until the recent war. Even today, the Iroquois, who are with us today, are our friends because of Conrad.

"Our colonies and England made many demands on Conrad and he was away from his home and family much of his life. However, his first love was his family and his farm. He sought to be just a farmer, but England and the American colonies needed him to continually negotiate peace with the Native Americans as we invaded their land. He served as the great advisor to William Penn, Sir William Keith, Robert Morris, Benjamin Franklin and James Logan. After the brutal raids upon our home in 1754 he again left his farm and formed an army that became the finest warriors of this war. He saved Tulpehocken and the surrounding area, and caused the Delaware to leave our land. He did this while remaining a brother with the Iroquois.

"Because of his friendship, the Iroquois remained loyal to our country and have helped us bring peace in North America. Many of the Iroquois today have traveled great distances from the Mohawk Valley to be with us. Our obligation, now that Conrad is gone, is to maintain peace with the Iroquois. ... ."

Benjamin concluded his remarks with one last request, "I represent one nation. Now I would ask Tawagwininto son of the great Chief Theyanoquin, who was Conrad's brother among the Mohawks, to come forward and represent the Iroquois Nation. He has asked to say a few words."

Chief Tawagwininto came forward with Lomasi, who would interpret for him. He was brief but talked about his relationship with Conrad and the brotherhood between Conrad and Chief Theyanoquin. He concluded with a remark that seemed strange to Benjamin and might be an omen for the future. "We are at a great loss and sit in darkness. Now that our friend has died, we might not understand one another."

The Death of a Patriarch
1762

———⊰⊱———

IT WAS CHRISTMAS EVE, 1761. The tradition continued for the Spyker family. Peter's house was aglow for the celebration. Outside the house there were lit candles that would lead the guests from the road up the lane and into the Spyker house. As Peter, Maria, and the kids lit the candles, Peter chuckled remembering a conversation with Benjamin Franklin during his last visit to Philadelphia for an assembly meeting. Peter was still staying at the Seidels. The Seidels had invited Benjamin to a dinner party the night after the conclusion of the assembly meeting. As they sat around the table with many candles, Benjamin Franklin said, "One day candles on a dinner table will be for romantic reasons only." All had looked at Benjamin wondering what he could be talking about. "My friends look above you at the dark ceiling. One day, you will see globes glowing with electricity. You will think you are having dinner outside just before the noon hour."

Gabriel Seidel had replied, "Don't laugh at 'Poor Richard,'" an often used referral to Ben's writings when he wanted to thinly disguise himself. "Mr. Franklin has already called electricity down from the sky."

Maria brought Peter back to the moment, "Peter, I'm worried about Jonny. Your father really looks frail these days. When he comes this evening we must be sure he stays warm. I've assigned his princess Maria to shower him with love."

As was the case in the days of yore, the Spyker Christmas Eve party attracted not only family members but neighbors from the community and often famous people outside the community. This year Peter had invited a special guest from Philadelphia. The guest was one of the most well known figures in Pennsylvania history, Isaac Norris. Isaac was the Speaker of the Assembly and had held that position since 1751.

At the conclusion of the dinner, the usual wonderful feast, Peter asked all to gather in the large living room. He looked lovingly at the over twenty people who were in his home that night including his father and Regina, and his brother, whom he admired greatly. With eyes of love he glanced at Maria, his wife of twenty years. His eyes shifted to their children, Benny, who was fifteen and becoming a man. He was like his uncle in many ways, particularly related to his love for the outdoors. However, he was different than his uncle in that he had a love for school and education. Wilhelm the Tulpehocken school teacher, who was also there that evening, said that Benny was his best student and had often given him the responsibility of teaching the younger children.

He looked at his two daughters and broke into a full smile. Anna, who was thirteen was on the verge of becoming a woman, and Maria his youngest was vibrant and confident and like her mother, in charge of the world. As Peter continued to survey the group he saw his two young boys Henry, nine and George six, sitting with their grandfather and Regina. Jonny had his right arm abound Henry and his left arm around George. Both boys were comfortable in the arms of their grandfather. After surveying the guests, he focused on his father. As Maria had mentioned, Jonny was frail, but still with a full head of gray hair and sat in his usual relaxed demeanor.

"Thank you for being with us in this time honored event. The eve of the birth of Jesus. The Spykers have hosted Christmas Eve in Germany and now America since 1650 and probably before. We have with us tonight two honored guests. I'd like to introduce my 'boss', Isaac Norris and his wonderful wife Sarah. Isaac is the Speaker of the Assembly, which I am so humbly a part. Isaac has been the Speaker since 1751. His father, also Isaac, was one of the people who made the colony of Pennsylvania possible. He fought successfully to have William Penn released from jail when the royalty disagreed with his Quaker ways. His wife Sara is the daughter of James Logan, the magistrate that admitted Jonny, Benjamin, and me to America in 1737. Mr. Norris asked to be with us tonight and I was honored. He comes into our home to present a special award. Family, friends, let me present Isaac Norris."

Isaac thanked everyone. "The Spyker family is the first family of the Western Frontier..." He continued to extol the Spykers and then explained his purpose for being here. "Each year the assembly gives the 'William Penn' award. This award is for a person that has helped make Mr. Penn's 'Holy Experiment,' a success. Mr. Penn founded a colony, which was a free society, instead of a society that tells us how to worship and live. The 'William Penn' award goes to the person that Mr. Penn himself would have chosen. Just a little over two months ago in our closing session of the assembly, we had our nominations for the 'William Penn' award. Many well known names were presented. I was hoping my name would have been mentioned." Speaker Norris said it in such a fashion that everyone laughed. All, however, wondered where Mr. Norris was going with this speech.

He continued, after a sip of Spyker's Riesling wine, "Then a young, well respected young man stood up and told his story of coming to America. He told of the trials and tribulations, not only of coming to America, to Pennsylvania, and the Western Frontier, but of building a home and keeping it safe. He lovingly described the person responsible for his family's success, the success of Tulpehocken, the success of the Western Frontier, the success of Pennsylvania, and ultimately the success of America. He described a man that allowed himself to stay out of the public eye, but use his wisdom and his example to accomplish the successes mentioned. This year the Assembly of Pennsylvania has unanimously selected Johannes Peter Spyker, Jonny, for the 'William' Penn award."

All stood and applauded and cried and even sobbed. Regina helped Jonny to the front. He beamed and finally said a few words. "I am so proud of my family. My father, who was one of the first settlers in Tulpehocken, paved the way for the Spyker family. My sons, Peter and Benjamin protected our homes and have allowed us to live William Penn's dream. My grandchildren will keep this dream alive. Thank you Speaker Norris and please thank the assembly for their kindness."

⸎

The award and speech by Isaac Norris proved to be an eulogy for Jonny as he died peacefully with his family around him in early February, 1762. After the death of Jonny, Peter and Benjamin discussed with Lomasi the possibility of her moving in with the Peter Spyker family. "Lomasi," said Peter, "you, Regina, Magdelena, and Christian will fit wonderfully into our home. Benjamin and I are concerned that there is not a man in the house. Christian is eight years old, and I think needs a father figure with him."

Lomasi, although eighty years old was still strong and vital. She maintained a garden that was still the pride of Tulpehocken. "Peter, Benjamin, thank you for your kindness. However, this is the only home I have known since your grandfather and I left Schoharie. I want to stay here until my soul meets the Lord and the Great Spirit. You and Benjamin are here often doing the farming, so we are seldom without a good man. I've talked to Regina and Magdelena and they wish to stay here. Magdelena will some-day leave and start her own home, but she wishes to stay here until her daughter is back or forever gone."

Peter and Benjamin were worried but would never go against the will of Lomasi. Soon they came up with an idea. After much discussion with Maria and Benny, they deceided Benny would live with Lomasi. Benny was sixteen. He was responsible and he was able to make good decisions. Also Peter would spend time with Benny most every day and Marie would often have Benny spend part of the day with her and Benny's siblings. They lived just five kilometers apart.

The Peace Treaty of Paris
1763

— ❦ —

THE WAR WAS OVER IN North America, but it dragged on throughout the world until finally a peace treaty between England, France, and Spain was signed on February 10, 1763. Peter and all the assemblymen were called to Philadelphia in June by Speaker Isaac Norris to understand the peace treaty.

Speaker Norris addressed those measures directly effecting Pennsylvania and the American colonies. He had a large chart on the wall of the assembly room and went through each of these treaty decisions with deliberation:

*France will cede Canada and all North American claims east of the Mississippi to Britain, but not New Orleans.

*France will cede the Western Territory of Louisiana and New Orleans to Spain.

*Spain will cede Florida to Britain.

*England will cede back to France, Guadeloupe and Martinique

*England will cede back to Spain, Cuba and the Philippines

After a brief explanation of the salient points by Speaker Norris, hands shot up asking to be recognized. Norris recognized first a young gentleman from Ridley, Pennsylvania. "Mr. Speaker, John Morton, Chester County, Pennsylvania. I am confused. We, our

Mother country, England, won the war. Why are we giving all these concessions to Spain and to France?"

Others joined in with their concerns. Speaker Norris, addressed these concerns with his opinion. "We have a new king in England, King George III. He had great fear of William Pitt becoming too powerful and he feared England was losing her domination of us, the colonies. Thus he wanted the treaty signed quickly."

Soon other concerns came up which indicated the colonists were not happy with their Mother country. "Mr. Speaker, George Brady, representing the city of Philadelphia. The war is over. Now, please tell the king, to take his bloody redcoats back to London. We in Philadelphia are tired of housing them and housing them for free. They eat us out of house and home and they have no respect for our daughters."

Several other assemblymen also echoed the concerns of the English taking advantage of the colonists. "Mr. Speaker, Samuel Foulks from Bucks county. We suffered more in this war than any Englishman. We paid dearly for supplies and many of our men paid the ultimate price and now we are being asked to reimburse our Mother country for the war efforts. What is it I don't understand?"

Speaker Norris couldn't get the meeting finished fast enough. It was turning into a revolution. "The meeting is adjourned until our next regular meeting in October. Good day, gentleman."

When Peter arrived back at the Seidels, he had a guest. "Colonel Bouquet, how nice to see you."

"Peter, I haven't forgot my pledge to your family, particularly to Regina Spyker and her daughter, Magdelena. The peace on the frontier will not be settled until the Indians bring back all their White captives that they kidnapped in raids. Please know I will advise you when we have regained those kidnapped by the Indians.

I will want Magdelena to come to Fort Pitt, once Fort Duquesne, and see if she can find her child."

As Peter rode home the next morning to Tulpehocken he had many thoughts: *"Will we find Regina? Regina was just ten when she was kidnapped. She would now be eighteen. Would she recognize her mother? If she's alive, horrible things must have happened to her; would she be able to face life in our community?*

Then Peter's thoughts turned back to the meeting. *"Will we someday wish to break away from England? Is the Peace Treaty of Paris just a prelude to other wars?"*

Peter, upon arriving back in Tulpehocken, went immediately to his father's home to see Magdelena. "Magdelena, I have talked with Colonel Bouquet and he is insisting that peace will not be granted to the French or their Indian allies in our country until all White captives are returned. He will notify me when the captives have been returned. It will take probably a year, but at that time he would want you to come to Fort Pitt to see if Regina is among the returned captives."

When Peter left to return to his home, Regina held Magdelena. "My darling daughter, I know you want Regina to be alive and in good health. We must pray for this, but also pray that if Regina is not found, our Lord will look after her."

The Paxton Boys
1763

———— ∞ ————

THE PAXTON BOYS WERE FROM Paxtang, Pennsylvania and probably should have been called the Paxtang Boys. They are not to be confused with the Paxton family who was massacred in the Tulpehocken area. Paxtang is about a three hour horse ride directly west of Tulpehocken.

The group of about two-hundred-fifty men was led by a preacher, Reverend John Elder. They were settlers at the base of the Blue Mountains on the Susquehanna River. They, as was true in Tulpehocken and other Western Frontier settlements, had suffered atrocities from the hands of the Indians during the Indian raids of the French and Indian War. However, the Spykers and Weisers were aware that many of the Native Americans, like the Iroquois, were not responsible for the Indian massacres.

"The Paxton Boys" believed an Indian was an Indian and the world would be better off without them. "Dear Congregation," raged the Reverend John Elder from the pulpit one Sunday morning in December of 1763, "we have been wronged by savages. They must die for their sins." He went on a tirade for almost an hour and then concluded his mad ramblings, pulling his rifle from behind the pulpit, and raising it above his head, "We will kill all the Indians in our area and all the way to Philadelphia. Who is with me?"

The first target was against a local Conestoga tribe who lived on land given them by William Penn since 1690. They were Christian and lived peacefully with settlers from the Palatines. After the hateful sermon of the Reverend Elder, the "Paxton Boys" with revenge in their heart attacked the defenseless Conestoga. They killed and scalped and completed their "victory" by burning down the camp.

The Reverend and the Paxton Boys attacked other Indians in their area and were able to claim over twenty scalps. With the "thrill of victory" and blood in their eyes they prepared to take their conquest to Philadelphia, where there were over one-hundred-forty protected Indians.

Before they decided to march on any and all Indians in their path to Philadelphia, they canvassed the Western Pennsylvania frontier to see who was "with them". The Reverend Elder and two of his Scots-Irish, Calvinist congregation traveled to Tulpehocken. He had heard about Benjamin Spyker and wanted the great Indian fighter on his side. Not knowing which was the Benjamin Spyker house they approached the house of Lomasi Spyker.

———— ✿ ————

Lomasi was amazingly spry for her eighty one years. She was admired by everyone in Tulpehocken. Lomasi was with her grandson, John Henry. John Henry loved to visit both Lomasi and his big brother Benny. They were the only ones home at the time of the visit by the "Paxton Boys." Benny, who was living with Lomasi, had left for a short hunting excursion to get a nice fat rabbit for his grandmother Lomasi to fix for their meal.

Lomasi saw three men approaching the house and was curious, but had no fear, as the men alit from their horses. They knocked and Lomasi answered with, "Greetings, welcome to the Spyker home. How can I help you?"

"Maam, I'm the Reverend John Elder of Paxtang over the Blue Mountain way. We're looking for Benjamin Spyker, the famous Indian killer."

The words 'Indian killer' did not sit well with Lomasi. "You must be talking about my grandson, who did defend us against the Delaware, but is a friend of all peaceful Native Americans. He's not here and I think it best that you depart from my house."

"You look like an Indian. Are you an Indian?" said the Reverend.

"I'm a Native American, an Iroquois to be exact, but I am also the widow of Johannes Peter Spyker, the mother of Jonny Spyker, now deceased, and the grandmother of Benjamin, the gentlemen you are seeking. I am also the grandmother of Peter Spyker, Magistrate of Tulpehocken. I am also a Christian. You say you are a reverend, are you not a Christian?"

"I am a Christian and I have been chosen by God to rid this country of heathen savages. We were hoping to have Benjamin Spyker join us in our path to Philadelphia. We are going to kill all Indians in our path and when we arrive in Philadelphia, we will convince the governor to assist us in this "holy" war. You are a heathen savage and you have no right to our America." At this the Reverend held his rife on Lomasi and said, "Come with us."

Lomasi was terrified and tried to close the door, but Reverend John Elder put his boot in the way and his two compatriots came at his command, "Bind this savage. We will take her to Paxtang and hang her in our church. She will be a sacrifice to our Lord and our God."

John Henry was standing behind his grandmother. When he saw his grandmother threatened, he sprang from the doorway and tried to tackle the interloper. Reverend Elder laughed and knocked him down with a hard swipe of his right hand, but he came right back and tried again to protect his grandmother. This time the Reverend swung his rife around and knocked him to the ground where he laid in a daze.

Benny saw the commotion at his grandmother's house and wondered who the three men were. First he saw the rough treatment of his grandmother and then he saw his brother fall from a gun swipe. Benjamin wanted to charge with his rifle, but then realized the necessity of using a rational approach. He dropped down and flattened himself out on the ground and crawled to the barn. Here he gained his bow and arrow and still retained his rifle. When he saw the men start to drag Lomasi to their horse, he shot an arrow through the shoulder of one of the men. The man fell with pain as the other two searched desperately for the Indian who had attacked them.

Reverend John, grabbed Lomasi, "See what your dirty savage brothers have done to my friend. This is why we must rid America of Indians. We simply came in peace to get the help of Benjamin Spyker and we find that Indians have taken over his home, but hopefully not his mind. One of your savages has wounded a God-fearing man."

While the Reverend's friend writhed on the ground the third member of the "peaceful" recruiting delegation approached Lomasi with a knife. As he reached to grab her long hair, an arrow whistled through the air and struck him between the shoulder blades. Now with Lomasi firmly in his grip the Reverend whirled around and around looking for the silent Indian. He had his rifle poised to defend himself. All of a sudden from nowhere came a rifle under his chin. *"My God,"* thought Reverend John, *a White boy, just a boy. Why would he be using bow and arrows? Why would he be defending an Indian?"*

"I don't know who you are mister, but you better get your friends on their horses and leave this part. As soon as I tell my uncle Benjamin Spyker about your attack on Lomasi, he will hunt you down and kill you. No one comes into our home and threatens my grandmother or threatens any of our Native American friends."

The Reverend left, helping his wounded friend on his horse and laying his dead companion over his horse and headed back to Paxtang. After making sure they were out of gun sight, Benny knelt down by his brother. John Henry was just becoming aware of what happened to him and had a swollen jaw and cheek.

When Regina and Magdelena returned to the house they found Benny consoling Lomasi, who was confused, but stoic in countenance. John Henry held a bag of ice to his swollen jaw. Benny told the story of the visit by the Reverend John Elder and some of the Paxton boys. Lomasi hugged Benny. He saved my life. He is amazingly brave and John Henry had no fear when they tried to take me away."

"Benny," Regina said while scanning the horizon, "ride to your dad's house and your uncle's house and ask them to come quickly. We may be in danger."

When Peter and Benjamin arrived they decided to have Benjamin and Benny stay to protect the family and have Peter ride to Philadelphia to alert the city and the government about the danger. There were sheltered Indians in Philadelphia that the Paxtons threatened to massacre.

Peter had Lomasi and her household, along with Benjamin, Henry, and Benny go to his house, and left immediately for Philadelphia. He did not stop until he arrived at the home of Benjamin Franklin. Franklin was the one person in the Pennsylvania government that Peter knew he could trust to stop a massacre of the Indians.

The governor was now John Penn. Governor Penn and Benjamin Franklin both wanted to stop the potential massacre. Governor Penn however did not want to lose the political support of the many followers of Calvin. The end result was that the governor agreed to hear the complaints of the Paxton Boys. He listened to them and agreed not to bring charges against the leaders of the mob, nor to stop them in their efforts to scalp Indians away from Philadelphia.

Although the Philadelphia massacre was averted and the mob disbanded, it was a dark day for Pennsylvania and America as it set the stage for the future treatment of the Native Americans.

Peter returned home and he and Benjamin Spyker now understood the statement made by the Iroquois at the funeral of Conrad Weiser, *'We are at a great loss and sit in darkness. Because he had died we might not understand one another.'*

Benjamin Franklin and the assembly, which was still dominated by peace-loving Quakers, were incensed by the decision made by the governor. Peter received a letter from Benjamin Franklin, thanking Peter for alerting him to the mob plans of the Paxton mob. Mr. Franklin concluded the letter with, "These things bring John Penn and his government into sudden contempt. All regard for the governor by the assembly is lost. All hopes of happiness under a proprietary government are at an end."

Regina Hartman
1764

AFTER THE PAXTON AFFAIR, THINGS settled down in Tulpehocken and all awaited the time when Colonel Bouquet would secure all the White captives from the Delaware. Lomasi's home with three generations although unusual, was a contented family. Benny was a big-brother figure to Christian, Magdelena's son, who was ten-years old. They had a wonderful relationship and Christian was becoming like Benny a good outdoorsman and an excellent student in Herr Leininger's school. Every Sunday the Spykers got together. They rode together on fine carriages to the "Church on the Ridge" to listen to Reverend Schmidt thank the Lord for His bounty. He was not the "fire and brimstone" preacher like his father. Reverend Filip always asked his congregation to forgive the French and anyone else that had, "transgressed against them". After the service, Reverend Schmidt would join the Spykers at one of the homes, Lomasi's, Peter's, the grandest home in the frontier; or the log cabin of Benjamin and Margaret Spyker.

These Sundays were grand affairs with wonderful Pennsylvania Dutch food prepared lovingly by all the women. While Sunday dinner was being prepared, the three men, which included a precocious Benny, who was now sixteen, talked politics, or farming, or particularly in the case of Benjamin and Benny, hunting and fishing. All seemed oblivious to the Peter Spyker children and Christian chasing each over the house or in good weather outside. As usual, Maria would come to give a report to her mother, "Mom, George and Christian are 'transgressing again.'"

At the dinner table when all were quiet they had a prayer and Reverend Schmidt always added, "Dear Lord if it be thy will, bring our child Regina back to our fold."

Finally the word arrived that hundreds of kidnapped children from the Western lands would be brought to Fort Pitt on September 13, 1764. Peter took Regina and Magdelena to Fort Pitt. The children, now many of them adults, were lined up on the parade ground and many happy reunions took place. There was no Regina. Magdelena, for the first time gave up hope and all rode silently back to Tulpehocken to try to forget her pain.

Just a week later, a rider came to Peter's house with a note from Colonel Bouquet. They had located fifty more captives. They would be brought to Carlisle, Pennsylvania, and be available for hopeful recognition on September 30. Peter rode to Jonny's house with the news.

"Oh, Peter," said Magdelena, "I'm not sure I can go through this again." However, soon with her mother's and Lomasi's counseling, Magdelena decided to go. She had little hope in her heart as she, Regina, and Peter traveled the three hour carriage ride to Carlisle.

The returned captives were again, as at Fort Pitt, lined up for a number of families to view. Colonel Bouquet was also there and escorted Magdelena up and down the line. There was no recognition in the eyes of Magdelena nor in any eyes of the captive White children, or adults, as now was the case in many circumstances. "My daughter is not here," she tearfully told Colonel Bouquet.

"Look again," said the Colonel.

"No," insisted Magdelena, "my daughter is not here."

"Isn't there some special way you could recognize her? A mark of some kind?"

"No," said Magdelena, "my daughter was perfect, unblemished in any way."

Colonel Bouquet kept being insistent. "Your daughter would have changed greatly in these eight years. She left you as a girl and now she would be a young women. "Perhaps a word, or a song that she would recognize?"

Magdelena had one last hope and she thought, *"I'll sing our song and then I'll forget forever my hopes of Regina's return."*

In a soft voice she started to sing, but feeling foolish, stopped quickly. "No, no," insisted Colonel Bouquet, "go on, go on."

"Allein, und doch nicht ganz allein; Bin ich in meiner Einsamkeit; Denn wenn ich ganz verlassen scheine,

An Indian girl, Sawquehanna, not always an Indian girl, but so long ago she barely remembered, heard the song, and it awakened a deep seated memory. Sawquehanna ran from the line toward her mother and joined in the song, *"Vertzeih mir Jesus selbst die Zeit; Ich bin bei Ihm und Er bei mir, So kummt mir gar nichs ein.–"He comes the weary hours to cheer, I am with Him and He with me, Even here alone I cannot be."* Regina was home.

This is based on a story from "The Life of Conrad Weiser" by Reverent C.Z. Weiser, 1899 publication.

The Passing of Lomasi
1765

———⊗⊗⊗———

IT WAS A STRANGE COLLECTION of people at the "Church on the Ridge". Reverend Paul Kurtz was now the pastor of the Aspach Lutheran Church. Filip Schmidt was retired, but he and his wife lived within view of "his" church. Filip was now eighty years old. He sat in the church on this afternoon in March, 1765 and wondered how the Lord had created such an amazing coincidence in his life. Reverend Paul Kurtz was the son of William Kurtz who was the pastor who took over for him in Aspach when he decided to emigrate to America in 1737. Reverend Kurtz was actually the pastor of two churches, one of which was just a few kilometers away in the settlement where Peter had his home.

Although Filip was sad as he viewed the body of Lomasi Spyker, he was sure that she was already in the hands of the Lord. Lomasi had died peacefully just after her eighty-fourth birthday. The church was filled for the funeral for the matriarch of Tulpehocken. Reverend Filip would be conducting the funeral ceremonies. Filip sat in the back with his wife close to the casket. While waiting for the ceremonies Filip enjoyed "the people watching" of all who came to honor Lomasi.

It was an auspicious crowd of Spykers and friends and acquaintances of Lomasi, including all the sons and daughters of Conrad

Weiser. It was interesting to see Conrad's daughter, Anna Marie with her husband Henry Muhlenberg. Oh how Reverend Schmidt admired Henry Muhlenberg. Henry was considered the "Father of Lutheranism" in Pennsylvania. The Lutheran churches, like Filip's, were isolated from one another. Henry Muhlenberg had formed the Lutheran Synod in Pennsylvania, giving churches like Filip's, a central organization. Henry had also unified the liturgy and basic beliefs of the Lutheran Synod. Many of the hymns in Filip's church were those consolidated by Henry. He couldn't wait to talk with him.

Lomasi's family of Regina, Magdelena and now young Regina, came walking arm in arm and all sobbing gently. It took many months for young Regina to adapt to life in a White community after her captivity with the Delaware. Regina's mother and grandmother with their constant love and patience helped immensely. But Lomasi, with her knowledge of Native American life had been the one most instrumental in helping Regina feel comfortable in the Tulpehocken culture. Young Regina had lost a dear friend and she was visibly sad.

"Just look at Regina," thought Filip, *"she is so beautiful. There will be many men vying for her hand. I just hope she marries a good Lutheran. No, Lord, just make that a good Christian and a good man."*

Filip continue to muse out loud as each person he recognized came to the casket and kneeled to pay their respects to Lomasi. "Filip," said Sara, his wife, "It's okay to talk to yourself, but must you also answer yourself?"

"There's the good doctor Jacob Lentz and his wife. Jacob has kept us all as healthy as possible over the years. He was holding the hand of Lomasi when she passed. His oldest son, Jacob, looks just like him. He's going to school in Philadelphia to be a doctor. I pray he comes back to Tulpehocken to help his father and some day take over for him. I wonder who he keeps looking at. Ah ha, it's young Regina." Filip was really enjoying his conversation with himself.

Walking solemnly past Filip, was a very tall native American, it was Chief Tagawininta. He was chief of the Mohawk tribe, once Lomasi's tribe. With him were a number of other Mohawk, both men and women. Although Lomasi was gone from the tribe many years, she was still a legend and still one they depended on to communicate with the White man.

Reverend Schmidt also noticed a Native American separate from the Mohawk. *"I wonder who he is and why he isn't with the rest of the Native Americans?"*

Benjamin Spyker was sitting with his wife, Anna Eve, head bowed and thinking about the years he had spent with Lomasi. He also noticed the singular Indian. Something about him seemed familiar. The Indian was not an Iroquois, most likely a Delaware, thought Benjamin. For some reason both were focused on each other. "Oh my God, it's Kitchi, my once great friend, my brother," said Benjamin to his wife. Benjamin stood and walked directly to Kitchi coming down the aisle. They looked at each other for a long time and then went forward and threw their arms around each other. "Kitchi, so long ago."

"Dear Demothi, I wondered if I should come. I loved Lomasi so much, but I knew the Delaware were not welcome in Tulpehocken."

They had a chance to talk. Kitchi explained that he was driven out of the tribe, because he refused to go on the attacks of the White man. He and his wife and son had left with others who did not want to go to war. They had settled in the Ohio Valley between the Little and the Great Miami Rivers. Kitchi had a trading station and had learned of Lomasi's death from an Indian trader from Tulpehocken. As they parted, Benjamin promised to come to Kitchi's home in the near future. It was a renewed friendship that would last until death. Funerals had a way of bringing friends back together.

There was a delegation from Philadelphia at the funeral. Peter through his long service in the assembly, had made good friends who had visited him in Tulpehocken. They each had met Lomasi and had the opportunity to talk with her about Native American relations. They all were together and dressed in fine suits. Filip knew some of them as they had joined Peter for Sunday services in "his" church.

Isaac Norris, now sixty-four years old, was still Speaker of the Assembly although this would be his last year. He had met Lomasi at the time of the 'William Penn' award presentation to Jonny and then had returned for the funeral of Jonny.

John Morton was Peter's best friend in the assembly. Peter had gone several times to John's home in Chester county and had taken Maria there as well. They usually got together at least once a year for a social occasion. John was forty-years old and had been in the assembly for over ten years. Because he chaired the committee on Native American Affairs, he had visited Lomasi a number of times. Each time John gave a committee presentation he always started out with "Lomasi says." Whenever, Isaac recognized John, he would say to the laughter of the body, "And what does Lomasi say today?"

George Bryan was the firebrand of the assembly. George was from Ireland and had a typical Irish temperament and brogue. At least once every meeting he would state a complaint about the English Parliament. His typical dialog would be, "They have no respect for us. They only care about what we can do for them. You can hear them say, 'what can we sell those farmers today? How can we squeeze another dollar out of their pocket?' I think it's time for – no I can't say it, but I've had it up to my neck."

Walking with George Bryan was Thomas Willing, Mayor of Philadelphia. Thomas had served in the assembly until 1763 when he became mayor. Although good friends, Thomas Willing and George Bryan disagreed often in the assembly. Thomas was very supportive of the British until the final days before the Declaration of Independence in 1774. When his friend, George Bryan, stood to congratulate him on being chosen mayor, he had said, "Finally, my friend, we have found a way to get rid of you."

Both Thomas and George and their wives had met with Peter and Maria each St. Patrick's Day in Philadelphia and then they all had gathered once a year in the summer at Peter's house in Tulpehocken. Both had visited Lomasi each time they came to Tulpehocken. George would always say in his exaggerated Irish brogue, "Ah, Lomasi, you are wise beyond your years." Lomasi would answer with a twinkle in her eye, "Does that make me one-hundred-and- ten?"

The last member of the delegation was unfamiliar to Filip. He was obviously a close acquaintance to Isaac Norris as he assisted him in walking down the aisle. Speaker Norris had been in ill health and walked with a cane. Filip could not help his curiosity as he leaned forward and tapped Benjamin Spyker on the shoulder. "Ben, who's that distinguished gentleman with Speaker Norris?"

Ben turned to Filip and whispered, "That's John Dickinson. He's also in the assembly with Peter. This is his first year. He's the son-in-law of Isaac Norris. He's here mainly to be with the Speaker as Isaac is in poor health. Filip, I should also mention he and Benjamin Franklin are at odds right now on Franklin's representation of Pennsylvania in London. Mr. Dickinson is very out-spoken. He doesn't think Franklin should represent Pennsylvania since he is at odds with Thomas Penn. John, like Thomas Willing, are two of the strongest supporters of King George and the English government."

All quieted as the pall bearers closed the casket and carried it to the front of the church at the foot of the altar. Peter, Benjamin, Benny, Samuel Weiser, Dr. Jacob Lentz, and Jacob Seltzer were the pall bearers. Reverend Schmidt, assisted by Reverend Paul Kurtz, conducted the ceremonies. It was as expected a reverent service. The service was highlighted by two songs. Magdelena and young Regina sang their family song, they sang in German, *Allein und doch nicht anz alleine...* .

At the end of the service, Chief Tagawininta came forward to the top of the altar area. He towered over both Reverend Schmidt and Reverend Kurtz. After several moments of silence he faced the casket and then turned to face the congregation, and began singing in a powerful and clear voice: *"Wleyuti tan tel-wltag; Kisi-wsitawjimk; Newt Keskaiap, Nike wejimk; Nek a pikwaisp nike welapi.*

"Wleyuti kisi-kinamatk nkamlamun. Ag pa kisikne walik; ank-mayiw ikaq wleyuti; teli-ngasek ketlamsitm."

As many in the church recognized the tune, they sang the rest of the verses along with Chief Tagawininta in their native tongue, both German and English: *"Twas grace that taught my heart to fear, and grace my fears relieved. How precious did that grace appear the hour I first believed.*

Amazing grace how sweet the sound that saved a wretch like me. I once was lost, but now am found, was blind but now I see. . ."

The Stamp Act
1765

This is the stamp that went on many legal documents
indicating a tax had been paid to the English government.

WEDDINGS AND FUNERALS WERE A time of gathering and reminiscing, but also a time of politics. The funeral of Lomasi was no exception. After the funeral, many gathered at the Peter Spyker house. Soon the talk started about the strained relationship with England.

Very quickly the talk among the men sitting in Peter's parlor, with cigars puffing away and most with a glass of stout or the Spyker's wine, turned to the Stamp Tax which had been passed by

Parliament in February, 1765. It was to take effect on November 1, 1765. The Stamp Tax was a duty placed on all legal documents in the colonies. Its purpose was to help defray the cost and the immense debt for the French and Indian War. Once taxes were paid, a stamp was placed on documents such as newspapers, liquor licenses, calendars, almanacs, certificates, diplomas, wills, and even decks of cards. If it was printed and circulated in the colonies it was taxed and stamped.

Naturally the Irishman George Bryan was the first to stir the pot. "If I came to your home and put a roof on your house and after completion, you looked at it and say 'very well done, thank you. Now you must pay me for putting up my roof.' What would you say?"

Benny, who was becoming old enough to participate in "men's talk", piped up right away. "I'd say, you must be 'blarney' to use your Irish expression. Then I'd ask my dad to sue you."

"That's telling him, Benny." said Benjamin with a wink to his nephew.

"Alright," continued George. "Let's say I gave my wagon, horses and food to help you defeat the French. And let's say that I also went with your officers to fight the war, and then when the war was over, you taxed me for giving my wagon, horse, food and soldiering to defeat your enemy, what would you say?"

Everyone quickly saw where the Irishman was going. "Well said," said John Morton. "You're obviously referring to the damnable Stamp Tax that's just been passed by Parliament. I feel it has one sole purpose, to squeeze money out of us colonists."

"My concern," said Speaker Isaac in a weak quiet voice, "is that we have a representative body that is willing to listen to the King and Parliament, but this tax came as a direct order. Why didn't the King and Parliament send the request to the legislatures, like our assembly, and let us debate and then if we find merit, approve the request. I fear we are having less say over our Pennsylvania affairs than ever before."

"I don't disagree with what has been said about the Stamp Tax, but I think it is important that we understand that we are colonies of the British empire. We can express our opinions but in the end we must respect and keep peace with our Mother county." No one was surprised by this statement by Thomas Willing.

"Gentlemen," said the distinguished looking John Dickinson, "Most of you know that I am loyal to the king. However, I disagree with the Stamp Tax because this is the first tax levied on us internally. Previously, the taxes were on trade from England to us and our trade to them. These were tariffs, which I cannot disagree with. However, this internal tax should only have come as a result, as mentioned by Speaker Norris, of our representative bodies approving such a tax. I also agree with Mr. Willing. We can only appeal to Parliament for justice, to repeal the Stamp Tax. We cannot let this destroy our loyalty to England. I fear some are getting too violent in their disapproval. A couple incidents recently have caused me to fear violence. In Massachusetts James Otis, a member of their assembly stood up in protest of the Stamp Act, and said 'taxation without representation is tyranny.' In Virginia a young man with a fiery temperament and fiery red hair stood up in the Virginia Legislature in opposition to this tax saying 'give me liberty or give me death.' I think debate is healthy, but we must express our disapproval in a respectful manner."

Peter had listened intently to each person. Finally he decided to give his opinion. "John, I know you are not presently in agreement with my friend Benjamin Franklin, but I think he made the most sense when he organized the Albany Congress. The colonies need to work together. Do you remember his drawing published in the *Gazette* of a snake cut into many pieces, "Join or Die?" I think the colonies need to meet together and talk about a plan of action."

The discussion continued, even getting heated, but quickly subsided when Margaretha had her daughter Maria, now thirteen, come into the parlor and announced dinner. Maria, always, the precocious comedian, came in holding her throat and faking a cough as if she was choking on cigar smoke and ordered everyone to dinner. With her antics all regained their good spirits and proceeded to the abundant Spyker buffet.

Pennsylvania Says Yes

1765

In September, 1765, Peter again went to Philadelphia for the assembly meeting. Although sad, that his father could no longer join him for his checker battles against Theodore Schnapps, he was glad to have his brother Benjamin with him. Benjamin was becoming very involved in the politics of Pennsylvania and the colonies. Whereas Peter was conservative, not wanting to ruffle the feathers of England, Benjamin was leaning toward independence. George Washington had contacted Benjamin by post and asked if he could come to Philadelphia and meet him and a friend. He wished to discuss military ideas between the two colonies, Virginia and Pennsylvania. Since the conclusion of the French and Indian War, Colonel Washington had kept a correspondence with Benjamin. He felt that Benjamin Spyker would be a man who could help the colonies form a united and competent military.

Gabriel Seidel had passed away and the Spykers now stayed in a fashionable hotel in Philadelphia, the Rittenhouse. It was the hotel where most of the out-of-town representatives stayed and often was a prelude to the order of business for the assembly. As at the reception after the Lomasi funeral, the Spykers, John Morton, George Bryan, John Dickinson, and several others got together after dinner and a few pints, for some "politicking".

"Peter," said John Dickinson, "I keep thinking about your thoughts of a union of colonies. I find myself more in agreement every day. I should also tell you that I have conversed extensively with your friend, Benjamin, and now understand his philosophy in representing our assembly in London. I think he initially tried to persuade Parliament not to establish the Stamp Tax by simply reasoning with them. I misunderstood his intentions and now we are one in agreement. I'm still loyal, but want to use the persuasion of the majority to help Parliament and the king to see the error of their ways."

Slowly it seemed all the representatives of the Pennsylvania Assembly were seeing themselves as Americans rather than British colonists.

The assembly opened its fall, 1765 session. Joseph Fox was the Speaker after the resignation of Isaac Norris. Joseph was a representative of the city of Philadelphia. Although from a Quaker family, he broke ties with many in his family when he supported the French and Indian War. Speaker Fox pounded the gavel, but the representatives were too involved in discussing the Stamp Act, which was to take effect in just a little over a month. Once again he pounded the gavel, "Gentlemen, gentlemen, Please, we have important business to address. You will have the opportunity for orations in due time as this is a representative body and each of you is an equal."

The crash of the gavel again brought the representatives to a respectful silence. "Gentlemen, before we begin our usual order of business I have a letter delivered to me from the Massachusetts assembly. It is ably written by James Otis. It is a call to action. Mr. Otis is an assemblyman from Massachusetts and author of many important tracts defining the role of government. Most notably he has recently authored "The Rights of the British Colonies Asserted and Proved" with the powerful statement, 'Whenever the administrators, in any of those forms, deviate from truth, justice and equity, they verge towards tyranny, and are to be opposed.' I read the following from Mr. Otis:

'My dear representatives of the Pennsylvania Colony. We, the Massachusetts Assembly, have calmly discussed the essence of the Stamp Act, passed by the English Parliament. We have agreement that taxes in the past were tolerable because they were external taxes mainly based upon our imports and exports from our mother country. This is a tax, which is totally internal, a tax on our documents with the stipend going directly to England, without benefit to the colonies.

It is not only that this is an internal tax that we have opposition, but that it is a tax levied on a free people without their consent. I personally feel, as I have stated, 'taxation without representation is tyranny.'

We feel this is an issue which affects all thirteen colonies. We the Massachusetts Assembly believe that through a consolidated effort, we might be able to convince the Parliament that this type of tax and this type of unilateral decision is not in the best interest of the colonies or England.

We invite representatives of the Pennsylvania Assembly to meet in collaboration with the Massachusetts and New York Assemblies and as many colony representatives as possible, October 5, 1765. The meeting will commence at 9:00 A.M. at New York City Hall. We would suggest that you send your Speaker and three other representatives. Please advise us of your decision at the earliest.

I am your honorable servant, James Otis.

P.S. Please note that if this letter was sent November 1, 1765 or later, it would include a stamp indicating we had paid a tax to England.' "

After the reading of the letter there was an extensive silence. Finally, Speaker Fox opened the floor. "My fellow representatives, what say you? Should we be involved in this conference realizing our King George III and Prime Minister Grenville will look disparagingly on this action? Do I have a motion? If not, this issue will die for lack of interest."

Very quickly, the outspoken Irishman, George Bryan rose to his feet. "Mr. Speaker, here is my motion. 'The Pennsylvania Assembly in their representation of the citizens of Pennsylvania will send delegates to this Stamp Act Congress'. "

"Thank you Mr. Bryan for your surprising motion," said the Speaker with a wry smile. "Do we have a second to the motion?" Many hands flew up and the motion was seconded and opened for discussion. The Speaker set the rules. "We will have discussion until each one of you have the opportunity to voice your opinion. At the conclusion of discussion, we will have a vote. Based upon our rules, any action which involves also our Mother country will require a two-third majority for approval."

The discussion ensued. Surprisingly all seemed in favor. Finally after the lunch break, came an unpredictable response which ended the discussion.

"Mr. Thomas Willing, you are recognized."

"Mr. Speaker, fellow assemblymen, you have always known that I am a loyal to England and his majesty, King George III. However, the Stamp Act is not in the best interest of our colony nor of our England. It is my hope that an aggressive action like the assertive discussion of the Stamp Act Congress will cause our King and Parliament to realize the repeal of this act will help maintain our loyalty. I feel Pennsylvania should send representatives to this congress."

Then the Speaker closed the discussion, "We will have a secret ballot vote and there will be no names denoted in the minutes as to do so might cause recriminations from our Prime Minister."

All voted. When all secret ballots were opened and tallied, Speaker Fox rose to give the results. "I have counted thirty six ayes and zero nays. It is unanimous."

There was no spontaneous reaction as all realized the seriousness of their action. This was only the second attempt to unify the colonies in a collective action. The Albany Congress, although establishing the possibility of unified action, had failed because of the fear of each colony losing their individual power.

Speaker Fox then said, "Immediately after the adjournment for today's session, I will meet with the Ways and Means Committee and tomorrow you will know the three delegates that will join with me in the Stamp Act Congress. We are adjourned until 9:00 tomorrow."

That night at the Rittenhouse Hotel, the representatives enjoyed a lively conversation of the pros and cons of the coming Stamp Act Congress. Peter always listened and rarely got into the lively discussion, but always had a cogent comment that usually drew nods of agreement. "I think it good that we gather and have a cohesive statement. One person's opinion or even one colony's opinion will not even draw a rebuttal, but if we have a large majority of the colonies making a statement, Parliament will take notice and must make a response."

Just as others were wanting to make a comment in support of Peter, in walked three gentlemen, one was well-known to all, one was known to many, and the third was at best a mystery guest. "Benjamin," said Peter, "I was hoping you would join us to night. It's wonderful to see George Washington as well. Why don't you introduce your friends?"

Peter and Benjamin, gave each other a brief hug and Ben said, "Thanks for letting us crash your discussion. We just heard about Pennsylvania's decision to send representatives and we have come to lend support, at least moral support, to this courageous decision. I'm sure all of you are familiar with the Commander of the Virginia military and representative of the Virginia Legislature, Colonel George Washington. I'll let George introduce our cohort."

George Washington had a presence that seemed to awe all the assemblymen. "Thank you Benjamin. We, Benjamin and I, and this gentleman, Patrick Henry have had a couple of days of discussion, considering a cohesive action as well, which I will brief you on after I introduce Patrick. Some of you are familiar with Mr. Henry's famous statement in our Virginia Assembly when discussing the Stamp Act. He is the one who declared, 'Give me Liberty or give me Death'. Patrick", said George Washington as he turned to him, "I think once Prime Minister Grenville hears your statement, you might well get your wish."

At this all laughed. Patrick Henry then responded in typical fiery fashion. "Dammit, George, I don't want a fight. I just want the opportunity for us to have the same representation in Parliament as my family members who still live in Scotland. We are equals, we are British. Why in God's name are we treated like servants? We the representatives of the Virginia Colony will not even get the opportunity that you in Pennsylvania have. We are forbidden by our Royal Governor to attend the Congress. My friend from Massachusetts has said it best, 'taxation without representation is tyranny.'" As he spoke, Patrick Henry's face became redder and redder and it seemed his bright red hair was on fire.

George put his arm around Mr. Henry and said, "Calm down Patrick, peaceful dialog will serve us best." With that George Washington explained the meeting he held with Benjamin Spyker and his young friend from Virginia. "Thank you for this opportunity to talk with you. After the French and Indian war, I have come to the conclusion that we, the thirteen colonies, need not only a unified body of representation, but a unified military force. I wanted to talk with Benjamin as he has an excellent military mind. I'm going to continue to talk with other military leaders in each colony and if I can get a consensus, I will travel to London and try to convince the King and Parliament of the need for a colonial army. We someday will again be threatened by the French and I think also the time will come when Spain will be a threat to England and her colonies."

There seemed to be a general agreement to George Washington's idea. The conversations of both his idea and the Stamp Act took them well into the night.

Speaker Fox opened the second day of the 1765 Pennsylvania Assembly. "The Ways and Means committee have chosen the three representatives to the Stamp Act Congress. When I call your name, please advise me if you will be able to fulfill this appointment. George Bryan, Representative of Philadelphia city. How say you?"

"Mr. Speaker, members of the committee, thank you for this great honor. I will be in attendance."

"John Morton, Representative of Chester County."

"Thank you and I will serve at the pleasure of the Assembly."

"John Dickinson, Representative of the County of Philadelphia"

"Thank you Mr. Speaker, Assembly, I will represent this body and inform you well of each step of the way."

Once again the Speaker addressed the assembly. "As Speaker, I was also to be a representative, but as of last night, an urgent family event has occurred that will take all of my time for the next month. I made the committee aware of this. They felt that it was important for Pennsylvania to have the maximum representation, i.e. four representatives. Thus they have chosen the person mentioned frequently along with appointed representatives. This would be Peter Spyker, representative of the Western Frontier. How say you Mr. Spyker?"

"I am honored and will be there."

After these announcements Speaker Fox addressed other orders of business. All seemed anticlimactic and the assembly was adjourned at noon.

The Stamp Act Congress
1765

—⟨∞⟩—

THE PENNSYLVANIA CONTINGENT TO THE Stamp Act Congress met at the Rittenhouse two days before the opening of the October congress. They each had canvassed many of the citizens from their area to understand their thoughts. Although each had their own personal ideas, they also realized they were representatives of the citizens in their district.

Together they rode to New York arriving at a hotel near the City Hall the evening before the first day of meeting. The official Stamp Act Congress lasted from October 7 to October 25, 1765.

Immediately, there was controversy regarding the chairman of the congress. All expected James Otis of Massachusetts, the main voice in calling for the congress to be the chairman. However, the Governor Francis Bernard of Massachusetts, wanted to do everything possible to limit the effectiveness of the congress. Before the congress met he made comments to keep Otis from being the chairman. In his conversations with as many of the delegates as possible, he stated, "Gentlemen, the congress will have no effect with Parliament as they do not respect Mr. Otis because he is too radical." Governor Bernard was effective in dissuading the election of Otis and the congress elected Timothy Ruggles of Massachusetts.

Mr. Ruggles was not in favor of any actions that showed disloyalty to England.

After much debate, and always with the caution of keeping their discourse acceptable to the ears of the king and the parliament, John Dickinson with the help of Peter Spyker and James Otis penned a resolution to be addressed to Parliament titled, "Declaration of Rights and Grievances".

"Mr. Chairman," stated John Dickenson, as he rose on October 19th, "we have written an agreement. We have worked diligently to represent all views. We maintain our loyalty to England but we also maintain our loyalty to these colonies that we represent. Let me read for your discussion our fourteen points of reasoning and grievances. For purposes of history we would like this document, "Declaration of Rights and Grievances" entered into the minutes of this congress. It is penned in my name, however, you the congress have written it. Particularly I would like to recognize Peter Spyker and James Otis for their input. James was the author of grievances and Peter the author of reasoning."

The first of the fourteen points met the immediate approval of the chairman:

*Colonists owe to the crown the same allegiance as subjects within the realm.

However, some of the points caused Chairman Ruggles and several others to frown and become more disgruntled as they were read:

*Colonists possess all the rights of an Englishman.

*Unless colonies have voting rights, Parliament cannot represent us.

*No taxation without representation.

From this date, October 19th until the end of the congress each of the fourteen points was debated heatedly. The most heated debate rose between Thomas McKean, a vigorous opponent of the actions of Parliament as related to the colonies, and Timothy

Ruggles, who felt every action of the congress was inflammatory to the Crown. When it came time to sign the declaration, two states, Delaware and South Carolina by previous state rule, were not allowed to sign. The declaration would be signed by six colonies. Massachusetts's assembly authorized all their representatives to sign, however, the chairman, Timothy Ruggles refused to sign. This incensed Thomas McKean, "Mr. Chairman, for three weeks we have hammered out an appropriate declaration. John Dickinson has a well written, succinct proposal. Now if the chairman does not sign, this declaration will be seen as just some petty grievances by a few."

"I will not sign," answered Chairman Ruggles, "and I suggest the declaration be sent without any one's signature. We must not be seen by the king and the prime minister as belligerent colonies."

"We are not belligerent, Mr. Chairman," said McKean, "but we are firm in these fourteen points. Particularly we want to make it forever clear that we will not allow ourselves to be taxed without representation. Your refusal to sign, Mr. Ruggles, highlights your performance throughout this congress. We might as well have had Prime Minister George Grenville as our chairman. You, Mr. Ruggles, are a scoundrel."

With those words the chairman charged Thomas McKean demanding a dual. The two were separated and later the duel demand by Mr. Ruggles was retracted. Chairman Ruggles had heard that McKean was undefeated in several duals.

The declaration would go forward without the signatures of Delaware and South Carolina, even though their delegates gave full verbal support, and without the signature of the chairman and one other delegate, Robert Ogden of New Jersey. How would it be received in Parliament? How would it be received by King George III? It would be weeks until the document arrived on the docket of the Parliament. It would be months until Parliament would make a decision.

October 25, 1765 Congress was officially adjourned seine die. Peter, John Morton, John Dickinson and George Bryan, all rode together the morning of the 26th to Philadelphia. Peter would stay the 27th with the Dickinsons and then take the trek to Tulpehocken. This gave them all the opportunity to unwind and express their optimism or pessimism.

"How do you feel your writings will be received in Parliament?" John Morton asked John Dickinson.

Dickinson still held high hopes that the problems could be resolved. "Our England is a country that has struggled for its own freedoms and representation. If only the king and the parliament agree with the one idea of the colonies having a fair representation in Parliament, we will be Englishmen forever. It seems so simple. Why would they not want to treat us like every other Englishman?"

"John," addressed George Bryan, "My fear is Prime Minister Grenville. He looks upon us colonists as serfs in the English empire. He also is obsessed with the debt occurred during the French and Indian War. For some reason he holds us responsible for the debt and responsible for ameliorating the debt; our blood and our treasure was not enough. He presently has the ear of King George III. I think the declaration will anger him and I expect retaliation. I feel it is the first step in a conflict that will someday come to civil war. I have no loyalties to England, but I will die for my colony of Pennsylvania."

Peter, ever observant and a listener, stayed quiet most of the trip, but finally after much introspection voiced his feelings. "I am German. My grandfather and my father have gained freedom from France and the Holy Roman Empire, but they have done so without help from England. Indeed my grandfather was often thwarted for his freedom by the English. We also hold no loyalties to England, but, George, we are peaceful people and philosophical followers of William Penn. We will do everything in our power to avoid conflict and violence, but we will not give up our freedom.

England must realize this. They cannot expect us to just accept their dictates when it is harmful to our well-being. I must do what is in the best interest of Tulpehocken and Pennsylvania."

The culture of America was starting to become clear, twenty percent of the citizens of the colonies were loyalists without exception and forty percent were patriots. The loyalists would never vote to sever ties with England. The patriots wanted independence. The other forty percent were torn and waited to be influenced by either loyalists or patriots. The decisions of the King and Parliament would decide the fate of that forty percent.

Home to Tulpehocken
1765

As Peter rode home on the 27th of October, he could not wait to get home to his family. He was tired and at fifty-four ready to enjoy a more peaceful existence than he had ever since he left Rotterdam on the St. Andrew in 1737. He longed to see his wife, who at forty-four was still youthful. He was always proud of her when they were in family and public gatherings. Besides being stunning in appearance, her personality charmed all and allowed him to be the quiet introspective person he enjoyed being.

As he rode over the final hill before seeing his stately home, he saw a cloud of dust as if a small army was riding toward him. At first alarmed and then with great joy he recognized his wife with her long hair flowing in the wind. Beside her was his son Benjamin, now a young man of nineteen and his sixteen-year-old daughter, Anna Elizabeth, who looked like a sister to her mother. Just behind them were his precocious daughter Maria and the new warrior in the family, twelve-year-old John Henry. They were all smiling and shouting their greeting. It had been almost a month since they had seen their husband and father.

They all dismounted and joined in a group hug. "Well, dearest," said Maria Margaretha "Have you straightened out King George and Prime Minister Grenville?"

"I've much to tell you Maria, but I want to hear all the tales of woe and joy that you and my children have engaged in this October. The reunion was joyful, beside Maria and the kids, his brother, Benjamin and his wife were there. They shared their stories at the dinner table. The meal was bountiful as all Spyker celebrations. "Peter," said Maria, "We have a new provider, both the turkey and wild boar you see on the table have come from the marksmanship of John Henry."

"Maria, will you lead us in the prayer," suggested Maria Margaretha. Maria, now thirteen- years-old was showing signs of the woman she would become.

"Let us hold hands and thank the Lord for my father's return. 'Come Lord Jesus be our guest and let these gifts to us be blest and dear Lord please let King George listen to my father. My father is the wisest man in the British Empire."

"I second that, Lord," said John Henry.

After the prayer and enjoyment of the dinner, Peter went into some details regarding the congress and tried to assure all that much was resolved. He particularly wanted to reassure his brother Benjamin, who was becoming a patriot. "If, Prime Minster Grenville, Parliament and King George III, accept the writings of my good friend John Dickinson, we should have great prosperity in the colonies and England will remain a great empire."

"Peter, I hope you are right," said Benjamin, but I put England and the Holy Roman Empire of my youth in the same category. I think ten years from now we will be a free and independent nation."

Maria Margaretha, quickly tired of politics and recognized that Peter was eager to hear about his family. "Peter, let me fill you in on the affairs of your children. You have remarkable children. Much has happened in the time you have been gone. I had to make an important decision and hope you will be okay with. Wouldn't it be nice if we had an instrument where I could talk with you in New York? You know Benjamin has completed as much education as Herr Wilhelm can offer him. In fact Herr Wilhelm relates that Benjamin has surpassed him due to his extensive reading.

Your friend Benjamin Franklin has always been interested in young Benny and impressed with his thirst for knowledge. I received a letter from him. He is still in England, but has offered Benny a scholarship to the school he helped found, the 'Academy and Charitable School in the Province of Pennsylvania.' If Benny was interested and if you and I permitted, I was to confirm accepting this scholarship for the school year starting in September, 1766. Benny was interested and I posted the letter and have already received the congratulatory letter from the department of education. Is this okay?"

Peter could not contain himself and eagerly left the table to hug his son. "Benny, I am so proud of you, and Maria thank you for your quick decision. You knew I would be delighted."

Congratulations went round the table. "Benny," said his uncle Ben, as he clapped him on the back. "You are good with the rifle and the books. I think the books are more important if America is to become a free country, rather than a collection of rifles."

───◦◦◦───

That night as Peter lay in bed with a sleeping Maria in his arms, he was content but could not help the thoughts that clouded his mind until the early hours of the morning. *"How blessed I am to have Maria. She is so much stronger than anyone I know, and yes, stronger than me. She has birthed ten children and three have died but she never displays her silent grief, but just keeps giving herself to me and to our children. She has made us a wonderful life."*

Peter's thoughts then went to his country, America. He like his brother, but not as hawkish, was starting to think about America as a country rather than a collection of colonies devoted to England.

Goading the Colonies
1766

———⌘———

OVER THE NEXT TWO YEARS from 1766 to 1768 it seemed like Britain, Parliament, and the prime ministers did everything possible to goad the colonies into a revolution. In April, 1766, Peter received a letter from Benjamin Franklin, who was still representing the Pennsylvania colony in London.

My Dear friend, Peter,

I hope this letter finds you and your family well. I have not seen you for a number of years as I have been in London battling for our colony's rights. It has been a struggle and I am afraid my efforts were not originally well received. Communication is very difficult between London and Pennsylvania because of mailing time and misrepresentation from others, both in London and in Pennsylvania. Some of it is innocent and some, I'm afraid, is intentional.

I do believe I am presently in good standing with your colleagues. Even John Dickinson has cancelled our impending duel. I have long admired the writings of John and he has advised me that he always asks for your input. It seems he and others find your sound judgment necessary to offset the rash statement and actions of others. It is good that I am presently appreciated in Pennsylvania as a number in Parliament and our beloved ex-prime minister would like to send me back to the colonies on the first ship out of London. I happily relate that George Grenville is Prime Minister no more. My friend, Silence Dogood, says with great glee, 'George has been put to pasture.'

This brings me to the intent of this letter. Sorry to ramble on, I again hear Silence saying 'By my rambling digressions I perceive myself to be growing old,' and I hear you say, 'get to the point, Benjamin.' The main reason for our friend, Prime Minister's fall from grace was his insistence on the Stamp Act. The Stamp Act has come under grave criticism by the merchants of England, who already see a severe decrease in their purses as "those damn colonists think they can get along without our goods."

Charles Watson-Wentworth, now called Lord Rockingham, has been "crowned" prime minister. I assure you he will seek to repeal the Stamp Act. However, do not celebrate quite yet. To get the Stamp Act repealed he must gain the votes of those in Parliament who resent the attitude of the colonists. With the final repeal, a "Declaratory Act" will be passed, which will state that Parliament has the right 'in all cases whatsoever' to enact laws for the colonies."

I stand by the above predictions, i.e. repeal of Stamp Act, Declaratory Act. Your Assembly will receive word of the actions probably in early May. Peter, the attitude in England now and the attitude in the colonies will someday collide unless some reasonable voices gain control of the Parliament and the Ministries. I still have hopes that the likes of your good friend and mine, William Pitt, and his followers will gain control of the government. Realize George III has little influence on the actions of the government. He has more cultural interests, 'he would rather play in his garden', than govern, and he is tugged by the ear in which ever direction the Parliament and Prime Minister desire.

My regards to Maria, your family, and your brother Benjamin, Your old friend, who is in the prime of — senility, Benjamin Franklin, Esquire

After reading the letter, Peter thought to himself, *The Stamp Act, The Sugar Act, the Quartering Act, The Townsend Acts, they just keep coming. It is though Grenville, Lord Rockingham, and Charles Townsend want rebellion."*

In May of 1767, Peter was working in his office on Center Street in Reading. Reading which had once been Finney's Fort, was established as a legally documented town in 1748 and became the county seat of Berks county in 1752. Peter was now the acting president of judges in Berks county. He had been a county judge since 1763. "Mr. Spyker." said Jane Smith, the court's secretary, receptionist, stenographer and gofer, "there is a gentlemen here to see you. I know you wished not to be disturbed, but he says he has 'fourteen rights and grievances' he wishes to discuss with you.'"

Peter was confused only for a few moments. "Send John Dickinson in and please bring us a bottle of sherry and two glasses." Peter was thrilled to have John visit him. They shook hands and as usual John got right down to business.

"Peter, Champagne Charlie has gone too far." John was referring to Charles Townsend, Secretary of the Treasury in the English government. "You are aware, he is literally the prime minister, while William Pitt, the newly appointed prime minister, is recovering from his mental breakdown. You are aware he has levied taxes on our merchants on the importation of lead, glass, paint, tea and paper. Are you aware that at least a third of these taxes go to those riffraff commissioners assigned by him, who are low-level human beings that care only about filling their pockets and making sure Champagne Charlie also gets rich?"

"I understand what you are saying and also am outraged," said Peter. "Are you going to tell me there's even more skullduggery than these acts."

"That's the issue I want to discuss with you. I come to you because of your splendid help on our 'Declaration of Rights and Grievances.' Here's the next chapter in the Charles Townsend Bible of hypocrisy. Mr. William Waddell from Philadelphia has a small fleet of ships that import glass and paint into the colonies. The commissioners failed to tax him on two shipments, then when his third shipment arrived last month, they not only taxed him on all three shipments, but gave him a heavy fine as well. William could not afford the total tax and penalty and thus his ships and cargos were seized and sold in foreclosure. Naturally the monies will not be spent to help the colonies but one third to the royal treasury, one third to Champagne Charley, and one third to the commissioner who conveniently neglected to collect taxes on the first two shipments.

"Peter I am going to write a letter exposing the exploitation of our colonies by our Mother country. It will be circulated throughout the colonies, circulated in England and circulated in France and other countries of Europe. I still want to strive for unity and fair treatment by England and hope that finally this letter will make them see they are forcing upon our colonies rebellion and possible revolution. I need your help. Will you help me write it? I want to have it written soon enough to get it initially published in the newly founded *Boston Chronicle.*"

"John, you are a brilliant writer. I only hope I can be a help and yes I will work with you right now until it's finished. Follow me to my home and spend as many nights with us as necessary until we have just the right message and tone to sound bells of warning to all of England."

"Thank you, Peter. I knew I could count on you and I have an ulterior motive, to visit with your lovely wife Maria." They left together for Tulpehocken to create a message that would not only sound a warning to all of England and all of Europe, but also the message that would bind together the thirteen colonies in one great cause. It was called "A Letter from a Pennsylvania Farmer". It was only the first of thirteen letters all of which were circulated throughout the colonies, published in the *Boston Chronicle* in December of 1767, published in England with help of Benjamin Franklin in May of 1768, and later published in France.

Schoharie to Tulpehocken Revisited

1768

———∞∞∞———

IT WAS EARLY SUMMER 1768. Wilhelm Leininger's school was out for the summer much to the joy of twelve-year-old George Peter, fourteen-year-old John Henry and sixteen-year-old Maria. Anna Elizabeth was planning her August wedding to Philip Gardner, and Benjamin was home from the academy. Peter and his sons had all the crops planted and the Berks county court was in recess until the first of July.

On the political front, the pot was still stirring. The letters of John Dickinson and the Massachusetts Circular letters of Peter's friend James Otis and patriot Samuel Adams were drawing mixed emotions in England. These letters were also causing the individual colonies to think as collective colonies.

In 1767 Peter had decided not to run for representative from Berks county for the Pennsylvania Assembly. In the last meeting of the assembly in October of 1766, Peter announced his decision. "Mr. Chairman,' addressed Peter to James Galloway and the assembly, "I have served on this legislative body for almost twenty years. I was first an ex-officiate representative appointed by Ben Franklin and then elected five times by my citizens from first Tulpehocken territory and then Berks County. It is time for 'new blood' to represent Berks county. This will be my last assembly meeting and I wish to thank my dear friends that I have made over the years." Peter, who was always a man of few words, simply sat down.

After a moment the entire legislative body stood up and applauded for what seemed to be forever. Peter could not help his emotions and shed a few tears and waved to all.

John Dickenson asked to be recognized, "Peter, we thank you, but we cannot get along without you. Your legal mind and your ability to help us frame our writings is indispensible. Would you consent to our call when we have need of your services? We promise not to overtax you as I know you wish to devote your time to Magistrate of Berks county, farmer, husband and father. Peter, will you answer the call when we are in dire need of you?"

Peter stood briefly and simply said, "Of course and thank you for those nice words."

⸺ ❧ ⸺

It was time for a vacation. For some time Peter had been researching and reading his grandfather's notes about his journey to the New World and eventually establishing the Spyker family in Tulpehocken.

"Maria, what would you think if I took John Henry on a canoe trip for a couple of weeks. It's something I've been thinking about for a long time. We would go to Schoharie where grandfather and Lomasi lived until the British kicked them out, then follow their path as they floated down the Susquehanna and the Swarta, connected to the Tulpehocken creek and settled where we live today. I want to reenact this journey and start writing the history of the Spyker family."

Maria, as always, was supportive. She particularly liked the idea of Peter bonding with John Henry. It seemed like Peter was always busy with his law practice, judgeship, and his responsibility in the assembly. He did not have the opportunity to spend as much time with John Henry as he had with Benjamin.

"How would you get there and where would you get the canoe?" asked Maria.

"Benjamin still trades with the Native Americans and although he has not been to Schoharie since the French and Indian War, he is confident he can lead John Henry and me there. He also speaks Iroquois and feels he can help us connect with Lomasi's tribe. We could ride together to Schoharie, and maybe spend a few days with the Mohawk. I'm sure we can buy a canoe from them and then make our journey. I think all together we would be gone for two weeks. We would travel light. We would just take some basic supplies and food and count on John Henry's skills as a hunter and fisherman to keep us from being vegetarians. I want to get as far away as possible from the problems with England."

John Henry was excited. He was a lad who loved the outdoors as did his uncle and his brother. He would be fifteen later in the summer and was eager to be recognized as an adult. His passion was hunting and fishing. He was okay in school, but not passionate as his brother Benjamin. "Dad when can we leave? I'm ready to go. I'm packed, two pair of pants and two shirts, my rifle, my shot, my fishing gear. Let's go."

Peter just laughed, tousled his son's light brown hair and said, "Son, easy, I'm as excited as you, but we must wait until your uncle is ready. We'll take our two sturdy horses. No need for speed. Benjamin will bring back the horses. He said that bringing back two horses will allow him to bring back furs and beaver skins that he can sell at the trading post in Reading.

On June 12th, 1768, the great adventure began. Benjamin, Peter, and John Henry trotted at a steady pace through trails which took them just two days to reach Schoharie and the settlement of the Mohawk. The Mohawk were still friendly with the colonists of the frontier. Upon arriving, Benjamin communicated with the guard who confronted them a short distance from the village. They conversed for what seemed like a long time. Then while the guard remained in front of the Spykers, the guard sent a runner into the settlement. After a wait of almost a half an hour, a tall elderly gentleman of great bearing approached them on a beautiful white horse with a headdress of flowing eagle feathers. On each side was a brave with a headdress of lesser elegance

Benjamin and the rider on the white horse communicated for a time with both smiling frequently and both being animated with obvious excitement. Finally, Benjamin turned to Peter, "May I present the chief of the Mohawk, Achachat, son of Atsila. Atsila was the chief who married Johannes and Lomasi. The story has been told many times at gatherings of the tribe. Lomasi is a legend in the settlement. There is even a song about the love between Johannes and Lomasi. Chief Achachat says you are welcome and he is honored."

With that introduction, Chief Achachat, Peter and Benjamin dismounted and approached each other. Benjamin and Peter extended their hands, which the Chief shook with a strong grip. Peter, then with the help of Benjamin, introduced John Henry, who was greeted with a bear hug, which caused him to momentarily lose his breath. The chief smiled as if reveling in his memory, and said, "Johannes."

That night there was a feast and a celebration, which for Peter would be a highlight in his biography of his grandfather. However, for John Henry it was the beginning of a wonderful memory that he would recall often in his life.

As Peter, Benjamin, and John Henry were presented to the tribe at the beginning of the celebration, Chief Achachat, brought forth a lady about Peter's age and a young girl about John Henry's age. Once again Benjamin interpreted for the occasion. "This is

Tehya, she is the daughter of Skenandoa, who was the younger sister of Lomasi."

Then the Chief took the hand of a girl, who appeared to be in her early teens and led her in front of the Spykers. "You have probably wondered what Lomasi looked like when she was very young. This is Lomasi seventy years ago." He then introduced Olathe. "This is the granddaughter of Lomasi's sister. She has heard the story of Lomasi and is excited to meet her family."

It was a night of eating, singing, chanting and dancing. At first, although exciting, it was bewildering to John Henry. Then later in the evening Olathe came to John Henry and took his hand and led him to a log just away from the large bonfire. It was a shock to John Henry to find Olathe spoke English. "You must tell me about Lomasi."

They carried on a long conversation where each learned about each other and about each other's family. At first John Henry was so shy he only talked in short sentences and avoided the dark eyes of the most beautiful girl he had ever seen. John Henry had paid little attention to girls and was similar to his father in being reserved. Slowly he warmed up to Olathe as she always smiled and held his arm when wanting more information. After the "getting to know you" conversation they started to entertain each other with their interests. John Henry found her enchanting.

"Do you like birds?" asked Olathe. "I love watching them and try to imitate their sounds. Does this sound like a cardinal, my favorite bird?" Then Olathe looked at the stars and called, "purdy, purdy, purdy, whoit, whoit, whoit, whoit."

"If I wasn't watching you make the cardinal call, I would be scanning the trees to find the red bird." They both laughed. It was one of the most enjoyable evenings of John Henry's early life.

That night Peter, smiled at John Henry, "You seemed interested in Olathe and I can understand why. You've never seemed that interested in a girl before. You told Mother and me that they just got in the way of your hunting and fishing." Soon father and son were drifting off to sleep, thinking about the wonderful evening.

"Purdy, purdy, purdy ... ." woke John Henry from his sleep. He thought, *"I love the sound of the cardinal now more than ever, because it makes me think of Olathe."* The bird call kept coming every minute or so, then John Henry thought, *"This is the first time I've heard a cardinal at night. It must be a night owl."* He almost laughed out loud at his joke. *"I'm pretty clever, maybe Olathe is helping me be funny. Won't my sisters be surprised."*

Then a thought rushed through John Henry's mind and he quickly put on his pants and shirt and went outside. There was Olathe with a smile on her face. "Hey sleepy head, I didn't think you would ever hear me calling you."

She led John Henry to a spot beside a small lake, just a few hundred yards away and spread out her colorful blanket for them to sit on. They talked and then became quiet, enjoying each other's closeness. Before the glorious night was over, John Henry had fallen in love and kissed his first girl.

On the second night, John Henry was again delighted to hear "purdy, purdy, purdy... ." However, after the second night Peter said, "Okay son, time to pack up and go. Chief Achachat has given us a fine canoe. He said it would not only take us down the Susquehanna but could also take us down the great river Misi Ziibe, which is many miles west of the Susquehanna. He told me the story of his father meeting a Father Marquette who described the great river that went to the bottom of America."

"Dad, I'm still tired from our ride from Tulpehocken. Maybe we should stay another night or two."

"Son, This is the first time you and I heard a cardinal singing at night. We'll stay one more night to hear if this strange occurrence happens again. Then we must leave to follow your Great Grandfather Johannes and Lomasi down the Susquehanna."

On the morning of June 17th they were packed. Chief Achachat would have one of his braves ride with the Spykers to take the canoe to Lake Otsego where they would start their journey down the Susquehanna. They gathered at the outskirts of the village to say their goodbyes. Nadi, the husband of Tehya had given John Henry a splendid bow with many arrows and Peter had given Chief Achachat one of the two horses that brought them to the Mohawk village. In the background Olathe smiled and gently waved. John Henry and Olathe both realized they would probably never see each other again.

They arrived at Lake Otsego, the source of the Susquehanna, late in the afternoon and camped there for the night. They said their goodbyes to Benjamin, who had the remaining horse loaded down with furs. While Peter was setting up camp, he sent John Henry to test his luck in fishing. It was not long when John Henry returned with a sizable lake trout, which made for a filling first night's feast. After a night's rest, interrupted with memories, they had their breakfast of hardtack and bacon and slid the canoe into the calm waters of Lake Otsego. Soon they left the lake and were in the narrow waters of the Susquehanna River.

It was a fulfilling experience for Peter and his son. Besides the companionship, Peter took many notes of their experience as he pictured his grandfather and Lomasi marveling at the same sights they were enjoying. Each night they ate well thanks to the hunting and fishing prowess of John Henry. Peter spent his evenings getting the camp ready and writing, while John Henry always brought back some game or caught the rainbow trout that was in abundance in the Susquehanna. On June 25th they left the Susquehanna and paddled north up the Swarta until they found a convenient place to make a portage to the Tulpehocken. It was getting dark when they beached their canoe almost in their back yard and the waiting arms of the family Spyker.

Benjamin Spyker (Benny)
1747 - 1819

⸙

Benny Goes to College
1766

—❧—

Two years prior to Peter's and John Henry's canoe trip down the Susquehanna it was time for Benny to go to the Academy. It was the last of August, 1766, and the Spykers were feverishly getting Benny ready to start college in Philadelphia. They had visited the school site and found accommodations for Benny in Mrs. Molly Cassidy's rooming house. She housed several students each semester and was known for her motherly care. Molly was a no-nonsense Catholic lady of about fifty-five years of age. She had come to Philadelphia with her husband, Martin, from County Galway in Ireland. Martin had passed away five years ago and this was her livelihood in the colony. Molly stood a little less than five feet tall and was almost five feet wide. Her former boarders always kidded her lovingly, "Molly, if you ever fell down on the Walnut Street hill you'd roll all the way down into the Schuylkill River." They also told her, "When you get your Irish dander up, you look six feet tall." She was a loving mother and a tyrant rolled into one small ball.

Molly sternly said at least five times to Peter and Benny, "I do not put up with any monkey business." After her pet phrase, she continued, "We lock the door at midnight and if you're not in you can sleep in the yard. The food is wonderful because I'm the best cook in Philadelphia. We eat breakfast at seven and dinner at seven. If you are not awake, no breakfast. If your are late no dinner. I'm Irish Catholic, but you can go to any church you want as long it is not Anglican. You are expected to go to church. When you leave each morning for school, I expect you to be clean and well dressed. Not rich well dressed, mind you, but clean well dressed. We have mainly boys who stay with me, but occasionally a girl. Boys stay in boy's room and girls stay in girl's room and never the 'twain shall meet. You understand me now. And one more thing, I love all my students. If you are having a problem come to me and we'll fix it pronto."

Peter was sold on the Cassidy boarding house, Benny was lukewarm, and Maria after hearing the report said, "My God Peter, isn't Benny to have some fun!"

They Spyker family left on August 30th. There was one more guest in the wagon, Catherina Lauer. Catherina, lived just a few miles from the Spykers. Her father was Michael Lauer the owner of "Sparky." The Lauers were great friends with the Spykers and had been at their Christmas Eve party every year. Her grandfather Christian was in the party with Johannes and Lomasi that came down the Susquehanna from Schoharie to Tulpehocken. Catherina was just a few years younger than Benny and said she was just a good friend. But Benny had said since he was sixteen, "One day, Catherina will be my wife."

Catherina was a tomboy. She was petite with raven dark hair, had a cute pug nose, and startling blue eyes. Benny and Catherina did everything together since she was twelve and Benny was fifteen. They rode horses together, they hunted together, they fished together, they sang together in the Aspach Lutheran church, and they went to Herr Wilhelm's school together. Although they were inseparable friends, they were also competitive. If Benny shot a pheasant, Catherina had to shoot two. If Catherina caught a forty-inch pike, Benny had to catch a forty-two inch pike. They often joked about who was first in Tulpehocken, Christian Lauer or Johannes Spyker. "My grandfather Christian was in the lead canoe and he arrived two minutes before your grandfather Johannes."

When getting ready for the journey to college, Benny insisted that Catherina come along, and Catherina was delighted. As they traveled the ten hours to Philadelphia, they sat huddled together, trying to joke, but both were sad as they knew they might not see each other for several months.

They met with Mrs. Cassidy and got Benny settled in. Molly was happy to see the whole clan, "You sure you're not Irish? I've never seen such a nice Irish family." After the introductions Peter said to Molly, "Make sure he studies every night." Maria then said to Molly, "Make sure he has fun." Catherina, who was almost as outgoing as Benny said, "Mrs. Cassidy, make sure he doesn't meet any girls."

Once Benny was situated in his room he would share with three other boys, he left with his family and Catharina for the Rittenhouse Hotel. The next morning the time came for parting and it was sad indeed. They all gave Benny one last hug and left on the trail to the Western Frontier. It wasn't long before Catherina was sobbing. Maria put her arm around Catherina and said, "You sure are sad. I thought Benny was just a friend."

"Yes he's just a friend, but he'll end up marrying one of those Philadelphia girls instead of marrying me like he promised."

Most colleges in the colonies had a traditional program to educate one to be a Christian minister. However, Benjamin Franklin, not being of the religious sort, though he tolerated Jedidiah, the famed Presbyterian preacher and his "fire and brimstone" sermons, was able to convince the founders to have a more rounded liberal arts curriculum.

By the time Benjamin would graduate he would have classes in the following: writing, arithmetic and mathematics; chemistry, navigation, astronomy, natural and mechanical philosophy; language study in Latin, Greek, English, French and German; history, geography, chronology, logic, and rhetoric.

Benny left Mrs. Cassidy's the next morning and walked the three blocks up Arch to Fourth Street to begin an experience which he treasured. Although he looked forward to his first day he was anxious. He wanted to do well. He wanted to learn everything the academy could teach him. As he approached the school, he took a mental picture of his place of learning for the next four years.

Academy and Charitable School in the Province of Pennsylvania

The Senior Year
1770

———— ⌖ ————

SCHOOL WAS A BLUR FOR Benny. His first three years he had little social life except when he returned home for Christmas, spring break, or summer vacation. Occasionally he would go out with friends to a pub and usually the conversation was politics or girls. When returning, his Philadelphia mother, Molly would grill him, "Benny, my boyo, tell me now. You haven't been out with those Philadelphia girls, have you? I promised that sweet Catherina that you would behave." After his assurance that he was a good boy, "Now you sit down there and have some of my Irish Dutch Apple Pie and some good Irish milk." Benny loved his Philadelphia mom and the feeling was mutual.

School always started the first Monday in September and lasted until the first of June. Benny loved school, but also loved his family and Catherina and was always anxious to get home. The Spyker's traditional Christmas Eve party of 1769 saw Benny get on his knees and propose to Catherina Lauer. Her answer was, "Well Mr. Spyker. It's about time." The wedding would be after Benny's graduation in June, 1770.

Benny returned for his final year and shared the news with Molly. "Well that's lovely. I still have lots of work to do. I've got to get you graduated and then married."

Although Benny had excelled in every course previously and was at the top of his class, he was concerned about taking a chemistry course. Benny was more verbally inclined, did okay in math classes, but had never had a science course. He was warned by fellow students that the teacher was new, was already a doctor and brilliant, and he expected his students to be brilliant as well.

It was with trepidation that he walked into his first chemistry class. Benny was early. He was always early to everything. Catherina had kidded him, "Benny, you will be early to your own funeral."

"Yes, my dear. I would hate to miss it." Benny had replied.

When Benny arrived there was just one other student. A young ruddy-faced boy, *'probably a little younger than me,'* thought Benny. "Hi there, I'm Benjamin Spyker, but everybody calls me Benny. This is my last year. I'm dreading this chemistry class. I hear the professor is a an egg-head and that he expects us to be almost like a doctor when we graduate."

"You think you're dreading it. I'm shaking in my boots. My name is Benjamin Rush. I don't think the professor is an egg-head. In fact I've heard he's not very smart."

The clock ticked to 3:30, the time the class was to commence. The 3:30 classes were always the last class of the school day. There were about twenty males in the class and zero girls. Finally a ruddy-faced young man went to the lectern and asked everyone to sit down. "My name is Benjamin Rush and I will be your chemistry teacher."

Peter tried to disappear behind the student sitting in front of him. *"I didn't really call him an egg-head, did I? My god he looks younger than me."*

Professor Rush seemed a little nervous, "I'll tell you a little about myself, but first I'd like to know you and I'm sure your fellow students are curious about you also. Would each of you stand, give us your name, tell a little about your academic standing, and your plans for the future?"

When it came to Benny, "Hello Professor Rush, I'm Benjamin Spyker and I understand that our professor is a brilliant, kind and understanding person, who forgives easily."

Benjamin Rush broke out laughing. "Ah, Benjamin, my good lad, we'll have a great time together." Benjamin Rush was an interesting person and the entire class was awed with his status and accomplishments. In 1760, he graduated with a bachelor of arts degree from the College of New Jersey. He served a medical apprenticeship for five years and then went to the University of Edinburgh in Scotland, where he studied from 1766 to 1768 and earned a medical degree. "I presently have a medical practice on Walnut Street. So if any of my students get ill, I will cure them in a blink of an eye, or again they may die." The students enjoyed his sense of humor and laughed with him. "I'm younger than some of you in here. I'm twenty-four and single and have no intention of tying any knots, unless they are of the umbilical nature."

After class Benny went to the desk of Professor Benjamin Rush to apologize. "Well, do you think I still have a chance to pass this course?"

Benjamin Rush stood up, slapped Benny on the back, "Mr. Spyker, your only chance to pass my course is to buy me an ale at the Commons."

Many days after class Benjamin and Benny would enjoy a frothy ale and a conversation. Frequently the conversation was about the politics of the time. Although they agreed almost completely on the politics, they did have some disagreement on religion. It seemed Benjamin Rush felt everything was the will of God. Benny was also religious but was more inclined to believe that God gave us free will, and we make our lot in life based upon our own conscience and inclinations. Both Benjamin and Benny were cerebral and this made for some interesting and introspective conversations.

"Benny, would you consider yourself a loyalist or a patriot? The reason I ask this is that the events of the last year, particularly in New York and Boston, are pushing me to become a patriot. I know you are aware of the Quartering Act."

This was an act passed by Parliament demanding that British soldiers in New York City be housed in private homes or the citizens of the city would need to pay for their quartering in public facilities. The New York Assembly had refused to appropriate funds for the quartering. They didn't want the soldiers there in the first place. Ostensibly they were there to protect the colonists. However, all believed they were there to enforce the various duties placed upon the colonists.

"Benny, are you aware the assembly was dissolved for refusing to appropriate funds for quartering the soldiers. It seems to me that England does not try to compromise. It's as though the colonies exist for only their purposes."

Benny nodded his head and replied, "Yes, I don't think compromise is in their vocabulary. Benjamin, I lean toward being a patriot, but do not want war. We are German and have never been fond of the English in our emigration history. They tried to thwart us in several ways, but we Germans are determined. Now, becoming a patriot, which means declaring our independence from England, I just don't know. My father, Peter, who was a Pennsylvania Assemblyman wants to avoid conflict, but I know he will never let the freedoms he has gained be taken from him. My uncle Benjamin Spyker is a patriot. He's ready to separate from England regardless of the consequences."

Benjamin Rush continued his concerns, "Another thing that worries me is that the assembly has organized again, but with just loyalists appointed by the Royal Governor. Recently they agreed to appropriate two-thousand pounds to quarter the English soldiers. This has polarized the New York colonists against each other, patriot or loyalist. The 'Sons of Liberty', extreme patriots, put up large signs criticizing the assembly for giving into the British. Besides the signs, they put up a liberty pole on Golden Hill as a sign of dissent. The British troops marched up Golden Hill to tear down the liberty pole. They were initially repelled by the 'Sons of Liberty', but finally overwhelmed them and tore it down. I tell you Benny, it's heating up. It's like a boulder rolling down our Walnut Street; the more it rolls the faster and more destructive it gets."

These types of conversation happened weekly. Often Benny and Benjamin Rush were joined by other students most of whom sided with the patriots, but many like Benny were not ready to commit to a conflict that might lead to a revolution.

The Boston Massacre
1770

—✸—

ONE DAY IN EARLY MARCH, Benjamin Rush approached Benny with an interesting proposal. "Benny, when we first started discussing the patriot – loyalist polarization, I told you I was leaning toward becoming a patriot. My uncle in Boston, Dr. Joseph Warren, the one who encouraged me to be a doctor, has invited me to Boston for our spring break. He wants me to go with him to a 'Sons of Liberty' meeting. I think I'm going to do it. Once and for all I want to see the extreme patriot side. Then I can decide if I want to take the next step; to get involved.

"I've told my uncle about you and he is familiar with your father, for whom he has great respect. He's invited you also. We would leave after class Friday and stay the better part of the week before it's back to dear old academy and even better old chemistry. By the way, you'll never be a chemist, but you're doing well despite that fact that I'm tougher on you. I don't want anyone to think I play favorites."

"I'd love to go to Boston. I'm not sure about the meeting. My father might not approve. Of course my uncle Benjamin would be all for it, and I know my fiancée would support me as she like me is interested in how the patriots feel about our relations with England."

Benny did go and also went to the meeting of the "Sons of Liberty." The meeting was chaired by a gentleman that looked to Benny to be about fifty-years-old.

"Before we get into the business of becoming a free and independent nation, I'd like to recognize our friend and one of our founders Dr. Joseph Warren to introduce the two young guests he has invited tonight."

Dr. Joseph Warren, one of the leaders of the "Son's of Liberty.

"Thank you Sam," said Dr. Warren, "gentlemen, let me introduce first my nephew, Benjamin Rush. Benjamin is following in my footsteps and is now a doctor in Philadelphia. He also is a professor of chemistry at the academy in Philadelphia. Next to him, and I'll ask him to stand, is Benjamin's friend, Benny Spyker. He is the son of Judge Peter Spyker of Tulpehocken, Pennsylvania. You possibly know his father as he was a distinguished representative from Pennsylvania to the Stamp Act Congress. Judge Spyker worked with John Dickinson in creating the fourteen points of 'The Declaration of Rights and Grievances.' If England and Parliament had heeded this historical document there would be no need for us to be here tonight.

"Both these young men are like us before we came together as 'Sons of Liberty,' not sure if our loyalties to England outweigh our thirst for independence. Gentleman, they must come to their own conclusions without our undue pressure." With that Dr. Warren sat down and the chairman again rose, shook hands with the doctor and approached the dais.

The chairman was at times bombastic but also very persuasive. He had a dry, but clever, sense of humor. "My fellow Americans, note, I did not say Bostonians or citizens of Massachusetts. I said Americans. It's time we start thinking of ourselves as a nation. It's time we start thinking of separating from our dictators. It's time we answer the question: Do we want England across the ocean to make our decisions, or do we want to make our own decisions?"

The chairman looked at the members and guests to see if there was any disagreement. "You all know, I once was a tax collector. I hated myself. The only person that loved me was my wife and that was just on collection days." After much laughter, he continued, "I found that taxation was a means of tyranny. My good friend, James Otis, said it best, 'taxation without representation is tyranny'. Let me introduce myself to our guests, I am Sam Adams, but as far as the British know, I'm Ben Franklin's,

"Silence Dogood", who is successful at doing nothing. It is best we keep it that way as I understand I'm more in demand in the English Parliament than the Christmas goose. The goose whose neck they'd like to wring."

Sam Adams continued for several more minutes stirring up the fury of the "Sons of Liberty." "Tonight we have a special guest who has joined our group. He has suffered a great deal of hardship at the hands of the British, even though he was trying to follow their precepts. I'll let him tell you the story. Let me present, John Hancock."

JOHN HANCOCK.

A tall distinguished looking gentleman stood up. He had great bearing. "I am a merchant and quite successful, thanks to God and my uncle. I have many ships doing import and export business with island countries as well as European countries. Although I disagree wholeheartedly with the extreme tariffs imposed upon me, not only because they harm me, but because the tariffs go to England and the British custom officials rather than to help our colonies. I have always paid my taxes to our beloved custom officials and bowed to each restriction no matter how lamed-brained. On May 9th my ship *Liberty* was seized by two English warships, that just happened to be in our Boston Harbor to impress some poor hapless seamen into the service of the king."

Mr. Hancock went on to complete the story and to thank Sam Adams and James Otis for interceding with the Royal governor of Massachusetts to release the *Liberty*, expel the British warships from the harbor and then eventually drop all charges against John Hancock.

At the close of the meeting, Sam Adams expressed his frustrations, "Does it ever stop, the Sugar Act, the Stamp Act, the Declaratory Act, the Townsend Acts, the Quartering Act, the dissolution of the New York Assembly, the Golden Hill incident, the Liberty incident. What will happen next to fully separate us from our love for the Mother country?" Sam Adams and the "Sons of Liberty" did not have long to wait.

———❦———

Other than the one meeting and discussions over dinner with Dr. Joseph Warren, Benny and Benjamin, relaxed and enjoyed the culture and atmosphere of Boston. On Thursday, March 5th, 1770, just two days before they would ride back to Philadelphia and the home stretch to graduation, they went to enjoy a dinner at the popular Green Dragoon Tavern.

Several times during the week Benjamin's uncle had warned them to be careful, "Benjamin, there's a lot of anger from our colonists toward the British soldiers who are stationed here. Please stay away from their posts as there are always some of our own hotheads who taunt them, and this could lead to violence."

They walked from Dr. Warren's house to Marshall street, which was close to the Boston Harbor. It was a cold miserable day and after gaining entrance into the very busy Green Dragoon they headed directly for the huge fireplace. It seemed like they would not find a place to sit, but at least they could warm themselves by the fire while waiting for a table to open. "Hey, young Benjamin Rush, over here." They looked around and were delighted to see John Hancock wave to them. "We've got room for two more. Paul and I are just discussing how we can get you young folks involved in our quest for independence. Let me introduce the best silversmith in Boston, Paul Revere."

They were happy to sit down with Mr. Hancock and Mr. Revere. Benjamin thanked them and said, "Mr. Hancock, you might have seen my friend Benny Spyker with me the other night at the meeting. I also recognize your friend, Mr. Revere from the meeting."

"Benny," addressed John Hancock, "I know more about you than you think. I've met your father during the Stamp Act Congress and he is the voice of reason. If ever, he decides to join us in our quest for independence, we will be sure we are on the right track. I also know you're getting married soon, so you should get to know my friend, Paul. He'll make you some fine silverware for your new bride."

It was a heady evening for Benny. He was impressed with both men. After their fine dinner of plates of oysters and all the trimmings, along with maybe too many pints of ale, they decided to walk home before it was too late. They wanted to heed Dr. Warren's caution and stay out of harm's way.

"Benjamin," said Paul Revere as they were standing to leave, "I'm headed your way also, home to my lovely wife, Sarah. If you don't mind, I'll walk along with you. Sarah will appreciate having two fine young men make sure I get straight home." They shook hands with John Hancock and headed out into the evening.

As they approached King Street they noticed a small group of people gathering around a customs house. There seemed to be an argument going on. Paul asked a bystander, "What's going on?"

The bystander, a young lad, very tall and heavy, eagerly filled Paul and the two Benjamins in on the details. "The guard, one of those lobsterbacks, got all insulted by my friend, Edward Garrick.

Edward's a wig maker and one of the British officers owed him money. He called out to the officer about the debt. The guard, although it was none of his business, yelled out to my friend that he should have more respect for an officer of the British guard. They started yelling at each other and the guard came down from his post and struck Edward on the side of the head with his musket. They've taken my friend away to a dispensary, but as you can see others are outraged. He had no right to assault my friend. It's getting to be a tense situation. I'm a bookseller at the store across the street and every day I see confrontations between the English guards and our citizens. I knew it would come to this. Let me introduce myself; I'm Henry Knox. I recognize all of you from the last meeting of the "Sons of Liberty" as I was there and am a member and a patriot. If this gets any more violent, please come in the bookstore for safety."

The crowd continued to build. At least fifty some people started throwing objects at the guard and yelling taunts such as, "You chicken, don't hide behind your red coat and musket. Fire the gun if you got any guts."

Fairly quickly a detail of a non-commissioned officer and six British soldiers with bayonets attached arrived at the scene. Soon the Captain of the Guard came and pushed through the crowd. He had his small detail form in a semi-circle with muskets aimed at the crowd. "God, said Benny to Benjamin and Paul, they're surely not going to fire are they? There must be three or four hundred people around here now."

Henry Knox, although he was just nineteen seemed to sense a potential tragedy. He jumped into the conversation and addressed the sergeant of the guard, "Sergeant, it would be best if you just have your men stand down. Eventually those being belligerent to the guard will calm down. If you provoke some of the crowd, anything can happen. We don't need an incident. Please tell your men to stand down and even to return to the barracks." It was of no avail as the sergeant of the guard was looking for action and had the look of revenge in his eyes.

Despite the threat of muskets aimed at them the crowd continued to shout and taunt the British soldiers. "Go back to England you lobsterbhacks. You eat our food, take our jobs and we must pay to have you here. We don't need you and we don't want you." This was one of the kinder taunts.

The riot continued. Then one of the rioters hit one of the guardsman with his cane and the guardsman lost control and fired into the crowd. This spurred several of the other guardsmen to fire. Benjamin, Benny, Paul, and Henry watched in horror as they saw several people fall, some fatally. Henry Knox grabbed Benny by the arm and the others followed, "C'mon let's go into the store." They went into the book store and watched as the melee continued. Finally, the shock of the event caused everyone to scatter and Paul encouraged Benny and Benjamin to go quickly to Dr. Warren's. They knew they could not help and might themselves be injured so they raced away from the scene to their homes. For Paul Revere, the scene left an image to him that he would later recreate in silver.

The bloody massacre as engraved by Paul Revere

The next morning Benny decided to visit the book store and talk with Henry Knox. He sensed that Henry could tell him more about the incidents with the British. Henry was glad to see Benny and they discussed the event. Benny was also interested in books as was Henry and they spent hours discussing the different books that were in the book store. Finally Benny went back to the Warrens and decided it was time for him to return home. The incident that would later be called, "the Boston Massacre, the "Sons of Liberty" meeting, and his discussions with Henry Knox pushed Benny closer to a position of being a patriot.

Graduation

1770

———— ✠ ————

IT WAS JUNE, 1770. BENJAMIN had graduated from the Philadelphia Academy in late May. His marks were stellar. For his senior year he received A in Latin, history, English, geography and writing. He did however, only get an A- in chemistry. "This is to keep you humble my friend," said his chemistry teacher.

Shortly after Benny returned, Peter asked his son to sit down with him for some talk about the future. Peter and Maria had inherited the house and the acreage of his father upon the death of Lomasi. This was the land and home originally of Peter's grandfather Johannes. The land was being held and farmed by renters, but the house was becoming run down and the fields were not being worked in the best manner for maintaining the richness of the soil. The family agreed that Benny and Catharina should live there and farm the land. However, eventually it would go into the estate for all the children. Benny was happy with the arrangements even though he longed for his own farm and home as soon as possible.

"Dad, I can't thank you enough for all you have done for me. To begin with, Catharina and I will stay in Tulpehocken, but some day we want to buy our own land. We want to buy a large amount of acreage and build our own home just as you did thirty years ago.

Maybe you have some ideas where we might find good farm land for sale?"

Before getting an answer from his father about land, Ben continued, "Also, you and mother know that I want to become a teacher. I've talked with Wilhelm Leininger and he says it's time our community has two schools and two teachers. He wants me to take the older students and he will teach the younger ones. So for the immediate future, I will teach and farm and Catharina will raise our family, keep our home, and help me farm. She's excited about the future and we want to start a family as soon as possible."

"Benny, those plans sound great. You've always been one who planned ahead. We are proud of you. I do have an idea for you to buy your own land. Maybe you can locate the land, and start a purchasing process where you can have ownership within a few years. You've met my friend Jonathan Hager and his wife Elizabeth. He was a great friend of mine on the St. Andrew and always listened to me when I was going through some rough times. He and his wife have been to our house several times and Maria and I have been to their home. Sadly his wife Elizabeth passed away a couple of years ago. Maria and I were at the funeral.

"Jonathan moved with his family from Philadelphia to an area that is about one hundred miles south of here. It's now just across the border in the colony called Maryland. Jonathan was very enterprising and he kept purchasing land. Today he has established a town named after his wife. It's called Elizabethtown. I'll talk with him and see what the opportunities would be for you."

———— ∞ ————

Besides planning for the future, Benny and his family along with the Lauers were busy preparing for a glorious event, the wedding of Benny and Catharina.

Benny's return to Tulpehocken also saw him in many political conversations with his father, uncle and brother about the events of the last year. Peter was still not convinced America should seek independence. Uncle Benjamin along with John Henry wanted separation immediately, even if it meant war, and Benny was caught in between his father and uncle. Although there was the fundamental difference between Peter and his brother, Benjamin, they were reasonable in their debate and both willing to listen to the other.

To celebrate Benny's graduation from the Academy, Peter and Maria had a special dinner and invited Benjamin and his wife as well as the Lauer family. This gave the men a chance to talk politics and the women to talk wedding arrangements.

"Dad," said Benny, "I witnessed firsthand the 'Boston Massacre.' There was no excuse for the British soldiers to fire into a mob. I realize the mob was taunting and some throwing things at them, but to fire into a mob who had no weapons was reprehensible. What has England done about it? Nothing. This situation is making me want to gain independence."

"Son, I understand your anger. It doesn't seem like anything at this time can reduce the hostility of patriots toward the English crown. However, one admirable thing came out of the aftermath, that should show to England and to the colonies that the best recourse is still the justice system. I believe, as a lawyer and a judge, that a person should be guaranteed a fair trial no matter the passions surrounding an incident. It was almost impossible to find a lawyer in the colonies to defend the captain of the guard, and the soldiers, eight all together. Finally, John Adams and Josiah Quincy volunteered to defend them. John Adams, cousin of Sam Adams, is a patriot, just like your uncle, but he believed in a fair trial. John and Josiah did such an admirable job that the jury, although they were colonists and some patriots, found the captain not guilty, since he did not order the men to fire. They also were able to find not guilty the soldiers who did not fire into the crowd. The three who did fire were found only guilty of manslaughter not murder since John and Josiah convinced the jury they were trying to defend themselves. They will however be in prison for many years."

Peter continued his thoughts about Mr. Adams. "I've had the opportunity to meet several times with John Adams.

He, like myself and our other Pennsylvania representatives, was opposed to the Stamp Act. We roomed in the same hotel in New York and we talked frequently about how to resolve the conflict between the colonies and England. Although he's just a young man of thirty-six and I'm an old codger, we seem to be of the same political philosophy. Benny, I've taken the liberty of inviting him to your wedding. He had mentioned he wanted to experience the frontier and understand more completely our interests and particular problems. He was delighted and I expect to see him. I hope that's okay with you."

"Father, it will be an honor to meet him. As you know I've met several 'Sons of Liberty,' Dr. Joseph Warren, John Hancock, Paul Revere, and a new friend Henry Knox. I also invited them along with my best friend Benjamin Rush. The wedding, I think, will be memorable and peaceful, but the reception afterwards will be lively and there might be some sparks flying. Perhaps, we should ask everyone to check their weapons at the door."

Everyone joined in with a good laugh and then Uncle Benjamin, who had been unusually quiet, gave his thoughts. "Peter, I agree that John Adams did an admirable thing and I believe a person deserves a fair trial. I do think, however, that if the incident was reversed and it had occurred in England, that our Americans would not have received a fair trial. If we want a country of liberty, fairness and justice, we must gain our independence from England."

Peter replied, "I don't disagree with you, but I hate to see war and hate to think of my sons going to war and perhaps losing their lives."

"Dad," said John Henry, who was now seventeen, "I want independence. I'm willing to die for the Spykers, Tulpehocken, Pennsylvania, and America."

While the battle of the political minds was meeting in the parlor, the women and a couple of captive gentlemen were meeting around the large table in the dining room. George Weiser was with them discussing the wedding cake and the bakery items for the reception. The wedding would be in the Aspach Lutheran Church, "The Church on the Ridge," with Reverend Johann Kurtz officiating. Reverend Filip Schmidt had passed away at the ripe old age of eighty, but had left "his" church in good hands.

The reception would be at the Spyker house with over eighty people invited. The beautiful grounds of the Spyker house, weather permitting, would be the area of congregation with the dining room being filled with food and bakery items from the Seltzer Tavern. Besides George the other gentleman at the wedding planning party was Jacob Seltzer. He and his staff would be doing the catering. Also, many of the guests from outside Tulpehocken would be residing at his public house.

All were admiring the wedding dress lovingly sewed by Regina Spyker, the widow of Jonny Spyker. "Regina," exclaimed Catharina, "It is just what I envisioned."

Regina accepted the compliment, "Your father provided me with the satin silk material. I think he canvassed every cloth maker in Philadelphia. I took this material and just kept thinking of you, a princess. My granddaughter Regina, recently married to young Jacob Lentz, helped me and was my model. You and she are just the same size. Now, Catharina, you will see in the back there is one stitch missing. You must sew the last stitch just before leaving for church." This was a tradition from Germany that was said to encourage good fortune.

After everyone admired the dress, then Catharina discussed the wedding party, "We will keep it very much in the family. "My maid of honor will be my sister, Eva Magdalena. My bridesmaids will be my sister Elizabeth and Benny's sisters, Anna Elizabeth and Catherine. Benny will also be keeping his groomsmen in the family with the exception of Benjamin Rush, his professor and friend from the academy, who will be one of the groomsmen. Besides Mr. Rush, his brother John Henry and my brother Johannes will be the other groomsmen. The best man will be his uncle Benjamin."

Wedding Day
1770

———— ∞∞∞ ————

IT WAS 10:00. GERMAN LUTHERAN weddings were in the morning. It was Wednesday morning. This was the most propitious day to get married. Saturday marriages brought bad luck, but Wednesday weddings brought good fortune and happiness. Catharina had sewed the final stitch in her white wedding dress, and was off to church with her family in their fine wagon and two black stallions. Matthew Lauer, Catharina's father, had the finest stable of horses in Tulpehocken, and he enjoyed showing off these two identical black stallions.

It was a sunny June morning and there was a stream of wagons as well as individual riders headed for "The Church on the Ridge". Maria loved gardening, not only vegetable gardening but also flowers. The church was filled with her flowers, particularly her red roses. At 10:00 precisely the church doors closed. The windows were open and the church was filled. Before the ceremonies, the Reverend Kurtz sat at the organ and played his favorite medley from Johann Sebastian Bach' s *Little Organ Book.*"

Before being ushered to the front pew, Peter looked and was amazed at all the well-known people who did him and his son the honor of attending the wedding. There, chatting amenably with each other were John Adams and some members of the "Sons of

Liberty," John Hancock, Paul Revere, Dr. Joseph Warren and Henry Knox. In another group were the good friends he worked with in the Pennsylvania Assembly, John Dickinson, John Morton, and George Bryan. Also with them was the new Speaker of the Assembly, Joseph Galloway.

Of course he was delighted to see his friends and families who were in the still active Tulpehocken Junto and other friends who usually came to the traditional Spyker Christmas Eve celebration. It was pleasing that his friend from the St. Andrew, Jonathan Hager and his two children were there. This, he thought, would be a good opportunity to talk with him and with Benny about the possibility of land in Maryland.

Just ahead of Peter and Maria, was Catharina's mother Emily. Johann Lauer with great pomp escorted her to the front pew on the right. Now it was time for John Henry to escort Peter and Benny's mother to her place of honor. Many were a little confused as he had Maria Margaretha on one arm, but also a short, round beaming lady on the other arm as if there were two mothers of the groom. Through the four years of college, Peter and Maria, as well as Benny and Catharina had become extremely fond of Benny's landlord, Molly Cassidy. They all called her Benjamin's "college mom" and Maria insisted that she should sit with her for the ceremonies.

The reverend completed his Bach music and the church became quiet before he began a traditional German Lutheran Hymn as Catharina came down the aisle escorted by her father, Matthew Lauer. All stood and sang along with Reverend Kurtz as he played the tune on the organ:

This is the day the Lord hath made; He calls the hours His own; Let heaven rejoice, let earth be glad, and praise surround the throne. ... .

It came to the part for the vows. First from Benny: "As God unites us in the presence of our family and friends, I give you my firm commitment to be faithful and loyal to you, in sickness and in health, good times or bad, in sadness and in joy. I do promise to love you unconditionally, to help you make your dreams come true and to respect and honor you. I cherish you, my dear Catharina for as long as we both shall live."

Next Catharina vowed: "I commit to never leave you, to follow you. For where you go, I shall go, and where you remain, I shall remain. Your people will be my people, and your God will be my God. Where you die, I shall die and be buried beside you."

Maria had suggested to Benny and Catharina this specific vow as it was the same one she and Peter had shared thirty years ago. With tears in her eyes, Maria reached over, hugged Peter and said, "Have you heard those words before?"

Peter replied, "No, never heard those words." Maria elbowed Peter so hard in the ribs that he almost lost his breath, but then he laughed, "Maria, my darling, I remember saying those exact words to you as though it was yesterday."

It was a grand wedding. It was a grand reception. The reception at the Spyker house was a celebration of the wedding with no politics. The children and adults acting like children played games and sang. There was dancing and eating with more than occasional imbibing. Later in the afternoon, Catharina did the "Dance of the Bridal Crown" and all the married women danced around her in a circle, while she guarded a wedding wreath on her head. Finally Christian Lauer broke through the circle and stole the bridal wreath off Catharina's head. Catharina made no attempt to keep it from him as it signified he would be married in a year.

The reception lasted until early evening. The guests from out of town along with Peter, Benjamin, and John Henry all went for a gathering at the Seltzer guesthouse and here the politics began. No one was killed, no one was harmed, and hardly a voice was raised, but they debated and debated the issues of the conflict with their Mother country until past midnight. It seemed most agreed that someday America should gain her independence. The main disagreement was in the means and the timing.

There was however, one dissenting voice. That was the new Speaker of the Assembly, Joseph Galloway. "Gentleman, I know you are dissatisfied with the events of these last two years, but the answer is not to seek independence but to become more a part of the English government. What would you think of the idea of England having two Parliaments, a Parliament in England and a Parliament in America? The American Parliament could make decisions for America and have veto power over any decision made by the Parliament in England if it affected America. Of course, both Parliaments would be subject and loyal to the Crown."

All paused and thought, until John Adams spoke, "Mr. Galloway, it is a noble idea, but I do not think the present Prime Minister and Parliament would consider it. It seems like they reject every olive branch we extend to them. I think, Joseph, the best recourse is for England to grant us our independence. We will become strong friends and support each other economically and also in the face of war. I propose a toast to independence as a peaceful conciliation from the Crown. Here, here, to England, to America, God bless the King, God bless America."

All raised their glasses with good cheer except Joseph Galloway. You could tell by the disgusted look on his face he did not favor independence. "Gents, it's never going to happen, nor should we want it to happen. Our strength is as a colony of England."

After the evening of ideas that served as a catharsis all went to bed, and the next morning all went their separate ways.

The Honey Moone
1770

———— ❦ ————

AFTER LEARNING THEY WOULD BE living in Jonny and Lomasi's house and farming the land, Benny and Catharina started cleaning, painting and preparing the house. Benny took over the farming and the raising of the livestock. He was grateful that his brother, John Henry worked with him many hours each day. By the time of the wedding the house had a new coat of paint inside and outside, a new roof, and all the floors, cabinets, walls, ceilings and fixtures were in good repair. It was once again, as in the time of Jonny and Lomasi, a comfortable and well kept family home.

Benny and Catharina stayed at the reception until the completion of the "Dance of the Bridal Crown" and then rode their horse and carriage just a few miles to Womelsdorf and their new home. The horse and carriage were a wedding gift from Uncle Benjamin. It was with great joy that Benny carried Catharina across the threshold and they entered their marriage chamber.

The next morning, just after breakfast, they carried their satchels and once again boarded their carriage. They were going to be away for a week; it would be, as they said in old England, a 'honey moone.' They would first go to Philadelphia and stay two nights in the Rittenhouse. Here they would be wined and dined by Benjamin Rush and his intended. They would also get the chance to visit with Molly Cassidy. They couldn't wait to take her to the finest restaurant in Philadelphia.

Benny had talked with Jacob Seltzer about ideas for the honey moone. "Benny, you should take your bride to a new place. My good friend owns an inn in Annapolis. That's in Maryland. It is a charming city on the river and close to the Atlantic. The inn is connected to one of the finest restaurants in all of the colonies. I hate to say it, but his inn and restaurant is even more grand than mine."

Thus the next stop on Benny and Catharina's honey moone was Annapolis. It was a city on Chesapeake Bay at the mouth of the Severn River. Jacob's friend was Robert Johnson, owner of the Calvert House. They had an enjoyable ride and visit to Baltimore before arriving at the warm and welcoming Calvert House. They stayed there three nights.

The second night of their stay in the Calvert house they went to the theatre and saw the production of the *"Prime of Parthia,"* Although it was not a Shakespeare play it had the basic elements of *"Romeo and Juliet."*

"Benny, my dearest, would you fall on a sword if I died tragically?"

"Catharina, my love, my darling, my apple strudel. I would jump out this window."

"You are so sweet, but we are on the ground floor."

They both laughed at their "play-acting." They were a happy couple in love.

The final night at the Calvert House they went to the Treaty of Paris restaurant. They were greeted by the maitre d' with a fine bottle of wine. The maitre d' first showed them the label:

Spyker Rießlingen
From the vineyards of the Peter Spyker farm, Tulpehocken

"Sir, Madam, this is an amazing wine that we have recently purchased from a frontier vineyard in Pennsylvania. I hope you enjoy it." With the wine was a note, *Please enjoy this wine and any menu you wish, compliments of Jacob Seltzer.*

They enjoyed first an appetizer, Maryland Crab Bisque, which was a tender jumbo lump crabmeat bisque with a hint of old bay and a touch of sherry. The appetizer was followed by Steamed Mussels sautéed with butter, white wine, scallions, garlic and Andouille sausage served with a toasted Baguette.

Next came the salad: baby greens with blackberries, strawberries and toasted pecans. At the same time as their salad the waiter brought a warm baked brie topped with caramelized brown sugar paired with fresh seasonal fruits and a toasted baguette topped with a rich truffle honey.

Between each course they sipped the Spyker wine and talked about their future. They were in no hurry and this was recognized by the waiter. After a lengthy pause to digest the first courses the waiter brought the main course. They had chosen Seared Arctic Char. A herbed crusted Arctic char filet served with a citrus lime reduction and jasmine rice. They finished the meal with a fine French brandy, an excellent tea from the West Indies, and each had chosen their own dessert. For Benjamin it was a Chocolate Ganache and for Catharina it was a Caramel crème Brule 'with fresh berries.

After the meal they thanked their waiter and the maitre d', and then waddled away and eventually walked along the shores of Chesapeake Bay. The three days in Annapolis, the Calvert Inn, the theatre, and the gourmet dinner was a story with which they would often regale their children.

Early the next morning they started the next leg of their journey, a journey that was to become a leg to their future. They traveled at a fairly fast clip to Elizabethtown, Maryland, and arrived in the evening. They were expected at the home of Jonathan Hager. Peter had introduced them both to Jonathan at their wedding reception. Peter had discussed with Mr. Hager the possibility of Benny and Catharina buying land around their community.

"Welcome to our home and welcome to Elizabethtown," said the gregarious Jonathan Hager. "The town is named after my wife, who passed away five years ago. These are my children Rosanna and Jonathan, Jr. " Elizabethtown, later to become Hagerstown, was founded by Jonathan Hager in 1762, in the Cumberland Valley. It nestles in between the Grand Appalachian Valley and the Allegheny Mountains.

The next morning they were off early to review the available lands in the Cumberland Valley. There were many areas that appealed to them, but none as fine as the land that Jonathan Hager owned. They mentioned this to him and he broke into a smile and said, "In a about five years I want to sell off at least half of my land. I'm fifty now and want to start relaxing. Even now it is difficult for me to farm all the land and take care of my business ventures. Jonathan is not interested in being a farmer of these many acres. He wishes to have a career in engineering. Already, although he is only fifteen, he is a mathematical genius. He wants to build bridges and has a dream of building canals to provide the frontier with cheap transportation for our products. In a couple of years he will go to Philadelphia and attend Ben Franklin's Academy."

They discussed the possibilities in a lengthy discussion. Finally it was agreed they would pay a deposit of five hundred pounds to guarantee ownership in 1775. "We will have your father draw up the agreement. I know your father well. We spent three intense months of our young lives together. We were on the St. Andrew and became friends along with Dr. Jacob Lentz. During the journey your father went through a gut-wrenching emotional experience which might have scarred him for life. Maybe, I shouldn't be sharing this with you, but your father fell deeply in love with a young lady on the ship. She died during an influenza epidemic. It was all Jacob Lentz and I could do to keep him from jumping off the ship to join his dearly departed in her watery grave. When I went to the wedding of your dad and Maria, I was overjoyed to see him so happy again. Your father was at my wedding to Elizabeth and also came for her funeral. And Benny I should tell you, your father is the best damn lawyer in the West. Our agreement will be as solid as these limestone ridges in our valley."

Although Benny was not sure he wanted to wait five years to be a landowner, Catharina said, "Benny, those years will go by fast. We will always have this beautiful land to look forward to, and hopefully by that time, we will be financially able to create our own homestead for our children."

Benny and Catharina
1771 – 1774

———— ⌘ ————

Life for the Spykers during the next three years was politically stable, but all kept their eyes on the East particularly Boston where Sam Adams and "The Sons of Liberty" kept the animosity toward England at a constant level. It was a strange dance for "The Son's of Liberty," they kept the population riled up and at the same time worked to avoid any mob violence, as they thought this might derail the unity they sought between the thirteen colonies.

Benny worked diligently in his two careers, farmer and teacher. Through the help of Peter and the Tulpehocken Junto, they raised the money and the manpower to build a second school, which was located in Womelsdorf. Wilhelm Leininger taught the students from eight to twelve and Benjamin had the teenagers. The Womelsdorf school opened in September of 1770.

Benny was a little nervous the first day of school. "Students," said Benny in his most strict manner, "I'm here to teach and you are here to learn. If you don't learn, we both have failed. There will be no monkey business in my class —" Before he could finish the statement a hand shot up from the back. In his nervousness Benny had failed to see the two students who entered quietly while he had his back turned writing his name on the slate. There in the back with their hair slicked back, like the other students who were groomed by their mothers for the first day of school, were Uncle Benjamin and John Henry.

Benny was momentarily stunned, but quickly recovered, "Yes, what was your question? I think this must be the twentieth year of schooling for your friend and he still hasn't graduated. Maybe this year. Go ahead with your question."

"I'm known for my nonsense." said John Henry, "What would be my punishment?"

Benny could hardly keep from laughing. "You two were tardy and that will not be tolerated. Students, class starts at 8:00. You are to be in your seats at least five minutes before 8:00. Here's what happens if you're late. You," pointing at John Henry, "stand in this front corner. And you, who look older than Moses, sit on this dunce chair in the back."

Both obeyed immediately. "Now students do you understand that I will not put up with any nonsense?" The class seemed to understand that if Benny would not tolerate monkey business from those two older students, they best behave. Both took their punishment, and at the end of the school day they advised Benny that he was too strict for them and they would not be back.

Besides helping Benny establish his discipline policy, one other positive came out of the first day of school. John Henry recognized Anna Marie Weiser. How she had changed since the families had last gotten together. She was now sixteen-years of age and was stunning in John Henry's eyes. He was allowed to leave his corner at recess and lunch and each time he made a beeline to visit with Anna Marie. John Henry at eighteen years old was only two years older than Anna Marie.

As in the case of all in the colonies, child bearing was fraught with anxiety. It would always be an extreme gamut of joy or grief. Benny and Catharina's first child, Eleanor, died only a few days after birth. However, in the fall of 1771, Elizabeth was born. They named her Elizabeth after Elizabethtown, the town that someday would be their home. They would have no more children in Tulpehocken.

Benny and Catharina were delighted to see Benny's two sisters Anna and Maria get married. They married the Gardner brothers, Philip and Jacob. The Gardners like the Spykers were large land holders in Tulpehocken.

Peter was the Magistrate, the president of the judges in Berks county. Berks county was founded in 1752 and included not only Tulpehocken but parts of Chester, Lancaster and Philadelphia county. The county was named by the Penns after their home in England, Berkshire. As Magistrate, Peter traveled frequently to Philadelphia. Also he occasionally went to Philadelphia and the assembly meetings at the request of John Dickenson, Joseph Galloway and others. As Magistrate of Berks county he frequently met with the proprietary representatives of the Penn family. Peter was constantly caught in the middle between the two factions of government in Pennsylvania. He seemed too moderate for many in the ssembly and two conservative for the proprietors.

With each incident that occurred in the colonies, where England treated the colonists as subservient, Peter moved more and more toward wanting independence. However, his religious beliefs, inherited from his father and William Penn, refused to accept the inevitability of armed conflict to bring about independence.

It was different for his son John Henry and his brother Benjamin. They wanted separation from England even if it meant conflict. As a result, Benjamin organized a chapter of the "Sons of Liberty" in Tulpehocken and John Henry was a willing member. Often, on the pretext of Benjamin's career as trader and saddler, and with his nephew John Henry as a frequent companion, they found themselves in Boston and in association with the Boston "Sons of Liberty." John Henry was gifted with numbers and was a real asset to Benjamin in his trading and saddle-making business. John Henry, who helped both Peter and Benny farm, also made himself available to businesses in Tulpehocken to do their book-keeping. However, Uncle Benjamin was his most exciting client.

Benny was leaning toward independence even if it involved armed conflict. However, he was too busy with his careers and his family to become involved on a personal level. He and his father talked frequently about the events and he understood his father's reticence toward war.

The Boston Tea Party
1773

THE INCIDENTS WHERE ENGLAND SHOWED a lack of consideration to the colonies were always publicized and embellished by Sam Adams and the "Sons of Liberty." One such incident was the Gaspee affair. The British ship the Gaspee was chasing a smuggler in Rhode Island when it ran aground. Often British ships on the pretext of apprehending smugglers interfered with legitimate shipping on the Atlantic coast, consequently the colonists did not want the British in American water even in a lawful pursuit. Members of the "Sons of Liberty," not happy to have a British ship in the Rhode Island harbor, boarded the ship and torched it.

England instituted a Royal Commission of Inquiry and established that the members of the "Sons of Liberty" that boarded and torched the Gaspee should be sent to England and tried for treason. Although later the case was dropped because of the concern for further antagonizing the colonists, Sam Adams and the leaders of the "Sons of Liberty" used this incident to further inflame the passions of the colonists.

Incidents like this kept alive the thirst for declaring independence. Sam Adams organized a Committee of Correspondence that disseminated all the incidents which threatened the livelihood and security of the thirteen colonies. Often it was more propaganda than fact, but the goal nevertheless, was to push the colonies to separation from England.

To appease the colonies, England dropped all taxes except the tea tax. They wanted to retain this just to establish the principle that they had the right to tax the colonies. The tax did not harm the colonists. They would be paying higher prices for smuggled tea than the tea from the East India tea company. England wanted to protect the East India company from bankruptcy and allowed them to provide tea to the colonies with low taxes and low prices. However, just the idea of taxation without representation galled the patriots. It seemed that England was rudderless. Each time they tried to help one of their colonies they upset another colony.

It was early December, 1773, when Uncle Benjamin asked John Henry if he wished to spend a couple of weeks in Boston. "John Henry, this is the time of the year that I do business with the Mahigan Indians in Massachusetts and you would be a help to me in both the trading and the selling of the merchandise."

The Mahigan was a tribe of Mohican Indians and friendly with the colonies. Even at this time the Native American Indians were split between loyalties to Britain and to the American colonies. The Mahigan, to some degree because of their relationship with Benjamin, were loyal to the colonies.

"It will also give us a chance to visit our friends in Boston," continued Benjamin. "Are you interested in traveling with me?"

John Henry was more than willing, he was always excited to go to Boston, "Where the action is."

"Uncle Ben, I've been talking to my brother Benny, and he mentioned if we ever trade in the Boston area, he would be interested in traveling with us if he could get away. This is a slow time for him; school is out until January and farming during the winter only involves livestock care. Would it be okay if we ask him to go also?"

Benny was able to get away and Catharina and Peter both encouraged him to go. "Benny," said Catharina, "you need some time away from your work, and by the way, wouldn't it be nice if I had a new bonnet and some fine cloth for Liz and me?"

Peter was also happy for Benny to have this opportunity, "Benny this will help you define your feelings toward independence. I believe you will see that the colonies are not always right and just in their treatment of Britain, but the goal of the "Sons of Liberty" and other patriots is simply, whether right or wrong, they want independence. I don't always agree with the actions of Sam Adams and the patriots, but when I think of you, my grandchildren and even further down the line, I know that an independent America is best.

"Benny, let me even get more philosophical; England went through its own civil revolution and gained freedom and the right to a representative government. However, the freedom enjoyed in England is slanted toward the nobility and always will be. It depends on the luck of your birth. I dream of a society and always have where a person can achieve the highest level of society no matter his level of birth."

"Thank you dad. I understand and agree. However, I do not see England ever granting independence. Eventually we will need to fight for our independence. I look forward to not only traveling with my uncle and brother, but getting into, as you say, philosophical discussions. I've been able to communicate with my friend, Benjamin Rush. He will come to Boston, and once again his Uncle Dr. Joseph Warren, has invited us to stay at his house. Dr. Warren, as you know, is one of the leaders of the "Sons of Liberty." So I am sure I will get his opinion during the stay. Also this will give me a chance to visit Henry Knox. He now owns the book store where he worked at the time of the 'Boston Massacre.'"

On the morning of December 10th, 1773, they loaded a wagon with guns, metal traps, metal kitchen utensils, and also decorative articles for the Native American women. They would be trading for beaver pelts and deerskins. The trip took them two days. They traveled to Stockbridge in the colony of Massachusetts, which was the main location of the Mahigan. Once the trades were made, they took their pelts and deerskins into Boston to be sold to merchants for money and goods.

Benjamin had visited Boston many times and he and John Henry would stay with his friend, the editor of the *Boston Gazette*, Benjamin Edes. Edes was in his early forties and a fervent member of the Boston "Sons of Liberty." His paper did much to galvanize the support for independence.

The trade with the Mahigan in Stockbridge went very well and on December 14th they went into Boston with their large wagon heaped with beaver and deer skins. Benny was amazed that his brother, John Henry, was able to keep an accurate accounting of every trade that was made.

Benny went to Dr. Warren's house and there was his friend, Benjamin Rush, to greet him. That evening they had a meal prepared by Dr. Warren's wife, Elizabeth. They shared the meal with the family including the Warren's children Elizabeth, Joseph, Mary and Richard. After grace, Elizabeth said, "Joseph and Benjamin I hope you enjoy the wine. It is a gift from Benny and his father Peter." Benny had brought two bottles of his father's wine.

While waiting for tea and strawberry scones, Dr. Warren started to bring up the latest concern of the Massachusetts patriots, "Boys you will not believe what our idiot governor..."

Before he finished, Elizabeth squelched him, "Joseph, we will not talk politics at the table and I don't want our children to go to church this Sunday and tell Reverend Clark that Governor Hutchinson is an – you know what."

"But Mom," jumped in Joseph Jr. "He is an idiot."

"Joseph, you can be excused. No scones for you."

After the meal Dr. Warren, Benjamin and Benny retired to the library for some brandy, tea and politics. However, they were pleasantly surprised that Elizabeth would join them. "Lizzie," said Mrs. Warren to her older daughter, "You help clear the table; mother is joining the "boys" for some politics."

"Gentlemen, and dear Elizabeth, I have a rare treat, courtesy of Samuel Adams. Sam brews his own beer and has gifted me with a number of bottles. Let's give Sam's pride and joy a taste." Benny, took the open bottle and gave it a good swig. One swig was enough. Benny grimaced in culinary agony and said, "Dr. Warren, perhaps Sam should give his beer to the English. They may no longer want American products and drop the export tax."

Benjamin Rush had a more violent reaction after his healthy swig; he sprayed the contents into a nearby spittoon. "My Gott, Uncle Warren, we no longer will need the death penalty, this is far worse."

Elizabeth just took a polite sip, crossed her eyes and said, "Dear hubby, tell Sammy we thank him so much. We no longer will have to use soap to wash out Joseph, Jrs. mouth when he says a bad word."

Dr. Warren, almost rolled out of his rocking chair with laughter. "Well that's the last you'll hear of Sam Adams beer."

They switched to a sniffer of fine French brandy and the politics began.

Dr. Warren turned serious. "I need to let you know that we in Massachusetts are at an impasse. We have three ships from the East India Tea company in the harbor loaded with tea. We will not pay the taxes on the tea and have advised our good governor, who I named so aptly at dinner, to have the ships depart. There is no reason for them to remain in the harbor since we in Boston will not purchase the tea. The governor insists the ships will not leave until the tea is unloaded. It's back and forth, the assembly is adamant and the governor is adamant."

Benny, thinking there had to be a solution, "Dr. Warren, surely Massachusetts and the crown can negotiate a way out of this mess."

"Benny," the doctor answered, "We can negotiate this situation and every other new law or restriction that is passed. We can negotiate for the next one hundred years, but to be truthful my young friend, we do not want a solution, we want independence."

The next day Benny and Benjamin went on a shopping trip. Benny had to get a bonnet and cloth for Catharina and then start working on his Christmas list. He also wanted to buy a book for his father. Naturally they went to Henry Knox's book store, the London Book store. Benny was impressed with the renovated book store, "Henry this is very nice, but why do you call it the London Book store when all I see on the signs in bold letter is HENRY KNOX?"

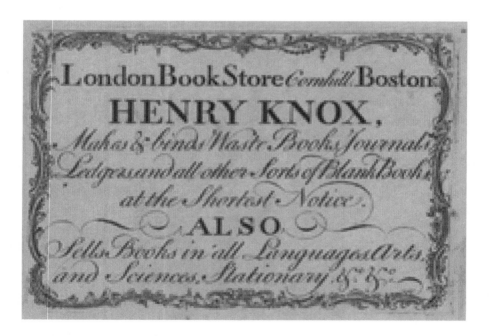

Henry closed his store for the day and accompanied Benny with his shopping. Soon they noticed and joined a large crowd outside the Old South Church. They saw Sam Adams and several others in a heated debate. Finally, Sam Adams went into the church and stepped up to the pulpit. The church was packed and the doors were open to the outside so the gathering throng could see Mr. Adams as he prepared to address the crowd. "My fellow Bostonians and all other Americans that are with us in our city, we have asked Governor Hutchinson for the last time to send the ships back fully loaded to India. He has refused. This meeting can do nothing more to save the country."

With that announcement the mob grew angrier and angrier and even started whooping like Indians. "I think some tea is going into the sea," rhymed Henry as he led them back to his book store.

The next morning, Dr. Warren called them into the library. "Boys, we had an incident last night that could lead to some drastic actions from England. Toward midnight, about fifty Mohawk, or those that looked like Mohawk, rowed into the harbor and boarded each of the East India ships. They proceeded to dump every tea chest into the sea. The harbor this morning is steeping in tea. I cannot tell you anymore details, but I would imagine you are wise enough to determine the real perpetrators."

The Spykers stayed just one more night and then all gathered at Benjamin's wagon which was loaded with goods to take back to Tulpehocken. It was a long ride back and no one said too much. Benjamin and John Henry took turns managing the two horses and wagon. While one took the reins, the other one slept. They seemed to be overwhelmed and extremely tired. Benny was quiet also, as he thought about the event of December the 16th. He was not surprised to see what looked like Indian war-paint smeared on both Uncle Benjamin's and John Henry's pants.

The Intolerable Acts
1774

———∞∞∞———

MASSACHUSETTS AND THE OTHER COLONIES waited for the hammer to fall. What would Parliament and the Crown do as a result of the "destruction of the tea" in Boston Harbor? Communications were slow because of the sailing distance to England. Also, it took time for King George, Parliament and his newly appointed Governor of Massachusetts, General Thomas Gage, to make the final decisions. General Gage thought he knew Americans best after having served successfully in America during the French and Indian war. He convinced the king of an appropriate action. "My King, Americans will be lions while we are lambs, however, if we are lions they will be as weak as lambs."

———∞∞∞———

Once Parliament reacted to the tea party, Peter was asked to attend the assembly meeting. After the meeting he carried the decision from the Parliament, along with many copies of the *Boston Gazette*, published by his Uncle Benjamin's friend, Benjamin Edes. These copies highlighted the events of December 16, 1773 and England's reaction to the "destruction of the tea."

Peter as magistrate got out the word to all of the representatives of the townships of Berks county to meet on April 25 at the county court house in Reading. After this meeting Peter would ask each representative to go back to their townships and discuss the information that he would provide. Although the meeting was for the township representatives, Peter had made it clear that all interested would be welcome. Many had seen one of the copies of the Edes article in the April 1, 1774, edition of the *Boston Gazette* and this had sparked their interest.

Boston, Massachusetts   *April 1, 1774*

HIGH TEA IN BOSTON HARBOR

British Troops Sent to Massachusetts

Band of "Mohawks" dump 342 chests of Darjeeling off Griffin's Wharf

FRANKLIN in LONDON feels the SPITE

ROOTS OF THE CONFLICT

BOSTON April 1, 1774 - King George III and Parliament responded decisively this week to The Boston Tea Party by closing the city port.

Four British regiments were sent to Boston, along with new Governor General Thomas Gage, who will replace the much-maligned Thomas Hutchinson.

Hardliners in the British government, looking for reasons to clamp down on the Bay colony, found their cause last December when the Sons of Liberty made a salty Darjeeling of Boston Harbor. 342 crates of tea were dumped into the ocean in response to a parliamentary act which imposed restrictions on the purchase of tea in the colonies.

Where Britain's actions will lead is the subject of wide speculation. While there is talk in America of some concerted effort on the part of the colonies to protest the closing of Boston harbor, historically, the colonies have been a diverse lot and many are skeptical whether they can unite in this cause. In any case, emotions are running high, and a sense of gloom is encompassing Massachusetts, and other colonies in America. One patriot mournfully observed, "Our cause is righteous and I have no doubt of final success. But I see our generation, and perhaps our whole land, drowned in blood."

⸺ ∞ ⸺

On the 25th, Peter, in his usual business-like manner, went through each action England would take as a result of the "destruction of the tea."

"First, the port of Boston will be closed. This means that at least one third of our importing and exporting will be handicapped. Despite the fact that ship flow will increase in Philadelphia and New York, this will harm not only the economy of Massachusetts but all thirteen of our colonies.

"Massachusetts will no longer have a representative government. They will still have the assembly, but members of the upper house will be appointed by the Royal Governor. The ablest representative in Massachusetts, John Adams, will no longer have a voice in the colonial government.

"Next, the assemblymen and most local officials will be appointed by the new Royal Governor of Massachusetts.

"Town meetings in Massachusetts, which are the core of self-government will be allowed to meet only once a year.

"Local courts will lose much of their jurisdiction. All capital cases will be tried in England or in another colony.

"The Quartering Act will be extended. More and more English soldiers will be permanently quartered in Boston.

Peter paused and looked out at the sixty or more people who were listening to him attentively. "Some of you are thinking that's Massachusetts problem, why should we be concerned? Gentlemen, we have come a long way since the Albany Congress and the French and Indian War. The thirteen colonies must become a cohesive unit. What affects one of the colonies affects all of us. There is no question that this is a warning to Pennsylvania and New York and all the others; step out of line and you will lose your hard-fought freedoms. It was not so many years ago that we had to ask your sons to go to war. We lost some of our young men to the French and the hostile Indians. I see on the horizon that we might have to ask you again for your sons." Peter was trying hard not to be so emotional, but he kept thinking of Benny, John Henry, the Gardner boys, and all others that he loved so dearly.

"I will not tell you how to think. You will not be chastised by me or other Pennsylvania officials if for now you decide to remain loyal to England. Neither will you be chastised for being a patriot, or like many of us, somewhere in the middle. I know there are many questions, many concerns. Finally, before opening up to these questions and concerns, I wish to advise you that the leaders of the Massachusetts colony and the Virginia colony are calling a congress to decide the actions that should be taken by the thirteen colonies. They will call it a Continental Congress. As you can see, leaders in the various colonies are trying to accomplish what Benjamin Franklin tried to do so long ago at the Albany Congress; that is, to get the colonies to work together for the good of each colony."

The meeting lasted another hour, but most left the meeting with a determination to be an independent country and to work with all the colonies in the interest of each colony.

First Continental Congress

1774

—❧—

THE CONTINENTAL CONGRESS WOULD BEGIN in Philadelphia at Carpenter's Hall on September 5, 1774. In all fifty-six delegates would attend from twelve of the thirteen colonies. Georgia had opted not to attend as they needed assistance from the English government and their military station in America to protect them from Cherokee raids.

Eight delegates from Pennsylvania were designated to attend including Peter's friends John Dickenson and John Morton. Also Joseph Galloway, who was still touting his "Plan of Union," was one of the delegates. All the Pennsylvania delegates had once again suggested to the new Speaker that Peter attend the congress and be an impartial legal mind whom they could question and receive unbiased interpretations.

The new Speaker of the Assembly was Edward Biddle, who was the representative from Berks county who replaced Peter in 1767. "Peter," requested Speaker Biddle, "it is essential that you be our lawyer during this congress. You will be the one to keep the peace among our delegates. We have chosen an even split in delegates, those for reconciliation and those like me for independence. We'll see if any of these change their positions during the congress."

Peter recalled the first time he had met Speaker Biddle. He was sitting in his law office in Reading when his secretary had informed him there was a young gentleman to see him. "Mr. Spyker, thank you for seeing me. I've just moved from Philadelphia with my wife to start a law practice in Reading. My father and Isaac Norris are good friends and Mr. Norris suggested that as soon as I get to Reading that I introduce myself to you. Mr. Norris has great respect for you. Also I know your brother Benjamin. We fought together in the battle of Quebec during the French and Indian War."

Peter became a mentor for Edward and encouraged him to run for the assembly. Edward also renewed his friendship with Benjamin Spyker. Edward like Benjamin, was determined to lead America to independence. He also became a member of the "Sons of Liberty" in Tulpehocken.

As was true of the Stamp Act Congress, much of the discussion and debate would go on outside the Congress chamber. Peter had asked his son Benny to be with him in the discussions outside the chamber. Benny was becoming involved in the politics of Tulpehocken and would represent the younger generation who might be called to bear arms.

Coincidently, one of the delegates from Virginia, George Washington, had asked his brother Benjamin to be a consultant to him. It was a distinguished list of delegates with both John and Sam Adams from Massachusetts and George Washington and Patrick Henry from Virginia.

The gavel was given to Peyton Randolph of Virginia to be the chairman of this august body of representatives. History would show that this was the greatest collection of leaders in American history. Peter was given the responsibility to be the legal advisor to the eight Pennsylvania delegates.

"Mr. Chairman," said James Galloway, delegate from Pennsylvania and past Speaker of the Assembly, "It is good that we meet together. We must put aside our jealousies between individual colonies and stand together and show England, King George and Parliament that we are of one mind and voice. However, it is essential that we present our grievances and get resolve rather than seek to separate from our Mother country. We need England's sea power and military might to keep us from being overcome by the other European powers such as Spain and France. Together with England we will have an 'empire that will never see the setting sun.'

"Gentlemen," continued Mr. Galloway, "as you are aware, I have authored a plan that will address the grievances we have with England and create an atmosphere of co-government and co-existence that will make our union inseparable. Mr. Chairman, I would like to put this in a form of a motion for discussion and eventually a vote for implementation:

"Resolve to create an American Colonial Parliament to act together with the Parliament of Great Britain.

"Resolve, on matters relating to the colonies, both parliaments, Colonial Parliament and Parliament of Great Britain, would have a veto over the other's decision.

"Resolve, The Colonial Parliament would consist of a President-General appointed by the Crown, and delegates appointed by the colonial assemblies. "

With the introduction of Galloway's "Plan of Union," the debate started. The debate continued on the floor, in the hotels, and in the restaurants and pubs of Philadelphia.

"The chair recognizes Mr. Jay, delegate from New York."

"Mr. Chairman, while I support in substance the motion in front of us as a long term goal; we must first address the grievances. Our rights of life, liberty, and property have been violated. Until England and Parliament have made amends particularly to the colony of Massachusetts and New York, there can be no plan of union.

"Here, here", was a resounding echo throughout Carpenter Hall.

"The chair recognizes John Adams from Massachusetts."

"Mr. Chairman, we can resolve this issue with some sort of compromise. We can propose Mr. Galloway's 'Plan of Union.' We can meet here at least once a year to resolve the next violation of our rights and the next year again to resolve another issue. We can do this for the rest of my life, the rest of my children's lives, my grandchildren's lives, etcetera, etcetera, etcetera. My fellow Americans we are independent, free thinking individuals. We crave more independence than any free English citizens. We are not just English. We are German, we are Irish, we are Scot, we are Swiss, we are Americans. It is time for us to look beyond ourselves. It is time to declare independence for our children's future. Let's not wheedle and bow to England. Let us become citizens of America a free an independent country."

Another round of "Here, here", resounded from delegates on the floor.

The debates continued on the floor, but the most interesting debates and discussions took place in the pubs, like the Tun Tavern. During the first week of October it seemed like Galloway's "Plan of Union" would be adopted. Peter, Benny, Benjamin and George Washington got together several times for dinner at the Tun.

They were just finishing up a fine meal of crabs, lobsters, and oysters all washed down with home-brewed Philadelphia ale. "George," said Peter, "You're a military man. You've planned military strategy and you've fought on the battlefield. Let me pose a question that has been on my mind for some time. I do not think the "Plan of Union" will resolve our differences with England. I think England will come down on us even harder and will send their best military force to keep us in line. I do not see any way we, a fledgling military without any national army and navy, can possibly defeat the strongest army and navy in the world. What should we do? Should we just capitulate and just try to live our lives the best we can under English rule?"

George Washington took a long time to respond. His intense blue eyes peered into the souls of the Spykers. "Peter, you are wrong. Your brother and I have discussed your exact concerns intensely during this congress. That is why I wanted Benjamin here. If we get in a war with England, there is no way we can lose. We have no choice but to win. We are fighting for our home. England is fighting to discipline one of their colonies. The will to win is the most important factor in battle."

George was frequently quiet in political debates, but one could tell he had thought many hours about this subject. This was George Washington in one of his most intense moments.

He continued, "We have other things in our favor. The ocean separates England from supplies including arms. America is foreign to most British military men. General Gage is an exception and he will be a strong opponent. However, he still is an Englishman with English ideas of warfare: Line up with red coats, march forward, kneel down, fire, next line march forward, kneel down, fire. We will not fight fair. We will hide behind trees. We will wear clothes that blend into the environment. France and other European countries will ally with us. We will have the eyes of our citizens always reporting to us on the enemies locations and actions. We cannot lose. We will not lose."

Benjamin and Benny kept nodding their agreement and for the first time Peter realized America could become independent no matter the resolve of England.

———— ⚬❊⚬ ————

"The chair recognizes Samuel Adams, delegate from Massachusetts."

"Mr. Chairman, fellow delegates. We in Massachusetts and particularly Boston have suffered the most from the coercive acts of Parliament. Our ports are closed, and it is only through the cooperation of the other colonies, and through the ports of Philadelphia and New York that Massachusetts has been able to survive. Also it is important to note that the province of Quebec has continuously shipped us wheat without the necessity of immediate payment. This has kept our households from hunger. It is my conclusion that England and Parliament have wanted us to beg and to come before them with our tail between our legs. 'Please open our ports, we will be good boys and girls.' They do not know the resolve of Bostonians or for that matter Americans."

Sam then relayed the most recent news from Boston. "While we have been debating the "Plan of Union," proposed by my friend Joseph Galloway, we in Boston and the colony of Massachusetts have decided on how we are going to react to the coercive acts or now called the Intolerable Acts. I have just received from my friend Paul Revere, who has ridden all night from Boston, the actions to be taken in our colony. Let me address them to you:

"Number 1", Samuel Adams, enumerated the actions of his county of Suffolk, which included the city of Boston, by signaling with each finger, "boycott British imports, curtail exports, and refuse to use British products.

"Number 2. Pay 'no obedience' to the Massachusetts Governor Act, which you know took away our representative powers and gave sweeping powers to the royal governor.

"Number 3. Do not obey the Boston Port Bill which barricades and blockades our port.

"Number 4. The royal governor appointed the representatives to our assembly. We demand their resignations.

"Number 5. We will refuse to pay taxes until the Massachusetts Government Act is repealed.

"Number 6. We will only support a colonial government in Massachusetts free of royal authority until the Intolerable Acts are repealed.

"Number 7. We will form a militia of our own people.

"Mr. Chairman", Sam Adams continued, "before we take a vote on the 'Plan of Union,' I propose time to debate and discuss the decisions made by Suffolk county and Boston and see if this is a better direction for our congress than the 'Plan of Union.'"

The congress immediately went into an uproar with both sides, those wishing legislative parity and those wishing separation, shouting and pointing fingers at each other. Chairman Randolph, who had argued both sides of the issues and was personally unresolved between the two contrasting sides, pounded the gavel. "Gentlemen, gentlemen, please. I would like a motion for adjournment until Monday. You can talk in your personal groups and on Monday we will have discussion and debate on the Suffolk actions. We will allow a day for debate on these actions, and before adjourning for the day take a vote on the Galloway 'Plan of Union.'" The meeting was adjourned.

Peter asked the eight delegates from Pennsylvania to meet in a special room of the hotel. It was an interesting meeting as the eight delegates were evenly split between legislative parity and separation. Peter did not participate in the debate but let each one have an opportunity to state their thoughts and try to convince the others of their opinion.

It was interesting in that two were Quakers, one Charles Humphreys who was dedicated to no war at any cost and Thomas Mifflin who was willing to separate from the Quakers to gain independence. Of the four conservatives, Peter's friend, John Morton was the most determined to favor the Suffolk actions. Naturally

Joseph Galloway, the creator of the plan for legislature parity was determined not to separate from England. John Dickinson was leaning toward legislature parity but not yet willing to commit to the "Plan of Union."

The meeting lasted all of Saturday and they met again on Sunday after each returned from their separate houses of worship. At the end, Peter summarized the discussion. "It is obvious that we are still evenly split on whether or not to accept the 'Union Plan'. I think it is impossible for Pennsylvania to cast its vote either way. Gentlemen, I think Pennsylvania should abstain. However, once a decision is made, our colony should support the Congress decision to our constituents. All eight nodded their heads in agreement.

On Monday the chairman opened the session and a discussion on the Suffolk actions. Despite the split between the "Plan of Union" and Suffolk actions the debate although intense was amenable. Chairman Randolph was very fair in his recognition of both sides. He had stated at the beginning of the day, "Delegates you will all get a chance to state your case and ask questions, but you only do so when I recognize you. You will not butt in on someone else's time and you will be respectful of each other. You may be from New York or you may be from South Carolina, but it is time you realize we are all from America."

At the end of the day the chairman stated, "Gentlemen, thank you. It has been an enlightening discussion. There need be no more debate. As I stated on Friday, we will not adjourn today's session until we have voted on Mr. Galloway's 'Plan of Union.' As suggested by Edward Rutledge of South Carolina and accepted by the majority, we will vote by colonies, with the representative of each colony voting as his delegation has so advised.

The motion, to accept Joseph's Galloway "Plan of Union," was restated by the secretary of the congress and the voting commenced:

"Connecticut" – Silas Deanne stood and said "Yes we are in favor of the 'Plan of Union.'"

"Delaware" – "Yes"

"Mr. Samuel Chase, how does Maryland vote?" – "We are opposed."

"John Adams, I think we know the Massachusetts vote." – "We will not support the Plan of Union"

"New Hampshire" – "We approve the plan."

"New Jersey" – "Yes"

"New York": There was a question in everyone's mind about the way New York would vote. Although it was fairly split among the delegates, John Jay stood and firmly said, –"We support Joseph Galloway's 'Plan of Union.' We don't approve of Parliament's actions, but we must try to reconcile."

"North Carolina": Also here there was doubt on how the colony would vote. John Hewes stood, –"Although I could support the 'Plan of Union', as a representative of my constituents, I must vote no."

There was a buzz in the Congress as those counting votes sensed a turn from what they expected.

"Pennsylvania" : Edward Biddle stood and explained– "We are evenly divided we cannot vote. We abstain."

Again a buzz went through Congress as many felt Pennsylvania being a predominate Quaker state would be for reconciliation to avoid war.

"Rhode Island" – "We vote no to the Galloway plan."

"South Carolina" – We vote no."

The vote stood at five to five and everyone knew how Virginia would vote.

"Virginia": All geared for a dramatic speech by Patrick Henry and they were not disappointed.

Patrick Henry "Give me liberty or give me death."

"Mr. Chairman, distinguished member of this Congress," With a flair and hands moving in concert with his comments, "it is natural to man to indulge in the illusions of hope. We are apt to shut our eyes against a painful truth, and listen to the song of the siren till she transforms us into beasts. Is this the part of wise men, engaged in a great and arduous struggle for liberty? Are we disposed to be of the number of those who, having eyes, see not, and having ears, hear not, the things which so nearly concern their temporal salvation?

"For my part, whatever anguish of spirit it may cost, I am willing to know the whole truth; to know the worst and to provide for it. I have but one lamp by which my feet are guided, and that is the lamp of experience. I know of no way of judging the future but by the past. And judging by the past, I wish to know what there has been in the conduct of the British ministry for the last ten years to justify those hopes with which gentlemen have been pleased to solace themselves and this congress? Gentlemen, we have done everything that could be done to avert the storm which is now coming. We have petitioned; we have remonstrated; we have supplicated;

we have prostrated ourselves before the throne, and have implored its interposition to arrest the tyrannical hands of the ministry and Parliament.

"Our petitions have been slighted; our remonstrance has produced additional violence and insult; our supplications have been disregarded; and we have been spurned, with contempt, from the foot of the throne. In vain, after these things, may we indulge the fond hope of peace and reconciliation? There is no longer any room for hope." Patrick then paused, looked at each delegation and then with a quiet, tired voice, said,– "Virginia votes no."

Once again the oratorical ability of Patrick Henry raised the emotions of his audience. Throughout the chamber, a chorus of "No" reached epic proportions.

Finally chairman Peyton Randolph banged his gavel repeatedly and got the congress back to order. "Gentlemen, we have rejected the 'Union Plan' of legislative parity. We must now come up with a unified plan of action. We have been given the task by our constituents to answer Parliament's Intolerable Acts. We must be sober in our speech and diligent in our action. Our very liberties and possibly the lives of our sons depend upon our decision. Let us adjourn and tackle anew the problem before us tomorrow morning. This session is adjourned."

The Congress remained in session until October 26, 1774. Finally on the last day when all debate was finished and decisions were made, the Chairman Henry Middleton, who had taken over for Peyton Randolph who became seriously ill, asked the secretary of the congress, Charles Thomson of Philadelphia to read the final decision.

"Mr. Chairman, members of this Congress. Here is our course of action as you have decided by a majority:

"We will boycott English goods until they have repealed the Intolerable Acts.

"We will require the same from our friends in the West Indies and will monitor their actions to make sure they cooperate.

"We will form a committee of observation to make sure all colonies and subjects adhere to this boycott.

"If England does not acquiesce and repeal the Intolerable Acts by September 10, 1775, we will cease all exports to England.

"And finally, we will have a 2nd Continental Congress on May 10, 1775, to evaluate the actions of England."

Christmas Eve

1774

———— ∞∞∞ ————

AGAIN IT WAS TIME FOR the traditional Spyker family Christmas Eve. It would be held at Peter and Maria Spyker's house in Tulpehocken. It was a time to celebrate the birth of Christ, but also a time to discuss the issues of the day. Peter, now sixty-three years old, was crowned with a full head of brilliant silver hair. Although still strong and in full stature, his face was wrinkled with the concerns of his country facing the possibility of war.

His son Benny and Catharina were there early in the morning helping to prepare the house and the food for the grand party. With them was their precocious three-year-old daughter Elizabeth, now called Liz. Liz was into everything, wanting to help pull the feathers from the turkeys, decorate the Christmas tree and asking a thousand questions.

Benny had returned from Boston with a new resolve, "Father, I am a patriot. I do not want compromise or reconciliation. I want independence for America."

Peter answered him, "At all costs, even war?"

"Even war. I do not want my children to be under the rule of any foreign nation. I want them to live in a free an independent nation. George Washington convinced me that America can be successful if it comes to a war of revolution. I know it may be a great sacrifice in life and treasure, but we must think of our future generations."

Guests started arriving in the middle of the afternoon. Although the party was at Peter's and Maria's, Benny and Catharina served as the greeting hosts. The first guest was not a guest, but a member of the household. "Hello, John Henry, and who's that beautiful girl you have on your arm?" John Henry blushed slightly as he led Anna Maria Weiser into his home.

"Anna," greeted Benny, "I thought I warned you about this delinquent student who makes his home in the corner of my schoolhouse."

Anna laughed and hugged John Henry's arm. "He's my warrior. He may march to war but before he does he's going to march me down the aisle." John Henry kept blushing, but you could tell he was pleased.

Other guests kept arriving and then came a huge gentlemen with a rotund wife. "Henry," said Benny as he reached up to hug Henry Knox, who was about six foot three and three hundred pounds, "I am delighted you are here, thank you so much, and who's this charming lady beaming at your side?"

Henry Knox in his revolutionary uniform.

"Lucy, I want you to meet my friend of controversy, Benny Spyker. Every time he comes to Boston he brings confrontation with the redcoats. I met him when several Americans were killed in front of the book store by lobsterback guards. Sam Adams has been successful in labeling it a massacre, the 'Boston Massacre.'

"Benny was also in Boston December 16th, just six months before our marriage. Do you remember some wild Mohawk, boarding East India ships and steeping a large cup of tea in the Boston harbor? This was the infamous event called 'destruction of the tea.' Now many are calling it the 'Boston Tea Party.'

"Benny," continued Henry who was capable of talking an hour non-stop, "this is my wife Lucy, the former Lucy Fluker. We were married on June 16th. I didn't invite you because we married secretly without the good wishes of Lucy's parents. Her parents are loyalists and her brother is in the British army."

Without stopping for a further explanation, Henry turned to Catharina, "I take it this lovely little flower next to you is Catharina. Catharina, Benny cannot finish a conversation without talking about his sweet Catharina."

With that, Henry reached way down to hug Mrs. Spyker. Lucy was almost as out-going as her husband and quickly hugged both Benny and Catharina. She was, however, not able to get a word in edgewise as Henry retained the floor.

"Benny, I've got lots to tell you about events in Massachusetts, but I know we need to wait until after dinner at cigar, brandy, and political time, and no, Lucy you can't come in but you and Catharina can listen from the door."

Lucy, quickly, chimed in with eyes rolling to the ceiling, "Who would want to gag on your cigar smoke and be bored with your tales of woe?" She laughed along with Catharina and gave her husband a big smooch on his rosy cheek.

Other guests kept arriving. Besides the adults, many children came in with their parents and grandparents and headed right to the Christmas tree where Liz was showing them all the decorations she had lovingly placed on the lower limbs of the huge fir tree.

Benny was happy to greet Edward Biddle and his wife Elizabeth nee Ross Biddle. "Mr. Speaker," addressed Benny to the Speaker of the Pennsylvania Assembly, "I'm Mr. Spyker." The name Spyker was pronounced Speaker and this was an old joke between Edward, Peter, and Benny. They played it to the hilt, "I'm Mr. Speaker." "No, I'm Mr. Spyker, you're Mr. Speaker," and so on. Catharina and Elizabeth just looked at each other as if to say, "doesn't this ever get old."

Shortly after Speaker Biddle arrived, Benny saw his friend Benjamin Rush coming up the lane. He didn't wait for the doorbell but went to meet him. He knew Benjamin was likely depressed as his fiancé, Sarah Eve, had died just a month before their planned wedding. "Benjamin, thank you for coming. I'm so sad about Sarah. She was a wonderful person."

"Yes, Benny, she was indeed. I hesitated about coming, but knew seeing you and Catharina might help cheer me up."

Benny, just put his arm around his good friend and led him to Catharina, who gave him a lengthy hug.

It was a beautiful cold day in Tulpehocken. The sun was shining brightly on over a foot of new fallen snow. The pond was frozen solid and both adults and children enjoyed the sledding and ice skating. The children helped John Henry build a snowman in the Spyker's front yard. All the children laughed when John Henry fashioned a crown, put it on top of the snowman, and pronounced that this was King George III. It became great fun to hurl snowballs and try to knock the crown off the king.

Just as it was starting to get dark, Maria rang the triangular medal ironwork that was hanging from the large tree in the backyard. She rang it with enthusiasm as she yelled, "Come one, come all, dinner is served." Immediately all activity stopped and the race began. All were eager for the Spyker Christmas Eve dinner that they knew would be a feast. They were not disappointed. Piled in front of them and on the side serving tables were golden brown turkeys with all the vegetable, fruits and pies. With the food were containers of fresh milk from the Spyker dairy herd and decanters of wine from the Spyker winery. It was a feast and all the children eyes were considerably bigger than their stomachs.

As the children started reaching for their favorite pie slices, Marie stopped them and said, "Children, we will have God's bounty before we have God's pies, and before either we will have a prayer. Peter has a special prayer."

Peter stood and asked all to hold hands in a continuous circle. They all bowed their heads as Peter gave the blessing, "Lord, bless our family, all of us now together, those who are far away and all who are gone back to you. May we know joy. May we bear our sorrows in patience. Let love guide our understanding of each other. Let us be grateful to each other. We have all made each other what we are. O Family of Jesus, watch over our family."

At the time of dessert, Peter, stood again and asked to address the family and guests. "I'd like to take this occasion to announce that a branch of the Spyker family will be moving from Tulpehocken to Maryland. My good friend, Jonathan Hager, who is with us tonight along with his son, encouraged Benny to come to his town, Elizabethtown, just across our border in Maryland. He wanted a strong German Lutheran family to move to Elizabethtown and particularly was excited about Benny enhancing the educational program of the Elizabethtown area. This week Benny and Catharina will finalize the land purchase agreement."

All stood and applauded the announcement and then Benny added, "Thank you, father; thank you, Jonathan Hager. We will make the plans and start building in the spring as well as plant our first crops and pasture our first livestock. Rest assured we will return many times to Tulpehocken and will not miss the Spyker Christmas Eve."

Maria could not help herself and started weeping silently. She went to her son and hugged him for what seemed forever and then hugged Catharina. Finally she regained her typical poise and sense of humor. "Enough tears; you men go smoke your horrible cigars and solve all the world problems, while we ladies clean up your mess and try to unearth some titillating rumors about all our community women who are not here to defend themselves."

The mass exodus began: the women stayed in the huge dining room to gossip, the young children gathered together for hide and seek and outside for tag, the teens gathered in the basement for a game of spin the bottle, and the men went with great purpose to the parlor for their smokes, brandy and political discussions and hopefully arguments. Some in the group would take the opposite side as they loved to argue. If some said it was dark outside others would say, "it's still light".

It didn't take long for the action to start in the parlor. Henry Knox, held court and gave everyone an update on the events in Massachusetts after the infamous rebuttal of the Intolerable Acts. Henry with his booming voice and great size filled up the parlor, and all paid rapt attention.

"Parliament and the Crown are being very sweet to every colony but Massachusetts. They are also calling every Massachusetts's patriot a traitor, but offering amnesty to all but Samuel Adams and John Hancock. They are going to allow all but Massachusetts to have their assemblies or legislatures make the decision on the taxes. We are being punished for the 'Boston Tea Party' and other of our decisions acts they deem rebellious. How does Pennsylvania feel about this?"

Peter immediately jumped in, "Henry, we are no longer thirteen independent governments. What affects one of the colonies affects us all. Parliament and King George are trying to drive a wedge between Massachusetts and us. It will not work."

Benny then stood and said, "We will be with Massachusetts when we are called. I have already assured Henry Knox that if he needs me I will be on my horse and headed to Boston the minute he calls whether I'm here in Tulpehocken or Elizabethtown. Catharina supports me on this. She is a strong women and wants independence for our child and our children to come. No matter the situation at home, she has told me to go to our country's needs."

John Henry quickly added, "And Benny knows I will be riding by his side."

Speaker Biddle then gave an official statement, "Mr. Knox, please tell Sam and John Adams, Dr. Warren, John Hancock and our other patriots, you can count on the Pennsylvania Assembly to support Massachusetts. Tell us what is going on in the Boston area? Are the redcoats making overtures of war?"

Henry Knox, broke into a smile, "Gentlemen, it is serious business dealing with an enemy and I do mean enemy that wants to take away our God-given liberties, but there are some jolly moments I want to tell you about. Our friend General Gage has little respect for us Yankees. He has told the King, 'Without rum they could neither fight or say their prayers.'"

Uncle Benjamin quickly jumped to his feet, "Friends, I propose a rum toast to General Gage." All raised their cups of tea or spirits as Benjamin said, "To General Gage. One Yankee with a tankard of rum is worth ten lobsterbacks. One Yankee with a cup of freedom is worth one hundred lobsterbacks. Take your rum and take your tea to your little island called England and don't let the sun set on your lobster backs."

"Here, here", became so loud several of the women rushed into the parlor to rescue their husbands from a dreadful fight.

After all had settled down after Benjamin's motivating toast, Henry again addressed the men, "I've got some unsettling and some amusing incidents to tell you about, which will answer

Speaker Biddle's question. General Gage, indeed, is concerned about the actions in Massachusetts. He knew the patriots were trying to stockpile cannons, guns and powder so he confiscated these supplies from arsenals in Cambridge and Charles Town. This prompted our Provincial Congress to appropriate monies for new military supplies. The Congress then organized a 'Committee of Safety' headed by John Hancock, to keep all patriots throughout the thirteen colonies informed. We have also organized a large militia. Coincidently, Benny, just mentioned he would ride to our needs the minute he's called that is why we call the militia 'Minutemen'. Our citizen army will be ready to fight the minute they are called. General Gage called our Congress a treasonable body. Maybe. However, once we finished our business, the Congress promptly dissolved and disappeared. Upon this action, John Adams related to General Gage, we have no body, how can we treasonable?'

"General Gage is also confused on how rum-filled Yankees keep sinking his supply barges, wrecking his provision wagons and even burning the straw meant to keep the beds of his men comfy. Sarah Tarant told me that General Gage and some of his officers were in her pub the other night, filled with rum, pounding their fists and heads on the tables and moaning, those 'Damn Yankees, Damn Yankees.'

With that bit of humor Benjamin again called for a toast to those "Damn Yankees,"

Henry Knox with an enthusiastic audience could not help continuing with his storytelling. "I've got to tell you about our first victory in this uprising, which will soon be war. General Gage decided to raid the arsenal at Fort William and Mary to make sure the Yankees didn't relieve the fort of valuable munitions. Sadly one night, for General Gage, several lobsterbacks with a tankard or two of the drink that Yankees can't pray without, were joking about it to the bar maid, Maggie O'Bryan. She went several tables over and whispered in the ear of Paul Revere. He quickly left, mounted his favorite stallion 'Boston Silver' and rode to see our patriot general, John Sullivan. Two days later with great confidence General Gage and his jolly troop rode into the fort only to face seventy-five Minutemen. The highly polished and beautifully attired redcoats quickly surrendered and with tails between their legs returned to their Boston barracks. There you have it gents, Yankees one, Redcoats zero."

All stood and applauded. That ended the evening and all went to their homes or Jacob Seltzer's Inn and dreamed of sugar plums and English ships sailing back to London.

Home in Elizabethtown, Maryland
1775

—∞∞∞—

SOON AFTER MAKING THE FINAL payment to Jonathan Hager and signing the legal documents, Benny and Catharina went for a visit to Elizabethtown, where they were guests of Jonathan. It was late January and there was snow on the ground, but they were able to plot out their house and barn. The house was easy to visualize as it would look similar to the Peter Spyker house.

With measurements and descriptions in hand, Benny and Catharina traveled to Philadelphia to visit her brother, Thomas Seidel, who was the heir of Gabriel's architecture practice. Before they left their meeting with Thomas they had the plans and a well designed picture of their home to be.

Author's idea of the plans for the Benny Spyker home in
Frederick County Maryland

In March they broke ground and worked through the spring both building and planting. John Henry and Catharina along with Jonathan Hager's son worked right alongside Benny. It did not take long for Benny and Catharina to make good friends of their new neighbors in Elizabethtown and Frederick county and some of these friends helped as well. As was true of Peter in building his house, Benny had craftsmen from Elizabethtown help create their home.

During this building stage they frequently traveled back to Tulpehocken. Benny kept hearing from his dad that they were getting closer and closer to a war of revolution. General Gage and his military kept insisting to Parliament that this was simply a minor disagreement that would soon be put down. After all, *"We are the strongest military in the world, and the colonists are like a small needle that keeps pricking our backside. Soon the needle will be back in the haystack."*

One evening in March, 1775, when Benny and Catharina had come for an Easter visit, Peter and his sons along with Uncle Benjamin were enjoying a pint of ale in Seltzer's Tavern.

As they were discussing the details of Benny's house in Elizabethtown, Edward Biddle, recently returned from the Pennsylvania Assembly meeting, came in to join them by the roaring fire. As soon as they had finished the "I'm Mister Speaker, you're Mister Spyker routine, Speaker Biddle regaled them with the latest conflict in Massachusetts. It was a humorous story, probably a little embellished by a typical politician.

"We are driving General Gage mad. He is getting very frustrated with his attempts to relieve our Minutemen of their weapons and munitions. The General, God bless his addled ego, heard from some loyalists that there was a large cache of cannons and munitions in Salem, Massachusetts. He sent two hundred and forty of his crack soldiers to relieve the Yankees of their war chest.

Unfortunately for General Gage, our patriot spies heard about the plan and informed our colonel, Timothy Pickering. Colonel Pickering quickly assembled forty Minutemen, had them begin to remove the weapons and put up the drawbridge leading into Salem. When the redcoats arrived at the river and the drawn-up bridge they saw facing them across the river the Minutemen. Both groups threatened with their weapons, the muskets in the hands of the British and the rifles in the hands of forty sharpshooters. It looked like the beginning of open conflict. However, Reverend Icabod Smithson of the Salem Lutheran church came to the forefront and with his hand on his black Bible, which actually was no Bible, but a copy of the church financial records, swore there were no cannons or munitions in the town. After he had stalled them long enough that all the weapons were removed, he invited them into the town to inspect. There were no weapons. Colonel Leslie, the British commander of the troops, apologized. "Reverend, we are sorry, I should have realized a man of the cloth would be telling the truth."

The Spykers and all in the tavern enjoyed the tale of Yankee ingenuity and guile.

Although Benny and Catharina enjoyed visiting their parents and siblings frequently during the days of establishing their home, they were happy to finally move their household furnishings as well as their livestock to their new home and pastures.

Soon after moving, Catherina had some special news for Benny. "My dearest you have given me a new home where we will have a wonderful life with our sweet Liz and her new brother, who will be here sometime in November."

Benny was happy but a little confused, "My darling bride, why do you say brother?"

"Don't you remember at Christmas when you asked Elizabeth what she wanted for Christmas and she said a little brother. When you asked her 'Why not a sister?' what did she say?"

"I remember," laughed Benny, she said, "we already have two girls. It's only fair that I have a brother."

"We are at War"
1775

⸻

"Congregation, this morning I will dispense with the sermon." Reverend Kurtz continued to address his worshipers on Sunday, June 25th. "Judge Peter has just returned from Philadelphia where the Congress is at recess for a week. He wishes to tell you the events that have occurred before the meeting of the Second Continental Congress and the actions that have been taken in the Congress."

The congregation remained silent as Peter made his way to the pulpit. Although Peter was considered a strong but silent personality, when in front of an audience he was an elegant and passionate speaker who was able to motivate all those listening.

"My dear friends in Christ, I've asked Reverend Kurtz for this opportunity, because we, Tulpehocken, Pennsylvania and our thirteen colonies need your prayers. We are no longer on the brink of war; we are at war." Peter paused to let this statement resonate with all in attendance. He could tell by their faces there was great concern, but also he could see the German Lutheran resolve, *"We will make the best situation out of everything that comes our way."*

"Let me take you through the most important events that caused our Congress to take arms against the British and the decisions they have made to win our independence. I do not ask you to not be afraid, but I want to assure you we will win our independence." The congregation that was always silent during the church services except in their lusty hymn singing and their recital of the Psalms and the liturgy, started to applaud timidly. Their timid applause continued to rise until it reached a crescendo that could be heard for miles. They were of one mind.

"The first battle of the war against the British occurred on April 19th in Lexington and then Concord. The British goal was to confiscate all munitions and weapons from Lexington and Concord, two cities close to Boston. It was to be a secret foray where the British would not only confiscate military supplies, but also arrest who they considered the two leaders of the patriots, John Hancock and Samuel Adams. The patriots have spies everyplace, barmaids, blacksmiths, hotel managers, market place employees and other people who had access to accommodating the British soldiers. Dr. Warren, the leader of the 'Sons of Liberty' heard about the British plot and asked his friend, Paul Revere, to alert the country side and to find Sam Adams and John Hancock and ask them to flee the Lexington area.

Peter continued to relate the news to an attentive audience. "The attack on Lexington did not surprise the fore-warned colonists. Minutemen were waiting for them and when the British troops secretly entered Lexington, lo and behold, church bells rang and rifle fire commenced. I wish I could tell you we repelled the British and won the battle. However, the British had reinforcements come in and overwhelmed our Minutemen. As the British left Lexington for Concord, our patriot commander Captain Parker, and eight of his Minutemen lay dead on the Lexington green.

"The British continued to Concord in hopes of arresting Adams and Hancock. Our Minutemen regrouped, more citizen soldiers joined them and we fared better at Concord. All along the route to Concord we sniped at the redcoats. Several times we caused them to retreat and gain reinforcements. At the end of the day, we lost almost fifty men and the British lost over one hundred. Blood has been shed. There is no turning back. On May 10th, as previously planned during the First Continental Congress, we gathered again in Philadelphia. However, when this date of the Second Continental Congress was set, we had no idea we would already be at war. We are fortunate to have many fine gentlemen on this Congress including our friend Benjamin Franklin. John Hancock has been elected as the Chairman. The Congress has established a Continental Army under General George Washington to prosecute the war for independence. General Washington and Congress have requested that each colony establish a militia and be ready to reinforce the present army which is the Massachusetts militia, known as the Minutemen."

Peter paused and then made a request. "Dear friends, we will need able-bodied men to join our military. We will also need money to arm our colony's militia. I ask you for the most generous donations possible. I have been appointed by the Provincial Government of Pennsylvania to be the individual responsible for raising this capital in Berks county. That is the reason I am talking with you this morning. In the weeks ahead I will be canvassing every household in Berks county to raise these funds.

Thanks to my brother, Benjamin, we have already established the foundations for our militia. He has formed an Association of Berks county for this purpose. The Colonel in charge will be John Patton, his first major is Joseph Thornburg and his second major is Christian Lauer. My son, John Henry, is the Major Adjutant. With your help we will be prepared to gain independence for America." With this summary of the events, Peter stepped down to sit with his family.

Reverend Kurtz returned to the pulpit for a prayer for guidance and then went to the organ and all joined in with great gusto, *"A mighty fortress is our God, a bulwark never failing; our helper he amid the flood of mortal ills prevailing. For still our ancient foe doth seek to work us woe; his craft and power are great, and armed with cruel hate, on earth is not his equal. . ."*

The Guns of Ticonderoga
1775

THE SIEGE OF BOSTON LOOMED ahead. General Gage and his British troops controlled the city. How could the colonies dismantle the redcoats from the city? They were looking at over a hundred British ships in the Boston Harbor and thousands of British soldiers. They needed a miracle to drive the British from Boston. Both the British and the Continental Army were playing a waiting game. The British kept bringing more and more ships into the harbor and the patriots kept beseeching the colonies for more recruits.

It was November 5, 1775. Benny and Catharina had just sat down to dinner. "Mama," said Liz, "When is baby Henrich getting here? I'm getting tired of waiting. It's been a long time since you said we would be having a baby. I've been looking under the cabbage leaves and now the cabbage leaves are gone. I don't think the baby is ever going to come."

"Who told you the baby would be under the cabbage leaves?"

"Grandpa Spyker."

Catharina laughed, "Wait until I get hold of Grandpa. Liz, the baby is in my tummy. Jesus put the baby in mother's tummy."

"Oh," said Liz, "I thought Grandpa was full of beans."

Neither Catharina nor Benny could keep from laughing at their precocious daughter.

"Liz, you must be patient," said Catharina who looked like she had swallowed a watermelon. "The baby will be here when he or she knocks on my tummy saying, 'let me out of here, I want to see Elizabeth.' It should be really soon. Put your hand on my tummy. Do you feel the baby moving around?"

Liz put her little hand on her mother's stomach and excitedly said, "Hi Heinrich, time to come out."

Catharina and Benny both laughed and enjoyed the sight of discovery, "Liz," said, Catharina, "we don't know if it will be a boy or a girl. We only hope the baby will be as healthy as you."

The Spykers enjoyed their well constructed home in Elizabethtown. The crops had grown well their first year. Benjamin, although content with his new life and homestead was ready to go to war whenever called. He was a Captain in the 1st Battalion of the Maryland Militia, called the "Flying Camp." They were a well trained unit and at the beck and call of General George Washington. Each weekend he went for training in Baltimore.

Besides the farm, Benny was once again in education. He was hired by Frederick county for the Elizabethtown area as the teacher of the older students. Fortunately he had no disruptive students like his uncle Benjamin and his brother John Henry. Education was not required but was a privilege that most parents took advantage of. All knew, and Benny had made it clear, if you misbehave you were sent home. If you were sent home for the second time you did not return for that school session. Also Benny had to make the students and parents aware that a time may come when school needed to be suspended at a moment's notice because of his position in the "Flying Camp."

On that evening of November 5th, they had just sat down for their dinner and Benny was telling Catharina about his day in school, when Liz interrupted them. "Daddy, why is my uncle John Henry coming to see us?"

Benny looked out the window and in the distance saw two riders coming toward their house. He recognized John Henry but did not immediately recognize the other rider on a black stallion.

They quickly left the table and went out into the cold and damp evening. They all stood together and waved, but were fearful that it might be bad news. As they got closer, "Catharina, it's Paul Revere, my friend from Boston and the messenger soldier for John Hancock and George Washington. I think it's time for me to go to war."

They unsaddled and Catharina and Benny both hugged their brother. "John Henry, wonderful to see you," said Benny. "Paul this is an honor to have you come to our house, but I fear it is not just for a social call. Come into the house. We have food for you, hot tea and maybe a little something to warm your innards."

Once settled in the parlor, Paul Revere addressed both Benny and Catharina, "Benny you and your brother John Henry are needed by your friend Henry Knox and this has been enthusiastically endorsed by General George Washington. This assignment may make the difference if we are to defeat the British in Boston. We cannot be successful in Boston without cannons.

"At the time of the meeting of the Second Continental Congress, Ethan Allen and the Green Mountain Boys captured Fort Ticonderoga on Lake Champlain. Reportedly the fort has numerous cannons and mortars. Henry went to General Washington with his idea of going to the fort and bringing back all the useable cannons and mortars. He also told the general he needed frontiersmen to help him navigate the route through the forests and mountains and specifically needed the Spyker boys.

"Benny, Henry knows that Catharina is due to have a child very soon and would not want you to leave her until you are sure she and the baby are fine. He did mention," Paul said with a smile on his face, "that Catharina will probably come through the birth much easier than you."

"Daddy's not going to have a baby," chirped in Liz. "It's in mommy's tummy and it is not under a cabbage leaf." Catharina just hugged little Liz and Benny just shook his head in wonderment at his outspoken little daughter.

Paul continued after enjoying the family scene, "John Henry is coming with me back to Boston. But we want you to go directly to Fort Ticonderoga when you are sure your family is comfortable. Lieutenant Knox, along with John Henry and twenty-some troops, will be there sometime in early December."

Catharina nodded, "Paul, thank you for thinking of me and the baby. I want Benny with me, but I also want as does Benny that we do everything possible to make sure this baby and my little Liz can grow up in a free and independent America. My mother and father will be here in two days to stay with me during this time. Also we have a wonderful doctor in Elizabethtown who stops to see me almost daily. Our whole community is excited about the first Spyker to be born in Frederick county."

After that night, John Henry and Paul Revere left directly for Boston, and Benny, Catharina and Liz waited for the arrival of Henrich or Lucretia, the name they had chosen in the unlikelihood Liz would be wrong.

On November 16, 1775 Henry Knox and his brother William along with John Henry Spyker and a small troop left Boston for Ft. Ticonderoga. This mission was to provide George Washington and the Continental Army with sufficient cannons and mortars to drive the British from Boston.

On November 16, 1775, Heinrich Spyker came into the world. One event gave America a chance to be independent, the other event assured that this author, Thomas B. Speaker would be able to tell this story.

Benny was in the barn milking the cows with Liz at his side. She enjoyed watching her father in his chore and only had about a hundred questions for her father. It was early, about an hour before he left for the schoolhouse, when his father-in-law came hurriedly into the barn. "Benny, it's time. You best go get the doctor." Immediately Liz started bawling as she raced to the house. Benny quickly saddled up and headed for the doctor's house and a quick note on the school house door, "No school today, another student is on the way."

Everything went smoothly and baby Heinrich entered a hopeful 'land of the free and home of the brave.' Mother and baby boy were fine and Benny soon recovered after the doctor administered him several shots of his medicinal eighty-proof home-brew. When friends and neighbors came to visit, Liz always was able to tell them, "My daddy is recovering nicely."

Ten days after the birth, Catharina and Benny went to the Frederick county court house and proudly filed the citizenship papers for Henrich and then Catharina sent Benny on his way.

"Dear husband, we are fine and Mom and Dad and my friends are taking wonderful care of us. I know that you are concerned about John Henry and want to be involved in their mission. Please go with my love and know that I'll be praying for you every day."

On November 26th, Benny saddled up his favorite roan and started his long journey to Fort Ticonderoga. He traveled north toward Albany, New York, and through the foothills of the Adirondack Mountains. He passed Lake George and rode beside the Hudson River, using that as his guide to get to the fort. Finally on December 2nd he sighted Ticonderoga and was greeted by the sentry, one of the Green Mountain Boys. He had been expected.

"Benjamin Spyker, I'm Ethan Allen and we have been alerted by General Washington that you might be here even before Henry

Knox and his troop. Lieutenant Knox has not arrived yet, but our scouts have informed us he is only days away." Benny was awed by the height and stature of Colonel Allen. He was well over six feet, even bigger than his friend Henry Knox, however, unlike Knox he was in great physical shape, tall, lean and muscular. Benny could tell how much the Green Mountain Boys respected their leader.

Ethan Allan commander of the "Green Mountain Boys".

That evening Benny sat with Colonel Allen at dinner and enjoyed the story of how Ethan Allen and the Green Mountain Boys had captured the fort from a dysfunctional British detachment.

"Benny, I would be lying if I was to tell you it was a great feat. Taking the fort was as easy as 'falling off a log.' We were unexpected guests. Only one man tried to fire on us and I slapped him aside as if he were a mosquito. I came upon the duty officer of the day, a Lieutenant Feltham, as he was pulling up his breeches after his daily constitution. After tightening up his belt he took me to the post commander, Captain Delaplace, who was outraged that we should interrupt his tea hour. 'Who are you and by what right do you and your raggedly dressed men have to come into our fort?'

"I answered him back, 'In the name of the Great Jehovah and the Continental Congress of America, I relieve you of your duty and your fort.' Both Colonel Allan and Benny laughed as they pictured the sight of the indignant Captain being relieved of his duty.

The next morning Colonel Allan and Benny evaluated the arsenal to be delivered to George Washington and the Continental Army. After their review and the advice of the quartermaster of the fort, Lieutenant Simpson, they determined that seventy-eight artillery pieces were fit and useful for the battle of Boston. One of the pieces was a cannon that shot twenty pound balls and weighed almost two tons.

"How in the world," questioned the Colonel, "are you going to get this mass of artillery to Boston? All together my quartermaster estimated the total weight will be one hundred twenty thousand pounds."

Benny had no idea but had confidence in his friend Henry Knox. "Sir, Henry has the ability to do the impossible. You will see when he arrives that he will have a complete plan for the delivery to Boston. I don't know how it will be done, but I know Henry can do it."

On December the 5th, 1775, Henry arrived along with John Henry and a small troop of twenty men. Henry Knox did not waste any time. Over the next four days he prepared the mass of artillery for shipment to Boston. "Benny, Colonel Allan," briefed Lt. Knox, "we will use boats, sleds, oxen, horses, and manpower and will get this precious cargo to Boston sometime in January. As I traveled from Boston I secured with our fellow patriots all that we need including their help to succeed in this venture. We will float down Lake George, sled on snow to Albany and across the frozen Hudson. Then the most arduous task which will take all my troop and the patriots along the way, will be to drag those sleds across the Berkshire Mountains. I can't wait to see the eyes of General Gage when we throw a twenty pound cannon ball into his lap."

On January 18, 1776 the artillery that saved the Continental Army in Boston was delivered. The British no longer laughed at the rabble of continental soldiers that could "only fight with a prayer and a tankard of rum." On St. Patrick's day, March 17, 1776, Boston and the Continental Army waved goodbye to one-hundred British ships and eleven-thousand soldiers.

It would be a long time of many defeats, retreats, and then victories until General Cornwallis surrendered to George Washington on October 18, 1781. It would not be until the Treaty of Paris was signed on September 23, 1783, that America could declare her independence.

The final treaty would not have happened if it were not for the victory of Boston or the leadership of George Washington, John Hancock, Sam and John Adams, Henry Knox and many other determined American leaders.

Independence would not have occurred without the leadership of each colony and the soldiers and patriots of each colony, including the Spykers and all the other Pennsylvania Dutch.

"You Will Always be a Pennsylvania Dutch"

1776

⎯⎯ ∞ ⎯⎯

AFTER HELPING HENRY KNOX SUCCESSFULLY deliver the massive arsenal of cannons, mortars, and howitzers to Boston, Benny and John Henry returned to their homes. John Henry was a major in the Pennsylvania Militia and Benny was with the Maryland special forces, called the "Flying Camp." Both had completed an important task in the history of the Revolutionary War but were eager to contribute further to the cause of freedom.

"Mommy, here comes Daddy," screamed Liz as she woke baby Heinrich into a startled bawling session. Catharina and her parents came out and waved to Benny in the distance as he eagerly approached his home. Baby Heinrich was two months old and had amazing lungs as he rang out his greeting.

Benny was thrilled with his new son and could not stop holding him and admiring God's work. "Catharina, did you get the birth certificate from the Frederick county courthouse? I want to have a grand baptism for our son and invite all of Hagerstown and Tulpehocken. After all Heinrich is a product of Pennsylvania and the first Spyker born in Maryland."

Catharina gave a strange answer to Benny's excitement of the grand baptism with hundreds of people. "A week after we registered Heinrich, father and I we went to get the document; his birth certificate was spelled 'Henry Speaker, born November 16, 1775. Son of Benjamin Speaker and Catharina nee Lauer Speaker.'

"I've waited until you returned to see what we should do about this misspelling."

"I will go to the courthouse tomorrow and correct this mistake. My son is Heinrich Spyker and will always be Heinrich Spyker."

Benny was successful in getting a new official document that read 'Heinrich Spyker, born November 16, 1775, son of Benjamin Spyker and Catharina nee Lauer Spyker.' Although the birth document was corrected, the future census reports used the name of Speaker at the time of Heinrich's birth and continued to use this spelling for all the descendants of Heinrich.

The baptism of Heinrich Spyker was a grand celebration. The celebration was on January 31, 1776, and Benjamin's house was filled with guests who had just witnessed the baptism of the first Spyker in Maryland.

After the celebration and all but family had left, Peter called the family into the parlor. He was in a melancholy mood and wanted to share his thoughts. Catharina was holding the next generation of the Spykers. Heinrich, was three months old, and seemed to realize his grandfather had something to say to him. Heinrich looked at his grandfather intently with large blue eyes.

"Heinrich, I have something very important to tell you and it's okay if your father and mother as well as your uncle and great uncle listen as well. Liz, you pay attention also. You are in this warm and beautiful home because your great, great grandfather, Johannes Peter Spyker had the courage to leave his home in Germany which had become so repressive he could not live or worship freely. Johannes got to meet William Penn a man that had a dream of independence and religious freedom, a man that founded the great colony of Pennsylvania. Penn along with Johannes Peter's teacher Wilhelm Leininger instilled in him the desire to be independent, to live and worship as he wanted. Johannes followed his dream with his friend, Conrad Weiser and his son, also Conrad. The Weisers were two of the greatest leaders of the emigration from Germany.

"Johannes Spyker and the Weisers tried to gain their freedom in New York along the Hudson, but they were only indentured servants to the Queen of England. Johannes said that's enough of this false promise and moved many families to the Mohawk Valley where they thought they had finally found freedom. In the Mohawk Valley they built a community, but once again it was snatched away from them, this time by the English governor of New York.

"They could have stayed in the Mohawk Valley, again as indentured servants, but once again your great, great grandfather, Johannes, said 'no; I want independence.' He met and married a soul-mate in the Mohawk Valley, your adopted great, great grandmother Lomasi. Johannes, along with Lomasi, again led families away from servitude. They journeyed many miles down the Susquehanna and came to Tulpehocken, Pennsylvania. Here they made a home for the Spykers.

"Your great, great grandfather thought he was in the land of the free and he sent for another brave man, Johannes Peter Spyker, same name, but we called him Jonny. He was your great grandfather. He brought his two sons, your great Uncle Benjamin and me, your grandfather to Tulpehocken. We became free and independent, but Heinrich, you cannot take freedom and independence for granted.

"Here in Pennsylvania, although we had freedom and independence, the French, with renegade Indians, tried to take it away from us. Your uncle, Benjamin, said 'no.' I said 'no.' We helped defeat the French and Indians, but now our freedom and independence is again threatened. England, like under Queen Ann, who indentured your great, great grandfather, wants to again treat us like indentured servants. We say 'no.'

"Your father and your Uncle John Henry have just returned from saying 'no' to England. They have risked their lives in one of the greatest feats in American history, bringing cannons, mortars and howitzers to George Washington to drive the English from Boston. It will be a long time to free ourselves from England, but it will be done, because of the courage of your father, your uncle, your great uncle ..."

Before Peter could continue, Benny interjected, "Heinrich, the most courageous man of all the Spykers, your grandfather, is telling you this story."

Peter nodded toward his son and continue, "Heinrich, everyone in the world will tell you it is impossible to gain our independence against the world's greatest military power, but I tell you, we will be free, we will be independent. We are determined because we are Pennsylvania Dutch. Heinrich, listen to me, just because you and your mother and father moved to Maryland changes nothing. You are Pennsylvania Dutch and you and your descendants to a hundred generations will always be Pennsylvania Dutch."

THE END (FOR NOW)

Acknowledgments

—⬡—

I HAVE SEVERAL PEOPLE TO thank for helping and supporting me in writing this novel:

William J. Palmer for his editing and suggestions. Without Professor Palmer this book might have been a disaster. William Palmer is an author well known for the "Mr. Dickens's" series of Victorian murder mysteries. He is also a Professor Emeritus at Purdue University.

My wife, Rosemary Cassidy Speaker, who listened to the readings of my novel and offered me many helpful suggestions. She is my biggest fan.

Maribeth Cassidy Schmitt, Ph.D., Professor Emerita, Purdue University for her dedication to make sure this would pass the standards of the many publications she has written and edited.

Robert C. Nelson, owner of the Peter Spyker House, a historical landmark in Stouchsburg, Pennsylvania. Robert sent me many pictures of the house, both exterior and interior, some of which are included in this novel. Mr. Nelson's encouragement and interest helped me complete this novel.

The following are the websites I explored that guided me to my roots, and the historical books that gave me the facts to relate the history of this story:

Websites:
archives.com and *Friede - Abrahamson Genealogy Site*

Books and Tracts:
Architect of a Nation, by John B. Trussel; *A History of the Speicher, Spicher, Spyker Family, 1737 - 1983* by Paul I. Speicher; *Benjamin Franklin: An American Life*, by Walter Isaacson; *The French and Indian War: Deciding the Fate of North America*, by Walter R Borneman; *1776*, by David McCullough; and *The Life of Conrad Weiser*, by Reverent C.Z. Weiser, 1899 publication.

Finally I want to mention the two excellent genealogy research libraries that provided me information for this historical novel: *The Allen County Library in Fort Wayne, Indiana* and *The Henry Janssen Library*, in Reading, Pennsylvania.

Made in the USA
Middletown, DE
10 August 2015